Lynne Graham was born in Northern Ireland and has been a keen romance reader since her teens. She is very happily married, to an understanding husband who has learned to cook since she started to write! Her five children keep her on her toes. She has a very large dog, who knocks everything over, a very small terrier, who barks a lot, and two cats. When time allows, Lynne is a keen gardener.

Melanie Milburne read her first Mills & Boon novel at the age of seventeen, in between studying for her final exams. After completing a master's degree in education she decided to write a novel, and thus her career as a romance author was born. Melanie is an ambassador for the Australian Childhood Foundation and a keen dog-lover and trainer. She enjoys long walks in the Tasmanian bush. In 2015 Melanie won the HOLT Medallion, a prestigious award honouring outstanding literary talent.

CINDERELLA'S ROYAL SECRET

LYNNE GRAHAM

HIS INNOCENT'S PASSIONATE AWAKENING

MELANIE MILBURNE

MILLS & BOON

First Published in Great Britain 2020
by Mills & Boon, an imprint of HarperCollins*Publishers*
1 London Bridge Street, London, SE1 9GF

Cinderella's Royal Secret © 2020 by Lynne Graham

His Innocent's Passionate Awakening © 2020 by Melanie Milburne

ISBN: 978-0-263-27817-0

MIX
Paper from
responsible sources
FSC® C007454

This book is produced from independently certified FSC™ paper
to ensure responsible forest management.
For more information visit www.harpercollins.co.uk/green.

Printed and bound in Spain
by CPI, Barcelona

CINDERELLA'S ROYAL SECRET

LYNNE GRAHAM

CHAPTER ONE

CROWN PRINCE RAFIQ AL RAHMAN of Zenara strode
into his uncle's private sitting room with an easy
smile. Even bending his proud dark head in a respectful bow, he towered over the older man, who stood
up in defiance of all protocol to greet his nephew.

'Rafiq,' the Regent said warmly.

'Sit down, sir, before you scandalise your guards,'
Rafiq urged uncomfortably.

'You were my King at twelve years old and always will be,' Jalil informed him quietly. 'And in
little more than eighteen months you will take your
rightful place when I step down.'

The reminder was unnecessary for Rafiq who, at
the age of twenty-eight, was chafing against the restrictions set down by the government's executive
council when Prince Jalil had been invited to become
Regent of the kingdom and raise his orphaned nephews to adulthood. Thirty had been set in stone as the
date of Rafiq's maturity and ascension to the throne
of his forefathers, but Rafiq had long been ready to
embrace that challenge. Yet feeling that way troubled

his conscience, because his uncle had been both an excellent ruler and a caring guardian—a man, indeed, infinitely more fit for the throne than Rafiq's late father Azhar had proved to be. Azhar's licentious ways and corrupt practices had plunged their hereditary monarchy into disrepute.

Without a doubt their parent's ugly history explained why Rafiq and his kid brother, Zayn, had had to endure a rigidly traditional, old-fashioned upbringing in which their every move had been hedged with prohibitions. Everybody had been terrified that Rafiq or Zayn might start revealing their father's traits although Rafiq himself had had little fear of that possibility, having been long convinced that his father had committed his worst excesses while in the grip of drug abuse.

'You said you had to see me immediately,' Rafiq reminded the older man gently, keen as he was to return to his own wing of the palace and enjoy a little relaxation before making an official report on Zenara's financial investments to the executive council. 'What has happened?'

Jalil breathed in deep and crossed the room to stand by the archway that led out onto a balcony from which a welcome waft of fresh air emanated and chased the heat of midday. 'I must ask you to speak to your brother about his marriage. He is proving… stubborn in the extreme.'

In receipt of that news, Rafiq stiffened and paled. 'You already know my opinion. Zayn is seventeen. He is too young.'

The Regent sighed heavily. 'I suppose that tells me very clearly how *you* feel about having been married off at sixteen.'

'No disrespect was intended,' Rafiq hastened to assert, discomfiture and guilt gripping him.

Yet how could he stand by and let his little brother pay the price of his own refusal to remarry? It was only two years since his wife, Fadith, had died but within weeks Rafiq had been approached by the council and asked to consider a second marriage. His marriage to Fadith, unhappily, had been childless and, although the medics had been unable to find anything wrong with either of them and had made much use of that catch-all phrase 'unexplained infertility', Rafiq was still in no hurry to enter a second union and very probably go through the same torturous process again. He was in no mood to apologise either for wanting to continue enjoying the freedom that had long been denied to him.

But, of course, that was not an excuse that his uncle either wanted to hear or would even understand. Jalil had married young and remained very happily married and, like the council, he feared the sexual liberty that all were convinced had been his late father Azhar's downfall and which had caused so many scandals. Azhar had preyed on the female staff and on the wives of his officials and his friends. No attractive woman had been safe in his vicinity. But Rafiq was neither a sex addict nor a drug addict in constant search of another high.

'Zayn *must* marry,' Jalil responded gravely. 'He must provide you with an heir.'

'In that case I will agree to remarry,' Rafiq breathed in a driven undertone, grimly accepting that he no longer had a choice.

He had withstood the arguments in favour of his remarriage for as long as he could, staving off the prospect of his brother being forced into a union while he was still too young for that responsibility. While he accepted that his remarriage was unlikely to lead to the much-desired heir, at least it would buy his little brother freedom for longer.

'I will remarry,' he repeated. 'But only on the understanding that my brother is given several more years before he is expected to take a wife.'

'Neither I nor the council would want you to feel forced into marriage against your own inclinations,' the older man protested in dismay.

'I will not feel forced,' Rafiq lied smoothly, determined to do the one thing he could to protect his kid brother from being compelled to grow up too soon. 'It is a necessity for me, after all, to have a wife. If there is to be a king, there must also be a queen.'

'If you are sure…' The Regent hesitated. 'The council will find this news of your change of heart very welcome indeed and who knows? In a second marriage a child may be conceived.'

'I think it is wisest to assume that there will *not* be a child,' Rafiq parried flatly. 'Of course, any potential bride will be aware of that likelihood from the outset.'

'Is there a woman for whom you have formed a preference?' his uncle prompted hopefully.

'Sadly not, but when I return from my next trip you may put suggestions to me,' Rafiq murmured, forcing a smile. 'I am a poor bargain for any woman.'

'A billionaire and future king feted on social media as the most handsome prince in the Middle East?' the older man countered feelingly. 'Social media is *so* shamelessly disrespectful!'

'There's nothing we can do to silence such nonsense.' Rafiq shrugged. Both he and his brother had long been barred from such public forms of expression, closed off in every way from their peers. And the movie-star good looks that he had inherited from his very beautiful late mother, an Italian socialite, merely embarrassed him.

It was a tribute only to Rafiq's force of will that he had completed his degree in business and finance with an executive council who had refused to see the benefits of an educated ruler. In so far as it was possible within the restrictions foisted on him, Rafiq had had a normal education, but nothing else about his life had been remotely normal. He was always surrounded by bodyguards and he was sentenced to travel with a cook and even a food taster because his father had died from poison.

Rafiq was much inclined to believe that that misfortune had had nothing to do with sedition but was much more likely to have been the act of an embittered husband, a vengeful woman or the consequence of an unjust settling of one of the many tribal disputes for which his father had favoured his cronies or demanded bribes. Unsurprisingly, his late father had had many, many enemies. In spite of keen investigation, nobody had ever been found to answer for his father's murder. Many had suspected various scandalous causes to have prompted his father's death but there had been insufficient evidence to fuel a prosecution and, sadly, his father's passing had been more of a relief than a source of grief to the executive council.

In comparison to his father, however, Rafiq was not only honest and honourable but also a skilled diplomatist. Not that that had helped him much in his role as a husband, he conceded with a near shudder, so repulsed was he by the concept of remarriage. He had absolutely no desire for another wife. Naturally he didn't want to feel trapped again. He had hated being married and knew that his attitude was a visceral reaction to what he had endured. He didn't want to be worshipped like a golden idol either and he certainly didn't want to be cursed a second time with a woman who wanted a child much more than she had ever wanted him. Yet he had remained faithful during his marriage.

Only after his wife had died had he been able to discover that there were other kinds of sexual experiences, casual encounters that could be fun and occasionally even exciting, where both partners walked away afterwards without a backward glance. No ties, no regrets, not even an exchange of phone numbers. That was what he liked the most but so aware was he of his father's addiction to sex that he rigorously controlled his strong sexual drive and rarely allowed himself to indulge his physical needs. But when he remarried, he would *never* enjoy unvarnished sexual pleasure again, he reminded himself grimly, knowing that he was going to find a woman on his next trip to the UK and spend mindless hours in bed with her. One last sin, he told himself wryly as he took his leave of his clean-living uncle, one last sin before his life and his privacy were stolen from him again…

Izzy groaned out loud when she checked her watch. She was late, she was *so* late and if the cleaning agency she worked for learned that she had missed a regular booking, she would be sacked without question. And she couldn't afford to be sacked, not with thousands of pounds of student loan debt already stacked up behind her and certainly not with parents who were always in need of a financial helping hand.

In truth, her twin sister Maya did most of the helping out, but then Maya didn't need to get down on her hands and knees to scrub floors to make money. No, Maya was a real brainbox in the mathematics field, so bright she was off the scale and had started university at the age of sixteen. Maya had qualified for scholarships and grants and had won awards throughout her education and if she needed to make some extra cash on the side there was always some special project keen to hire Maya to juggle numbers and work her special magic. Unfortunately, Izzy had none of those advantages and had to do menial jobs so that she could chip in with much smaller amounts to help keep their family afloat.

Izzy didn't mind though because she adored her family, especially her little brother, Matt, who was disabled and in a wheelchair. Her father, Rory Campbell, was a jovial, optimistic Scotsman with a shock of red hair and a lifelong habit of focusing all his hopes on get-rich-quick schemes and then borrowing money when things went wrong, as they invariably did. Her mother, Lucia, was Italian and had grown up in a very wealthy family, who had disowned her after she fell in love with Rory, got pregnant and ran off with him, turning her back on a far more profitable and socially acceptable marriage to another rich Italian.

In truth, Izzy could not remember a time when money and debt had not been serious issues in her family. Had it not been for her parents' insistence that she and Maya further their education both girls would have gone straight out to find a job after finishing school. But in the light of that parental insistence, the twins had concentrated hard on getting good educations and focusing on goals that promised decent graduate jobs. After all, the main reason why their parents were so often in a financial bind was that neither one had had the benefit of the kind of education that equipped them for steady employment.

And while there was no doubt whatsoever that the twins' ambitious plans had been perfect for Maya, Izzy had found reaching her own goals much more of a struggle. Maya had gained entry to Oxford University, but Izzy was completing her studies at a local college in the same town, which enabled the sisters to share accommodation. She wasn't super clever like her twin and academic study didn't come naturally to her. Even worse, exams freaked her out and she didn't do her best work in that state. The need to sit the first of her final exams that very morning had been the reason she'd missed cleaning the penthouse apartment and in the aftermath of that daunting experience, she was wrung out and panicking that she had failed. Losing her job on top of that would be even worse.

When she walked into the elegant apartment block, the security guard looked surprised to see her. 'What are you doing here at this time of day? It's almost lunch time,' he pointed out.

'I had an exam this morning. I'm running late.'

'I've just come on duty,' he replied, smiling at her because she was a very pretty girl, but particularly because she was also a very small girl and she was one of the very few women whom he could look down on. 'I'll have to check if the guests have arrived yet. I'm not supposed to give out the key for maintenance after eleven.'

'*Please* give me the key,' Izzy begged in desperation. 'If the guests arrive to an uncleaned apartment, I'm toast!'

'Just this once,' he conceded, stepping back to reach for the key and passing it across the desk, catching her hand in his to add, 'Fancy a drink some night?'

'Sorry, I'm seeing someone,' she lied, rather than turn him down cold when he was doing her a favour in turning a blind eye to her late arrival.

'Let me know when you're free again,' he urged with a wink as she stepped into the service lift that ran up to the rear entrance of the apartment.

In the lift, Izzy dug her pink uniform tabard out of her bag and donned it, smoothing a hand through her mane of tumbled red curls to prevent them from standing on end. She sighed, thinking she couldn't remember when she had last had a date. Keeping up with her studies, working several cleaning shifts a week and visiting her family at weekends left her with little free time. Indeed, a free night was a big enough treat and usually given over to curling up with a good book or watching a movie with Maya, with whom she shared a small dingy flat. Yet there was her father always telling her that the years of youth were the most fun-filled years of her life! So much for that, she thought wryly, wishing she had at least fancied the security guard because she had yet to meet any man who sparked her interest in that field.

Maya was the beauty in the family with her straight blonde hair, long legs and flawless face. Izzy was red-haired, five feet nothing in height and curvier than she liked. In the street men turned their heads to look at Maya and rarely even noticed Izzy by her side. The sisters might be twins but they were far from identical.

Inserting the pass key in the lock of the rear entrance, Izzy hurried into the apartment and extracted her cleaning box and the fresh linen from a storage cupboard. She spared the kitchen only a quick assessing glance. Although she would clean it before she left, the cooking facilities rarely required much attention because the tourists and business people who normally used the apartment either dined out or ordered in takeout food. As a rule, she spent most of her visit ensuring that the bathrooms were immaculate and, that objective in mind, she headed straight for the *en suite* bathroom off the main bedroom to start there.

Rafiq had suffered a very trying morning. An accident leaving the airport in the early hours of the morning had put two thirds of his protection team and his cook into hospital. Fortunately, none of his staff had been badly hurt but Rafiq had spent hours at the hospital and he was tired and hungry. He had been in no mood to deal with his uncle's panic at the mere idea that his nephew was abroad with only two men left to watch over him. The Regent had insisted that outside security be hired as a precaution even though Rafiq was only in Oxford to open the research facility he had funded at the university and would be flying home the following day.

A strange woman walking into the bathroom at the exact moment he stepped out of the shower was just about the last straw and he erupted into an angry tirade in his own language, demanding to know who she was, how she had gained entrance to the apartment and what she thought she was playing at.

And then he focused on her as he furiously secured the towel round his lean hips and fell abruptly silent, because she looked more like a child than a woman and her tiny body was rigid with fright and surprise, her face telegraphing her concern at the blunder she had made.

Izzy came to a dead halt as she registered too late that the bathroom was actually occupied and a huge bronzed guy in a very small white towel was stalking out of the shower to confront her for her impertinence. She stared at him in shock, her stomach turning over, and she couldn't stop staring because he was—*literally*—the most beautiful man she had ever seen. A shock of black tousled hair enhanced his extraordinary dark deep-set amber-gold eyes. He had lashes long enough for a woman to trip on, blade-sharp cheekbones that rivalled a supermodel's and a five o'clock shadow that huskily accentuated his strong masculine jaw line and wide sensual mouth. He was gorgeous. Even as that inappropriate thought occurred to her, hard hands were clamping into her shoulders from behind and pulling her backwards and her face was burning up with embarrassment.

'I'm so sorry!' she began apologising. 'I thought the apartment was empty.'

'Who are you?' Rafiq demanded impatiently.

'The cleaning and changeover service,' Izzy confided, shooting a glance to either side of her at the man mountains holding her fast. 'Steady on, guys. I'm not about to attack anyone!'

'How did you get in?' Rafiq shot at her while also directing the overzealous guards to loosen their grip on her. She reminded him of a doll with her white porcelain skin, bright blue eyes and that strangely coloured hair that brought to mind highly polished copper, a wild mop of curls spiralling around her heart-shaped face like question marks and tumbling to her shoulders. But she was not the child he had initially assumed, he registered, scanning the ripe full curve of her breasts and hips with a hunger that he struggled to master because it had been way too long since he had had company in his bed.

'W-with the pass key.'

An exchange in a foreign language took place over her head.

'You could not have come through the front door without being seen,' Rafiq countered.

'I'm not supposed to use the front door,' Izzy argued. 'I used the service entrance off the kitchen—'

Another incomprehensible vocal exchange took place.

'We were not aware that the apartment had a second entrance,' Rafiq admitted gravely, shifting a large brown hand in an imperious gesture to indicate that she should be removed from his presence.

'Look, I'm *really* sorry about the mistake. I shouldn't have been here this late in the day but if you report me, I'll lose my job!' Izzy exclaimed.

'And why would I care about that?' Rafiq asked,

stalking lazily into the bedroom as lithe as a panther prowling through the jungle.

'Because I've already had a really horrible day! I'm sitting my final exams and I ran out of time before I could finish the paper, so I might've failed,' Izzy told him flatly.

'You're a student?'

Izzy nodded jerkily.

'Wait next door while I get dressed,' he instructed. 'I'll speak to you then.'

Izzy drew in a quivering breath, deposited her pile of fresh linen on the ottoman at the end of the bed and backed out, the two goons on her heels.

'Can you cook?' the guy in the towel asked her abruptly.

Izzy blinked in bewilderment and turned her head. 'Yes…er…but why?'

'Later.' As she was herded into the spacious reception area, the bedroom door thudded shut behind her.

'You sit there,' one of the goons told her in a thick accent.

'I'll get on with my job,' Izzy overruled without hesitation, trundling her box of cleaning supplies into the other bathroom to start work.

Why on earth had he asked her if she could cook? Of course, she could cook. Learning had been a necessity with a mother who could barely handle toast without burning it. Both she and Maya had been making meals from an early age. Even her father was handier in the kitchen than her mother was, but she didn't blame her mother for that failing because in all the ways that mattered in making children feel loved, appreciated and safe, Lucia Campbell excelled, she thought fondly.

She would finish the bathroom, head into the kitchen and then hopefully the bedroom would be free for her to change the bed, she planned, refusing to allow her brain to dwell on what had occurred… that guy, that totally unbelievably, indescribably gorgeous guy. Izzy blinked, shocked and mortified by her brain's inability to suppress the images still shooting through it on constant repeat. Yes, like any normal woman she noticed attractive men but certainly not to the extent she had noticed bathroom guy, whose wide-shouldered, lean-hipped, long-legged perfection had imprinted on her like ink she couldn't wash off.

In fact, until that very day she had never realised that a guy in all his half-naked splendour could even appeal to her in such a very physical way. She had truly believed that she was a little cool on that side of things because no previous man had ever sent an embarrassing flush of heat washing through her entire body and welded her attention to him as though there were nothing else but him. There in the midst of her most embarrassing moment she had been wholly mesmerised by those eyes of his, those hard, dark perfect features, that sleek bronzed torso indented with lean muscles that shifted with his every movement, not to mention the fabled V that ran down from his hip bones… Sucking in a steadying breath, Izzy blanked her mind and got on with the cleaning while scolding herself for behaving like a convent school-girl who had never seen a real man before.

There she was, an unapologetic feminist being sexist in the most mortifying way, she thought, shamefaced. She had objectified 'bathroom guy' in exactly the same way women complained that men did women, without seeing him as a person, an individual. And sheer lust had dug painful claws into her body, her nipples snapping taut, an awareness she had never felt before slicking over every inch of her exposed skin as insidious heat curled up from her core. It had been mind-blowing, terrifying to feel gripped by something that seemed so much stronger than she was. She had never dreamt that sexual attraction could be that powerful or that instantaneous. Way out of control, not at all the sort of thing she had ever expected to feel.

She had always been far too sensible for stuff of that nature, not remotely like Maya, who, for all her genius, remained a romantic dreamer at heart. No, Izzy was a realist and knew very well that such a very good-looking man would never look back at her with the same hunger. She also suspected that he was, very probably, another woman's husband or boyfriend and guilt at that likelihood made her shudder at his effect on her. He was far too spectacular to be running around on his own, she thought crazily. No, had he belonged to Izzy he wouldn't have got more than twenty feet from her and he certainly wouldn't be stepping almost naked out of a shower in front of some random strange woman!

Rafiq strode out of the bedroom in search of his quarry and asked one of his guards where she was.

'She doesn't listen to orders,' he was told.

Rafiq grinned at the sight of her bending over the bath, her peachy bottom twitching as she energetically scrubbed it. He had never gone for really skinny women. He loved curves and softness and femininity. The lush feminine swell of flesh above and below her tiny waist turned him on hard and fast. He checked his watch and lounged in the doorway. 'So,' he murmured softly, making her jump nervously and twist round. 'Can you cook an omelette?'

Rattled at being taken by surprise yet again, Izzy threw back her stiff shoulders, wishing for only the fiftieth time in recent years that she were tall enough to be taken seriously and not so small that she was regularly taken for an adolescent rather than the woman of twenty-one years that she actually was.

'Yes…but why would you ask me that?' she asked impatiently as she swung round to be welded to the spot by dark-as-midnight velvet eyes that had remarkable intensity.

Her mouth ran dry. He was lodged in the doorway, rampantly masculine in his infuriatingly complete relaxation.

'I want you to cook for me. You have an hour before I have to go out to keep my appointment.'

'Why wouldn't you just order food in?' Izzy prompted in wonderment.

'I don't eat junk food. I like a freshly cooked meal

served in private,' Rafiq told her, strangely entertained by the new experience of being treated like an equal by someone who clearly had not the smallest suspicion of his true status.

'I'm only here to clean and change beds,' Izzy pointed out abstractedly, taken aback by the demand.

'But I could throw you out of here and complain about your intrusion if I so desired and you could lose your job,' Rafiq reminded her with silken immediacy. 'In return for my generosity in overlooking that offence, you could cook lunch for me and everybody will be happy.'

'Is that so?' Izzy gasped, shattered by the ease with which that blatant blackmail attempt had emerged from his perfectly shaped lips.

'And if lunch is good, you can also cook dinner for me this evening and I will pay you handsomely for your services,' Rafiq completed levelly.

'How handsome is handsome?' Izzy pressed tautly.

Rafiq almost laughed at her upward glance of sudden interest. 'I'm very generous when it's a question of my comfort and convenience away from home.'

Izzy nodded slowly. 'So, I'll cook lunch.'

'I thought you would argue.'

Izzy rolled her bright blue eyes. 'Not a chance if you're offering to pay me and keep quiet about my late arrival here. I'm not too proud to admit that I'm as poor as a church mouse and that when money talks, I listen.'

Rafiq liked her frankness even if he was a little

turned off by it. Of course, he was accustomed to gold-diggers with a little more flair at hiding their true natures, the type that admired diamond jewellery, designer clothing or dropped loaded hints to ensure that they benefitted richly from any time they spent in his bed. Yet the minute his thoughts went in that judgmental direction, he was angry with himself. This particular woman was an ordinary woman working in an equally ordinary job to make a living, a person far removed from the polished models and spoiled socialites of his experience. On her terms, money was a basic need to cover real-world expenses like shelter and food and clothing.

'You said I've got an hour?' Izzy checked, peeling her tunic off up over her head, copper curls bouncing as she went for the challenge. 'There's no food here but there's a supermarket across the street. You'll have to tell me your likes and dislikes first.'

With difficulty, Rafiq dragged his attention from the bounce of her full breasts beneath her faded tee shirt as she removed the overall. His groin throbbed as though a blowtorch had been turned on him, the hunger, the need almost painful and at that moment he reached a decision. If everything went the way it should, he would take her to his bed and spend the night with her. Cruising clubs for a suitable pickup wasn't really his thing. Drunken or loud women turned him off. His guards drew attention to him. Photos would be taken. Discretion was always a problem. Conscious that those sapphire-bright eyes were still locked to him with an air of expectancy, Rafiq stopped plotting and replied.

Izzy checked her watch. 'First, shopping,' she told him.

'One of my guards will accompany you,' Rafiq informed her.

'That's really not necessary.'

The dark eyes went cool and hard. 'I decide what's necessary around here.'

'Oh…' Izzy succumbed to an involuntary grin as if his innate dominance was somehow amusing. 'Do you want me to call you "sir"?'

Rafiq thought about it since, after all, that *was* what he was accustomed to in company. Yet, there was something ridiculously refreshing about her playful irreverence. It lightened his mood and stimulated his sense of humour because he had not the slightest doubt that she'd be 'sir'-ing him all the way if she knew that he was a crown prince.

'No. You may call me Rafiq,' he informed her smoothly.

'Do you live in the UK?'

'No. I live in Zenara,' he divulged with greater reluctance.

But Izzy wasn't even looking at him; she was gathering up her cleaning tools. 'Never heard of it,' she told him apologetically.

'It's in the Middle East,' Rafiq felt moved to explain with amusement. 'I gather you're not a geography student.'

'No, I'm doing English. My final year, final exams,'

she burbled with a wince, sidling past him, her hip bumping his. 'Sorry, but I had better get on with that shopping…'

And just like that Rafiq's attention was dismissed by a woman. Irritation and surprise and something perilously like pleasure warred within him because a woman had never walked away from him before. No, they *always* lingered, chatting, flirting, batting eyelashes and desperately trying to hold his interest. She wouldn't be a pushover, that was for sure, he acknowledged with satisfaction, at that moment loving the prospect of a challenge.

As soon as she crossed the street, a hefty bodyguard at her side, Izzy unfurled her cheap mobile phone and rang her sister, Maya. *'Well,'* she said cheerfully in a voice laden with sisterly mystery and promise. 'Have I got a story to tell…'

CHAPTER TWO

'I'M NOT USED to you describing a guy as "hot",' Maya complained worriedly. 'Are you sure you'll be safe with him in that apartment? Is he the sleazy type? All over you like a rash?'

'Totally not. I'm not even sure he's noticed I'm female,' Izzy burbled, with the phone tucked between her chin and neck as she settled eggs and butter into the trolley, which was being steered by the guard. He had looked at her aghast when she'd thrust it at him. But as far as she was concerned if she was stuck with him, he might as well make himself useful. 'I was just there in the right place at the right moment when he wanted a cook, and you know we need the money.'

'Don't we always?' Maya sighed. 'Look, I'm heading home for a couple of nights. Mum has a chest infection and she'll need help with Matt for a couple of days. It's not serious but you know how out of breath and tired she gets.'

Izzy nodded while piling vegetables into the trolley for a side salad. 'Give them my love,' she urged, cruising by the milk and then the coffee, adding sugar and then condiments, reminding herself that she was returning to a totally empty kitchen while wondering if she should be shopping for dinner ingredients as well. No, for that she would require the official stamp of approval, she decided, because he might be a really picky eater, in fact probably was... for goodness' sake, who didn't eat takeout food? Nobody *she* had ever met.

On the other hand, she had never met anyone who used bodyguards either. What was the security all about? Maybe he was a diamond dealer? A dangerous criminal with a lot of enemies? An assassin on a top-secret government mission? Izzy entertained herself with such colourful ideas while she finished the shopping, anxiously checking her watch because the time limit Rafiq had given her was approaching fast.

It was a relief when the guard pulled out a card to pay at the checkout and, suddenly, she realised why he had been sent with her. Izzy flushed, embarrassed that she had contrived to overlook the reality that she wouldn't have been able to cover the costs that week because she had had to cut back on shifts while swotting for her finals. Once again Maya was picking up the slack because her earning power was so much greater and Maya had already almost completed her doctorate. Still, Izzy only had one more year of living on a student budget to face, she reminded herself, but, of course, that plan was reliant on her passing her degree at an acceptable level...

There was no sign of Rafiq when she returned to the apartment and whirled around the kitchen like a maniac, quickly discovering the deficiencies of a kitchen space that nobody really expected to see much actual use. And when, rising above those deficiencies, she slid a bowl of side salad and a plate containing a perfect crisp golden omelette down on the table in front of him, she was justifiably proud of her achievement, but it still wasn't what she would have considered to be an appropriate meal for a powerfully built man who stood at well over six feet tall.

'You should've asked for something more filling,' she scolded him helplessly. 'I could have bought sourdough or added potatoes or rice. Of course, maybe you watch your weight or count carbs or something…'

As her flood of speculation dragged to a halt, their eyes collided and for Izzy it was like being speared by a trident. Suddenly her chest was constricted, and she couldn't breathe and the saliva in her mouth had dried up and her heart was hammering fit to burst.

'*Are* there men who count carbs?' Rafiq asked with sudden interest, utterly ignoring the hovering guard who was supposed to first taste every dish set in front of his Prince and hoping he took the hint that that rule was finally being broken.

'The bodybuilding ones do. For goodness' sake, I know men who wear more make-up than I do!'

Deeply entertained by the conversation, because the people he met were usually very careful to steer the dialogue through safe, very conservative and often boring channels calculated not to offend him in any way, Rafiq sent her a flashing smile of appreciation. 'Sit down and talk to me while I eat,' he urged.

Taken aback by the suggestion and spellbound by that smile that lit up his lean, darkly handsome face like the sun, Izzy hovered, feeling overheated and oddly boneless as if her knees had somehow lost all necessary contact with her lower legs and feet. 'Well…er… I was about to make you coffee and you haven't much time.'

'Skip the coffee. The water is fine and the omelette is superb,' Rafiq asserted, leaning back to yank out the dining chair to his right. *'Sit,'* he said again. 'Do you realise that I don't even know your name yet?'

'Izzy Campbell. Izzy is short for Isabel but I've been called Izzy since I was a baby.' Stiff with indecision, Izzy settled down into the seat. She was so close to him that she could smell him, and he emanated an inexplicably attractive aroma of sandalwood and soap and clean fresh male. For a split second she was tempted to bury her nose in him as if he were a pile of fresh laundry and colour ran up her throat to tinge her cheeks. He affected her in the weirdest ways, she acknowledged ruefully.

'So, tell me about the men who wear make-up,' Rafiq encouraged in the humming silence, recognising her discomfiture but spellbound by the strong zing of sexual attraction dancing in the air between them. On her part, it seemed so natural, so real, so utterly unforced and practised.

His lashes were as long and lush as black velvet fringes, Izzy noticed abstractedly as she told him about an acquaintance who, to impress a girl, had had a spray tan done in such a way as to fake the muscle definition he lacked, and Rafiq laughed in seeming astonishment. As well he might, Izzy conceded, when his own body was a masculine work of art, roped with lines of lean, strong muscle and hard abdominal definition. And then she mentioned a good friend who regularly used eyeliner to accentuate his pretty blue eyes.

With a sigh of annoyance, Rafiq checked the time on his phone and thrust away his empty plate. 'I must leave for my appointment.'

'You never said where you were going,' Izzy dared to remark.

'A business appointment,' Rafiq lied, because the instant he mentioned the Zenara research facility he was officially opening at the university he too had attended, the game of secrecy and discretion would be blown to the four winds. And once she knew that he was who he was—Zenarian royalty—it might change her, might change the way she behaved and the way she treated him, and he already knew that he didn't want that to happen.

Springing upright, Rafiq gazed down at her with a flare of scorching gold brightening his eyes as his scrutiny rested a second too long on her full pink lower lip and his imagination went crazy. Long brown fingers clenched hard on the back of the chair he had sat on because it was that much of a challenge not to reach for her and drag her into his arms. But it was too soon for that, way too soon when she wasn't even flirting with him yet. And if she didn't flirt, what then? It dawned on Rafiq then that he was too habituated to sure-fire hook-ups in very definite hook-up places and that for the first time he was trying something distinctly different. The realisation unnerved him just a little, for his entire experience of women outside marriage came down to eighteen months and a handful of one-night stands…

'This evening,' he breathed huskily, fighting off those uncharacteristic doubts, 'you will make dinner for us both and you will join me for the meal.'

Her smooth pale brow furrowed. 'Are you sure you want that?'

'Yes,' Rafiq delivered without hesitation. 'I would enjoy your company.'

Rafiq departed with his guards and Izzy continued to operate on automatic pilot by immediately abandoning the messy kitchen to complete the cleaning tasks she had still to accomplish. She changed the beds, cleaned the en suite bathroom and pulled out the vacuum cleaner and all the time she was fighting off constant feelings about Rafiq's invitation. It *wasn't* a date, it was just what he had called it, 'company', she told herself repressively, a totally casual arrangement. Even so, that still meant that he *had* to be interested in her to some degree, she reasoned. She glanced down at her worn jeans and tee. Did she want to eat with him looking so very obviously shabby? Even so, she didn't intend to get all dressed up and trowel on the make-up either lest she look madly keen. But, hey, there was nothing wrong with tarting herself up a little…

Izzy walked home at speed to the flat she shared with Maya and rifled frantically through her slender wardrobe before extending her search to her twin's. Some of Maya's stuff fitted her, even though Maya was taller and thinner. And it was one of her sister's dresses that she ended up choosing to wear. After washing her hair in the fastest shower on record, she put on the dress. It was green, stretchy and it hugged her curves but it was rather too long; however, it was the best option she had. At least it wasn't glittery or too short or too low-necked, which would give her the look of a woman who was trying too hard to impress, she reflected ruefully.

Even if she *was* trying the hardest she knew how to impress, a little voice prompted in the back of her head. She reddened as she added a little subtle cosmetic enhancement and crammed her feet into a pair of her sister's shoes. For dinner with a guy *that* hot, it was normal to make a big effort, she told herself forgivingly.

On the way back to the apartment she was forced to go shopping for the meal. She regretted her reluctance to buy the ingredients earlier because she didn't have much in her bank account and that reality shrank the range of meals that she could cook. Having settled on a Thai curry, she utilised the pass key she had yet to return and walked into the kitchen.

She had only been there about five minutes before

Rafiq strolled in with a bottle of wine in his hand as if he had been awaiting her arrival, which bucked up her self-esteem no end. 'How was your afternoon?' he enquired lazily.

And she thought, God bless him, he doesn't have a clue. It didn't even cross his mind that she had spent the majority of his absence cleaning the apartment. Izzy simply smiled forgivingly, recognising that he came from a vastly different level of daily life from her own and she was tickled by that revealing question. 'Nothing special,' she said quietly, choosing not to embarrass him with an honest response.

'Let us hope this evening will be different,' he murmured almost awkwardly, settling the wine down on the counter right in her way where she was dicing vegetables. 'Where are the glasses?'

Yes, totally clueless, she thought with even stronger amusement, like a guy who had never been in a kitchen in his life. Rafiq was not accustomed to a woman cooking for him and even less accustomed to the working requirements of a kitchen in the midst of the preparation of a meal. She reached into the china cabinet to withdraw wine glasses and set them out for him while trying not to stare at him, because he had dressed down for the occasion. The formal business suit that had fitted him with designer-tailored perfection was gone, replaced with form-fitting denim jeans and a black shirt open at the neck. He still looked amazing. She reckoned he could even have rocked a dustbin bag with that lithe and powerful physique of his and those startling, stunning good looks. She no longer marvelled at her own susceptibility, reckoning that no man would ever provide her with so much temptation. Rafiq was in a class of his own: he was unique.

He poured a foaming golden liquid into the glasses and she squinted at the label on the bottle and her brows flew up. Champagne, the very best! She felt out of her element, watching him out of the corner of her eye as he lounged up against the hob where she was trying to cook, and almost groaned, recognising that she was dealing with a guy who was acting as if he had never been in a working kitchen in his life. It was weirdly cute, him striving to look cool and relaxed when the tension in his stance revealed that he was anything but relaxed and she took pity on him.

'Why don't you go and sit down next door while I finish up here?' Izzy suggested gently as she lifted her glass and sipped.

Rafiq's wide sensual mouth compressed, a muscle tightening in his strong jaw line. 'If that is what you want...but it doesn't seem very sociable to leave you alone.'

'It's fine,' Izzy murmured soothingly, wanting to smooth away the frown etched between his brows. 'I'll only be a few minutes.'

'You look amazing in that dress,' Rafiq breathed thickly, scanning her shapely figure with a hungry intensity that she could feel.

For an instant that appraisal unnerved her and then that anxious feeling evaporated. Only a few weeks earlier she and her twin had talked about whether or not they were too choosy about men and how uncomfortable, immature and secretive it felt to be the only virgins they knew. They had decided that they were too fussy, too busy holding onto something that that they had got tired of holding onto while everyone else their age moved on into another, seemingly more adult phase of life. When they were teenagers, they had assumed that Mr Perfect would come along, Mr Right, but now they were no longer so naïve about the society they lived in. The men they met weren't looking for sexual innocence and wouldn't place any value on it and as a result both of them had reached the conclusion that their restraint was pointless.

After all, even their mother hadn't waited until she was married. Lucia had been very honest about her life experience, freely admitting that she had got to twenty-five years of age zealously conserving what her traditional parents had assured her she had to conserve. But she had tired of respecting the social belief that to be valued she had to remain 'pure' even though the men she met were far from pure and, having fallen head over heels for their father, she had never lived to regret that decision, in spite of her judgemental family's shocked rejection of her.

So, when Rafiq shot her an all-encompassing look that almost ate her alive, Izzy went pink with awareness but, on another level, she thought, yes, I *could* with *him*, and she felt positively wicked and forward and shameless, but she couldn't help the heat that mushroomed up through her quivering body, because the desire that he was unafraid to show was coursing through her as well. And why should she be afraid of showing it? Of feeling that way? He made her body come alive in a way it never had before. He made her want what she had never wanted before. And who knew how long it would be before she met another man who had that effect on her?

Striving to act as cool as she knew how while struggling to handle all the different responses assailing her, Izzy set out the simple starter on the table and they sat down. 'So, how did your appointment go?' she enquired casually.

Rafiq shrugged a broad shoulder in dismissal. 'Nothing unusual. I would prefer to talk about you. Tell me about yourself…'

In a few words, she described her family. He asked about her brother, Matt.

'Was he born disabled?' he asked with a frown.

'No, he fell off a ladder when he was very young and broke his spine. He's paralysed from the waist down. He's eleven now and because he's been in the wheelchair for so long he bears it very well,' Izzy told him with quiet pride. 'But caring for him is tough on my parents so Maya and I help as much as we can. Hopefully I'll be able to do more when I can finally start full-time work.'

'That will be soon?' Rafiq assumed.

'Well, no, if everything goes according to plan, and I get a good enough pass in my degree, I'll have a year's teaching training course to do next,' Izzy explained. 'I want to be a primary school teacher. Maya will probably take a high-flying job in the city. She's very good with numbers.'

Of course, she wasn't about to tell him the embarrassing truth that their parents were almost drowning in the amount of debt they had accrued over the years and at risk of losing their home, which had been specially adapted for her little brother's needs. All their choices always seemed to come down to money, which was mortifying, but Izzy felt sorriest of all for her sister because Maya had no desire to be a high-flyer in the stock market but since that kind of work paid the best, she would have to take it. At least Izzy, being the less academic twin, would be able to follow the career she wanted.

'Where are your guards?' she asked curiously, keen to get off the topic of future plans when she couldn't tell him the truth.

An almost imperceptible hint of colour honed the high cheekbones that lent Rafiq's lean dark features such powerful impact. The four guards hired at his uncle's insistence had been banished from the apartment while the remaining pair, who had long been in Rafiq's employment, were enjoying a night off that they would never mention to anyone. It outraged his pride that even as a fully grown adult male he was obliged to utilise such ploys to escape the intrusive nature of his security arrangements. 'They're off duty tonight because I'm not going out.'

'Tell me about Zenara,' Izzy suggested.

'Even though you've never heard of my country

before?' Rafiq murmured with a touch of a raw edge to his intonation.

Izzy went pink and then lifted her chin at an angle. 'I offended you, didn't I?'

'Of course not,' Rafiq countered, noting how that extra colour in her cheeks merely brightened the sapphire blue of her eyes.

'Yes, I did. Well, I'm sorry, but we all have moments of ignorance,' she pointed out in her own defence. 'I expect I could come up with a topic that would leave you floundering too…if I *tried*.'

'Not in basic geography,' Rafiq told her drily.

Izzy compressed her soft pink mouth and shifted a narrow shoulder. 'Yeah, bet you could have completed the science paper I tanked on this morning too. I'm not gifted at science or general knowledge.'

Rafiq frowned. 'I thought you were studying for a degree in English?'

'To complete my degree I had to study a couple of different topics this year and everybody said the basic science course was easy-peasy.' Izzy's lip curled at the memory. 'Well, Maya could probably have aced it at five years old but even after swotting hard I couldn't answer some of the questions.'

'Hopefully you managed to answer enough to gain a pass,' Rafiq said encouragingly. 'It's a mistake to do a major post-mortem after an exam. People tend to underestimate their own performance unless they're exceptionally confident in their abilities. And by the sound of it you have been overshadowed your whole life by a very clever sister, which must have been difficult.'

'No, it wasn't!' Izzy protested defensively as she rose to fetch the main course. 'I was never envious of Maya. She always tried to help me whenever she could.'

Rafiq registered that he had entered a conversational minefield. 'We'll talk about Zenara instead,' he informed her, disconcerting her by that total change of subject.

In the wake of her protest, Izzy had paled, her innate honesty tugging at her conscience. 'No, what you said was right, although I never envied her,' she admitted reluctantly as she reappeared from the kitchen. 'Sometimes it *was* difficult being Maya's twin because people would make comparisons and have expectations that I could never meet. But I love her, and I would never admit that to her. It wasn't her fault.'

'Of course, it wasn't. I have a teenaged brother and I am equally protective of him,' Rafiq confided.

Set at ease again, Izzy smiled at him, appreciating his insight and intelligence. His glorious black-lashed dark eyes shimmered like gold ingots in the subdued lighting and butterflies leapt and soared in her tummy, so that she felt almost intoxicated even on a glass and a half of champagne. 'Nothing's more important than family,' she remarked.

Studying her animated face and the smile that illuminated her porcelain-perfect skin, Rafiq gritted his even white teeth because she *still* wasn't flirting with him and he didn't know how the conversation had become so serious, as though they were on a date or something. And how would he know what *that* was like when he'd never been on a date in his life? But when he looked at her, let his attention linger on those big sparkling blue eyes, that wickedly luscious pink mouth full of promise, the delicate little slice of pale skin below her collarbone where a tiny pulse was beating, he burned for her as he had never burned for a woman, the hardness at his groin a constant nagging ache. He wanted to plunge his fingers into that amazing curly hair the glittering peachy colour of a desert dawn.

'You were going to tell me about your home country,' Izzy reminded him.

Rafiq pushed his plate away because they had finished eating.

'My goodness, I'm so busy talking I'm forgetting about the dessert course!' Izzy exclaimed, leaping out of her chair and vanishing into the kitchen.

Rafiq didn't want dessert. He wondered what would happen if he simply walked into the kitchen, snatched her up into his arms and carried her into his bedroom. She could thump him, she could say *no*. Right at that instant, he felt he could handle either negative reaction better than he could handle being passive when he was much more an aggressive, action-orientated kind of guy. He had been raised to take charge, to steer negotiations and wasn't sex a form of negotiation? An exchange in which both partners knew the score? She could not have come to the apartment to be alone with him for the meal and have expected any other kind of conclusion… could she? How the hell did he know?

In a blaze of frustration, Rafiq stared at her, catching the glow of awareness in her eyes as she looked back at him. He thrust back his chair and sprang upright. Izzy emerged from the kitchen again carrying bowls of fruit or something. His innate good manners warred with his lust and that seething hunger won hands down, sweeping away every other consideration. As she set down the bowls he stalked around the table and hauled her entire body up into his arms, the pleasure of finally touching her engulfing him in a heady surge.

Izzy blinked and gasped in complete shock. One minute her feet were on the ground and the next she was airborne, and he was kissing her.

'I am only hungry for you now,' Rafiq husked in a ragged undertone as her tiny frame quivered in his arms, huge sapphire eyes now locked to him with an appreciation he could no longer misinterpret.

After that explosive kiss, Izzy's heart was pounding so hard inside her chest she couldn't get breath into her lungs, and while on one level she felt that pouncing on her like a panther and lifting her off her feet wasn't quite what she had expected, on another secret level she was thrilled by the glow of wildness in his smouldering gaze and that urgent mouth on hers. It was so exciting, the most exciting thing that had *ever* happened to her and wasn't that sad, she chided herself, at her age? And Rafiq was *that* hungry for *her*? That was a thrilling assurance for a young woman who had never seemed to inspire passion of that strength in any presentable man before. And he wasn't just presentable, he was downright drop-dead gorgeous…

CHAPTER THREE

RAFIQ CARRIED IZZY into the bedroom and laid her down with great care on the bed.

'This…it is what you want too?' he was careful to check.

Izzy sat back against the leather headboard, still a little stunned by the speed and mode of her arrival into a more intimate setting. Rafiq was being very direct and of course she understood why it had to be that way. No man could risk a misunderstanding in such a scenario. Even so, colour ran up her face like a banner because the decision she had acknowledged earlier in the kitchen still felt so new and fresh to her; she would sleep with him, finally discover what sex was all about, only, if she was honest, she hadn't really expected it to happen so fast between them.

'Yes…this is what I want too,' she almost whispered, ramming down all her insecurities with ferocious determination because she was convinced that a wildly desirable opportunity with someone like Rafiq was only likely to happen once in her lifetime and she wasn't planning to squander it. 'But

I'm a little shy, not very experienced,' she added in cautious warning, in case his hopes were focused on more erotic thrills than she was likely to deliver.

Suddenly, Rafiq felt as though he could finally breathe again. The idea of her walking away, turning her back and rejecting him had been a fear strong enough to freeze him in his tracks because there was something about her, presumably a very *sexy* something, that totally set him on fire with lust. He wondered if it was those huge blue eyes or possibly that ripe pink mouth or even the crazy copper curls surrounding that triangular face. Perhaps even the reality that shy didn't turn him off, as her face said she feared, it actually turned him on *more*. Indeed, it meant that he was much less likely to be taken by surprise by anything *she* did.

'That doesn't bother me,' he admitted, hitting the buttons to close the blinds on the window and dim the lights even though, by choice, he would have put her under a spotlight, but her comfort, her ability to relax with him, were more important. He kicked off his shoes and vaulted onto the bed beside her. She startled and his flashing smile tilted his shapely mouth again, his hand coming up to frame her face as he lowered his head and tasted her mouth again with all the urgent demand he was struggling to hold back.

Izzy travelled from nervous tension back into a paradise where everything seemed to be about just one perfect kiss because he was one hell of a kisser. In that line, she was plenty experienced, even though no man had ever kissed her and made her very toes curl until Rafiq. It was as if he lit a spark somewhere down deep inside her, a spark that fostered a spread of warmth in her pelvis and made her thighs tighten. Her whole body turned liquid, her breasts swelling inside her bra, the peaks tightening and pushing against the lace.

His lean, long-fingered hands roamed slowly over her, cupping, touching, moulding, and she quivered, heat roaring through her in an almost unmanageable surge. Her hands lifted and found his wide shoulders to explore and then the long sweep of his back, the literal heat of him burning through the silk of his shirt.

'Take it off,' he told her.

Izzy went for the buttons, unwilling to break the kissing to look, and she must have been too slow at the task because with an earthy groan he pulled back from her and just ripped off the shirt, buttons flying everywhere.

'I guess you don't value your clothes very much,' she muttered helplessly.

'Not when they get in the way of what I want, which is your hands on me,' Rafiq growled, taking that moment to reach down for the hem of her dress and lift it up and over her head.

Disconcerted to find herself so swiftly reduced to her bra and panties, Izzy tensed, lacking the confidence in her body that was required to feel calm beneath his smouldering dark golden gaze.

'You are *so* gorgeous,' Rafiq breathed raggedly.

She glanced up at him in stark shock and it was there in his appreciative gaze that he truly believed that.

It wasn't quite enough encouragement for her to lie back and preen herself like Cleopatra on a ceremonial barge, but it certainly made a difference to the way she generally viewed herself as the *plain* twin. After all, it had been said within her hearing many times when she was a child because people weren't careful about making such statements around her, and it was a role she had unconsciously accepted and assumed to be the truth.

Empowered by Rafiq's statement, however, Izzy went back to taste that wickedly sensual mouth of his for herself and he reacted with flattering enthusiasm, pressing her back against the pillows and kissing her breathless, lean fingers sliding beneath her to release her bra in what she believed to be the smoothest move ever. And then he was curving his big hands to the swell of her full pale breasts, touching, smoothing, rolling and squeezing her achingly sensitive nipples, sending piercing shards of pleasure travelling straight to her groin.

As he drove a thigh between her legs, pushing against the most sensitive spot of all, her entire body jackknifed upward, a muffled cry wrenched from her throat as the excitement rippling through her rose in a blinding, stabbing wave. His mouth travelled down the slope of her neck, kissing a path down to the erect buds, dallying there with lips and tongue and teeth until the breath was sobbing between her lips, and he crushed her mouth under his again, his tongue delving deep, twining with hers, only partially answering the desperate, fevered craving controlling her.

'You want me…' Rafiq savoured with satisfaction.

'Wouldn't be here if I didn't,' she gasped, lost in those dark dramatic eyes gleaming with sparks of gold in the low light, marvelling that he felt the need to state the obvious, because who wouldn't want him? His eyes were absolutely beautiful—*all* of him was absolutely beautiful, she acknowledged dizzily as he snaked his hips back from her to unzip his jeans and take them off, the generous bulge thrusting against his boxer briefs making her stare for a split second. He looked a little larger than she had been counting on, she conceded, but Mother Nature had fashioned men and women to fit, so there wasn't likely to be a problem in that line, she told herself.

His sensual lips sought hers again as he whisked off her panties, pulling her onto his thighs as he threw back the duvet and settled her on the sheet. He gazed down at her with wondering thankfulness because she was full of passion just like him and it wasn't an act to impress him or even a ruse to take a photo of him, making him the boastful virtual equivalent of a show-and-tell. He smoothed hungrily grateful hands over her, his very *last sin*, and she was perfect, a perfect doll as she lay there looking up at him with those wide-open cerulean-blue eyes, as clear as the Zenarian sky in summer, against her pale redhead's skin. He threaded long fingers through her wonderfully soft, silky ringlets and shifted down the bed to tug her to him and crush her luscious mouth under his again.

His hands wandering over her curvy bottom, pulling her to him, he rejoiced in her softness and smoothness and responsiveness as he slid down the bed to spread her thighs and assure that she got as much pleasure out of the encounter as he expected to. Startled by that move, scolding herself as the most appalling wave of awkward embarrassment washed over her, Izzy threw her head back on the pillows and closed her eyes tight. If she didn't see what he was doing, it would be more bearable, more difficult to recall that he was looking at her...*there*.

Yet that first lick from his tongue over her feminine core sent a wave of heat shooting through her as hot as a lava flow and every nerve ending she possessed screamed into immediate response. Nothing had ever felt that good, nothing had ever felt so necessary to her that if he had stopped, she would have screamed even louder in frustration.

Involuntarily one of her hands closed into his black hair and it was like thick silk between her fingers, and those eyes of his when he looked at her, yes, somehow her own eyes had opened, well, it was somehow the sexiest thing ever. Her extreme self-consciousness died away because she knew she wanted him more than she had ever wanted anything and that there was nothing wrong with feeling how she was feeling. And finally, she relaxed, although possibly relaxed wasn't the right word to describe how exquisite sensation sent her a little crazy and out of control.

Her body took over without her volition, her hips rising in tune with a racy beat that was new to her, little shudders of reaction tingling through her from her pelvis. The shudders increased to a level of devastating pressure that tightened and tightened around her womb until she thought she would go insane. The ferocious need that clawed at her was unbearable and it tore breathless little whimpers from her throat until finally she reached a peak and it felt as though she were internally combusting with pleasure from the outside in, rippling pulsations of sheer delight shooting through her to leave her limp and no longer on what seemed to be the same planet. The total experience was infinitely more sensational then she had expected.

That was fortunate, she soon learned, because as Rafiq came over her—having reached for protection, she noted with relief—what followed was not quite so enjoyable. She went from pliable to stiff as he nudged at her damp centre, easing in. As he groaned with apparent satisfaction at how tight he said she was, Izzy was concentrating on the newness of sensation, and then he tilted up her hips and thrust deep and it hurt. She hadn't been expecting an actual pain, had assumed there would possibly be a sting or a faint twinge of discomfort but not anything that truly hurt, and she cried out at the pain of it.

And everything stopped: *he* froze, *she* froze.

'It was my first time,' she heard herself gabble in

mortification. 'Maybe I should've mentioned it but it's done, so let's finish.'

'I don't think so,' Rafiq growled, thrown into a loop by the unwelcome news that he had bedded a virgin, which to him meant that he had taken advantage of someone more vulnerable, more innocent, in short a woman he should never have touched.

Unexpectedly, Izzy found that she was amused because in the blink of an eye Rafiq had transformed from passionate lover into a naked masculine pillar of censorious disapproval, the gorgeous eyes angry, the strong jaw line clenched, the sensual mouth flattened. 'It's not your choice, it was mine and it's a little late to be a party pooper,' she told him staunchly, absolutely refusing to be embarrassed after what they had already shared.

'Izzy...' Rafiq began, astonished to see the sparkle of laughter in her sapphire gaze and disconcerted yet again by her.

Izzy tilted back her hips and wrapped her legs round his hips. She didn't have very long legs, so it was a struggle to execute that imprisoning gesture that told him what she didn't have the words to tell him because she really didn't understand herself at that moment either. But he wasn't going anywhere, not until he had finished. 'Well, see if you can fight your way free,' she urged with a helpless giggle.

And Rafiq's ready sense of humour came to the rescue because it was a ridiculous suggestion when she was so tiny and he was so much bigger. Involuntarily, he smiled and she rested her fingers against his softened lips and murmured, 'That's better. It's not your fault it hurt, not your fault you're over-en-dowed.'

It was involuntary again but Rafiq laughed. 'And how would you know whether I am or not?'

'I'm assuming that's why it hurt, because you weren't rough,' she said very softly.

Something about that tone, or possibly it was the worryingly anxious plea in her bright blue gaze, shot every other thought out of his mind. He angled back his tousled dark head and contrived, with admitted difficulty because of the difference in their heights and their still thoroughly joined bodies, to kiss her, the fierce tension draining out of his lean, powerful body as though it had never been.

He had never wanted anything as much as he had wanted her and now it seemed a cruelly appropriate punishment for his conscience that he had taken a virgin as his last sin. Defying that punitive thought, he stamped it down and shifted his lean hips, revel-ling in the feel of her, the ache at his groin climbing with every tiny movement she made. The hunger and the need burned like a fierce flame through him and he couldn't resist her. At least that was what he told himself: that she was more temptation than any nor-mal man could be expected to withstand. Only on another level, he knew he wasn't a normal man, that he was supposed to be stronger, tougher, harder: the guy raised and expected to always do the right thing.

But *still* he didn't do it. He surrendered to the overpowering hunger, driving into her again with caution but also with deep physical satisfaction, delighting in the way her eyes clouded over again and her heart-shaped face relaxed to reveal pleasure. Never had he needed so badly to give a woman pleasure and even though the lust riding him was brutally strong, he took his time, measured his pace, watched her for every tiny sign of response.

The heat in her lower body rose again, the flood of excitement unleashing as her heart hammered so fast inside her chest she could barely breathe. Izzy felt ridiculously happy and didn't know why. Because he had listened to her? Because she had got him out of that grim mood that had promised to wreck everything and transform her adult decision into a big messy mistake to be regretted? She didn't know—knew only that she had accidentally discovered that her 'bathroom guy', as he would be in her brain for ever, had an unexpectedly *very* serious side to his nature.

Something deep inside her quickened and her body clenched around him as little tremors of blissful excitement mounted. His every movement became all important, stoking the pulses of hot sensation in her pelvis until the fire rose again, throwing her on a wild cry of pleasure into climax again, and she fell back against the pillows, her hand smoothing over the long, damp, satin smoothness of his flexing spine.

'That was amazing,' Rafiq said breathlessly, pulling back from her to flop back on the bed beside her, leaving her feeling strangely abandoned.

Lighten up, Izzy, she urged herself ruefully. Stop piling silly expectations on him and then feeling sad when he doesn't deliver. Nobody had asked *him* if he wanted to play a leading part in her most romantic fantasies, the fantasies that until that moment she would've said were more her twin's department than her own. Striving to act casual, she watched him vault out of the bed and head into the bathroom, belatedly appreciating that he was disposing of the contraception and marvelling that she had forgotten that practical aspect in favour of wishing for a hug. They were still essentially strangers, she reminded herself doggedly. Maybe hugging was too much too soon…

In the bathroom, his thoughts very far removed from the subtleties of sexual aftercare, Rafiq was wrestling with his essential streak of honesty. He *should* tell her…but why? Nothing could come of the accident but still…

Rafiq came to a halt in the doorway.

Izzy contemplated him with a helpless smile. There he was, tall and bronzed and naked and beautiful and he had given her a lot of pleasure. She had definitely made the *right* decision.

'The condom split,' Rafiq admitted flatly. 'But there is no risk involved for you. I have never had unprotected sex and I cannot father children.'

Izzy was shocked by the sheer size of that admission and the hard, shuttered look on his lean, darkly beautiful features as he made it. 'How do you know you can't father children?' she couldn't help asking.

'Because I was married for a long time and it

didn't happen,' he confided tautly. 'So, no risk involved for you in that field.'

End of discussion, she recognised, shaken that he had been married for what he deemed a long time when he was still seemingly so young. 'How old are you?' she prompted helplessly.

'Twenty-eight.'

So a very youthful marriage that had presumably ended in divorce—not her business, she had to remind herself when other questions threatened to brim from her lips, and she swallowed them back hard to reassure him with her information.

'I'm on the pill,' she told him quietly.

Rafiq frowned in surprise. 'But…why?'

Hugging the sheet, Izzy sat up, copper corkscrew curls springing up like a halo around her flushed face. She wasn't prepared to tell him the whole truth, not when it revolved around her mother. 'My sister and I know someone who had an unplanned pregnancy and we never wanted it to happen to us that way, so we chose instead to be prepared for all eventualities.'

'Are you staying?' Rafiq enquired, ignoring the explanation that only emphasised to him that they lived in very different worlds, he in a world where pregnancy would have been an unashamed joy but she in one where it would have been an apparent punishment of some kind.

Just being asked that question freaked Izzy out. In ten seconds, she was out of the bed and gathering up her clothes at the speed of a fleeing squirrel.

'I was hoping you would stay,' Rafiq rephrased, accepting that he had been clumsy. 'But I have to leave very early in the morning and would likely be gone by the time you awake.'

'Leaving the UK?' Izzy queried tightly, without warning feeling as though he had buried an axe between her shoulder blades.

'Yes…'

Izzy slid past him into the bathroom and shut the door. He knocked on it and with reluctance she opened the door a crack.

'I don't want us to be so brief…but I don't have a choice.'

'Why? *Why* don't you have a choice?' Izzy pressed in desperation.

His ridiculously long black lashes shielded his stunning gaze. 'I can't explain that.'

'You know what? That's fine. I'm going to have a shower and go home,' Izzy told him with quiet dignity even though her stomach was already in the mood to heave.

It was *over*. In fact, it had been virtually over even before it had got to begin, she reckoned, stricken. She had dimly assumed that she was on a date when in reality she had been succumbing to a one-night stand and that made her feel very, *very* stupid and naïve. She hadn't realised that he was only in Oxford for one night and that tomorrow she would be receiving a text from the cleaning agency to do the changeover clean again. Best not to be in the apartment alone when that text came, she reasoned dully, as no doubt sleeping with the client was yet another fireable offence.

Dear heaven, how had she contrived to be so dumb? How had she managed to decide to sleep with him and somehow idealise the decision into something it wasn't and could never be? And she had *believed* that, of the two of them, Maya was the romantic dreamer?

Showered and dressed, Izzy emerged from the bathroom in record time.

Back in his jeans but barefoot, Rafiq extended the handbag she had left behind in the lounge, proving that he was surprisingly at home with a woman's needs. The gesture only increased her suspicions. 'Are you sure you're not still married?' she demanded thinly.

'I am not married but—' Rafiq breathed in deep, like a male mustering his strength '—I will be married again some time soon.'

'You bastard…you're engaged and you slept with *me*?' Izzy exclaimed and she hit his shoulder with her handbag as she swung it like a weapon.

Rafiq said nothing because there was nothing he could say without revealing his true identity. Being struck by someone for the first time ever shocked him, but not enough for him to rebuke her because the evening had turned into an irrefutable disaster and he didn't blame her for the way she felt. He was rigid as he extended an envelope to her.

'What's this?' she questioned.

'The money I promised you,' Rafiq advanced warily. 'I pay my debts.'

'I don't want the money now!' Izzy framed shakily, her face very white. 'Not after what we've just done!'

In a sudden movement, Rafiq snatched the bag out of her nerveless hand, opened it and dug the envelope into it before handing it back to her.

'You do realise that this is the last straw…the biggest insult?' Izzy shouted at him, stricken. 'You're paying me off like I'm a hooker or something!'

'We both know that it was not like that between us,' Rafiq framed in a raw undertone.

'But that's what it *feels* like now!' Izzy slung back at him as she stalked out of the bedroom, out of the apartment and back to her own life with the knowledge that she should never have strayed from what she understood and what was familiar because, without those guidelines and boundaries, it was easy to get badly hurt.

And she *was* hurt. On the way home she took her daily contraceptive pill from her handbag where she kept them, not wishing to trust in the convictions of the guy who had already let her down. But it had been *her* hopes he'd disappointed. He hadn't promised anything, hadn't broken her heart with lies either. He was engaged though, had been unfaithful to some other woman with her, which made her feel soiled, tainted by association. That wounded like another knife twisting inside her…how could it not? That took her right back to basics and she wasn't the slightest bit surprised that, when she got back to the apartment, she was horribly sick on her empty stomach and never had she been more grateful that her sister was not around to see her at her lowest ebb.

CHAPTER FOUR

MAYA RETURNED FROM her visit home and stayed in the bedroom most of the evening, clearly in no mood to chat, and Izzy was grateful, if not discomfited, by her twin's preoccupation.

'How's stuff at home?' she asked over breakfast the following morning.

Maya grimaced. 'The usual mess and Dad saying that everything's going to be all right even though there's no way it will be.'

'Dad doesn't change.' Izzy sighed. 'How's Mum?'

'Keeping faith in Dad as usual,' her sister said wearily.

'So, what do we do?'

'Anything we can do,' Maya breathed tautly. 'And that's not a lot at the moment.'

Izzy hugged her own misery to herself in silence because Maya had quite enough to be contending with at present and Izzy had no plans to add to her burden. Undoubtedly her sister would share once life had lightened up a little, she thought tiredly, while still wondering how someone like Rafiq, whom she

had only known for less than twenty-four stupid
hours, could dent her usually cheerful nature to the
extent that she felt as though an armoured tank had
run over her. Even so, there was no point beating herself up continually over events she had no power to
change, most especially when she was in the midst
of her final exams, she reminded herself squarely.

Over the subsequent month, Izzy swotted hard and
sat exam after exam, worrying every step of the
way and then discovering a different and an entirely
more frightening possibility dawning on her when
her period was two weeks late. Could Rafiq have
lied to her about being infertile? Well, he hadn't
been decent enough to mention that he was engaged, had he? By that stage, Izzy was willing to
believe any evil of Rafiq. He had left her two thou-
sand pounds in that envelope for cooking two meals
for him and presumably, whether he was prepared
to admit the offensive fact or not, for being a willing bed partner. He had treated her exactly like a
hooker, thrusting cash at her as she departed, and
her blood still boiled over that truth. But she didn't
understand either how she could possibly have conceived while she was taking the pill; she hadn't
missed one…had she?

The ice queen of a doctor at the student health
centre soon disabused her of that conviction with the
reminder that she had been on a course of antibiotics
for a mild infection only a couple of weeks earlier
and that it was stated quite clearly on the leaflet that

came with the pills that antibiotics could interfere with birth-control medication and that in that situation extra precautions should be taken.

'Yes...but who reads those leaflets?' Izzy had mumbled while the lady doctor looked at her as though she was an idiot when she already felt like one.

It was too late but, devastated by the confirmation that, yes, she was indeed pregnant, Izzy read that stupid leaflet on the bus on the way home and learned that even that episode of sickness she had had that night after leaving Rafiq would have lessened the effectiveness of her birth-control pills. It seemed to her that every piece of happenstance bad luck she could have had had all visited her on one day but she blamed Rafiq most of all for that lie about infertility, for parting from her without even giving her his surname or any means of contacting him. *Of course, an engaged man wouldn't want any comeback from his one-night stand, would he?* she thought nastily. And why should he get to walk away from her pregnancy when she *couldn't*?

There was another side of the coin to Izzy's feelings about her pregnancy. She adored babies, had always hoped that there would be children in her future *but...?*

At that precise moment in her life, a pregnancy was nothing short of a disaster, she acknowledged unhappily. She needed to be able to complete her education with a teaching qualification to earn a decent living and how was a baby going to factor into that?

And what about the costs involved in raising a child? Everyone knew that babies, sweet and wondrous as they were, cost a fortune to bring up!

The more Izzy thought about what Rafiq had done to her, the angrier she became, because he had walked away afterwards, deliberately ensuring that she had no chance of identifying him or contacting him for support or anything else.

She accepted that a sneakier approach to her dilemma was required. Determined to identify Rafiq, Izzy called in at the rental agency that managed the penthouse apartment she cleaned and got into a cosy chat with the receptionist. In tones of wonder, she described the absolutely gorgeous guy with his bodyguards whom she had supposedly seen when leaving the building.

'That must've been the Prince…' The receptionist sighed, hanging on her every word. 'I never saw him, of course. People that important don't make their own bookings but when his staff contacted us on his behalf, I looked him up on the website because I was curious…a prince, you know, and he *is* very, very good-looking, isn't he? I wish I'd seen him in the flesh.'

'The Prince?' Izzy repeated chokily. 'Like a *real* prince?'

'Heir to the Zenarian throne. It's all on their website,' her companion told her abstractedly. 'He's something special.'

Izzy was gobsmacked. A *prince*? A freakin' prince? And now she understood the bodyguards, the air of imperious expectation, the cash, the reluctance to tell her anything about himself, which she had only registered afterwards, when it was far too late to see that attitude as suspicious. She raced home purely to look up the website that had been mentioned and, true enough, there Rafiq was in a photo along with his uncle, the Regent, the heir to the blasted throne of the whole country! Even worse, there was a very small reference to a rumour that the heir could be getting married again soon.

Breathing heavily, Izzy paced the room, relieved that once again her twin was back in London with their parents, attending job interviews. Sooner or later she would have to come clean about her problems but, right now, Maya had more than enough on her plate and Izzy was determined not to lean on her sister as well. It was a wonder, she thought guiltily, that Maya hadn't already drowned with the sheer weight of them all clinging to her, constantly looking to her for advice and support.

No, on this occasion, Izzy would deal with her own issues and act like an adult. Not like the time she had been bullied at school. Not like the time Maya had rescued her from drowning in a winter river and almost drowned herself. Not like the time Izzy had broken her leg and Maya had sat up all night in hospital with her. No, just for once, Izzy would handle herself.

She would fly to Zenara using the money Rafiq had given her to cover the cost of the flight. She had to tell him that she was pregnant *before* he got married. That was only fair to him and the woman he was planning to marry. It would be mean to withhold such information until a later date. In any case, the child she carried was his baby as well, and, while he had a responsibility towards his fiancée, he also had a responsibility towards Izzy and his child. Rafiq would have to man up and handle the situation and that was *his* problem, *not* hers!

It cost a small fortune to book a flight to Zenara and, by the time she had booked and paid for a hotel for three nights as well, she didn't have enough money left to book a return flight. But she was quite sure that bathroom guy with his private jet and his reputed billions would ensure that she swiftly got home again, she thought bitterly. He would want her smuggled out of the country again where she couldn't cause His Royal Highness any further embarrassment!

Rafiq had *lied* to her, she reminded herself, because it wasn't like her to be bitter and angry but that was what the whole experience of Rafiq, his lies and evasions and an unexpected pregnancy had done to her. Instead of feeling able to rejoice in the baby she carried, she felt ashamed because love hadn't featured in that conception, not as it had in her parents' case. And Rafiq had hurt her pride and her heart, of course he had. She had been well on the way to tumbling into an infatuation with him. She hadn't realised that she wasn't on a level playing field. She hadn't even suspected that she could be dealing with a real VIP, a foreign royal, no doubt accustomed to taking his sexual pleasure where he found it even if it meant wining and dining a humble student cleaner to seduce her into bed!

Izzy couldn't understand what the problem was at the airport in Zenara. She had disembarked from the plane, shown her documentation and then somehow everything had gone wrong and, instead of being left free to go about her business, she had been ushered into a small office for an interview.

The heat was killing her, the small fan on the desk in front of her making little impression on her condition. Her cotton top and linen trousers were sticking to her perspiring flesh and her brow was damp.

An older man entered and gave her a small tight smile. 'Miss Campbell. I am sorry for this inconvenience,' he told her.

Izzy went limp with relief at finally meeting someone who could speak her language. 'I don't understand why I'm not being allowed to leave the airport.'

'We have certain entrance requirements for unaccompanied single women and I'm afraid you don't meet the regulations,' he told her.

Izzy tilted her chin, not in the mood for some silly form of bureaucracy after sitting trapped in that claustrophobic room for more than an hour. 'In what way?'

'You have not stated your business in Zenara.'

'I said I was a tourist,' Izzy protested.

'You have booked a hotel for only three nights and have not booked a return flight. Unfortunately, this sends up certain flags in our system. If you have any friends or connections in Zenara who could vouch for your character, please give me their details now and I will contact them.'

Izzy blinked. 'The only person I know in Zenara is Prince Rafiq...'

The silence of shock that fell then pleased her because she was so tired, so hungry and so darned hot that she was utterly miserable and all she wanted was out of the blasted airport into the air-conditioned cool of a hotel.

'And this...er...acquaintance?' the older man began very awkwardly, clearly not sure how best to proceed when it came to questioning someone with a possible link to the royal family.

Something in Izzy snapped then, something like the last link to her sanity, because she had just had enough and she breathed wearily, 'He is the father of my child.'

At that point the world around Izzy went crazy as cries of disbelief, shock and rapped-out exchanges in a foreign language broke out over her head. Overpowered by it all, she stood up because her back was aching and she was feeling queasy. An ocean of darkness instantly enfolded her, and she dropped without a sound into a dead faint. Pandemonium broke out while she was unconscious and rushed into an ambulance with a police escort.

* * *

Izzy surfaced back to consciousness in a bedroom so splendid that she was disorientated. Not a hospital, not a hotel either. Still fully clothed, only her shoes removed, she was lying on a grand four-poster bed with a trio of doctors standing at the foot of it, giving names that she instantly forgot while assuring her that she was in the safest of places because she was in the *royal palace*.

Frozen back against the pillows by that startling information, she blinked rapidly, wishing that she could think clearly and less like a zombie. Without warning, the bedroom door opened and heads started dipping in a show of respect and Rafiq strode in, the proud lineaments of his bronzed and flawless features inhumanly calm and collected for a single man who'd had a woman announce at the airport that he was the father of her child. The airport, for goodness' sake! Izzy could feel hot colour sweeping from her head to toes, her fury with Rafiq eclipsed entirely at that moment by the situation she was in. He had to think she was a madwoman but nothing that he might be thinking or feeling was showing on the surface.

Involuntarily, her attention lingered on him. The high cheekbones and strong hollows, the blade-straight black brows, the stunning deep-set eyes fringed by those outrageous thick lashes. Get over it, he's gorgeous, it's not relevant right now, she scolded herself anxiously as he sank down with fluid grace for so large a man in the chair by the bed and reached for her hand in a startlingly supportive gesture.

'How are you feeling?' Rafiq asked graciously, for all the world as though they had only parted as close friends in recent days, instead of the weeks that had passed since their last explosive meeting. Her fingers trembled in the light grasp of his.

'Groggy,' she muttered truthfully, gently removing her fingers from his hold while striving not to make a production out of the withdrawal. She was painfully aware that they were not alone, and she was keen to follow his example and behave as though everything between them were normal. 'Think I'm just tired…'

'You must rest, of course,' Rafiq murmured quietly. 'Beforehand, however, the doctors are asking if they could have your consent to carry out an ultrasound procedure…?'

In awe of his self-assurance, his ability to act as though there were nothing crazy about the situation, she nodded jerkily. 'Yes, that would be fine, I suppose. Though it might be too early to see much…'

He was sheathed like a rapier blade in a pale grey suit teamed with a white shirt and a red silk tie. Her eyes continually tracked a path back to him, connecting with scorching gold semi-screened by his black lashes, and in the depths of his steady gaze she caught the merest glimpse of all the strong emotion and reaction he was suppressing for the sake of appearances, she assumed. He was so strong, so self-disciplined, she recognised, uncomfortable with that moment of truth and deliberately turning her head away. What on earth had got into her at the airport to say such a thing? Inside herself, she cringed at her reckless impulsive revelation, recalling the astounded response she had drawn from her audience before she fainted.

An ultrasound machine was wheeled in for the scan. A nurse rolled up Izzy's cotton tunic top a few inches and Izzy lifted her hips to enable the stretchy waistband of her casual trousers to be rolled down a little, baring her still-flat stomach. The transponder ball rubbed over her exposed skin and goosebumps broke out on her skin as a galloping heartbeat began to thunder through the room and she gasped, peering in wonder at the screen the operator was indicating to her, breaking into a flood of words in her own language with a huge smile.

'T-twins…' Rafiq stammered in a hoarse undertone. 'You are carrying twins. It is too early as yet to know the gender, but the doctor believes that they are fraternal, not identical.'

His hand had found hers again, she didn't know when or how, was, indeed, in too much shock to notice anything beyond the screen where the operator was beaming and chattering away, outlining the two tiny vague bean shapes while their heartbeats went on thundering. Twins, she thought in wonderment, with an undernote of panic because her mother had shared what a challenge it had often been to raise two babies. And yet there they were, already part of her, she acknowledged, struggling to concentrate as

Rafiq translated the information she was being given as well as the round after round of hearty congratulations delivered to them both as though they were a proper couple.

In the aftermath of all that excitement, Izzy felt drained and her head flopped back heavily on the pillow. Although their audience had melted away with the promise of pictures of the scan to be brought back later, Izzy was too exhausted to deal with Rafiq and all the many complications that their situation would unleash. Mercifully he seemed to understand that because he released her hand and stood up.

'You should rest now. We will talk later,' he murmured unevenly, something ragged in his voice that tugged at her, but her eyelids were too heavy to open and she drifted off to sleep on that last abstracted thought.

Rafiq had been plunged into a state of earth-shattering shock. In fact, he had to walk out of the palace into the ornamental garden that fronted it to deal with that shock because he didn't have the slightest doubt that, when Izzy had conceived within such a time frame, *he* was responsible. That far, he had innate trust in her. He was going to be a father. His bodyguards waited at the edge of the garden, watching Rafiq wander around the lavender-edged paths that traversed the tranquil stretch of green grass, maintained at such huge expense of water in the Zenarian heat. Throughout that aimless wandering he was battling to adapt to the idea that he could truly *have* a *child* of his own.

And it was an *enormous* shock because Rafiq had long accepted that he was infertile, and that fatherhood would never be an option for him. Yet, one little contraceptive accident and Izzy had conceived. How likely was that? What had happened to that birth control she had been taking?

But he genuinely didn't care. He was *so* grateful, so ecstatic that it *was* possible for him to father a child that he could barely catch a breath. Such a development lifted all the weighty responsibility from his little brother's shoulders because Zayn would no longer be expected to marry to provide an heir to the Zenarian throne. Zayn would be left free as Rafiq had once dreamt of being and, in being free, he would set Rafiq free of guilt and concern.

In fact, Izzy's pregnancy totally changed everything Rafiq had once taken for granted. A child, *two* children indeed, he recalled almost dizzily. The palace staff had automatically assumed that Izzy was his wife, married abroad, it being the default position of a conservative culture to believe that a man of his background could only have achieved parenthood within conventional boundaries.

But she *wasn't* his wife, this amazing woman who had contrived to conceive his children. *Children*, he savoured, child in the plural. Nobody else could possibly understand what that single word meant to Rafiq, long accustomed to viewing himself as the inadequate husband who had denied his wife her basic, *desperate* need to have a child. It transformed his entire view of life in a way that only *he* could understand. He had to marry Izzy, as soon as it could possibly be arranged. There was no other choice.

But even as he came to terms with the wonderful change Izzy had brought to his life, stark fear underlined that new knowledge. As a boy, Rafiq had seen his mother die in the aftermath of his brother's birth. In the panic of rushing, fearful staff, struggling to deal with an emergency they were not medically equipped to handle, the presence of the quiet boy hovering at the back of the room had been overlooked. He remembered every moment of that experience and it had chilled him that the arrival of new life could bring death in its wake. Pregnancy and delivery could still be dangerous for a woman. Concern for Izzy gripped him, but it was not a concern he would share with her because the last thing a first-time expectant mother needed was a nervous partner even more fearful than she was.

'What time is it?' Izzy asked of the friendly female face that came into view as she lifted her head, registering that she felt truly rested for the first time in days. Of course, the stress she had been under meant that she hadn't been sleeping and hadn't been eating very sensibly either.

'Early evening, Your Royal Highness. Would you like a shower or a bath?' she was asked.

'I would love one and a change of clothes,' Izzy responded pleasantly, reluctant to enquire about that strange appellation. Why would anyone anywhere think that she was royal?

But even as she slid her legs slowly out of the bed, she remembered afresh that startling announcement of hers at the airport. It had erupted from her as panic took a hold. She had told them that Rafiq was the father of her child and she suspected that official label, that assumption that they could only be married if that were the case, was linked to that and she almost cringed in mortification, wondering what had come over her and why she had had to finally give way to her overload of stress in front of an audience. That was why she had been brought to the palace and a trio of doctors had arrived to attend to her. Airports and palaces, full of gossiping, chattering employees, were very public places. That was why Rafiq had felt constrained to act as though her arrival and everything that had happened since were normal. Move on by, nothing to stare at here, she paraphrased numbly.

The maid showed her into a reassuringly modern bathroom. Her suitcase already sat in readiness for her on a stand and she dug into it to extract a clean outfit and headed for the shower, stripping off her badly creased clothing and letting the garments fall to the floor. She freshened up in record time, keen to see Rafiq again and get things sorted out, say what she had to say while hopefully remaining civil if he planned to have a relationship with *their* children. That was the problem, she acknowledged ruefully—everything she said and did now would have repercussions that could impact on the happiness of the babies she carried. It would be unwise to be as unpleasant as she had originally intended. Yet, sadly, she was still so angry with him that just the thought of him enraged her.

Walking back into the bedroom to find a small table set with food by the window would have been most welcome, because she was really hungry, had Rafiq not been seated on the other side of the table awaiting her appearance. He flew upright, a very tall well-groomed and powerful figure in a designer suit that fitted his impressive physique to perfection. And then he made the very great mistake of smiling at her.

'Don't you dare smile at me, you...you creep!' Izzy launched at him in disbelief at that smile. 'You *lied* to me. You told me you couldn't father children! You are also engaged to another woman! I don't want to even think about how *she* feels about this mess!'

In the face of that attack, Rafiq breathed in deep and slow. She looked amazing, a glow in her pale cheeks, bright eyes like sapphire stars contrasting with those glossy copper curls that glinted in the sunlight. She wore a strappy vest top with trousers, a top that only hinted at the bounty of her lush breasts and the shadowy cleft between but that thought was all it took for his groin to tighten and the throb of arousal to set in.

'It was my genuine belief that I was infertile,' Rafiq murmured and he spread his lean brown hands in a graceful gesture that emphasised his acceptance of that conviction. 'Although nothing was ever found wrong with me or my wife, we were together for ten years and we were unable to conceive a child.'

'Ten years? You must've got married very young,' Izzy heard herself comment without having meant to.

'I was sixteen. Fadith was seventeen. We were far too young, but our guardians chose to believe otherwise,' Rafiq countered levelly.

'What happened to her? Are you divorced?' Izzy pressed.

'She caught a chest infection that turned into pneumonia and died. It happened very fast,' he clarified.

'I'm sorry…' Izzy whispered awkwardly, disconcerted by his explanation.

'Come and sit down now and have something to eat…'

'I have a lot to shout at you about,' Izzy argued, struggling to recapture her nerve.

'You can shout after you have eaten,' Rafiq pointed out smoothly. 'I promise not to deprive you of the opportunity.'

A laugh almost bubbled out of Izzy's throat but she swallowed it back, determined not to be manipulated or charmed or fooled or anything she didn't choose to be. 'I am very, very angry with you,' she confided as she sank down in the chair he had yanked out for her. 'But I'm also very hungry, so we'll take a rain check on the shouting for now. Aren't you joining me?' Izzy prompted as he too sat down but there was no food at his place, only a cup of coffee.

'I have already eaten.' And it had not been an enjoyable meal with his uncle, the Regent, Rafiq reflected, his mind sliding back to that uncomfortable experience.

'Twins!' Jalil had pronounced, rubbing his hands together with incredulous glee. 'This is a very special young woman you have brought to us.'

Rafiq had dug deep to extract his innate honesty and had said what he knew would cause distress. 'This is a young decent woman, with whom I spent one night…'

His uncle surveyed him with tolerance. 'But Allah saw more clearly and saved you,' he breathed with genuine emotion, glossing over his nephew's sinful encounter. 'This woman is *meant* to be your wife.'

A little less naïve, Rafiq nodded, accepting that necessity. He was a crown prince and he wasn't stupid. He knew that the next generation was as important to the stability and popularity of the monarchy as he was. All those years wed to Fadith he had known he was a failure in providing that necessity, in fulfilling that occasionally despairing need a woman could have when it came to conceiving a child. He still could not *quite* accept that he could have unborn children on the way because, on his terms, it *was* a miracle…with difficulty, he dragged himself back into the present.

Izzy spared Rafiq a single glance but his lean, darkly handsome features stayed stamped on her brain like the ultimate blueprint of perfection. Her hands a little unsteady, she picked up her knife and fork.

'So tell me about the fiancée,' she invited, sweetly sarcastic.

'There isn't one. I'm *not* engaged. I did not contradict your misapprehension in Oxford because I was not in a position to explain that I had, however, recently agreed to remarry and why. As future King I am expected to take a wife. But no particular woman has yet been put forward for the role.'

While relieved that no other woman was involved in their plight to be hurt by her pregnancy, Izzy still made a stabbing motion with her knife in his direction. 'You didn't tell me who you were! You left me with no way of contacting you,' she condemned thinly. 'I had to go and talk to the receptionist at the rental agency to discover your identity. Why weren't you honest?'

In a powerful surge of energy, Rafiq rose from his chair and strode across the room, wheeling round before swinging back to face her again. Already, he was fighting the sensation of feeling trapped. 'Honesty would've changed everything between us. Pretending that I was an ordinary businessman kept it relaxed.'

Unimpressed, Izzy lifted her chin. 'The truth is always preferable,' she told him.

'I also liked the fact that you treated me as an equal and that you would have no reason to go and report your night with a prince to the tabloid newspapers who deal in such sleaze.'

'I didn't get a night. I got an hour in bed,' Izzy breathed tightly, wondering if he had been subjected to tabloid exposure of that nature at some stage, resolving right there and then to look it up and devour every word of sleazy revelation. She lifted cool hands to her hot cheeks, wondering what was wrong with her brain, why she would even *think* of doing such a crazy thing.

'And it was a wonderful hour,' Rafiq sliced back at her provocatively, his resolve to be calming taxed by her prickliness and the wall of distrust etched in her once clear eyes.

'It was an hour that destroyed all my future plans,' Izzy told him, furious that he was wriggling adeptly out of all her accusations. He had more lives than a cat, she decided resentfully. 'I love children but I wasn't planning to have any until I was much older. I wanted to finish my education and get my career started before I even thought of settling down. Now that I'm pregnant my ability to follow those plans has been seriously compromised.'

'I agree. Children will certainly limit your freedom, which is why I have every intention of ensuring that that accident of fate does not destroy your future,' Rafiq intoned silkily. 'This is not a development which either of us foresaw but we must make the best of it.'

'I doubt that a royal prince knows very much about making the best of anything!' Izzy parried angrily.

'I didn't *choose* this life, Izzy,' Rafiq fielded almost harshly. 'I was born into it and it imposed frustrating limits even when I was a little boy. Couldn't do this, couldn't do that, couldn't be seen to do many things as future King, couldn't be allowed to do anything that might seem too bold or different or aggressive or dangerous. There was an endless list of prohibitions and rules to follow, so, yes, I *do* know a great deal about making the best of a situation.'

Disconcerted by that flood of blunt explanation, Izzy lost colour and dropped her head. 'I'm in a snippy mood…but look on the bright side, at least I'm not shouting.'

Rafiq moved closer, his extraordinary eyes a mesmeric pure gold fringed by well-defined inky lashes. 'Must we dispute? Cannot we…even for one short minute…*celebrate* the conception of our children?'

'C-celebrate?' Izzy stammered and stared back at him in stark disbelief.

'Yes, celebrate,' Rafiq countered forcefully, leaning back against the footboard of the bed. 'You said that the truth is always preferable and I will not lie to you. That you have conceived feels like a miracle to me. It is amazing news and I am overjoyed…'

'Overjoyed,' Izzy almost whispered in her astonishment.

'I thought I couldn't have children,' he reminded her drily. 'And because of that inability, my younger brother was going to be forced to marry young to provide me with an heir to the throne.'

Izzy frowned. 'Why can't *he* be your heir?'

'It doesn't work that way in Zenara's constitution. Zayn's child being accepted as an heir would have been a big enough change to the usual direct line of succession from the eldest son. That I have conceived my own child makes life simpler for everyone,' he completed.

Her heart had been warmed by the notion of her conception being worthy of celebration. Such an attitude radically changed everything because it was far removed from her far more prosaic expectations, which had run the gamut from Rafiq utterly denying that he could be the father to his having her conveyed back to the airport with a suitcase of cash to keep her quiet.

'Aren't you even about to ask me how it happened when I told you that I was on the pill?' Izzy prompted.

Rafiq shrugged. 'Does one question a miracle? I believe in fate.'

'Apparently a course of antibiotics can stop birth control working properly, so that may be what contributed to the...er...miracle,' she extended awkwardly. 'And the episode with the condom, of course.'

'Twins,' Rafiq pronounced with a slashing smile, ignoring that reminder. 'Could be boys, could be girls, could be one of each. That's even more exciting.'

'I'm surprised but delighted that you're pleased about the development. However, it doesn't sort out the problems,' Izzy remarked stiffly.

'There won't be any problems to worry about once we're married,' Rafiq countered with supreme assurance. 'Any problems you foresee will vanish.'

'And I'd vanish too if that were the *only* solution,'

Izzy declared dizzily, stunned at that response, that apparent assumption that marriage was the only possible answer to their dilemma. 'I'm only twenty-one. I don't want to get married to anyone. I haven't even started living my life yet. For goodness' sake, I only had sex for the first time a couple of months ago!'

Rafiq registered that he had a problem and one he had not foreseen. For too long he had been encouraged to view himself as a matrimonial prize in terms of rank and wealth, his apparent infertility his only flaw. But the immediacy of Izzy's rejection showed him that rank and wealth meant nothing to some women. It was a supreme irony, he conceded grimly, that even though he didn't want to marry any woman her lack of greed and ambition might also have raised a tiny spark of enthusiasm in him for the venture.

'We will discuss it tomorrow,' he breathed in a driven undertone, emotions he didn't want pulling at him, refusing to allow him to embrace his usual cool-headed thought processes. He had learned to be unemotional during his first marriage, had learned that it was the only safe way to cope with doing his duty. He could not change that mindset, not when once again he had no other choice but to surrender his freedom. Lightning *could* strike twice in the same life, he acknowledged, but at least this time he had the joy of becoming a father to lighten the load…

CHAPTER FIVE

A COUPLE OF hours after Rafiq left Izzy alone, she slid into the big bed with a sigh of appreciation for its comfort.

She couldn't believe that she was tired again after napping throughout most of the afternoon but that had been one of the warnings given by the doctors. A multiple pregnancy would take more out of her than a singleton one and she would need more rest and a very healthy diet. She smiled, fingers creeping across her stomach as she thought about her babies.

It was an escape to think of them rather than the bombshell that Rafiq had dropped on her! Marriage? That didn't fit in with her plans or expectations at all. Rafiq was out of touch. Women didn't have to get married simply because they were pregnant these days, she soothed herself. Although being forced to take Rafiq to bed for the rest of her life could be an encouragement, she conceded guiltily, shocked and then amused by her drowsy reverie.

But then the bedroom door opened again and Rafiq strolled in, dark golden eyes widening a little when he saw her still awake, sapphire eyes rounding above the sheet with surprise, her hair tumbled across the pillow like a copper question mark.

'It's after midnight,' Izzy pointed out a little unsteadily. 'What are you doing here?'

'This is my bedroom.' Rafiq dropped the news without apology because he had a campaign to mount. Like it or not, freely choose it or not, he had to *make* Izzy marry him and he would do whatever he had to do to achieve that end result.

Izzy was so taken aback, she sat up against the pillows in a sudden movement. '*Your* bedroom? Why was I put in your room?' she gasped.

'Because everyone thinks we're married.'

'But we're *not*!' she protested vehemently.

'We know that,' Rafiq conceded. 'But to make a major announcement of the truth that you are pregnant and we are *not* married would kick off a huge scandal and I'm not prepared to do that.'

'Oh…' Izzy kind of saw his point, which only infuriated her. Unfortunately, it was *her* fault that everyone knew that she was pregnant.

'I owe Prince Jalil, my uncle and the Regent, more than that scandal after the hard work he has done to ensure that the Zenarian royal family is viewed with affection and respect again.'

'*Again?*' Izzy queried and then she shifted a hand, dismissing that mystery to concentrate on the here and now, which seemed rather more important. 'Couldn't you use another bedroom with the excuse that I'm pregnant and you don't want to disturb me?'

'No. Although it has been assumed that we were married in the UK, everyone also knows that we must have been apart for many weeks and to sleep anywhere but *with* you would look strange.'

Izzy breathed in very deep and compressed her lush pink lips. 'Then it looks like we're stuck with this sharing but it's not as though I'm planning to stay long, so I'm sure we can cope until I leave again. Then you can say we're divorced, can't you?'

Rafiq said nothing at all because there *was* nothing to say to that unwelcome suggestion. If it hadn't been for the twins she was expecting, they could have taken that road, but then they wouldn't have been in the situation in the first place had it not been for her pregnancy. His brain, which until that moment had been very much preoccupied with the prospect of becoming a father, took a sudden jolting hike in another direction as Izzy stopped hugging the sheet as though he were a potential rapist and let it fall to her lap. She was sporting something made of thin white cotton, the material so fine it outlined the ripe curves of her unbound breasts and displayed the darker circles of her pouting nipples. Rafiq went instantly hard as a rock and turned away lest she notice the desire his neatly tailored trousers could not conceal.

Izzy shifted over to what she had chosen as her side of the bed and told herself that she was *not* going to watch Rafiq undress. But she did, while for the entire space of each nail-biting second assuring herself that she would naturally close her eyes and stop peeking, *perving* on him like some sort of sex-starved woman.

After all, she was no longer that naïve any more, she told herself briskly. Unhappily, for some inexplicable reason, having seen Rafiq naked before didn't seem to be enough to satisfy her renewed curiosity or her fresh interest. The shirt dropped to the floor and her gaze hungrily roamed over his muscular brown torso as if she had never seen a man's chest in her life. A sort of invasive heat source entered her pelvis at the same moment as she appreciated the corrugated musculature lining his eight-pack, not to mention that Adonis belt of a vee that magically appeared as he began removing the suit trousers. Her nipples peaked and her body shifted restively below the sheet as she noted the dark arrow of hair disappearing below the waistband of his boxers and the sizeable bulge still covered there. And that was the point where shame made her shut her eyes tight, castigating herself for her inability to do so earlier.

Was it her fault that he was so absolutely magnificent naked that she wanted to put her hands all over him? Explore, touch, trace, *tease*? She buried her burning face in a pillow, praying for her composure to return before he registered how ill at ease she was simply sharing a bed with him again. After all, been there, done that, got more than a T-shirt out of it, why should sleeping with him in the same bed seem so much more dangerously intimate?

Rafiq went for a shower, a freezing-cold one, keen to dispel the treacherous pulse of arousal in case his condition gave her the impression that he wanted more. *Of course*, he wanted more of the best sex he had ever had, he scoffed at himself, but he wouldn't do anything about it or make any kind of approach. He might have taken advantage of her once, but he wasn't about to repeat that mistake. The mother of his unborn children deserved better than that; she deserved his respect, his consideration. And the streak of dark, highly sexed wildness in him that he always kept chained up and suppressed would not get a single chance to escape, he swore inwardly.

Taut with discomfiture from her most recent reflections, Izzy waited until she felt his weight depress the mattress before stretching out a hand to switch off the light. She couldn't expect him to sleep with the light on all night as she had planned to do because she didn't like waking up anywhere strange when she was half-asleep. She wasn't a kid any more. She could sleep fine in the dark in an unfamiliar place, she told herself irritably.

Even so, it seemed to be taking her a very long time to fall asleep because she was so very aware of his presence in the bed. The bed was wide, long, the perfect fit for a wide-shouldered, long-legged male, but he put out heat like a furnace and she swore she could feel that unwelcome heat warming her back and it made her all twitchy and uneasy, a tightening deep inside her nagging at her nerves.

'Go to sleep, Izzy,' a voice murmured in the merciful darkness. 'I'm not about to jump you.'

In silence, her teeth gritted and she wouldn't let

herself screech something back. He thought she was afraid of him now, did he? How dared he? She wasn't a scared little kid! She compressed her lips and, cursing him thoroughly, lay as still as a corpse and eventually that did the trick and she drifted off to sleep.

Feeling too warm woke her up again. Moonlight was casting a little clarity into the room and she could see that it was still dark but that was the least of her problems, she registered, because she was welded up against a very masculine body like a second skin and, yes, he was too hot but, on another level, he felt *incredible*. Yet again her teeth clenched together even as a tiny little quiver thrummed through her. It was a case of mind over matter. It was perfectly normal to be attracted to him but, in the circumstances, it would be totally wrong to do anything about it. So, even though she wanted to flip over and investigate that warm hair-roughened, sun-darkened skin with all the wanton attention of a complete pervert, she wasn't about to do it, was she?

Even if she wasn't the *only* one of them with that kind of idea and physical urges at play? After all, she wasn't stupid. His arousal was aggressively firm against her hip. In fact, she felt rather smug about the truth that he wasn't impervious to her either. Why should she be the only one suffering?

'If you don't stop twitching and shifting, I'll…' Rafiq ground out in frustration.

'You'll what?' Izzy positively snarled as she flipped up into sitting position. 'Go on! Threaten me with some ghastly medieval punishment for breathing!'

'I was not about to threaten you but you're certainly not making this easy!' Rafiq snapped back thickly.

'Oh, excuse me,' Izzy said snarkily, flipping back the sheet to slide off the bed, the nightie flipping up to reveal the stretch of shapely legs for his bemused appraisal. 'You're the one who had an arm round me!'

'I thought that if I held you, you might stop moving around so much and keeping me awake!' Rafiq grated. 'I'm sorry. I'm not used to sharing a bed with anyone.'

'You were married for ten years,' Izzy threw back at him. 'How is that possible?'

'We didn't share a room,' Rafiq ground out.

Disconcerted by that admission, Izzy swivelled back to the sofa by the wall that she had been considering for what remained of the night hours. With a sigh, she curled up on it and closed her eyes. 'What sort of a marriage was it in which you didn't even share a room?' she prompted with helpless curiosity.

'I will not discuss that.'

Rafiq swore in his own language and sprang out of bed. Izzy opened her eyes again on over six feet of angry naked masculinity stooping over her and snatching her up off the sofa to settle her firmly back down on the bed. 'You are not sleeping any place else but *this* bed!' he thundered down at her.

'Rafiq...the domestic tyrant,' Izzy murmured softly. 'It's kind of sexy.'

Seriously perturbed by that unexpected comeback, Rafiq froze, for that was one word he would never have applied to himself. He shook off the label again. It was a superficial, silly comment, not intended to mean anything, certainly not any kind of invitation when she was so angry with him. 'We'll talk over breakfast,' he breathed in a driven undertone.

He would lay the facts out for her then. After all, the woman he remembered had been reasonable and rational. Presumably she retained those traits, even if she wasn't displaying them at the moment. Of course, he reminded himself ruefully, just like him she was struggling to deal with a situation she had not foreseen and the sudden destruction of her immediate plans for the future. If he made it clear that she could still walk away and *have* that future, he would be offering her a practical solution.

Izzy wakened and, finding herself alone in the bed, wasted no time in taking advantage of the privacy. Showering and washing her hair, she chose capri pants and a tee to wear, her small case and even smaller wardrobe for a hot climate not offering much of a choice. Her brain felt clear again and her anxiety level soothed, leaving her feeling equipped to deal with whatever Rafiq had to throw at her over breakfast.

The quiet little maid was waiting in the bedroom to escort her out into a long stone corridor and through a doorway into very bright light. The heat engulfed her like a blanket, disconcerting her after the air-conditioned cool of the interior of the building. She was ushered down a flight of steps and into the merciful shade of palm trees to find herself standing in a very pretty courtyard, crammed with lush tropical plants.

'I didn't realise how hot it would be,' she muttered, suddenly plunged back into awkwardness as Rafiq, immaculate in yet another designer-cut suit, sprang up from the table set beneath the trees. 'I haven't been abroad very often. Well, we only ever had one foreign holiday,' she told him reluctantly, not wanting to sound like a deprived child because she loved her parents very much and did not want to sound in any way critical of them.

No way was she about to tell Rafiq, with the kind of wealth she assumed he had, that money had *always* been a problem in her family and that the single holiday to more exotic climes she had enjoyed only a couple of years earlier had occurred when one of her father's business ventures unexpectedly did well. Of course, the doing well hadn't lasted—it never did—and the business had eventually gone down in a torrent of debt, plunging them back into the normality of being a family for whom a holiday was a dream luxury.

'Where did the holiday take you?' Rafiq murmured easily, accustomed to setting people at ease in his presence, watching her settle nervously into the chair tugged out by one of the servants hovering.

'Spain. Matt was able to get down in the sand and act like a little boy for a change,' she recalled fondly of her little brother, whose need for a wheelchair prevented him from enjoying many of the pursuits available to an able-bodied child.

'You are close to your family,' Rafiq gathered, having watched her expressive face light up. 'I am very fond of my brother. I will introduce you to him soon. He is at school right now.'

'School's not something I miss,' Izzy muttered in what she knew had to sound like a gabbling rush but, really, continuing to look across the table at a guy who took your every single breath away at one glance was challenging. 'Maya was horribly bullied because she was so beautiful and clever. I was average.'

'I don't see you as average,' Rafiq cut in.

Izzy shrugged a tiny thin shoulder and ignored that pointed remark. 'You said we were going to talk. You don't need to work through this getting-to-know-you stuff to be polite with me.'

Rafiq breathed in deep and slow. 'Our children can only be recognised here if their parents are married. Obviously I want the children to have that option, to be able to take their place in Zenara as royals if they wish.'

Izzy had tensed and she sipped at her tea. 'But when you were talking yesterday, you didn't make it sound like being royal in Zenara was really that enjoyable,' she reminded him drily.

'I was raised in a totally different way from the way I will raise my own children. It was a different time in my country's history and a different set of circumstances. But neither of us can know what our children will want when they are grown up,' Rafiq reasoned. 'Don't you want them to have a free choice?'

Grudgingly, Izzy nodded because she hadn't thought through the royal connection. 'You're referring to titles, like you being a prince.'

'No, Izzy. I'm talking about much more. The first-born of those twins will be my heir to the throne. I will be King when I reach my thirtieth birthday in eighteen months and my child will be the next in line, which is a very important role. If you don't marry me, both our children will be automatically excluded by law from an official role in Zenara. Yet they need to be living here to learn our language, our culture and to get to know their people.'

Izzy released her breath in a long sigh because she hadn't grasped just how deep that royal connection could go. Rafiq was going to be a *king*? Yes, she had already known that. So, how on earth had she contrived, even briefly, to forget such a fact? There she had been squabbling with him last night in bed as though he were just any ordinary Joe, when really he was anything but!

'In the light of that reality, I have a suggestion to make,' Rafiq murmured levelly.

Izzy looked up from the piece of fruit she was slicing and let herself greedily focus on him, only for a few seconds, she bargained with her conscience. He had the same effect on her, she reckoned, as a major crush would have on a teenager. Only she had never experienced one of those crushes. During the teen years, she and her sibling had been far too busy handling family problems like bailiffs and debt collectors and keeping food on the table with part-time work as shop assistants. It was just there was something so ravishingly perfect about those lean dark, chiselled features and those eyes, *stunning*, gleaming with gold highlights, and then there were the lashes: inky, lush and curling. Her body heated to such an extent that she thought she might expire.

'A suggestion?' she said jerkily, dredging her attention off him again to concentrate on eating the fruit, which was much safer and more sensible, she told herself fiercely, exasperated by the manner in which her brain kept on wandering around him.

'That we marry now to legitimise our children and stay together until they are born,' Rafiq outlined with clarity. 'I need to be with you until the birth to support you, to be a *responsible* father.'

'You're a literal throwback to the Dark Ages,' Izzy muttered helplessly. 'But in an odd way, it's kind of sweet.'

'*Sweet?*' Rafiq growled.

'Most of the men I meet would run away from that level of responsibility,' she extended, reluctant to offend him. 'You're the opposite. Sorry, I interrupted you. You were suggesting that we stay together until after the birth…and then?'

'You and I go our separate ways,' Rafiq framed, releasing his breath. 'That agreement between us would leave all options open for all of us.'

Izzy nodded very slowly. Marry purely for the sake of that legal bond and then split up again? Yes, that did make sense to her. It *would* settle the essentials. It would give the twins their choices, whatever they might be, when they were adults and it would also leave both her and Rafiq free to continue with their lives. Even so, it certainly didn't feel like the answer to her every prayer and she didn't understand why it didn't.

'I think that would be almost perfect,' she told Rafiq, because her brain believed that and she squashed the sense of unease already threatening to rise inside her. 'After all, you can't be any keener on the idea of marrying a virtual stranger than I am.'

The strong lines of his fabulous bone structure went taut, showing off the intriguing hollows, and her heart jumped behind her breastbone. 'No...' he conceded almost guiltily half under his breath. 'I will always do my duty but my first marriage was not a happy one.'

Rafiq froze up even more as he felt those words slip from him because he had never once admitted to anyone what he had just admitted to her. Even so, the sky didn't fall, and no piercing shard of disloyalty pained him because he had long since adjusted to the absence of a woman who had, in truth, been as absent in life to him while alive as she was after she passed. 'I shouldn't have said that!' he breathed in a roughened undertone of discomfiture.

'Why not, if it's the truth?' Izzy murmured quietly, skating a soothing finger down over the clenched fist lying within her reach. 'All this will be easier if we try to be honest with each other.'

'Yes,' Rafiq conceded, censuring himself for that moment of weakness, that moment of unguarded frankness that was very unlike him. Something about Izzy encouraged him to break free of his normal reserve and self-discipline. He would have to watch himself around her and not make a habit of such vulnerability.

Women disliked weak men and only weak men revealed emotion, he reflected grimly. He had learned that as a child when his mother pushed him away and told him that boys didn't cry and cling to their mothers. He had learned it as an adult when he tried to reason with his childless wife and referred to his own feelings and she went off into hysterics, outraged that he could dare to mention *his* side of their story and verbally abusing him for that mistake.

'I will arrange the wedding.'

'Wedding?' she exclaimed in dismay.

'Not a normal one,' Rafiq qualified. 'A little ceremony, which will only be witnessed by a couple of people in a quiet room here in this wing of the palace.'

Izzy's frown evaporated. 'Because it has to be secret,' she guessed. 'Well, that's lucky. I don't have anything to wear for a proper occasion.'

'I will have appropriate attire brought to you. My uncle will be one of the witnesses and a bride in a dress of some kind will feel more normal to him. He is a kind man, a good man but out of touch with the modern world. Our situation has troubled him deeply,' Rafiq confided again, compressing his wide sensual lips on the suspicion that once again he was saying too much, revealing too much.

Izzy nodded agreement and made herself munch through a piece of toast very slowly because she was feeling a little queasy and hoping that something a little more solid than fruit would settle it. Unhappily, the ruse didn't work and a few minutes later, she found herself plunging out of her seat like a madwoman and racing up the stairs and back to the bedroom again to find the bathroom.

She was genuinely horrified to glance up when she had finished being sick and discover Rafiq in the doorway. 'This is par for the course,' she pointed out defensively as she rinsed her mouth at the sink and reached for her toothbrush.

'The doctor will still visit. The palace has its own medical clinic. Now,' Rafiq breathed, suddenly at her elbow and bending down to scoop her up like a doll. 'You should rest until you feel a little better.'

He lowered her back down on the bed.

'But we will have to get some food into you that stays down,' he remarked worriedly. 'I will consult the doctor.'

And with that, Rafiq was gone, leaving her to dizzily study the space where he had been.

CHAPTER SIX

THEY WERE GOING to marry and, by the sound of it, quickly, Izzy reflected in a daze.

It wouldn't be a real marriage, of course, but it would enable her to build a proper foundation for her babies' futures and she wouldn't be fit to *be* a mother if she wasn't willing to make some sort of a sacrifice, would she? After all, her own mother had given up a life of comfort and ease to live on a shoe-string for the sake of the twins she'd carried and to be with the man she loved.

Rafiq was clever too because he had stripped the facts down to the basics and left her without a leg to stand on with regards to the suggestion that they marry. She rolled her eyes at recognising how he had won the concession he wanted from her.

When the maid knocked and entered with another, explaining that they had brought an outfit for her to wear to meet the Regent, she was even more impressed by Rafiq's shrewd cover-up. Staging a secret wedding in a place stuffed with gossiping staff would have to be done with care but there could be no better excuse for her to get all dolled up than for the important occasion of meeting her husband's uncle, the Regent and current ruler of Zenara.

Evidently, there was a need for them to marry at speed before anyone could suspect that they were actually *not* married. She could only assume that any kind of scandal was viewed as a major catastrophe in the Zenarian royal family and suppressed a sigh. Her mother would have understood that viewpoint better than Izzy would have, considering that becoming an unwed mother-to-be had led to her mother being thrown out of her family. That same attitude, however, struck Izzy, the child of a different generation, as prehistoric.

Even so, if that was the way it had to be in Zenara she would play along for her babies' benefit, and in the bathroom she put on the long blue richly embroidered dress she had been brought. It was pretty but it looked like one of those national dress outfits people wore to dance in at country festivals and she smiled, returning to the bedroom to be draped in jewellery and have her hair fussed over. In the end she did her hair herself because her corkscrew curls had a mind of their own and putting them up in a more formal style took a familiar pair of hands. The jewels in the box opened for her perusal were utterly spectacular, she reflected, smoothing a reverential finger over the diamond and sapphire necklace at her collarbone, which was accompanied by matching earrings.

Rafiq strode into the bedroom and she froze because for the first time she was seeing him out of Western dress. He wore a long white tunic and cloak and a red-checked turban, the ends of which draped over his shoulder like a scarf. It was a mode of apparel that made him look very different, very...*very* fantasy sexy, she decided abstractedly, studying the clean sculpted lines of his devastatingly handsome features in awe. She stood up, her knees suddenly weak.

'You look amazing,' he told her.

Her eyes danced with amusement at his reaction to what felt like fancy dress to her but presumably seemed much more ordinary to him.

'Why are you laughing?' Rafiq demanded in bewilderment.

'Back home, only a micro miniskirt and a very revealing top would get me that reaction from a man,' she whispered.

Rafiq frowned. 'Do you dress like that when you go out?'

'No, never been a fan of putting it all out there,' she told him as he grasped her hand in his and led her down the corridor. The first thing she noticed was all the guards lining that corridor and then they were walking into a big sunlit room and a little portly man with a huge smile was coming towards her with an extended hand of welcome. The door closed behind them. Rafiq translated his uncle's warm greetings because the older man didn't speak much English, but it didn't matter because his smile and his twinkling dark eyes were wonderfully friendly and relaxed. Prince Jalil did not stand on ceremony.

A robed elderly man approached them and he spoke words to them both before directing them over to a table where Izzy and Rafiq were instructed to sign the marriage contract. Indeed, the wedding ceremony happened so fast and was completed so quickly that she almost asked Rafiq if that was really all there was to it. Happily, however, she was on her very best behaviour in such exalted company and engaged instead in replying to the Regent's polite questions about her family while Rafiq remained at her side, deftly translating.

'What now?' she murmured as Rafiq accompanied her back down the corridor.

'Now we escape the goldfish bowl of palace life,' Rafiq told her with resolve, guiding her downstairs and across an unbearably hot open space towards a helicopter.

'To go where?' she exclaimed. 'I haven't even packed!'

'You have nothing to pack. You brought hardly any clothes with you!' Rafiq pointed out. 'I have taken care of that problem.'

'Have you indeed? But—' Her voice broke off as he scooped her up in his arms to stow her in the helicopter and the rotor blades began spinning, making further conversation impossible.

Seated in the back of the helicopter, Izzy surveyed Rafiq in frustration. He hadn't told her where they were heading. He had implied that he had bought her clothes to wear. He had no right to do that, no right to make decisions without her input. They might be married but she was still struggling to accept the idea that bathroom guy, the father of the twins she carried, could now be her husband. And apparently, she had landed herself a bossy, I-know-best style of husband even if it was only for the next seven months or so…

She supposed he planned to visit their twins when he was in London on business and that they would both be very polite and civilised following the divorce. After all, what else but a divorce could he be planning?

Thirty minutes later, she was peering out of the window beside her when she saw a huge building loom up ahead of them and she blinked in astonishment because initially she thought she was hallucinating. They had flown over endless miles of desert, only occasional rock formations and black tent encampments interrupting the emptiness, and then all of a sudden she saw the giant construction looming ahead. Cream and gold in colour, it had a great domed entrance and a forest of tall turreted walls. It resembled a fantasy cartoon castle yet the lines of it were modern, but it was still an utterly out-of-place property to find in what seemed to be the middle of nowhere.

'Where are we?' she questioned as the craft dropped down onto a helipad on a flat roof.

'Alihreza,' Rafiq informed her, his exotic bone structure taut, his intonation indicating some strong emotion but not one she could label. 'It has been mine since my father's death but I don't use it.'

'Then why now?' she prompted as he assisted her from the craft to urge her through the blinding heat of exposure towards the building.

'Being here frees us from the goldfish bowl of palace life and gives us privacy. You can have your own room. I can go back to work and you can sun yourself by the pool and if we only meet once a day for dinner, nobody will even notice,' Rafiq completed with audible satisfaction.

Well, with her classic redhead's skin, quick to burn, she was unlikely to be sunning herself beside any pool, Izzy conceded, dazed by the piercing sense of hurt that assailed her in the wake of that little speech. He had brought them to this out-of-the-way spot so that he could reclaim his freedom and ignore her existence.

Why on earth *should* that make her feel hurt and rejected?

Hadn't they been honest with each other about their feelings? Rafiq was no keener on being married than she was, and it was natural that he would want to return to his normal way of life. He didn't want to be one half of a couple and feel forced to share a bed. He didn't want the annoyance of having to be seen to entertain a woman people believed was his wife.

It might hurt her pride, but she needed to come swiftly to terms with the reality that she was only a wife on a legal document and not in any other meaningful way.

Rafiq didn't owe her anything more and he wasn't pretending that he did either. That was honest, fair, she told herself firmly. They had had a one-night stand, not a relationship. A one-night stand and an accidental conception did not make a relationship.

An assembly of staff greeted them with a near reverential respect, which made her feel more of a fake than ever because she wasn't truly Crown Princess and future Queen—she was only a stand-in, a temporary aberration, Rafiq's contraceptive mishap… or miracle, depending on one's viewpoint, she adjusted ruefully.

A hail of polite introductions and smiles welcomed them to Alihreza before they were ushered into a lift that was as over-the-top opulent in mirrored design as the gilded marble corridors and staircases she had glimpsed.

'This place is spectacular,' Izzy murmured, staring in wonder at the tiers and arcaded terraces of carved stone walling that surrounded the huge central courtyard that sported a swimming pool, luxury seating areas and glorious vegetation.

'It is a monument to excess and corruption,' Rafiq contradicted between compressed lips as he strode through grand double doors into a bedroom.

Thoroughly taken aback by that lofty judgemental statement, Izzy directed a bewildered glance at him.

Rafiq was poised by the window, his bronzed face in sunlight as he removed the ceremonial turban, running long brown fingers through his black luxuriant hair, that hair that *felt* like silk between her fingers. He was so beautiful at that moment that he made it hard for her to breathe, and something intimate tightened and clenched at her feminine core to send colour flying up into her cheeks.

Unnerved, Izzy made a show of examining her surroundings. It was a superb bedroom, awash with a jaw-dropping amount of luxury. In the simmering silence she ran a fingertip over the gilded trim on a nightstand and along the smooth crease of a delicate embroidered silk curtain.

'Your room is next door,' Rafiq informed her tautly, striding across the room to pull open the connecting door in invitation because the more he was exposed to her, the more he wanted her, which meant that keeping his distance made better sense. And he was *always* sensible, he reminded himself with resolve.

He couldn't have her, not now when their marriage was only supposed to be an empty charade, and it was a retrograde step to appreciate what he could not have. He saw that lush pink mouth and he craved it. She was like a fire in his blood, heating him up every time she came too close yet blissfully unaware of the effect she had on him. She had gazed back at him incredulously when he told her she looked amazing in that dress, utterly unable to see how the tight bodice cupped her full breasts and how the drape of the fabric outlined the curve of her generous hips, equally incapable of comprehending how a man who had already seen her naked could picture her shapely legs…*spread*.

Rafiq gritted his teeth at that crude thought and image, particularly at experiencing it in the place most notorious for his father's carnal transgressions. Maybe the blood in him *did* run true, only fortunately for him his clean-living uncle had contrived to have more of a sobering effect on his principles than his dysfunctional parents had. Such troubling concepts and suspicions and insecurities had haunted Rafiq since he had been a teenager. Every time he craved sex for the sake of it, every time he wondered what it would be like to be with a woman who wanted him outside those few short days when she had the greatest chance of conceiving…

As if that declaration about her separate room hadn't punched what remained of her breath back out of her lungs, Izzy pinned a bright smile to her face since it seemed to be what Rafiq expected and she didn't like to disappoint him. Or maybe she wanted to hang onto what remained of her pride, a more cynical inner voice suggested as she strolled over to the open doorway, and then what he had said only minutes before roused her curiosity afresh and she turned back to him and probed inquisitively, 'A monument to excess and corruption?'

Lean, devastatingly attractive features grim, Rafiq turned brooding dark eyes back to her, thinking that she just had to go *there*, where nobody else dared in his radius. 'My father built this palace and ploughed millions into it, so that he could have some-where *very* private and luxurious to entertain.'

'Well, maybe he was extravagant but surely in an oil-rich country that's not a hanging offence,' Izzy remarked uncomfortably, beginning to wish by his grave demeanour that she had left the sub-ject alone.

Rafiq studied her with shielded eyes and de-cided it was time to tell her what was already widely known in Zenara, where his father's name was never ever mentioned in polite company. 'He held drug-fu-elled orgies here with porn stars and hookers.'

'Oh...' For a split second, Izzy was frozen to the floor by shock and then she blinked rapidly, and a startled strangled snort of laughter was wrenched from her, her hand flying up to her parted lips in sincere apology and dismay. 'S-sorry,' she stam-mered. 'I was just thinking that this is one place where you wouldn't want to say, *If only the walls could talk*!'

Rafiq surveyed her in utter disbelief.

'I'm sorry, I'm sorry, but you're standing there like a pillar of doom,' Izzy told him helplessly. 'All ashamed and disgusted and miserable at having to tell me that. Why are you still so sensitive about it? Your father's gone! It *is* the past you're talking about, not the present, and you're not responsible for your father's choices.'

'It is not that simple,' Rafiq argued fiercely. 'He disgraced the royal house. There is no depravity he did not explore, no extravagance he did not commit!'

'When did he die?' Izzy asked more gently.

'Sixteen years ago...' Rafiq admitted flatly.

'And you're still angry, but you shouldn't still be feeling that so personally,' Izzy countered with conviction. 'It happened and can't be changed but the sins your father committed weren't yours and you should make the decision to let go of it all. Make that decision for your own sake. It *is* that simple.'

Rafiq was shaken by that straightforward and practical approach to the sordid heritage that had haunted and humbled him throughout his life.

'I mean, *every* family has secrets,' Izzy commented more thoughtfully. 'Some secrets are embarrassing, some are hurtful, some may even cruise close to illegality but there's nothing you can do about that. If it's your family, you're stuck with them and that background, but you certainly shouldn't feel guilty about their mistakes, particularly not if you choose to lead a different life from theirs. I mean, you *do*, don't you?'

Even more surprisingly in response to that enquiry, Rafiq found himself breaking out into spontaneous laughter that she could even ask such a question of him. 'Definitely not into orgies and the like,' he confirmed with a flashing smile, relishing her indifference to what he had told her and the obvious fact that it didn't change her attitude to him. 'But some people *do* believe that such behaviour as my father's is the result of bad blood and that such a man's children may follow in his footsteps.'

'Only really, *really* out-of-touch, prejudiced people,' Izzy opined confidently.

'I am not oversensitive on the subject,' Rafiq felt the need to declare even though he knew he was glossing over the truth, indeed possibly outright lying. After all, his father's sins had been used like a stick to beat him with throughout his life, changing him, marking him, rebuking him, warning him of the danger of excess in any field. Having someone simply laugh inappropriately and remind him that his father's mistakes were not his to repent was a little like being suddenly busted out of a prison cell with bars that he hadn't even realised existed.

'Well, if this is my room, I'll leave you to it!' Izzy breezed, stepping through the doorway and beginning to close the connecting door.

'No!' In an abrupt movement, Rafiq crossed the room and dragged the door open again.

'No?' Izzy queried in surprise as she spun back. 'But I *thought*—'

'This far we have not had much of a wedding day,' Rafiq breathed in taut continuation. 'No celebration, nothing…'

Izzy shrugged a tiny dismissive shoulder, her head high, her chin at an I-can-cope-with-anything angle. 'We're not a real couple,' she pointed out quickly.

'We may as well be,' Rafiq countered, brilliant dark-as-Hades eyes locked to her triangular face, lingering on her pale flawless skin and the brightness of her bluer than blue eyes. 'Tonight, we will do something different…'

'Don't think there's a lot of *different* around this neck of the woods,' Izzy warned him ruefully, having only seen sand and more sand out of any of the windows that looked beyond the walls and the courtyard. And Izzy didn't *like* sand, had never liked sand, whether it was sand on a beach or sand in a sandpit when she was a kid. Sand in giant rolling dunes that formed the entire landscape left her cold.

'We will dine in the desert this evening,' Rafiq proposed, striving to think feminine, romantic, even frilly and getting absolutely nowhere in his imagination because he had absolutely no experience in that line. Instead he was forced to settle on an experience that he was pretty sure she could not previously have encountered.

'Oh…' Izzy was just quick enough to kill the grimace threatening her facial muscles. 'Well, that would be different, *special*,' she added hastily, not wanting to be picky or ungracious because there truly wasn't much available in the way of alternative options.

'The stars are amazing at night,' Rafiq told her with sudden warmth, his smile illuminating his bronzed features like the sun and dazzling her. 'The desert at night is wondrous.'

Engulfed by that astonishing smile, Izzy decided she could bear to picnic in a mud puddle should that be what was required of her.

Vanishing back into his own room, Rafiq stripped for a shower and wondered why he had suggested dinner in the desert. It was surely basic courtesy to ensure that his bride enjoyed her time in Zenara and for him to act as a considerate host? *Even though he had planned to avoid her?* his hind brain prompted. And beneath the beat of the shower, Rafiq groaned, comprehending his change of heart with a clarity that surprised him.

Izzy was *not* Fadith. In nature, she was not remotely similar to his first wife. She was a totally different woman. Just as the handful of women he had had sex with in recent years could also have been dissimilar, only he had never given them the chance to prove that, had never got to know them in any but the most superficial of ways. He had never spent the night with anyone until Izzy and had never allowed an encounter to stretch into a second night.

Izzy, however, was a unique case. *'We're not a real couple,'* she had said, and while in one essential way that was true since they did not plan to remain together, in other ways it was quite distinctively untrue, Rafiq reasoned seriously. Of course, his outlook on marriage was very different from hers. Weddings were fun occasions in the West, associated with romantic love and deeply optimistic hopes. But being born royal, Rafiq had never expected that kind of marriage. He had always known that he was unlikely to get to choose his wife for himself and that he would have to simply make the best of whichever woman he married. That awareness had made him realistic and practical.

What Izzy had yet to accept was that, even without those Westernised notions of hers about marriage, she was *still* his wife and was *still* the mother of his unborn children, a bond that would create an unbreakable lifelong tie between them. And when she did reach that real-world state of acceptance, how would she feel then? How could he possibly know?

He was still marvelling that she was willing to surrender custody of their offspring and leave her children behind in Zenara while she returned to the UK to pursue her career plans. She was a lot younger than he was, he reminded himself, and still defiantly determined to reclaim the life she had expected to have, and he understood that tenacious streak of hers. Even so, she had seemed softer, more sentimental and had made it very clear that family meant a lot to her...

But then what did he know about a mother's emotions, most particularly a career-orientated modern mother? he asked himself cynically. Having birthed him, his own mother had not seemed to care whether he was alive or dead, having never shown any further interest in him. At a very young age he had realised that not all women were maternal. It wasn't *every* woman who wanted to raise her own child, take on that responsibility for another being's welfare and limit her own freedom accordingly. He had not the slightest doubt that, had it not been for the royal nursery staff, he would have starved and cried without comfort as a baby. He wasn't making a poor judgement of Izzy's character, he assured himself staunchly, just as he hadn't judged his mother for the same lack of interest. After all, he freely acknowledged that his father had been no more concerned than his mother about their son's well-being. And with his private jet at her disposal, Izzy would be able to come back and visit their children any time she wanted…

In the bedroom next door, Izzy cradled her mobile phone and tried to work out what she could afford to tell her sister when she called her. And she *had* to call Maya because they had never been out of contact for so long.

'Where the *heck* have you been?' her twin shrilled down the line with worried emphasis. 'I've been worried sick! You *vanished*… I mean, who can afford to do that on our income?'

Izzy registered that she had to come clean. 'I found out that I was pregnant,' she told her sister baldly.

'How the hell—' Maya exclaimed and then added with startling insight, 'Bathroom guy? I *knew* I wasn't getting the whole story.'

'Bathroom guy,' Izzy confirmed, grateful for once that her sibling was that quick on the uptake.

'Right, so you're *pregnant*,' her twin murmured with laden stress on that condition. 'And right now, I'm…er…working in Italy.'

'You got a job abroad?' Izzy gathered with admiration. 'Congratulations. I expect, considering how fast your talents have been snapped up, that the position pays very well?'

There was an unexpected silence before Maya responded brightly, 'The benefits are unbelievable. My stay in Italy promises to free Mum and Dad from *all* their financial problems!'

'My goodness,' Izzy muttered, undeniably impressed by her twin's superior earning power. 'But what a shame that the dream job has to be abroad!'

'Well, can't have everything,' her twin sighed feelingly. 'So, where are you?'

'Zenara,' Izzy admitted.

'Where's that?' Maya questioned, delighting Izzy with her ignorance. 'And you're living there with this guy?'

'Yes.' Izzy grimaced, reluctant to tell fibs to her sister and hoping she wouldn't ask too many more difficult questions. She would tell Maya the whole story when she got home again but if she spoke up now, her twin would be worried sick, and she didn't need that stress when she had just embarked on a demanding highly paid job in a foreign country. But sooner than that she would definitely have to tell Maya about Rafiq's true identity and share the news that they were married.

'He wants us to stay together until the babies are born,' she admitted.

'Babies…like *more* than one baby?' Maya exclaimed in excitement.

'Twins,' Izzy confirmed. 'But it's too soon to know the gender yet.'

'Heavens, I'm going to be an auntie!' Maya cried with satisfaction and the dialogue veered off awkward questions into territory that Izzy could more easily cope with.

'All right, you're being suspiciously silent here about the important stuff. Tell me all about bathroom guy.'

'He's…he's gorgeous.'

'You're not that shallow,' Maya told her.

Izzy reddened at her end of the phone. 'He's very responsible, decent, maybe a little old-fashioned.'

'Nothing to complain about there when you fall accidentally pregnant,' her twin commented bluntly. 'Why shouldn't he be responsible? They're his kids too. At least he's not trying to run away.'

'Rafiq is not the running-away type.'

Having completed her call, Izzy walked into the ridiculously large and luxurious dressing room off the bedroom and opened doors and drawers, amazed to find them packed with brand-new garments and she leafed through them in awe. Rafiq had *said* she had no clothes because she had only brought along a couple of casual summery outfits in her carry-on case and he had made good on that deficit, *so* good indeed that she was staggered by his generosity. There were drawers full of fine lingerie, rails lined with dresses, both long and short, and all appeared to be maternity wear. It was good that he was aware of that issue with clothing, she told herself even while her instincts shrieked no, no, *no*, don't want that aspect to be so important that it shadows everything else for him.

So, you go and say thank you like a well-brought-up woman, she reflected, reasoning with her less grateful self, crushing it down because she was being *unreasonable.* After all, he wouldn't have needed to marry her or clothe her had she not been pregnant, therefore it was downright irrational to be annoyed that he was quite *that* aware of her condition. And it was not as though she could afford to buy a hot-climate wardrobe for herself or any maternity wear, she reminded herself. In any case her cropped jeans were already straining at her thickening waist and all her bras were too tight.

Knocking on the door politely, she walked into his empty bedroom.

'Rafiq!' she called lamely, knowing in frustration that there was no way she could track him down easily in the giant building and simply hoping against hope that he was still somewhere within hearing distance.

The bathroom door opened and he emerged, wrapped in a towel, and she grinned.

'So, back where we started, with you half naked,' she commented cheerfully, rejoicing in the vision of him standing before her, all lithe and bronzed and damp. 'I like it.'

Rafiq was shocked by that earthy honesty and struggled to hide it. Odd as it seemed, it had never really occurred to him that a woman might like to look at a man naked as much as a man liked to look at a woman and, acknowledging that, he felt off-puttingly out of his depth even though he was incredibly flattered and aroused by the appreciation that glowed in her sapphire eyes. That unabashed glow in her gaze had an immediate effect on him and he gritted his even white teeth, striving to suppress his arousal.

'I wanted to say thank you for the clothes…but there are so many,' she exclaimed. 'I'm never going to get to wear all of them!'

'You will be here for months,' Rafiq pointed out levelly. 'Through the hottest season.'

Izzy tried and failed to swallow as she studied him, her attention involuntarily glued to that tall, lean, powerful physique of his, the muscles indented in his torso that shifted with his every slight movement, the flatness of his stomach and the little dark silky furrow of hair there that snaked down out of sight below the towel. Her mouth ran dry. 'Not as hot as you,' she mumbled while thinking, I didn't just say that, *I didn't*.

'You find me…hot?' Rafiq breathed without any thought at all.

Colour claiming her cheeks in a feverish surge, Izzy simply nodded with a jerk.

The silence seethed, dark golden eyes welded to blue like heat-seeking missiles, and she felt her whole body leap into awareness, jolting her with embarrassing sensation as her breasts swelled and the peaks tightened and that hollow hungry pulse throbbed between the slender thighs she pressed tightly together.

A phone rang, breaking in like a sudden bucket of

ice water flung over her heated skin, and she turned away in haste as he reached with a stifled apology for the mobile phone lying at the foot of the bed. She was crossing back into her own room again when he murmured abruptly, 'It's cold in the desert in the evening. Wrap up warm,' he advised.

Cold *and* sandy, she thought dolefully. Oh, joy.

CHAPTER SEVEN

THE NIGHT SKY was a great arching black velvet expanse spangled with white glittering stars and it was, indisputably, very beautiful. The fire crackled and burned with blue and orange flames that were almost hypnotic, light leaping and casting shadows over the robed and armed men guarding the encampment. Dinner in the desert with a crown prince demanded a substantial number of people in support and protection roles, Izzy reflected ruefully.

There was the cook and his helpers, who had slaved over a brazier to provide a wholly impractical elaborate meal that ran to several courses. There were also Rafiq's bodyguards, the maid hovering for Izzy's benefit, lest she might need some service carried out. There was a black cloth tent behind them for their comfort and given the excuse she would have retreated to it because it looked cosy and she *was* horribly cold, in spite of the layers she wore. Across the fire, musicians pounded skin drums softly, another man plucking at a stringed instrument that resembled a mandolin while two more wielded flutes.

The music was rhythmic and melodic, the muted beat of the drums humming through her bones.

'My brother will visit us tomorrow. He is eager to meet you,' Rafiq told her quietly, after they had eaten.

With their backstory, Izzy winced a little at the prospect. 'What have you told him about us?'

'Very little. He has no interest in the details. Let me be blunt—you are the answer to Zayn's every prayer,' Rafiq declared with amusement. 'With me married and on track to have an heir, he finally has the freedom to do as he likes. He will join the army, train at Sandhurst, abseil down cliffs, shoot and blow up things. The active life of a professional soldier has always been his dream, but it was deemed too dangerous for the younger son who still had to marry and produce an heir and he was barred from it until now.'

'It's good to know that our...er...misfortune will bring someone else a happy result.'

'Our children are *not* a misfortune,' Rafiq sliced in with ruthless bite, grasping her slender fingers in emphasis, and then his ebony brows shot up and knotted into a frown. 'Your skin is like ice...why didn't you tell me that you were so cold?' he demanded, vaulting upright and carrying her up with him in the sudden movement. 'We'll use the tent.'

He urged her inside and she blinked rapidly, momentarily blinded by the brilliance of the many intricate jewelled glass lanterns that hung from the poles above them and sprinkled the soft rugs on the floor with slanting shards of rainbow colour. He tugged her down onto an opulent sofa scattered with cushions and rubbed her slender spine as if he could somehow force heat into her chilled bones.

Taking in her luxury surroundings, she laughed. 'Your people can't really have carted around all this furniture when they travelled into the desert.'

'Of course not, but this is what my father taught the staff at Alihreza to do. He never set foot out in the desert without insisting on every possible comfort,' Rafiq told her wryly, arranging a velvet throw round her shoulders and then laughing as he looked down at her, touching the pink tip of her small nose. 'You're bundled up in so much cloth you look like a baby being swaddled!'

Izzy gazed up into stunning dark golden eyes fringed with black curling lashes and her heart skipped an entire beat, her body engulfed by such a wash of heat that she broke out in nervous perspiration and quickly shrugged her shoulders to emerge from the cocoon of cloth she was wrapped in. 'Just being in here warms me up,' she muttered awkwardly, ducking her head down to break that visual connection in case he guessed what being that close to him did to her wretched hormones.

Long brown fingers pushed up her chin and their eyes met again, colour warming her cheeks, her lips softly parting. A growl broke free low in his throat as he scanned that pink pouting invitation and his mouth crashed down on hers with a raw hunger that stole her breath away.

'I'm burning up for you,' he breathed raggedly as

he finally wrenched his mouth from hers to allow her to catch her breath.

Staring at him, Izzy sucked in oxygen like a drowning swimmer until instinct drove her back for more of his mouth, hunger sizzling through her like a forest fire that had only required a spark to blaze. Her hands slid up over his shoulders and locked in the lush depths of his hair, a gasp sounding from her as his tongue tangled with hers and then plunged deep, sending a piercing shard of need arrowing to the very heart of her.

Without warning, she was on her back on the sofa and Rafiq was engaged in impatiently extracting her from her clothes and removing his own. Nothing had ever felt so desperate for her as that overpowering need to feel *his* skin against *her* skin.

'We weren't going to do this,' Rafiq growled the reminder as he straddled her in the act of pulling off his T-shirt before jerking down the zip on his jeans.

'Shut up,' Izzy said resolutely, running exploring hands appreciatively up over his bare bronzed torso and rejoicing in the sheer heat and masculinity of him.

Rafiq came down to her again like a man compelled by an unseen force, seeking her parted lips again, fiercely exploring and plundering. Izzy moaned low in the back of her throat as his wide chest crushed her throbbing nipples and his pelvis sank into contact with hers but she still had way too many clothes on and her hips bucked upward as she fought to shimmy out of her tailored wool trousers. Rafiq rolled off her onto the floor with a stifled groan. 'This is crazy!' he ground out in frustration.

Izzy rolled upright and shimmied with shameless haste out of her trousers. 'Only if you overthink it.'

'I always overthink stuff,' Rafiq admitted hoarsely.

Izzy had the cure for him, she decided as she sank down on her knees in front of him and tugged at the waistband of his jeans. The boxers went down with them, exposing the thick length of him. She licked her lips and just went for the challenge, hoping enthusiasm was more important than experience and from his first husky sound of pleasure she was lost in a sensual daze.

'I want to come inside you,' Rafiq husked, his deep voice soft and hoarse as he pulled her back up to face him again.

Unexpectedly, he then dropped down on his knees to peel her panties out of his path and nuzzle against the tender flesh between her slender thighs. All control was torn from her as he explored the swollen dampness at her core where she was so unbearably sensitive.

Izzy quivered with excitement and shook until he lifted her, hands cupping her hips and, in a feat of strength that took her breath away, brought her down on him with an urgent hiss, his body meeting hers and thrusting home with an efficiency that sent her heart racing like a bullet. He went down on the floor and hooked her legs over his shoulders and began to move with awesome speed and ferocity, grinding down into her receptive body with all the urgent demand and force she craved. As frantic as he was in that driving need for completion, she writhed under him in a frenzy, rising up to welcome every thrust.

The pressure tightening within her was an uncontrollable force of nature that dominated everything. When he sent her soaring and, with a harsh gasp of completion, buried his face in her tumbled hair, she felt as though she blacked out at the apex of her climax because it was so blinding, so utterly intense. Shaken by that raw physical intensity, she trembled as spasms of delight continued to ripple through her in pulsating waves.

Rafiq lifted himself off her in a fluid movement and then hunkered down to lift her up into his arms.

He stalked into the bathing facilities tacked onto the back of the tent and pressed the shower lever. Water streamed down her overheated body, plunging her from one temperature into coolness. She shivered and used the shower gel to freshen herself up as quickly as she could. As she emerged, Rafiq engulfed her in a giant towel and dried her off.

'I was rough. Did I hurt you?' Rafiq murmured, those glorious eyes locked to her and visibly anxious.

'No, I *love* your passion,' she confided in an involuntary rush, still stunned by the entire experience they had shared.

'And I yours,' Rafiq murmured thickly, scooping her damp naked body into his arms and holding her close. 'But I didn't intend this to happen.'

'Shush…' Izzy urged, resting a finger against his wide sensual mouth.

'I thought we could manage our relationship most effectively by becoming friends.'

Izzy rolled her eyes as he tugged a throw over her to keep her warm. 'We're never going to be friends. I'm too attracted to you,' she told him baldly, shaken by her own boldness but preferring to be honest. 'I know that's a complication we don't need but, since you seem to be feeling the same way, we might as well just go with the flow for the present.'

'I don't think I've ever gone with the flow with anything,' Rafiq admitted, black lashes lowering over his beautiful dark golden eyes as he studied her. 'How attracted is attracted?'

'Hungry for compliments…right?' Izzy grinned up at him, absolutely charmed by that need she saw in him then while she was in her relaxed state and able to be observant.

'It is a serious challenge for me to keep distance between us,' Rafiq confessed.

'Well, we just lost that battle,' Izzy pointed out without too much concern, relieved as she was to know that he was struggling with the concept of a platonic bond in the same way that she was. 'You're accustomed to rules and following them. But you can't make decisions on my behalf. I couldn't do friends with you right now…maybe some time in the future when we're a little more distant from recent events. Let's just keep it casual.'

Rafiq released his breath on a slow measured hiss.

In relationships, he preferred a pre-set agenda with every aspect carefully considered in advance. That approach left little room for misunderstandings or sudden emotional squalls. In comparison, he had never extended casual to more than one night with a woman and to be married and involved in a casual sexual relationship with his wife struck him as all kinds of wrong and dangerous, indeed much more likely to cause confusion and toxic feelings when they finally separated. And yet he still wanted her, he *wanted* Izzy more than he had ever wanted anything, and the knowledge that she carried his children only turned him on even more and made it even harder to take a step back. He lounged back on the sofa, cradling her in his arms, and struggled to relax while his libido was stirring him again to renewed hunger for her.

'You're so tense,' Izzy sighed against his chest, revelling in the damp musky scent of his skin, one hand idly stroking a satin-smooth shoulder. 'Tell me about your parents. What's your last memory of them?'

Rafiq groaned at that unfortunate question, which nobody had ever asked him before, but he was in the mood to be honest, shedding the guilt that that recollection always imbued him with. 'I was hiding behind a pillar and listening to them having a violent argument about the fact that my mother was pregnant with Zayn. She wanted a divorce and an abortion. She didn't want another child.'

'Good grief...' Izzy whispered, lifting her head to

look down at him, concern palpable in her troubled blue eyes. 'What age were you?'

'Ten or so.' Rafiq compressed his lips, feeling his tension drain away as he shared that memory. 'I was spying on them because my parents were virtually strangers to me. They spent almost all their time abroad and I was insanely curious about them.'

'Naturally you were. Does Zayn know about what you overheard?'

'Of course not. I would never have shared that scene or what was said then with him.'

'Why didn't they take you abroad with them?'

'A child wouldn't have fitted in with their lifestyles. My father was an unrepentant drug addict and my mother loved to party. Neither of them had any desire to settle down and be parents. By that stage my mother was tired of my father's infidelities and she wanted out of the marriage, but if she divorced him without his agreement, she would have lost the unlimited spending power she enjoyed and in the end she couldn't face that prospect.'

'So, they stayed together,' Izzy gathered.

'And she died of pre-eclampsia when Zayn was born. My father was negligent in not ensuring that she had the very best medical care. But by then they were already living separate lives.'

'Why was he like that? *So* uncaring?'

'I don't know. His mother died young and his father was elderly, which meant that he was only twenty when he came to the throne, too immature to have such power and wealth. He neglected his duties to chase a jet-set lifestyle across Europe and quickly fell into drugs. He built Alihreza because he was getting pressure to spend more time in Zenara, and he could only face that if he could have a very private bolt-hole where he could continue to indulge in drugs and sex.'

'Did he die from an overdose?' Izzy whispered.

'No, someone poisoned him, which is why I have a food taster.'

'A *food* taster?' she gasped in disbelief. 'But those times *I* cooked for you...'

'I broke the rules set by the executive council for my upbringing,' Rafiq murmured with amusement glinting in his dark golden eyes. 'How could I have explained a food taster while I was posing as an ordinary businessman?'

'Why was he poisoned?' A shiver ran through Izzy. 'That's seriously scary.'

'He had made so many enemies. He was a notorious womaniser. He slept with just about every woman around him and it's unlikely that they were *all* willing partners. I've always believed that it was a revenge killing. His death was exhaustively investigated but nobody was ever brought to trial. Now may we please talk about something else? I have answered all your questions.'

Izzy had lots more to ask but she suppressed the words bubbling in her throat because she could see that trudging through that weighty back story of his had loaded him down with unhappy recollections. And she didn't blame him—she really didn't blame

him. Although he had been born into almost un-
imaginable status and wealth, he had not enjoyed the
love, support and security that all children needed
to thrive.

'So, both your parents were gone and that's why
your uncle had to raise you and your brother,' she
summed up quietly.

'And we could not have had a better guardian,'
Rafiq sighed. 'Becoming Regent and agreeing to
raise his nephews was a huge responsibility for Jalil
to take on and he has never been a man who enjoyed the limelight, yet he did it because he felt it
was his duty.'

Gently settling her down on the sofa, he stood up
and began to get dressed. 'Let's return to the palace,'
he urged. 'It's getting late and you must be tired.'

But Izzy wasn't tired. As she was shuttled back
along a rough track in a four-wheel drive, Izzy's
brain was teeming with thoughts. They had become
intimate again. She hadn't planned that, hadn't truly
had time to consider that aspect of their marriage because one minute they had been two separate people
and the next they had been married. Keeping it casual wouldn't come naturally to her, she acknowledged ruefully. But, somehow, she had found herself
saying what she believed that Rafiq needed to *hear*
to relax with her.

He had felt trapped in his first unhappy marriage.
He hadn't said so, but she had guessed how he felt
about those years, years spent with a woman she
didn't believe he had loved. She definitely didn't

want him to feel trapped with *her*. She wasn't going to attach strings just because sex with Rafiq was mind-blowing. She wasn't about to tell him that though, wasn't an idiot. What had started out as a random, utterly unexpected first-time sexual experience had turned into something more for her, but she wasn't about to share that either. Her feelings were getting deep and complicated where he was concerned. Feelings that made her feel attached and involved in a way she was terrified of being but somehow couldn't help, feelings that were stronger than common sense and self-preservation. But was that really so surprising when the man she had married was also the father of the twins she carried?

Right now, her hormones had to be firing on all cylinders because of the pregnancy, she reasoned anxiously, and that might well be why her emotions were all over the place. It was even possible that she could be imagining the sense of attachment pulling at her.

Closing a firm hand over hers, Rafiq urged her into his bedroom with him and closed the door.

'What am I doing in here?' she muttered. 'I thought you liked your privacy.'

'Not when you're around,' Rafiq said succinctly, staring down at her with hooded dark golden eyes alight with sexual heat, his well-defined jaw line taut and beginning to shadow with stubble, accentuating his beautiful mouth. He looked so hot, her knees wobbled, butterflies flying loose in her stomach. 'Give me one good reason why I'd want to sleep alone.'

'Thought you preferred it that way.'

'Thought the same about you,' Rafiq incised, lean brown fingers rising to frame her flushed face. 'Got that wrong, *very* wrong.'

Enthralled by the dark liquid sexiness of his deep voice, Izzy tilted her head back to have a better view of him and that was a mistake because her mouth ran dry when she met the scorching heat of his appraisal. Her body reacted instantly, nipples tightening, pelvis clenching, that hollow ache between her thighs stirring afresh.

'Five minutes after I have you, I want you again,' Rafiq husked.

Her hands lifted and settled at his narrow waist to steady herself and she shifted closer, feeling the heat of his lean, powerful physique soak through the barrier of their clothes. She shivered, the strength of the pull he exercised over her unnerving her as she tried to fight it. It was the work of an instant for him to haul her fully into his arms and detach her from the cloak she had been wrapped in, casting it aside to unbutton the tunic she wore beneath.

'Rafiq…' she began.

'Tell me you don't want me.'

Her breath snarled up in her throat because she couldn't lie to him, couldn't lie to herself, had never in her life before realised that hunger could be so overwhelming that she could barely think, never mind speak in the grip of it. 'Can't do that,' she muttered in a pained whisper.

He gathered her up into his arms and brought her

down on the big bed. 'A little taste of you only makes me want more. It makes me greedy.'

As his lips closed around a straining pink nipple, her spine arched, and she gasped helplessly in response. Shimmering dark golden eyes surrounded by dense black lashes gripped hers and her heartbeat hammered, liquid heat shooting straight to her core. He spread her over the bed and worked a skilled path down over her squirming body, teasing at the more receptive spots, lingering at his leisure when her response was more immediate, toying with her as her movements grew more agitated. It was a slow burning torment after the swift release he had granted her earlier when his dominant masculinity had been exactly what she craved.

Her control was hanging by a thread, tiny tremors rippling through her as she stayed poised on the edge of climax, frantically seeking that ultimate goal. He swiped his tongue across her exquisitely sensitive bud and her whole body rose in a whoosh of sensation, fierce arousal linking with bone-deep craving and the clenching tightness in her pelvis to combine in a rapturous rush of pleasure that sent her careening into space, splintering delight shockwaving through every sense.

'Wow...' she framed in the aftermath, weighted to the mattress like a stone statue out of its element, gazing up at him with stunned eyes. 'Didn't know I could feel like that.'

'Didn't know I *could* make a woman feel like

that,' Rafiq traded with a flashing grin of satisfaction. 'I'm experimenting with you.'

'I'm like a session in the lab? Homework?'

'Infinitely more exciting than that,' Rafiq breathed, sliding between her spread thighs and lowering his head to snatch a breathtakingly demanding kiss that sent her fingers diving into his silky black hair to hold him close.

He surged into her, her body stretching to send sublime messages of pleasure through her quivering length. 'Do that again,' she said raggedly, struggling to breathe.

And he *did*.

And it was even more amazing because he slowed his pace to tease her, sending sensation slowly, oh, so slowly, sending her every nerve-ending into screaming overdrive to the height of excitement and craving. He flipped her over like a rag doll, ground into her from behind at the same time as he strummed that tender bud, and that fast she hit another orgasm, shrieking his name, out of her head, out of control, almost frightened by the drowning onslaught of sheer physical pleasure.

'So, no more separate bedrooms,' Rafiq murmured raggedly as she lay in his arms afterwards. 'Waste of time. Waste of opportunity. Waste of everything that we can be.'

'But we still have an end date,' she reminded him helplessly.

'Everything has an end date,' Rafiq qualified, deciding then and there that he would do everything within his power to stave off that end date for as long as was humanly possible.

'True.' And it was only sex, *casual* sex, she reminded herself, nothing that she needed to get all worked up about. It didn't matter that she didn't know anything about having a casual relationship because presumably he *did* and a few months down the road, she would barely remember him or the ecstasy, she told herself fiercely.

She was young and she was strong, no man's patsy, no man's fool. She would move on, write off Rafiq to the accident of fate he had been. She couldn't call him a mistake because it wasn't his fault that she had conceived, but they didn't belong together. He was going to be a king, for goodness' sake, utterly removed from her in every way, just as their twins would be in their relation to him, she registered belatedly, titled royals with a commoner mother with no claim to fame.

Long powerful fingers splayed across her stomach, which was no longer quite flat. 'I still think they're a miracle,' he murmured levelly. 'And I'm already so curious about them.'

'I suppose you're hoping for a boy to be your heir,' Izzy remarked, involuntarily touched by that miracle reference coming her way again.

'The firstborn will be my heir. Gender is irrelevant. A warrior queen here in the eighteenth century put that kind of sexism behind us. A future queen in waiting will be as acceptable as a king.'

'A *warrior* queen?' Izzy exclaimed, startled by that news.

'And reputedly a tougher negotiator than all the tribal heads put together!' Rafiq extended with amusement. 'It is many years since there was a constitutional bar to a woman taking the throne in Zenara. Zenara may strike you as a conservative country but, in some fields, we've always been quite free thinking.'

That assurance was a huge surprise to Izzy and not an entirely welcome one because in the back of her mind she had already been guilty of thinking that if she gave birth to two girls Rafiq might choose to be less involved with them and seek less regular access. Her cheeks coloured with shame at that ungenerous thought because it *was* selfish of her to want to keep the parental sharing to the minimum. Their children would benefit most from having *two* interested parents.

'Are you planning to visit the children here on weekends and school holidays?' Rafiq enquired curiously, wondering and in great surprise at himself if it could even be vaguely possible to run a marriage on such a part-time basis.

And Izzy froze as if a fire alarm had gone off and sat up with a sudden jerk, a befuddled expression stamping her triangular face as she shook her head. 'Visit them…*here*?' she repeated in disbelief. 'Why would I be *visiting* my children when they'll be *living* with me?'

A silence laden with electric undertones fell and

Rafiq gazed back at her with much of the same frowning disbelief.

'I mean, I know we never actually talked about the arrangements in any *detail* but I naturally just a-assumed,' Izzy stammered, watching the dark tension clench his lean, devastatingly handsome features taut with a sense of foreboding.

Rafiq was very still. 'And I assumed that you would be leaving the children here in Zenara with me to be raised as royals,' he breathed in a raw undertone. 'I thought you understood the situation. It is not solely of my choosing that they should live here but how else can they learn the language and how to integrate with our life if they only make occasional visits?'

Izzy had already heard more than enough. She snaked out of the bed like an electrified eel, stooping in haste to gather up her discarded clothing. Her hands snatched at her panties in desperation and she struggled to climb into them. Her hands were shaking. She could not credit, *refused* to credit that he could have thought for one moment that she would be prepared to walk out on her children with only occasional visits back to see them on offer.

'What sort of a monster do you think I am that I could agree to walk away from my kids?' she demanded wrathfully.

Lean, strong face hardening, Rafiq also left the bed. 'I did not attach such an offensive label to you. This is an emotive subject and you need to calm down.'

'I don't need to do anything I don't want to do!'

Izzy slammed back at him furiously, outraged to register that she was on the brink of tears.

'Izzy.'

'You made horrible assumptions about me and got me to marry you on false pretences!' she condemned in gritty interruption. 'When I leave Zenara in a few months' time I will be *taking* my children with me!'

'Not without my consent,' Rafiq slung back at her without hesitation as he hauled up his jeans and zipped them.

Izzy froze. She was in a mood, fit to be tied, wholly unable to rationalise the rage and hurt and sense of threat she was experiencing and that declaration of his was the last straw. 'Not…without… *your*…consent?' she questioned incredulously.

'Not without *my* consent,' Rafiq repeated with unapologetic emphasis.

'Well, we'll just see about that!' Izzy flung back wildly, dragging open the door between their rooms and slamming it shut again with a thunderous crash.

CHAPTER EIGHT

'YOU CAN'T JUST get into bed and ignore this!' Rafiq raked down at her as she lay in her bed.

Izzy spared him a brief glance that couldn't quite contrive to take in all of him for, clad only in jeans, a shirt hanging open on his bronzed torso and with his feet still bare, there was an awful lot of tall, lethally well-built Rafiq to encompass.

Izzy parted her lips. 'Watch me,' she urged curtly.

Rafiq stalked across the room like a predator ready to spring on prey and she watched even though she didn't want to. Something about that fluid prowling, loose-limbed grace of his tugged at her every sense and, gritting her teeth, she turned over and buried her hot face in the pillow. She was a mess of conflicting feelings. Rage and hurt. Lust and self-loathing. Fear and resentment.

'We *have* to talk about it,' Rafiq grated.

'Nothing to talk about,' Izzy said mutinously. 'We're not going to take a twin each and call it quits, are we? And since no sane parent would *do* that to their children that leaves us standing in conflicting corners.'

Rafiq flung back the sheet covering her and she flipped over in disbelief, her sapphire eyes alight with fury. He scooped her up, ignoring her struggles, and planted her down on the side of the bed.

'We *will* talk about this,' he said again fiercely.

Bridling like a cat that had been stroked the wrong way, Izzy smoothed a hand down over the silk and lace sleep shorts and strappy top she had put on, uneasily aware of how much skin she was exposing.

'How could you think for one minute that I would walk away from my babies?' she demanded rawly.

'I spent my formative years with a mother who continually walked away. Yes, I saw other maternal examples, in my uncle's home in particular, but I have always been aware that, just as there are men who can walk away from their children, there are also women who choose to do the same thing,' Rafiq completed in a driven undertone.

Izzy could not argue with that statement, but she still flung her head back to look at him, unable to accept that explanation for his assumption about her. 'But you *know* me. I can't believe that you thought *I* would do that.'

'You said you wanted your life back the way it had been. When you married me, you were very set on retaining your freedom and the choices you had already made. I can understand that outlook,' Rafiq conceded grimly. 'It was not for me to judge you.'

'Oh, don't come over all tactful now!' Izzy interrupted angrily. 'You assumed that I would give up my children pretty much completely to do…*what*? Train as a teacher? My children are more important and if you don't get that, you don't get anything about me!'

'It may be that I *was* guilty of wishful thinking, of hoping that there would not be conflict between us over this issue.'

'Oh, you'd better believe that there's going to be conflict!' Izzy hissed.

'But there were no false pretences,' Rafiq insisted. 'There *was* a genuine misunderstanding. I took too much for granted when you agreed to marry me. I was too keen to persuade you to marry me for the sake of the children, too relieved by your agreement to go into the matter in proper depth. Neither of us clearly expressed our wishes or intentions.'

'It should've been obvious to you that I always intended to take my children back to the UK *with* me.'

Rafiq raised a lean brown hand in an infuriating silencing motion. 'They are *my* children too.'

'I'm their mother,' Izzy stated vehemently.

'And I am their father. Why should I be any more willing to be deprived of my children than you are?' Rafiq demanded wrathfully, stunning dark golden eyes ablaze with anger.

'I wasn't planning to deprive you of them. You would've been free to see them any time you liked!' Izzy fired back.

'And how much time do you think I have to travel to the UK?' Rafiq prompted. 'In eighteen months, I will be King. My uncle only leaves Zenara for state visits, which are tightly scheduled, and he has little free time for travel. I will no longer be travelling on business. Even now I am bound to a very tight itinerary. I am not and I will *not* be free to do as I like.'

Izzy breathed in deep and threw her head back, copper curls dancing around her porcelain-pale face. 'I'm sorry if that is the case but, considering that we agreed to separate before we married, your problems are not *my* problems,' she declared, suppressing the guilt his arguments had unleashed inside her and the sensation that she was being unfair. 'And if you are likely to be *that* busy, surely the children will be much better off living with me.'

'For them I will make time, I will *always* make time,' Rafiq framed with fierce conviction. 'Probably because few people made time for me as a child.'

And her heart clenched inside her because she knew that he would make that effort, knew it for sure even while still furiously, bitterly resenting his willingness to believe that she would have been prepared to accept only an infrequent role acting as a mother to her children.

'This pregnancy may not have been planned but, now that it has happened, I'm fully willing to change and adapt,' she told him curtly.

Rafiq thrust impatient long fingers through the black hair still tousled by her clutching hands. Her face flamed and she looked hurriedly away from him as if by so doing she could block such thoughts and memories.

'It's too late in the day for this conversation,'

Rafiq murmured flatly. 'I can see that I have offended you and that was not my intention. Perhaps
tomorrow we will both be in a more reasonable state
of mind.'

'I still don't understand how we're going to work
anything out when we both want the same thing,'
Izzy breathed tightly.

'We'll work it out because we're both adults,'
Rafiq countered impatiently. 'And adults negotiate
and compromise.'

Izzy almost urged him to speak for himself because she wasn't in the mood to compromise, not
when it came to being a mother to her own children. That wasn't negotiable, was it? In that field,
she wasn't prepared to make concessions because she
couldn't afford to bend. It would break her heart to
walk away from her babies and deny them her full
love and attention. How could he think otherwise?

'I won't surrender my rights,' she whispered
tightly as Rafiq reached the connecting door that
separated their bedrooms.

Rafiq skimmed dark golden eyes back to her in
an electrifying moment of silent communication.
'We'll see.'

No, we won't see, she told herself as she punched
her pillow and got back into bed. She wasn't about to
change her mind, no matter what he had to say. Some
wedding night, she thought prosaically, cringing at
the recollection of the intimacy they had shared before she realised how he saw her. Well, monster *was*
an exaggeration, she conceded grudgingly, but Rafiq

certainly did view her as less than the feminine ideal of caring motherhood and that had bitten deep. Why had it hurt so much? Why on earth did she care so intensely about *his* opinion of her? Why was she so vulnerable when it came to him? Why couldn't she grow a thicker skin?

In the morning she was heavy-eyed and still at odds with herself. It was both a relief and an annoyance to walk out into the courtyard where breakfast was to be served and be greeted with an apology on Rafiq's behalf and the news that a major fire in a hotel in the capital city, Hayad, had demanded his presence early that morning. Braced to see him again and deprived of the expectation, she stiffened and her back went rigid. She would be much happier without him, she told herself staunchly.

She was still deep in that uneasy mood when a young man strolled out from under the trees shading the table. He extended a confident hand in greeting. 'May I join you for breakfast? I'm Rafiq's brother, Zayn.'

Momentarily, Izzy froze because in the midst of all the drama she had forgotten about his visit. But there he was, tall, lean and as dark as Rafiq in colouring and unmistakeably her husband's sibling. Dark eyes inspected her with unhidden interest.

'I had to see for myself if you could live up to Uncle Jalil's acclaim,' he admitted as he gave a nod to a hovering servant and smiled with Rafiq's easy charm while breakfast arrived at full tilt, offered in a bedazzling choice of dishes.

'Acclaim?' Izzy queried with a look of surprise.

'My uncle believes that you are exactly what my brother needs. Considering that he once believed that Fadith was the perfect wife for Rafiq, who can blame me for being a complete cynic and refusing to trust in his assessment?'

'Fadith,' Izzy echoed uncomfortably, now feeling very much under scrutiny, for Rafiq's kid brother was making no attempt to hide his scepticism. 'Rafiq rarely mentions her.'

'Rafiq never rats on anyone. It's a point of honour for him. An amazing trait for someone who was shafted at birth and cursed to pay for our late, unlamented father's sins,' Zayn continued with bite. 'He deserves better now.'

'Yes,' Izzy agreed, dry-mouthed, feeling under fire and unsure how to respond with anything other than honesty. 'And you want to know if I'm a better bet, but I'm afraid only Rafiq could answer that question.'

'You think?' Zayn lifted a black brow and scoffed, '*Twins?* My brother already thinks you are the eighth wonder of the world!'

Izzy reddened and continued to carefully eat the muesli she had selected. She was tempted to tell Zayn that no woman wanted to be valued purely for her fertility but that was too private a thought for sharing. 'Lucky me,' she murmured a shade flatly.

'Do you love him?'

Izzy glanced across the table in consternation. 'You can't ask me that!'

'I just did. I want my brother to be happy. It's that simple,' Zayn declared unrepentantly.

Feeling under pressure, Izzy pushed her curls back from her damp brow. 'I don't know how I feel. Everything's happened so fast. One minute I was single, the next I was married and expecting twins, for goodness' sake! I've hardly had time to catch my breath.'

'So, that's a no, then,' Zayn assumed, his mouth down curving.

Izzy looked back down at her plate, struggling to concentrate. In truth she didn't know what she felt for Rafiq, only that she felt *too* much in too many different ways, not all of which made sense. Last night, he had left her feeling angry and hurt, but she had still come down to breakfast with a helpless sense of anticipation. The disappointment that had infiltrated her once she learnt of his absence still rang like a hollow bell of warning inside her, reminding her that she couldn't afford to get too attached to the man she had married, not when their marriage wasn't expected to last.

'It's a marriage of convenience,' she told Zayn baldly since he had been so blunt with her. 'And it's early days for us.'

'Only my unlucky brother would get to make *two* marriages of convenience,' Zayn ground out and, glancing at her, he saw her surprise and curiosity. 'No, it wasn't a teenage love match with Fadith. But you need to ask him for the details.'

'I wasn't going to ask you,' Izzy said, thinking *I*

so was, her face colouring afresh. Like most people she preferred to avoid contentious issues and it was obvious to her that Rafiq didn't want to talk about his first marriage. Getting the story from Zayn would have been easier, most particularly when she and Rafiq were currently at daggers drawn.

Evidently accepting that he had got all he was likely to get from her, Zayn engaged in normal conversation for what remained of the meal. He was much less guarded than his older brother, yet very mature for his age, only his sudden boyishly enthusiastic smile betraying his youth. She understood his loyal protectiveness towards Rafiq because she was equally attached to her twin and two orphaned brothers, regardless of the age gap between them, were almost certain to be close.

They sat in the shade playing poker, Izzy working up a tally of losses that hugely amused Zayn.

'It's lucky for you that we agreed not to play for money,' he teased. 'You're a hopeless card player.'

'It's been a long time since I played,' Izzy admitted ruefully.

'I'd take you for a drive in the desert but Rafiq thinks I'm reckless at the wheel and you're too precious a cargo for me to take the risk,' he told her cheerfully.

They ended up playing a board game then, which Zayn played with the same ferocious spirit of competitiveness. When he departed in a helicopter before lunch, he and Izzy were on easy terms and she was sorry to see him leave. After lunch she felt queasy and went for a nap, but it didn't help. Her pregnant stomach was determined to be oversensitive and feeling under par was a side effect she assumed she had to accept. It was a surprise when a doctor was shown in by her maid, who had evidently contacted him. Where he had come from, she had no idea and she was taken aback to be told when she asked that he was the doctor 'in residence' at Alihreza. A herbal tea was prescribed and Izzy sipped it throughout the afternoon, pleasantly disconcerted to discover that it did definitely help the nausea and reduced it to a more bearable level.

She dozed through the hottest hours of the day, wakening to learn that Rafiq was on his way back. She went for a shower to freshen up, enjoying the cool sprays hitting her overheated skin before rifling through her new wardrobe to pick a casual cotton blue-and-white maxi dress that was both cool and comfortable. It was unnerving how fast her body was changing, she thought ruefully. Her breasts had swelled at least a cup size and her once neat waist was vanishing as her stomach pushed out.

When she heard another helicopter flying in, she was reading a magazine in the shade of the courtyard. Eventually, Rafiq came striding across the courtyard towards her and by that stage she was seriously tense and mentally walking on eggshells.

Sheathed in jeans and an open shirt, his bronzed skin shadowed by stubble, his stunning eyes gleaming at her from between lush lashes, Rafiq was a lethally lustrous and rawly masculine presence. Instantly her senses went on high alert, her heart rate increasing and, that quickly, she wanted to slap herself until she wised up. It was one thing to be attracted to the man she had married, quite another to break out in a girlish fever just because she was seeing him for the first time that day.

'My uncle sends his profuse apologies for dragging me back to Hayad for the day and leaving you alone here.'

'The fire…was it serious?'

Rafiq nodded grimly. 'A club popular with our young people. Although there were few deaths, many serious injuries were caused by the panic that broke out once the alarms and the sprinklers went off. I have been dealing with distraught parents and fire officials all day,' he confided heavily, studying her with appreciation. 'It is a relief to come back here and find you sitting calmly beneath the trees looking as fresh as a daisy.'

'But not feeling calm,' she muttered awkwardly, never able to be comfortable accepting a compliment and cringing because that made her feel as gauche as an adolescent.

'I understand that Dr Karim needed to attend you this afternoon.'

'Yes and he's very charming,' Izzy responded with a stiff smile. 'Why is there a resident doctor?'

'Because you're here and my uncle is very mindful of your health and keen to ensure that, should there be any kind of emergency, expert care is on hand,' he admitted. 'But while the doctor is here, he is also treating the staff and the local Bedouin. He will have a constant procession of patients requesting his attention.'

Izzy relaxed a little more and watched Rafiq take a seat opposite her, the sheer vibrancy of him that close tugging at her with invisible cords.

Rafiq drank in the sight of her, as pretty as a picture, and swiftly looked away again, troubled by the shuttered look in her once clear eyes and her defensive posture. He was responsible for that change in her, he reminded himself broodingly. She no longer trusted him. He had made a huge error with his assumptions and destroyed any faith she had had in him. He had screwed up royally and now he had to redress the damage at the same time as he concentrated on achieving the end goal *he* wanted.

'Now, tell me,' he urged. 'Are you well?'

His air of gravity made her frown. 'It was only a bit of sickness, Rafiq, nothing serious, nothing unexpected. Please don't fuss over me. I'm young, strong and healthy.'

'I don't see concern as fussing,' Rafiq countered. 'Obviously, I will worry about your well-being. I am keenly aware that what we discussed last night was destructive. Now you don't trust me. You may even fear that I could be planning to try and take our children from you.'

Izzy turned pale at that suggestion and gooseflesh cooled her arms as fright gripped her. 'No, I hadn't got quite that far yet but I don't want to even hear you *say* such a thing.'

'Fears voiced aloud cause less concern than those that remain secret and unspoken,' Rafiq murmured. 'I don't want you worrying about anything at the moment. Stress is bad for you.'

'Stress is an integral part of being temporarily married to and pregnant by a…a stranger,' Izzy muttered in an apologetic rush. 'You don't *feel* like a stranger to me. Somehow you never did but how much do I really know about you and what you could, ultimately, be capable of? And where do we go from here?'

Disconcertingly when she least expected it, Rafiq smiled, a flashing charismatic smile that warmed her chilled and anxious body from the inside out. 'We will work it out, Izzy. I promise you that we will work it out without any harm or hurt to anyone,' he assured her.

His sheer confidence blasted out at her like a force field, the controlled power of the nature he hid behind a cool, measured facade lacing his stunning dark eyes and flawless masculine features as he studied her.

'That's a lovely idea but I don't think it will prove possible in the long run,' Izzy countered heavily. 'We're going to fight—'

'We are *not* going to fight,' Rafiq sliced in with conviction as she shifted, the hem of her dress lifting to reveal delicate ankles wrapped in impossibly feminine ribbon ties. It was the ribbons that he found sexy, he told himself, unable to imagine any ribbon attached to Izzy's body that he wouldn't want to tug loose and untie. Hardening, he shifted position, regretting his tight jeans. 'I may have been apart from you today but, believe me, I didn't waste my time. I considered all our options and we have many more than you seem to think.'

'Options?' Izzy repeated, her brow furrowing. 'Like maybe…we separate now before everything gets even more complicated?'

His dense spiky lashes dipped to screen his gaze and he almost swore in frustration at that startling suggestion. 'That definitely wasn't one of my options,' he admitted.

Her attention lingered on his full sensual mouth, framed and accentuated as it was by a blue black shadow of stubble. A hot liquid sensation tugged in her pelvis and she pressed her thighs together, sudden painfully intense hunger gripping her like a dangerous drug. 'Well, what was…er…*your* preferred option?' she prompted, dry-mouthed, so tense that she couldn't even swallow.

The silence simmered like a haze of heat on a hot day, blurring her surroundings and the clarity of her thoughts but fully centring her attention on him.

'Easier than yours… I think,' Rafiq husked, springing upright with that lithe, fluid grace that stabbed her with a longing she could not control.

'Easier?' she questioned breathlessly.

Without the smallest warning, Rafiq bent down and scooped her up off the padded sofa into his arms. A startled sound of surprise was wrenched from her and she gazed up at him with huge sapphire-blue eyes. 'Rafiq…what are you doing?'

'What comes most naturally to me,' he murmured, settling back on his seat to cradle her across his lean muscular thighs, his arms caging her in place. 'You chose a pessimistic option. *I* choose a more positive one.'

'Oh…?' she gasped, heart hammering, body striving to melt into the pure heated allure of him that close in spite of her attempt to remain stiff and discouraging.

'We continue as we are,' Rafiq breathed in hoarse extension. 'Last night wasn't planned. Nothing that has happened between us has been planned. The attraction is too powerful to be ignored and too rare to be discounted or suppressed.'

'A-attraction? *Rare?*' Izzy exclaimed, sapphire eyes welded to glowing gold.

'I have never wanted any woman as much as I want you,' Rafiq confirmed without hesitation.

'You said…*continue* as we are?'

'Give our marriage a decent chance while we await the birth of our children,' Rafiq extended. 'We see if we can make it work and if *we* work, we stay together to raise our family.'

'You mean…like a *real* marriage?' she almost whispered as he stroked his fingertips across a slender ribbon-bound ankle.

Beautiful dark golden eyes held hers fast and hard. 'I want to keep you *and* our children but there are still other variations on the same theme available, which, if you wish, we can discuss. I am prepared to be flexible.'

His hand was sliding up her calf and she was lost in the sensations darting to more tender areas of her body. Indeed, the stroke of his knowing fingers against the sensitive soft skin of her inner thigh fired up every sense. That fast she wanted to rip off his shirt and sink down on the male arousal pushing boldly against her hip. Her face flamed. Rafiq brought out every shameless urge she possessed, introducing her to a side of herself she had not known existed until he appeared in her life.

Variations on the same theme, though, God bless him, she thought helplessly, her soft mouth quirking, recognising that he had approached her armed with every possibility he could muster, like a businessman engaged in trying to finalise a very important deal.

He didn't know how to do romantic, didn't even try. *But* without a doubt he wanted to *keep* her, and that truth smashed down Izzy's barriers and flooded through her defences to wash them away. The craving inside her, which she had been fighting to the very last ditch, was released like a sudden storm. Without a single word, she snaked up her hand to spear her fingers into his luxuriant black hair to drag his beautiful sensual mouth down to hers.

His lips smashed down on hers with an urgency that thrilled her to the marrow of her bones. He wanted her, he desired her as no man had ever desired or wanted her and, in that moment, the simple knowledge that he wanted her as much as she wanted him was sufficient to silence every other insecurity. Rafiq was going to be hers, absolutely hers for ever, because she wasn't prepared to let him go. His tongue plunged deep into the damp interior of her mouth and she moaned low in her throat.

'Dinner will be late tonight,' Rafiq breathed raggedly as he leapt up with her still clutched in his arms and strode towards the lift below the arches. 'Very, *very* late.'

Her entire body still buzzing from the provocative stroke of his fingers, Izzy was simply out of her mind with the same desire that powered him. Only he had the nerve that she lacked, she acknowledged, burying her hot face in a wide strong shoulder as he stalked past the servants hovering on the terrace, unconcerned by their scrutiny, unashamed of his passion. In the lift, he pinned her against the mirrored wall and kissed her breathless and she rocked against him like a shameless hussy, craving the arousal he couldn't hide from her, needing that physical contact in that instant as much as she needed air to breathe.

'You're amazing,' he told her thickly, laying her down across his bed. 'The most amazing woman I've ever met.'

It's only sex, her brain warned her, but she silenced that voice at supersonic speed because she was living in the moment—*revelling* in the moment, if truth be told—as Rafiq stood back and stripped, all urgency and hunger and appreciation, revealing a lean bronzed torso taut with muscle definition, exposing long powerful hair-roughened thighs.

It didn't get better than this, she told herself dizzily, it would *never* get better than this…

CHAPTER NINE

THE FOLLOWING DAY at Alihreza, Rafiq rose early, kissed her brow and headed for his office to catch up on work.

Izzy lay in bed feeling exceedingly foolish for her complete capitulation the night before. Her intelligence hadn't featured much in that decision, she acknowledged with a wince. Reality was, however, now staring her in the face. She was falling in love with Rafiq. What had started out as an infatuation had transformed into something much deeper and more long lasting. The instant he had offered her the chance to stay and become a normal wife rather than a temporary one, she had snatched at the offer, hadn't even hung back long enough to ask to hear the *other* options. She raised cooling hands to her hot face and groaned in chagrin.

She had agreed to stay married to a man who didn't love her and who would probably never love her. A man already familiar with the limits of a marriage of convenience, a man whose sole driving interest was in retaining custody of his unborn children. There it was: the awful truth she didn't want to face. Rafiq's primary objective was keeping his heir and spare in Zenara and raising them in his own home. She was a prized incubator to be tended, not a woman with thoughts and needs of her own. Realistically, Rafiq was likely to tell her whatever it took to keep her in Zenara. And how did that bode for their future? Or her happiness? Could she settle for that?

'Of course, you can't settle for that,' her sister told her sternly on the phone an hour later. 'I'll be flying in to see you in a few weeks.'

'The plane fares to Zenara cost a fortune!' Izzy warned her twin.

Maya laughed but it was an almost bitter laugh that made Izzy frown because she didn't get the joke. 'Money's not a problem for me now,' her sister declared. 'We have a lot to catch up on but I'm concentrating on the fact that I've settled Mum and Dad's problems for all time and no sacrifice is too great to achieve that, is it?'

'If you're the sacrifice, I'm not sure,' Izzy sighed. 'Oh, Maya, do you truly *hate* this job?'

'It's not a typical job. We'll talk when I see you. Face to face is always better.'

But the weeks passed and in the end Maya wasn't able to visit. First, she fell ill and said she didn't want Izzy to visit her in Italy, which hurt but had to be accepted. And then in the aftermath she said she didn't feel either like travelling or entertaining and that had to be accepted too, Izzy conceding that for the very first time her twin was asking for space from her.

Maybe it was part of growing up and attaining adult independence, she reasoned worriedly, wondering if she had been coming across as a little too clingy and demanding in the sibling stakes while resolving to let Maya get on with forging her own path.

In the meantime, life went on in Zenara. Izzy was able to satisfy her curiosity about Rafiq's first marriage as he began talking more freely to her. 'The guilt after Fadith's death was the worst burden.' Rafiq sighed, smoothing long fingers over the firm swell of Izzy's pregnant stomach as they lay in bed a few weeks later. 'In truth the marriage was miserable for both of us. Fadith never attained what she most desired…a child or even the status of Queen.'

'Was that so important to her?' Izzy queried, running a hand down over his flat, taut stomach to stroke him with tender possessive fingertips and smile as he stretched and groaned half under his breath, loving the effect she could have on him. 'I mean, I can understand her desire for a child, particularly when the two of you were hoping for an heir to the throne, but I don't really understand why being Queen was so important.'

'Because that was why she married me. Status meant a lot to her and her family.'

'I can't understand that outlook.'

'No, but then you're different, wonderfully different,' Rafiq growled, rolling her over to pin her beneath him. 'Fadith never loved me, never wanted me for me. A passionate clandestine romance with one of her brother's friends before our marriage set that in stone. He died in a car crash and she decided that she'd never love again, which is why she agreed to marry me.'

'So, she wasn't a virgin,' Izzy remarked in surprise.

'No but she was honest enough to tell me that before I agreed to marry her. I was shocked, out of my depth because I was much more naïve than she was and although virginity isn't demanded, it is rather taken for granted in a marriage at our level. Girls are sheltered, guarded in our society,' Rafiq confided. 'I was more surprised that she had loved someone else.'

'Oh, dear,' Izzy whispered reflectively. 'That was far too much for you to take on at sixteen.'

'I wasn't jealous because she felt more like a sister to me than a wife for months after we married,' Rafiq admitted wryly. 'That brought problems too. All she ever really seemed to want from me was a baby and, sadly, when she didn't achieve motherhood she blamed me for it. She was totally convinced that if there was anything wrong with either of us, it had to be *my* problem, my flaw.'

Izzy winced, imagining what that must've been like for them both when the expected development failed to materialise over ten long years. 'For me, babies were always something I knew I wanted but it was also something that was planned for way in the distant future,' she told him absently. 'But now that it's something very much in the present, I've adjusted.'

They had moved back to the royal palace outside

Hayad and Rafiq had taken up his usual duties, taking her with him on official activities when it was appropriate to do so. After a couple of engagements at schools, Izzy found herself becoming interested in the education system and she agreed to take those visits on. A second ultrasound revealed that she was carrying two girls. She flew over to London twice to visit her family with Rafiq by her side and found her parents and her little brother hale and hearty, her father talking with enthusiasm about some new sales job he had managed to get. The visit, however, had been dominated by Izzy needing to come clean and explain to her family who Rafiq was and that they were married. She told Maya on the phone, where Maya dropped her own marriage bombshell, telling Izzy about a whirlwind romance with her new Italian boss. Something in Maya's story didn't quite sit right with Izzy, but Maya deflected her twin's worried questioning, choosing instead to concentrate on Izzy's own news.

As her pregnancy advanced, the nausea vanished but Izzy went out less, aside from a short trip back to the UK to spend a weekend with Maya and her new husband and their extended family. The fact was that Izzy was embarrassed by her increasingly cumbersome body. Her beautiful cunningly shaped maternity clothes could only do so much and she still thought she most closely resembled a barrel because a twin pregnancy on her slight frame was enormous. Rafiq might tell her that she was 'glowing' but she couldn't find it within her heart to quite believe his sincerity and when her ankles swelled up unattractively, and even her face began to show the same tendency, the doctors advised more rest and she did exactly as she was told.

Rafiq was wonderfully supportive every step of the way. He did not leave her alone for longer than a night, but she felt increasingly less desirable as her pregnancy progressed and the doctors warned them that, with her rising blood pressure and other symptoms, sex was best taken off the menu until the delivery of their twins was safely accomplished. Rafiq acted as if the bar on the seething passion that had once united them was no great loss and she blamed his easy acceptance on her swollen stomach, assuming that he no longer found her quite so attractive.

No longer, however, did she kid herself about her own feelings. She adored Rafiq and, although it embarrassed her, it was still a struggle to keep her hands off him. He still shared a bed with her every night, and she cherished that intimacy, loving the way he still held her close even when she complained, tongue in cheek, that he made her too warm. While they had still been lovers, she had felt needed by him, necessary, *desired*. Without that physical connection, she felt bereft, unimportant, insignificant aside of the reality that she was carrying their children.

Did he feel anything for her at all, beyond the reality that his children's well-being rested on hers? Was her only value to him based on her ability to bring the twins into the world? What about her personally? Was there another dimension to his care of her, beyond that of her pregnancy? Those were the fears that tormented Izzy with every passing day.

She studied the ever-growing collection of her jewellery and picked sapphires to wear over diamonds. Earlier in life it could never have occurred to her that such luxurious choices would one day be hers. But Rafiq's generosity and frequent gifts had endowed her with a fabulous collection of priceless jewels. She donned a pair of loose flowing pants with a tunic and high heels, reckoning that she would look like a ship in full sail but aware that she had no real choice in the clothes department, having developed a girth that normal garments could not encompass.

Rafiq was always giving her stuff but the superb nursery being put together down the corridor in a previously unused section of the palace was even more telling. She had picked a bright jungle print and primary colours to provide their twins with a stimulating decor. Rafiq had taken an interest in every single choice she made, unashamedly enthralled by the prospect of being a father. His enthusiasm both warmed her heart and hurt her at the same time. If only he could have focused that emotional intensity on *her*…and why shouldn't she *ask* him where she stood in his life? What was she so afraid of? If all he cared about was the babies she carried, she had the right to know that and he would probably be honest enough to tell her. So, she would *ask*…

She was about to leave her bedroom when a cramp gripped her stomach and she fell still, her hand pressing against her abdomen. When a damp sensation assailed her, she rushed into the bathroom to check herself. Horror gripped her when she saw the bright red blood.

Oh, dear heaven, was she losing her babies? She had believed she was safe this far on in her pregnancy—well, as safe as any woman could ever be in her condition. In a panic, she stabbed the button on the household line that would summon Dr Karim…

CHAPTER TEN

EVERYTHING THAT HAPPENED over the next hour was ever after a blur for Izzy.

Dr Karim came running and then she was being swept off in an ambulance, Rafiq hanging onto her hand, as pale as someone of his bronzed complexion could be. He looked like a man in the grip of his worst nightmare and, ridiculously, she wanted to smooth his tumbled black hair from his brow and soothe him.

'We're going to deliver the babies now,' Dr Karim told her gently, after she had been separated from Rafiq and a nurse had helped to undress her and slot her into a hospital gown. 'But I'm afraid it will be a C-section, because one of the babies has moved into a breech position.'

'It's too early!' Izzy gasped, stricken, frantically worrying about the survival of her twins.

Mr Abbas, the English-speaking consultant obstetrician engaged for her delivery, whom she had already met on several occasions, joined them and answered her.

'No, it is only a couple of weeks early and we were prepared for this development by your most recent ultrasound. We have every prospect of achieving a safe delivery,' he declared with immense confidence as she was wheeled into the operating theatre and monitors were attached to her. The epidural was administered without any pain.

Rafiq reappeared by her side, gowned and masked, his lean, darkly handsome features rigid with fierce tension.

'Mr Abbas…' Rafiq urged half under his breath. 'Whatever happens, my wife must come through this procedure safely. *She* must be your first priority.'

Izzy blinked rapidly, her eyes dazed, because she was certain she had to have either misheard or misunderstood that instruction.

'Try to relax, Your Royal Highness, I fully intend to bring all three of your family safely through this experience,' Mr Abbas informed him as the doors of the theatre swung open and an entire medical team trooped in to join them and a series of checks was carried out.

Rafiq squeezed the life out of her hand. He looked terrified.

'A lot of women have to have this,' Izzy felt it incumbent on her to state.

'This is you,' Rafiq rebutted hoarsely. 'There is only one you.'

A sheet was erected, cutting off her view of her lower body. Her fingers went numb in Rafiq's fierce hold. She felt that she was being touched and then there was a little pressure but absolutely no pain. What seemed like only a few minutes later a baby's wail broke through the silence and a cross little face topped with a shock of dark hair appeared for an instant before disappearing again.

'That's Leila,' Izzy whispered in total awe.

'She's…' Words seemed to fail Rafiq entirely at that point.

'And that's Lucia,' Izzy added when a second baby made a brief appearance above the sheet.

She wasn't able to hold them. The operating theatre was too cold for them and the babies had to be checked and wrapped up warm to be borne off. As she turned to comment on the fact to Rafiq, there was a crashing sound and she caught a narrow glimpse of him sprawled on the floor before aides rushed to lift him and help him out.

'He will be fine, Your Royal Highness,' Mr Abbas murmured gently. 'The emergency was a little too much for your husband's nerves. The Crown Prince has been very concerned throughout your pregnancy.'

'Has he?' Izzy muttered in surprise, because she genuinely hadn't realised that Rafiq was actively worried, had simply assumed that he viewed caring for the needs of a pregnant wife as his duty and responsibility.

'A not unexpected reaction from a man who saw his mother die after his brother's birth. That delivery was a sadly botched business and I'm sure it left a mark on our future King to have witnessed such a tragedy as a young child.'

She was moved into the recovery room and asked if she required anything for pain. She didn't, and when two nurses came in wheeling tiny cribs that held her babies, she was entranced. Leila had Rafiq's hair and Lucia was blonde, a sort of sandy strawberry blonde that might or might not turn red. Izzy cradled each baby to her in turn and smiled, so very relieved that everything had gone well and quite in awe of her children. When Rafiq appeared in the doorway, still looking pale, she beamed and extended a hand to him encouragingly. 'Come and see them properly,' she urged.

'I'm sorry,' he breathed tautly, his stunning dark golden eyes full of regret. 'I wasn't able to be there for you as I should have been.'

'No, I'm the one who should be apologising,' Izzy told him ruefully. 'It never crossed my mind that you could be so wound up about this.'

'I didn't want to alarm you with my fears. My anxiety was better kept to myself,' Rafiq pointed out stiffly.

'I didn't know that you *saw* your mother die,' she muttered with regret. 'I wish you had told me that.'

'*Not* while you were pregnant. All I could do was ensure that you had the very best medical care available,' he countered gravely. 'And look after you.'

And look after her he *had*, continually fussing over what she ate and how much she rested and how she felt, she acknowledged, reckoning that she had been blind not to suspect the very real fear that he was concealing on her behalf.

'I won't tell anyone that you fainted,' Izzy murmured, reaching out to close a hand over his.

'With the number of staff that witnessed my collapse, it will be a well-told story the length and the breadth of Zenara,' Rafi responded in a wry tone of acceptance. 'I am simply grateful that both my wife and my daughters are safe and healthy.'

'Would you like to hold them now?' Izzy proffered.

Rafiq sank down in the chair beside her bed and Leila was placed in his arms. He studied the tiny face under the pink beany hat and Izzy watched him swallow hard and blink rapidly, but the sheen in his lustrous gaze was unmistakeably emotional. He touched a careful fingertip to her little cupid's bow mouth. 'So tiny…'

'I'll have you know that they are both a very good weight and isn't it wonderful that, even though they've arrived a little early, they don't need to be put in incubators?' Izzy proclaimed with pride. 'We'll be able to take them home with us as soon as we're ready.'

'I would like you to spend two nights here within the care of trained personnel…just to be safe,' Rafiq admitted quietly as Leila was returned to her mother and Lucia was brought to him.

'So precious,' he muttered with deep appreciation. 'I think they are going to have blue eyes and this little lady may even have inherited your hair. My uncle and aunt and Zayn would like to visit this evening. Do you feel up to that? Feel free to ask them to wait until tomorrow.'

'No, I'll be fine. I want to show my daughters off,' Izzy admitted with a rueful grin. 'But I have to phone my own family first.'

'Perhaps I could contact your parents for you, and you could take care of your sister. I hope that she will come to meet her nieces. I know you have been worrying about her and that you would enjoy that,' he completed thoughtfully.

It was one of those moments when she almost dropped her guard and told him that she loved him but she swallowed the words, recalling the guy who had been trapped for ten years in an unhappy marriage and who had settled, for the sake of his children, for a second loveless marriage without complaint. If she told him how she felt about him, he would feel that once again he wasn't delivering what his wife wanted and needed because he didn't love her back. She couldn't do that to him, she just *couldn't* do that, not when he already made such an effort to be caring and supportive. She must have imagined those instructions he had given the doctor about making her safety a priority during the birth. Surely the children, his heirs, must always have come first on his scale? Obviously she had got it wrong because he could never have uttered such a heresy, she reflected, not when their entire relationship was based on the importance of the babies she had conceived.

Three days later, thoroughly rested, she travelled back to the palace in a limousine flying the Zenarian flag. She showered and dressed slowly, careful of the occasional twinge from the site of the incision and pleased to see that as her stomach receded a hint of a waist was already beginning to show again. The arrival of the twins in the nursery was a real event in the palace because it had been so many years since there had been babies in the royal family. The staff were very excited and flocked to see the little girls.

A week later there were many appreciative sighs over the picture Leila and Lucia made when they were dressed in white broderie-anglaise camera-ready outfits for the official family photograph session that was expected of them. Rafiq argued that it was too soon, and that Izzy needed more time to recover from the birth, but Izzy was well on the road to recovery by then and said she would sooner get the photo call over and done with.

After all, Izzy thought, little was expected of the Zenarian royal family in terms of public exposure and, after the years of scandalous headlines and rumours generated by Rafiq's misbehaving father, the family had all chosen to follow a low-key lifestyle. They were expected to appear at ceremonial occasions and official events, but the private life of the royal family remained private and there were no paparazzi hunting them in the hope of digging up dirt. The birth of the twins, however, fell into the realm of public interest and the populace needed to see the children.

'And their future Queen,' Rafiq reminded Izzy gently as she gave her opinion to him. 'You should put on some jewellery.'

'I'm never going to be able to pull off *regal*,' Izzy opined with a grimace, smoothing down her tailored cream dress while her maid was directed by Rafiq to lay out diamonds for her to put on.

'Your beauty and our children are more than enough to impress,' Rafiq assured her with amusement. 'Leila and Lucia are the next generation of an unbroken line that our people never thought to see continued except through Zayn and that would have required a change in the law.'

The Regent awaited them in the same elegant reception room where their wedding ceremony had been staged. Izzy's daughters delighted her by falling asleep for the session and the photographer was quick to take advantage. Within twenty minutes the photographs were complete, and the twins were being settled back into their cradles.

'You know, you never did tell me what those other options concerning our marriage were,' Izzy remarked as they walked into his bedroom, which had somehow become *their* bedroom, except when she was getting dressed because her wardrobe was stored in her room next door.

Rafiq froze where he stood. 'Why are you asking about those options now?'

'I'm just curious,' she told him truthfully.

Rafiq nodded his proud dark head, his stunning dark golden eyes resting full on her face. 'It's a little late in the day to discuss those options now,' he began tautly.

'Only if you are already taking it for granted that our marriage is working and that I'm going to stay in Zenara for good,' Izzy pointed out defensively.

'You would hold me to ransom now that our children are born?' Rafiq demanded, disconcerting anger flashing in his strained gaze, warning her that he had not been in any way prepared for such a dialogue.

Izzy straightened her slim shoulders. 'It's not a question of holding you to ransom,' she framed with distaste. 'Maybe I think it's time for us to have a conversation about where we go from here. Not talking about it makes me feel like I'm still on trial in the wife stakes!'

Rafiq stared back at her in apparent disbelief. 'How could you ever have thought for one moment that you were *on trial* with me?' he demanded rawly.

'Well, isn't that the right label for the way we've been living for the past few months?' Izzy prompted tartly, although she was trying hard not to lose her temper. 'You made the deal. You set the rules. You said we'd see if we *worked* as a couple and you've never mentioned the subject since!'

'Evidently I'm no good at making deals or agreements with you!' Rafiq retorted in a savage undertone. 'I always get it wrong and now you're asking about the options I referred to at the time. They were of a more short-term nature than long-term.'

'I'd still like to know what they were,' Izzy pressed, seriously unnerved by the storm she had unleashed with her awkward questions.

Rafiq stalked over to the window, his strong jaw line clenched hard. 'I could have asked my uncle for permission to base myself in the UK for a few months while you followed your teacher-training course. I would've bought a house there, but I would have asked you to return to Zenara for the birth so that our daughters would be born here.'

'OK. That was a…a considerate option,' Izzy acknowledged, struggling to come up with the right words in response to that surprise possibility that he had chosen not to share with her at the time.

'Another choice would have entailed you doing your studies here. As you know, we have classes at the university taught in English,' he reminded her doggedly. 'Both options, as I'm sure you have noted, involved us remaining together as a couple. Had the Regent and the executive council refused to agree to my spending so much time abroad, I would have joined you in the UK every weekend instead.'

'So…' Izzy mused thoughtfully, mulling over what he was telling her. 'None of the options let me walk away free and clear.'

His bold, strong profile went rigid and he swung back to her, golden eyes blazing like flames. 'No,' he agreed without apology. 'I wasn't prepared to let you go free and if you'd run away, I would have followed you and endeavoured to persuade you into returning. There is nothing I would not have done to keep you.'

As she listened Izzy's heart was hammering and ridiculous hope was suddenly blossoming inside her tight chest to such an extent that it was a challenge to breathe. 'And why was that?'

'I do not think I could live without you in my life,' Rafiq grated between his teeth, as though the words were being torn from him under the pressure of the cruellest torture. 'You have transformed my life and I will do just about anything not to return to the life I led before I met you. It was empty, joyless. My sole focus was becoming King, and my sole interest was this country. Now…wrong though it is in my position…*you* are my main focus!'

'Well, I don't see what's wrong with that or why you should get so worked up about sharing that with me,' Izzy told him softly. 'I think what you're saying is that you love me.'

'You don't love me when you can ask about those options all these months on!' Rafiq shot at her rawly, his pain and vulnerability palpable to her.

'No, I just wanted to know where I stood and now I know that I'm standing exactly where I want to be,' Izzy murmured gently as she crossed the room to his side. 'Because I love you too. I started falling for you the day we met but you walked away, and I would never have seen you again if I hadn't traced you because I'd fallen pregnant.'

'I wouldn't be so sure of that. Misguided and unwise though it was when I was being expected to take a wife again, I had your name and your address and sooner or later I would have used that information to see you again because I don't believe that I could've stayed away!' he confessed in an emotional surge. 'I wanted you the moment I first saw you and I never stopped wanting you, not for a moment. I didn't even look at another woman after being with you.'

Izzy stretched up tender hands to frame his lean, devastatingly handsome features. 'It was pretty much the same for me. Is that why you said that you believed in fate?'

'Yes, I believe we were fated to meet, fated to be together,' he told her raggedly. 'You really do love me?'

'You're so very easy to love,' she murmured, her heart lurching at the longing, the need for reassurance that she could see in his beautiful eyes, this man, who had known neither the love of his mother nor the love of his first wife, who did not even understand or fully believe that he *could* inspire love in any woman.

His essential humility had fooled her into crediting that he was merely staying married to her to preserve the status quo and keep his heirs in Zenara. How much blinder could she have been not to recognise that a man who still held her all night even when there was no prospect of sexual satisfaction had to truly *care* about her?

'So at the hospital when you said, "There is only one you"—'

'I was admitting that I loved you and that you are irreplaceable,' he proffered tautly. 'I was so scared that something would go wrong, that the staff would automatically prioritise the heir to the throne's survival over yours...should there have been that horrible choice. We could, conceivably, have other children but I could not replace you, the woman I love, with anyone. I have never known such fear.'

'Oh, Rafiq,' she sighed, wrapping both arms around him, rejoicing in the strength of his tall, well-built physique. 'If only you had told me sooner how you felt.'

'My mother and Fadith showed me that women don't appreciate men who get too emotional,' he confided in a tight undertone. 'I didn't want you to think less of me. I didn't want to appear weak in your eyes. Weakness is not an attractive trait and I was trying to win your love.'

'And all the time you already *had* my love,' she whispered with a huge smile bright with happiness. 'Just as I couldn't recognise your feelings, you couldn't recognise mine.'

'I've never been in love before, only in lust, and that only briefly and never with anyone who mattered to me beyond that level. But it was different with you from the start. I began falling for you the minute you told me about the guy who wore eyeliner because nobody ever chats to me about stuff like that,' he admitted ruefully. 'I loved how natural you were with me. I didn't want to tell you who I was. I didn't want to walk away from you, but I wasn't free to do what I wanted. I had promised my uncle that I would remarry so that Zayn could have another few years of freedom before being forced to marry and procreate for my benefit. And in the light of that promise, it would have been wrong for me to seek to see you again.'

'And yet you still went to the trouble of finding out where I lived. How did you find out?'

'I suspect that someone at the rental agency you worked for was bribed. I didn't ask for the grubby details. I just wanted the information even though I knew I was only tempting myself with what I couldn't have, because seeing you again would only have made the idea of marrying some other woman more of a nightmare than it already was.'

Rafiq freed her and strode over to open the safe in the wall, extracting a small box from it. 'I was saving this for your twenty-second birthday next week but now seems more like the right moment,' he breathed with a flashing smile as he handed the box to her.

Izzy lifted the lid on a glittering diamond eternity ring, and he removed it from its velvet mount and eased it onto her finger with an air of satisfaction. 'It's beautiful,' she whispered appreciatively. 'I love you so much.'

'You fill my heart to overflowing,' Rafiq breathed, stroking his fingers down the side of her heart-shaped face, making her shiver. 'You are everything I never dared to dream of in a woman and a wife. You make me amazingly happy and for the first time I am at peace with the future, content to become King when it is the right time, in no hurry to rush ahead and miss or waste a single moment of being with you and my children.'

Izzy gave him an intoxicated smile and watched the sunlight sparkle a rainbow on her ring. 'You're really very romantic.'

'No, I'm not,' he protested instantly, a tinge of colour scoring his high cheekbones. 'Not at all.'

'Nobody but me needs to know what you're like behind closed doors,' she pointed out softly.

Rafiq brought his mouth down hungrily on hers. 'I'm starving for you!' he groaned, instantly breaking away from her again. 'But we should wait until the doctor has advised us that—'

'Well, we still have a few weeks to wait,' Izzy informed him ruefully, shimmying out of her fancy frock with a tantalising smile to expose curves embellished by silk and lace lingerie. 'But that doesn't mean that we can't do other things,' she pointed out shamelessly.

Rafiq hovered for a split second as if he couldn't quite believe that he was allowed to touch her again and then he stalked forward and lifted her into his arms to kiss her with fierce urgency. 'All those nights we couldn't.'

'All those nights,' she agreed on the back of a sigh of recollection. 'But you held me close anyway and I really loved that about you. I wouldn't have blamed you if you'd shifted me back to my own room.'

'I like being close to you even if I can't make love to you,' he breathed raggedly as he shrugged free of his jacket and tore off his tie with flattering enthusiasm. 'And by the way, you don't *have* your own room any longer.'

Her brow furrowed. 'How don't I?'

'Why would you need your own room? We'll turn it into a dressing room for you. From now on, you will always share my bed. I've got used to having company,' he confided teasingly.

'I suppose I'll always have the sofa to escape to when you annoy me,' Izzy told him playfully.

'And I'll snatch you off it again,' he promised, amusement dancing in his eyes, a new relaxation in his lean, darkly handsome features as he feasted his beautiful eyes on her smiling face. 'I love you, Izzy. I love you like I never thought I could love anyone...'

Silence crept in, broken only by occasional murmurs as discarded garments fell to the floor and they rediscovered each other and the passion that had first brought them together in a blaze of glory that consumed them until the real world crept back in. Izzy realised that it was feeding time for the twins and she needed to put some clothes on again. The buoyant happiness that had flooded her peaked as Rafiq threw on jeans and watched her with loving admiration brightening his keen gaze.

'You and our daughters have become the very centre of my world,' he murmured with satisfaction.

EPILOGUE

Two years later, Izzy hurriedly clasped her son Nazir to her bosom and tugged her playful daughters into the lift with her, one after another.

Leila chattered in voluble toddler-speak and Lucia listened, her little fingers twisting at her copper curls and her thumb creeping into her mouth until her mother pulled it out again. Nazir, replete after a feed, snored gently below his mother's chin.

'Auntie Maya,' Leila framed. 'Like Auntie Maya.'

'I should hope so.' Izzy was almost bouncing with excitement at the prospect of seeing her twin and the rest of her family.

It was their twenty-fourth birthday and Maya and Izzy were having a joint celebration at the Alihreza palace. Helicopters had been flying in all afternoon, ferrying loads of VIPs to the party being staged.

Having ascended the throne and become King, Rafiq had become less sensitive about his father's troubled legacy and the sleazy goings-on he had once associated with the desert building. After all, he and Izzy, their girls and their newborn son, Nazir, were now very much a family and Alihreza was the perfect place to unwind after a busy week of activity at the royal palace. It also provided an even more perfect backdrop for a large party because it offered plenty of luxurious accommodation for family members, who were staying on for a holiday.

Nazir had not been a planned baby. Traumatised by the twins' emergency birth, Rafiq had announced that two children were quite sufficient for them and that there was no way he would allow Izzy to risk herself again with a second pregnancy. Even though Izzy had wheeled in medical support to underline the truth that she had simply been unlucky and that twin pregnancies were more likely to encounter complications, Rafiq had taken an immoveable stance. That had been a shock to Izzy's system as usually Rafiq was willing to move heaven and earth just to give her whatever she wanted.

In fact, they had had heated discussions for weeks over whether or not they should have another child and then fate, that Rafiq was generally so fond of, had intervened and Izzy had discovered that she was expecting again. Of course, she wasn't taking contraceptive pills any longer because the several brands she had tried after the twins' birth hadn't agreed with her and Rafiq had taken charge of the contraception. She had been three months pregnant by the time she finally appreciated that once again she had conceived. She had been overjoyed by the surprise but Rafiq's reaction had been more shock and concern for her well-being.

Mercifully none of his fears had come to fruition during her second pregnancy. She had suffered minimal nausea and the delivery had been straightforward. Happy now to consider their family complete, she was even more grateful for the fact that Nazir was a wonderfully easy, good-natured baby, who slept when he should, ate at regular hours and smiled beatifically at everyone.

Leila had needed very little sleep and after a few weeks of sleepless nights they had hired an official nanny. It had amazed Izzy that Lucia could slumber on peacefully even though she was only feet away from her screaming sibling. But the twins were very different, Izzy conceded fondly. Leila was altogether a louder personality, a little extrovert in the making. Copper-haired Lucia was quieter and prone to wandering off to amuse herself with imaginative games with her toys, leaving Leila the one to follow her. Leila went looking for her twin the minute she moved out of sight, but Lucia was more independent. Izzy loved seeing the children's different personalities emerging.

At that moment her mother, Lucia, walked up and stole Nazir out of her elder daughter's arms, rocking him and murmuring sweet nothings to the sleeping bundle. 'I swear an earthquake could go off and this child wouldn't notice!' she carolled appreciatively. 'Matt is so excited about being put forward for the stem cell treatment, Izzy. We'll never be able to thank Rafiq enough for doing that for him, even if it doesn't provide either an improvement of his condition or a miraculous cure.'

Izzy swallowed hard. It had been Rafiq who had suggested that they sought stem cell treatment for her kid brother's paralysis. Her family could never have afforded the costs involved. Matt had recently undergone a series of tests, which had concluded with him being offered a place in ground-breaking trials. She was married to a man with a huge heart, even if it was a heart that he often felt he had to bury deep and hide from notice, and if anything two years of marriage had only made her love her husband more deeply than ever. The happiness their relationship gave her was infinite.

Izzy watched as Rafiq snatched Leila back in the nick of time from the edge of an ornamental pond and scolded her. The little girl threw a massive tantrum and Rafiq just stood there watching it play out while Lucia sucked her thumb and stared. Izzy began to move in their direction. She gave her father a fond hug on the way, teased Matt about the latest piece of technology he was playing games with and greeted and kissed Rafiq's uncle and aunt on the cheek, pausing to chat with the older couple for a few minutes. By the end of it, Leila was still stubbornly going strong.

'Leila...' she intervened sharply.

The tantrum died with Izzy's arrival, but Leila ran off in a sulk instead, causing Rafiq to roll his eyes and groan out.

'It'll blow over,' Izzy told him soothingly. 'It's the

result of too much excitement and the annoyance of me choosing what she had to wear today.'

'She's very wilful,' he said with a frown.

'She'll learn, just like we all have to learn how to behave,' Izzy countered. 'Just don't tell her any more stories about the warrior queen who preceded her in case it gives her ideas.'

Laughing, Rafiq tugged her back under an archway onto the shaded terrace. 'You look pretty spectacular in that dress,' he remarked huskily. 'Dark blue suits you, matches your eyes.'

Izzy lounged back against a sandstone pillar and preened herself like an old-style sex siren, looking up at her husband cheekily from beneath her lashes. She leant closer to walk her fingertips up over his shirted abdomen, one at a time, the spirit of wantonness personified as she stroked his lean muscled torso, appreciating his physical beauty with every fibre of her being and loving that he was all hers for ever. She watched his gorgeous eyes light up as golden as the sun and noticed with a wicked little grin how he shifted position to contain his arousal.

'I married a shameless hussy.'

'And you love that shamelessness, Your Majesty,' she whispered, gazing up at him with her heart in her eyes.

'I do and I always will. I will cherish my memory of the virgin who told me not to be a party pooper for ever,' he husked, lowering his head to claim a single burning kiss that lit her up like a firework.

'I love you,' Izzy said sunnily, squeezing his hand.

'You may be a king but you're still my bathroom guy...'

Rafiq winced. 'Are you ever going to let me forget our first meeting?'

'Probably not.' She laughed as they joined the festivities to mingle and chat and ensure that their guests had as good a time as they planned to have for the rest of their lives.

* * * * *

HIS INNOCENT'S
PASSIONATE
AWAKENING

MELANIE MILBURNE

Dedicated to Rachel Bailey—
a fellow dog-lover, romance writer
and awesome brainstorming partner!
Thanks for being such a wonderful friend. xxxxx
Licks and cuddles from Polly and Lily too.

CHAPTER ONE

ARTEMISIA BELLANTE STARED at her father's lawyer in abject horror. 'But there must be some mistake. How can Castello Mireille be…be *mortgaged*? It's been in my father's family for generations. Papa never mentioned anything about owing money to a bank.'

'He didn't owe it to a bank.' The lawyer, Bruno Rossi, pushed a sheaf of papers across the desk towards Artie, his expression grave. 'Have you heard of Luca Ferrantelli? He runs his late father's global property developing company. He's also a wine and olive producer with a keen interest in rare grape varieties, some of which are on the Castello Mireille estate.'

Artie lowered her gaze to the papers in front of her, a light shiver racing down her spine like a stray current of electricity. 'I've vaguely heard of him…' She might have spent years living in isolation on her family's ancient estate but even she had heard of the handsome billionaire playboy. And seen pictures. And swooned just like any other woman between the ages of fifteen and fifty.

She raised her gaze back to the lawyer's. 'But how did this happen? I know Papa had to let some of the gardeners go to keep costs down and insisted we cut back on housekeeping expenses, but he didn't mention anything about borrowing money from anyone. I don't understand how Signor Ferrantelli now owns most, if not all, my family's home. Why didn't Papa tell me before he died?'

To find out like this was beyond embarrassing. And deeply hurtful. Was this her father's way of forcing his shut-in daughter out of the nest by pushing her to the verge of bankruptcy?

Where would she find the sort of money to dig herself out of this catastrophic mess?

Bruno shifted his glasses further up the bridge of his Roman nose. 'Apparently your father and Luca's father had some sort of business connection in the past. He contacted Luca for financial help when the storm damage hit the *castello* late last year. His insurance policy had lapsed and he knew he would have no choice but to sell if someone didn't bail him out.'

Artie rapid-blinked. 'The insurance lapsed? But why didn't he tell me? I'm his only child. The only family he had left. Surely he should have trusted me enough to tell me the truth about our finances.'

Bruno Rossi made a shrugging movement with one shoulder. 'Pride. Embarrassment. Shame. The usual suspects in cases like this. He had to mortgage the estate to pay for the repairs. Luca Ferrantelli seemed the best option—the only option, considering your father's poor state of health. But the repayment plan didn't go according to schedule, which leaves you in an awkward position.'

Artie wrinkled her brow, a tension headache stabbing at the backs of her eyes like scorching hot needles. Was this a nightmare? Would she suddenly wake up and find this was nothing but a terrifying dream?

Please let this not be real.

'Surely Papa knew he would have to eventually pay back the money he borrowed from Signor Ferrantelli? How could he have let it get to this? And wouldn't Luca Ferrantelli have done due diligence and realised Papa wouldn't be able to pay it back? Or was that Ferrantelli's intention all along—to take the *castello* off us?'

Bruno leaned forward in his chair with a sigh. 'Your father was a good man, Artie, but he wasn't good at managing finances, especially since the accident. There have been a lot of expenses, as you know, with running the estate since he came home from hospital. Your mother was the one with the financial clout to keep things in the black, but of course, after she died in the accident, it naturally fell to him. Unfortunately, he didn't always listen to advice from his accountants and financial advisors.'

He gave a rueful movement of his lips and continued.

'I'm sure I wouldn't be the first person to tell you how much the accident changed him. He fired his last three accountants because they told him things had to change. Luca Ferrantelli's offer of financial help has meant you could nurse your father here until he passed away, but now of course, unless you can find the money to pay off the mortgage, it will remain in Luca's possession.'

Over her dead body, it would. No way was she handing over her family's home without a fight, even if it would be a David and Goliath mismatch. Artie would find some way of winning.

She *had* to.

Artie did her best to ignore the beads of sweat forming between her shoulder blades. The drumbeat of panic in her chest. The hammering needles behind her eyeballs. The sense of the floor beneath her feet pitching like a paper boat riding a tsunami. 'When and where did Papa meet with Signor Ferrantelli? I've been Papa's full-time carer for the last ten years and don't recall Signor Ferrantelli ever coming here to see him.'

'Maybe he came one day while you were out.'

Out? Artie didn't go *out*.

She wasn't like other people, who could walk out of their homes and meet up with friends. It was impossible for her to be around more than one or two people at a time. Three was very definitely a crowd.

'Maybe…' Artie looked down at the papers again, conscious of warmth filling her cheeks. Her social anxiety was far more effective than a maximum-security prison. She hadn't been outside the *castello* walls since she was fifteen.

Ten years.

A decade.

Two fifths of her life.

As far as she knew, it wasn't common knowledge that she suffered from social anxiety. Her father's dependence on her had made it easy to disguise her fear of crowds. She had relished the role of looking after him. It had given her life a purpose, a focus. She had mostly avoided meeting people when they came to the *castello* to visit her father. She stayed in the background until they left. But barely anyone but her father's doctor and physical therapists had come during the last year or two of his life. Compassion fatigue had worn out his so-called friends. And now that the money had run dry, she could see why they had drifted away, one by one. There wasn't anyone she could turn to. Having been home schooled since her mid-teens, she had lost contact with her school friends. Friends wanted you to socialise with them and that she could never do, so they, too, had drifted away.

She had no friends of her own other than Rosa, the housekeeper.

Artie took a deep breath and blinked to clear her clouded vision. The words in front of her confirmed her worst fears. Her home was mortgaged to the hilt. There was no way a bank would lend her enough funds to get the *castello* out of Luca Ferrantelli's hands. The only job she had ever had was as her father's carer. From fifteen to twenty-five she had taken care of his every need. She had no formal qualifications, no skills other than her embroidery hobby.

She swallowed and pushed the papers back across the desk. 'What about my mother's trust fund? Isn't there enough left for me to pay off the mortgage?'

'There's enough for you to live on for the short-term but not enough to cover the money owed.'

Artie's heart began to beat like a wounded frog. 'How long have I got?' It sounded like a terminal diagnosis, which in some ways it was. She couldn't imagine her life without Castello Mireille. It was her home. Her base. Her anchor.

Her entire world.

Bruno Rossi shuffled the papers back into a neat pile. 'A year or two. But even if you were by some chance to raise finance to keep the estate, the place needs considerable maintenance. Costly maintenance. The storm damage last year showed how vulnerable the *castello* is. The north wing's roof still needs some work, not to mention the conservatory. It will cost millions of euros to—'

'Yes, yes, I know.' Artie pushed back her chair and smoothed her damp palms down her thighs. The *castello* was crumbling around her—she saw evidence of it every single day. But moving out of her home was unthinkable. Impossible.

She literally *couldn't* do it.

Panic tiptoed over her skin like thousands of tiny ants wearing stilettoes. Pressure built in her chest—a crushing weight pushing against her lungs so she couldn't take another breath. She wrapped her arms around her middle, fighting to hold off a full-blown panic attack. She hadn't had one for a while but the threat was always lurking in the murky shadows of her consciousness. It had followed her like a malevolent ghost ever since she came home from hospital from the accident that killed her mother and left her father in a wheelchair.

An accident that wouldn't have occurred if it hadn't been for *her*.

The lawyer cleared his throat. 'There's something else…' The formal quality of his tone changed and another shiver skittered down Artie's spine.

She straightened her shoulders and cupped her elbows with her hands, hoping for a cool and dignified stance but falling way too short. 'W-what?'

'Signor Ferrantelli has proposed a plan for you to

repay him. If you fulfil his terms, you will regain full ownership of the *castello* within six months.'

Artie's eyebrows shot up along with her heart rate. And her anxiety grew razorblade wings and flapped frantically against her stomach lining like frenzied bats. How could she ever repay those mortgage payments in such a short space of time? What on earth did he require her to do? 'A plan? What sort of plan?' Her voice came out high and strained like an overused squeaky toy.

'He didn't authorise me to discuss it with you. He insists on speaking to you in person first.' Bruno pushed back his chair, further demonstrating his unwillingness to reveal anything else. 'Signor Ferrantelli has requested a meeting with you in his Milan office nine a.m. sharp, on Monday, to discuss your options.'

Options? What possible options could there be? None she wanted to think about in any detail. Ice-cold dread slithered into her belly. What nefarious motives could Luca Ferrantelli have towards her? A woman he had never met? And what was with his drill sergeant commands?

Nine a.m. Sharp. In his office. In Milan.

Luca Ferrantelli sounded like a man who issued orders and expected them to be obeyed without question. But there was no way she could go to Milan. Not on Monday. Not any day. She couldn't get as far as the front gate without triggering crippling, stomach-emptying, mind-scattering panic.

Artie released her arms from around her body and gripped the back of the nearest chair. Her heart was racing like it was preparing for the Olympics. 'Tell him to meet me here. It's not convenient for me to go to Milan.

I don't drive and, from what you've just told me, I can't afford a taxi or even an Uber.'

'Signor Ferrantelli is a busy man. He expressly told me to tell you he—'

Artie stiffened her spine and raised her chin and ground her teeth behind her cool smile. 'Tell him to meet me here, nine a.m. sharp, on Monday. Or not meet with me at all.'

Luca Ferrantelli drove his Maserati through the rusty entrance gates of Castello Mireille on Monday morning. The *castello* was like something out of a Grimm brothers' fairy tale. The centuries-old ivy-clad stone building was surrounded by gardens that looked like they hadn't been tended for years, with overgrown hedges, unpruned roses, weed-covered pathways and ancient trees that stood like gnarly sentries. The *castello* had loads of potential—years of running his late father's property development company had taught him how to spot a diamond in the rough.

And speaking of diamonds...

He glanced at the velvet box on the seat next to him containing his late grandmother's engagement ring, and inwardly smiled. Artemisia Bellante would make the perfect temporary bride. Her father, Franco, had emailed Luca a photo of his daughter shortly before he died, asking Luca to make sure she was looked after once he was gone. The photo had planted a seed in Luca's mind—a seed that had taken root and sprouted and blossomed until all he could think about was meeting her—to offer her a way out of her present circumstances. Young, innocent, sheltered—she was exactly the sort of young woman his conservative grandfather would deem suitable as a Ferrantelli bride.

Time was rapidly running out on convincing his grandfather to accept the chemo he so desperately needed. Luca had a small window of opportunity to get Nonno to change his mind. Luca would do anything—even marry a poverty-stricken heiress—to make sure his elderly and frail *nonno* could live a few more precious years. After all, it was his fault his grandfather had lost the will to live. Didn't he owe Nonno some measure of comfort, given how Luca had torn apart the Ferrantelli family?

A vision of Luca's father, Flavio, and older brother, Angelo, drifted into his mind. Their lifeless bodies pulled from the surf due to his reckless behaviour as a teenager. His reckless behaviour and their love for him—a lethal, deadly combination. Two lives cut short because of him. Two lives and their potential wasted, and his mother and grandparents' happiness permanently, irrevocably destroyed. No one had been the same since that terrible day. No one.

Luca blinked to clear away the vision and gripped the steering wheel with white-knuckled force. He couldn't bring his father and brother back. He couldn't undo the damage he had caused to his mother and Nonna and Nonno. His grandmother had died a year ago and since then, his grandfather had lost the will to live. Nonno was refusing treatment for his very treatable cancer, and if he didn't receive chemotherapy soon he would die. So far, no amount of talking, lecturing, cajoling or bribing or begging on Luca's part had helped changed his grandfather's mind.

But Luca had a plan and he intended to carry it out no matter what. He would bring home a fresh-faced young bride to give hope to his grandfather that the Ferrantelli family line would continue well into the future.

Even if that was nothing but a fairy tale.

Artie watched Luca Ferrantelli's showroom-perfect deep blue Maserati come through the *castello* gates like a prowling lion. The low purr of the engine was audible even here in the formal sitting room. The car's tinted windows made it impossible for her to get a proper glimpse of his face, but the car's sleek profile and throaty growls seemed like a representation of his forthright personality.

Didn't they say a person's choice of car told you a lot about them?

Artie already knew as much as she wanted to know. *More* than she wanted to know. That would teach her for spending the weekend trawling over the internet for any mention of him. Her research had revealed him as a flagrant playboy who brokered property deals and broke female hearts all over the globe. Barely a week went past without a gossip page featuring Luca Ferrantelli with a star-struck sylph-like blonde draped on his arm.

The powerful sports car came to a halt at the front of the *castello*. Artie sucked in a breath as the driver's door opened, her heart giving a sudden kick, her eyes widening as a vision of potent, athletic maleness unfolded from behind the wheel. The internet photos hadn't done him justice. How could it be possible to be so spectacularly attractive? Her pulse fluttered as if someone had injected her veins with thousands of butterflies.

The good-looks fairy godmother had certainly excelled herself when it came to Luca Ferrantelli. Six foot four, lean and athletic, with wavy black hair that was casually styled in a just-out-of-bed or just-combed-with-his-fingers manner, he was the epitome of heart-stopping handsome. Even though she was looking at him from a distance, Artie's heart was stopping and starting like a spluttering engine. How was she going to be when he was in the same room as her? Breathing the same air? Within touching distance?

As if Luca Ferrantelli sensed her gaze on him, he took off his aviator-style sunglasses and locked gazes with her. Something sprang open in her chest and she suddenly couldn't breathe. She quickly stepped away from the window and leaned back against the adjacent wall, clutching a hand to her pulsing throat, heat pouring into her cheeks. She had to get a grip. And fast. The last thing she wanted to do was appear gauche and unsophisticated, but, given she had been out of society for so long, she was at a distinct disadvantage. He was the poster boy for living in the fast lane. She was a wallflower who hadn't been seen in public for a decade.

It was some minutes before the housekeeper, Rosa, led Luca Ferrantelli to where Artie was waiting to receive him, but even so, her pulse was still leaping when the sitting room door opened. What if she became tongue-tied? What if she blushed? What if she broke out in a sweat and couldn't breathe? What if—?

'Signor Ferrantelli to see you,' Rosa announced with a formal nod in Luca's direction, before going out of the room and closing the door behind her with a click.

The first thing Artie noticed was his hair wasn't

completely black. There were several strands of steel-grey sprinkled around his temples, which gave him a distinguished, wise-beyond-his-years air. His eyes were framed by prominent eyebrows and were an unusual hazel—a mix of brown and green flecks, fringed by thick, ink-black lashes. His amazing eyes were a kaleidoscope of colours one would normally find in a deeply shadowed forest. His jaw was cleanly shaven but the faint shadow of regrowth around his nose and mouth hinted at the potent male hormones working vigorously behind the scenes.

The atmosphere of the room changed with his presence, as if every stick of furniture, every fibre of carpet and curtains, every portrait frame and the faces of her ancestors contained within them took a collective breath. Stunned by his looks, his commanding presence, his take-charge energy.

'*Buongiorno*, Signorina Bellante.' Luca Ferrante's voice was like the sound of his car—low and deep, with a sexy rumble that did something strange to the base of her spine. So, too, did seeing his lips move when shaping and pronouncing her name. His lower lip was full and sensual, the top lip only marginally less so, and he had a well-defined philtrum ridge beneath his nose and a shallow cleft in his chin.

Artie slipped her hand into his outstretched one and a zap of electricity shot from her fingers to her core like a lightning bolt. His grip was strong and yet strangely gentle, his fingers long and tanned with a light dusting of dark masculine hair that ran over the backs of his hands and disappeared beneath the cuffs of his business shirt and jacket. Armani, at a guess. And his aftershave an equally intoxicating blend of citrus and spice and sophistication that teased her senses into a stupor.

'*Buongiorno*, Signor Ferrantelli.'

Artie aimed for cool politeness but sounded more like a star-struck teen in front of a Hollywood celebrity. She could feel warm colour blooming in her cheeks. Could feel her heart thumping like it was having some sort of medical crisis. Could feel her female hormones responding to his male ones with little tingles and pulses deep within her body.

Let go of his hand!

Her brain gave the command but her hand was trapped in some kind of weird stasis. It was as if her hand had a mind of its own and was enjoying being held by his warm, dry one, thank you very much. Enjoying it so much, she could feel every whorl of his skin as if it were being engraved, branded into hers.

Luca removed his hand from hers but his gaze kept hers tethered. She couldn't look away if she tried. Magnetic. Enthralling. Mesmerising. His eyes seemed to draw secrets from within her while concealing his own.

'Firstly, allow me to offer my condolences on the recent passing of your father.'

'*Grazie.*'

She stepped back and waved her still-tingling hand in the direction of the sofa. 'Would you like to sit down? I'll call Rosa to bring in coffee. How do you take it?'

'Black and strong.'

Of course you do.

Artie pressed the intercom pad and summoned Rosa, surreptitiously eyeing him while she requested coffee from the housekeeper. Everything about Luca Ferrantelli was strong. Strong, determined jaw. Strong, intelligent eyes. A strong and muscled body that hinted at a man who wasn't afraid of pushing himself to the limits of endurance. A man who set goals and didn't let anyone or anything stop him from achieving them.

Artie ended the intercom conversation with Rosa and sat on the nearest sofa, and only then did Luca take the seat opposite. He laid one arm along the back of the sofa in a casually relaxed pose she privately envied. She had to place her hands on the tops of her thighs to stop her knees from trembling. Not from fear but from a strange sense of fizzing excitement. She tried not to stare at his powerfully muscled thighs, his well-formed biceps, the flat plane of his stomach, but her gaze kept drifting over him of its own volition. Drinking in the planes and contours of his face, wondering what was going on behind the screen of his gaze, wondering if his firm lips would soften when he kissed…

Artie blinked and sat up straighter on the sofa, crossing her legs to try and control the wayward urges going on in her lower body. What was wrong with her? He had barely exchanged more than half a dozen words with her and she was undressing him with her eyes. She curled her hands into balls on her lap and fixed a smile on her lips. 'So, how was your drive from Milan? I hope it didn't inconvenience you too much to come here?' Who said she couldn't do small talk?

Luca's half-smile and his glittering forest floor eyes made something slip sideways in her stomach. 'It didn't inconvenience me at all. But we both know that was your intention, was it not?'

Artie forced herself to hold his penetrating gaze. 'Signor Ferrantelli, I am not the sort of woman to jump when a man says jump.'

The dark gleam in his eyes intensified and a hot trickle of something liquid spilled deep in her core. 'You may have no choice, given I now own nine tenths of Castello Mireille, unless you can buy me out within the next twenty-four hours.' There was a don't-mess-with-me warning in his tone that made her want to mess with him to see what would happen.

Artie disguised a swallow, her heart picking up its pace. 'My father's lawyer informed me of the unusual financial arrangement you made with my father. One wonders why you didn't buy all of it off him while you had the chance.'

His gaze was unwavering. 'He was a dying man who deserved some dignity in the last months of his life.'

Artie gave a cynical smile while her blood boiled in her veins and roaring anger bubbled in her chest. 'Do you expect me to believe you felt some measure of compassion for him? Even while you were systematically taking his home away from him ancient stone by ancient stone?'

Luca didn't change his casual posture on the sofa but a ripple of tension passed across his features, tightening his jaw, flaring his nose, hardening his eyes. 'Your father approached me late last year for help. I gave it to him. It was a straightforward business deal. And now I have come to collect on my investment.'

Artie shot up from the sofa as if someone had pressed an ejector switch. She glared at him with the full force of her fury, chest heaving like she had just completed a marathon without training first. 'You can't take my home off me. I won't allow it.'

Luca Ferrantelli's gaze was diamond-hard. 'My intention is to give the *castello* back to you—after a time. And for a price.'

Something heavy landed on the floor of her belly. 'What price? You must know I can't possibly raise the necessary funds to pay out the mortgage?'

He held her gaze in a lock that made the backs of her knees tingle. 'I will erase the debt and give the deeds of the *castello* back if you agree to be my wife for six months.'

CHAPTER TWO

ARTIE STARED AT HIM in open-mouthed shock, her heart pounding like it was going to punch its way out of her chest. Had she heard him correctly? Was her imagination playing tricks on her? Putting words in his mouth he couldn't possibly have said? Had he said *wife*? W.I.F.E? The woman a man chose to spend the rest of his life with in a contract of love and commitment?

'Your…*what?*'

He hooked one ankle over his bent knee, his finger idly flicking the zipper toggle on his Italian leather boot. *Flick. Flick. Flick.* So relaxed. So casual. So confident and in control it was maddening.

'You heard—I need a wife for six months. On paper.' The note of self-assurance in his voice made her dislike of him go up another notch.

On paper? Her eyes widened while her feminine ego shrank. She might not be a social butterfly or model material, but as far as she knew she hadn't broken any mirrors lately. 'You mean a marriage of convenience?'

'But of course.'

Why 'but of course'? It was ridiculous to be affronted

by his unusual proposal, but what woman wanted to be dismissed outright as a potential lover?

But why would he want you? the voice of her conscience sneered. *Who would want you? You killed your mother, you maimed your father—all for the sake of going to a stupid party.*

Rosa, the housekeeper, came in at that moment carrying a tray with cups and saucers and a steaming percolator of freshly brewed coffee. Rosa handed Luca a cup before turning to give one to Artie. But as soon as Rosa left the room Artie put her coffee on a side table, not trusting her shaking hands to bring the cup safely to her tombstone-dry mouth. Her conscience was right. Why would he want to marry *her*? Why would anyone?

Luca lowered his crossed ankle to the floor and, reaching for his cup, took a sip of his coffee as if this was a regular old coffee morning. Not one in which he had delivered a bombshell proposal to a virtual stranger.

'May I ask, why me?' Artie inserted into the silence. 'You surely have no shortage of far more suitable candidates for the role.' Socialites. Supermodels. Not a shut-in like her.

Luca put his cup back in its saucer with unnerving and methodical precision. It hinted at the man he was—self-assured, focused, confident he could get anything he set his mind to. 'Your father was the one who planted the idea in my—'

'My *father?*' Artie choked over the words.

'He was concerned about your future, given how badly his financial situation had become and how it would impact on you long-term. He wanted you well provided for, so I devised a plan to make sure we both

got what we wanted. You get to keep the *cas...
a temporary wife.'

Artie clasped her hands together, trying to keep c...
trol of her galloping pulse. Her legs were threatening to
give way beneath her but she was reluctant to sit back
down, because it would bring her closer to him than
she wanted to be. 'But why would you want me to be
your...your wife?' Saying the word felt strange on her
lips and yet her mind ran with the image it evoked. Images popped into her head of her wearing a white dress
and standing next to Luca at an altar. His arms going
around her, drawing him closer to his muscled body.
His mouth slowly coming down to seal hers in a kiss...

'You're exactly the sort of woman my grandfather
would approve of as my bride,' Luca said, his gaze drifting to her mouth as if he was having the same thoughts
as her. About kissing, touching, needing, wanting.

Artie arched her eyebrows. 'Oh, really? Why is that?'

His lips curved in a satirical smile. 'You're the sweet,
homespun type—or so your father led me to believe.'

What else had her father told him about her? She had
made him promise not to tell anyone about her social
anxiety. Had he broken that promise? She was pretty
sure he hadn't told Bruno Rossi, the lawyer, otherwise
he would have mentioned it yesterday. It was her shame-
ful little secret. Her father's dependence on her since the
accident had made it easy for her to hide it from others,
but with him no longer here...

Artie kept her expression neutral but on the inside,
she was seething. How dared her father set her up for
auction to this incorrigible man? It was positively feu-
dal. And why did Luca Ferrantelli want to please his

grandfather? What was at stake if he didn't? 'Look, Signor Ferrantelli, I think there's been some sort of misunderstanding between you and my father. I can't think of a single set of circumstances in which I would ever consider marrying you.'

Luca's mocking smile broadened. 'Perhaps not as sweet and biddable as your father said.' His tone was musing, the lazy sweep of his gaze assessing. 'But, no matter. You will do.'

She straightened her shoulders and sent him a look so frosty icicles could have formed on her eyelashes. 'Please leave. We have nothing left to discuss.'

Luca remained seated on the sofa, still in that annoyingly relaxed pose. But his eyes contained a glint of intractability that made her wonder if she was wise to lock horns with him. She had no experience in dealing with powerful men. She had no experience, period. Any fight between them would be like Tinkerbell trying to take down a Titan.

'The way I see it, you don't have any choice. You will lose the *castello* if you don't agree to marry me.'

Artie ground her teeth and clenched her fists, anger flicking along her nerve endings like a power surge of electricity. It was all she could do not to slap him. She pictured herself doing it—landing her palm against his lean and chiselled jaw with a resounding slap. Imagining how his rougher skin would feel under the soft skin of her palm. Imagining how he might grasp her by the wrist and haul her closer and slam his mouth down on hers in a passionate kiss…

Eek! She shouldn't have watched *Gone with the Wind* so many times.

She stretched out one arm and pointed her index finger towards the door. 'Get. Out.'

Luca raised his long, lean, athletic frame from the sofa with leonine grace and came to stand in front of her. She fought not to step back, determined to show he didn't intimidate her with his commanding, disturbing presence. Even though he did. Big time. She had to crane her neck to maintain eye-contact, and give her traitorous body a stern talking-to for reacting to his closeness with a hitch of her breath and an excited leap of her pulse.

'I'll give you twenty-four hours to consider my proposal.'

Artie raised her chin to a defiant height. 'I've already considered it and flatly turned it down. I'll give you the same answer tomorrow, so don't waste your time or mine by coming back.'

His lazy smile ignited a light behind his eyes as if her refusal had thrilled rather than disappointed him. 'You have a lot to lose, Signorina Bellante.' He swung his gaze around the room before bringing it back to meet hers. 'Are you sure you want to throw all this away for the sake of your pride?'

'Pride has nothing to do with my decision. If and when I marry, it will be for love.'

The loud cackling of her conscience rang in Artie's ears like clanging bells.

Marry for love? You? Who's going to love you?

His eyes flicked to her mouth and lingered there for a heart-stopping moment. 'You love this place, do you not? Your family's home for how many centuries? If that's not marrying for love, I don't know what is.' The deep, mellifluous tone of his voice had a mesmerising effect on her. She had to fight to stay focused on resisting him. It would be so easy to say yes. To have all her problems solved by agreeing to his plan—even if by doing so it threw up new ones. Dangerous ones. Exciting ones.

Artie pressed her lips together. 'Of course I love it. It's the only home I've ever known.'

The only home I can ever know.

His eyes meshed with hers. Dark, mysterious, unknowable. 'If you don't marry me, you will lose it. And I won't lose a wink of sleep about taking it off you. Business is business. I don't let emotions cloud the issue. Think about it, hmm?'

She tried to ignore the cynical gleam in his eyes. Tried to ignore the slippery eels of panic writhing in her belly. Tried not to think about her home being lost for ever. Of it being made into a plush hotel with strangers walking through every room, occupying every private space, every special corner made into a flashy showpiece instead of a private sanctuary where her most precious memories were housed. 'You can't force me out of my home. I have some rights, surely?'

'Your father signed those over to me when he begged for my help.'

Artie raised her chin, summoning every bit of willpower she possessed to stand up to his monumental ego. 'You came here expecting me to say yes, didn't you? Does anyone ever say no to you?'

'Not often.' He reached inside his jacket pocket and took a velvet box and held it out to her in the middle of his palm. 'This might help you come to a decision.'

Artie reared back from the box like it was a cock-roach. 'You think you can bribe me with diamonds?'

'Not just diamonds.' He flicked open the velvet box with his thumb and a glittering sapphire and diamond engagement ring winked at her. 'Take it. Try it on for size.'

Artie brought her gaze back to his, her mouth tightly compressed. 'No, thank you.'

There was a beat or two of silence.

Luca snapped the lid of the ring box closed and placed it on the coffee table. If she had offended him with her point-blank refusal then he didn't show it in his expression.

'I'll be back for your decision tomorrow. *Ciao.*'

He gave a mock bow, and without another word he walked out of the salon, closing the door on his exit.

Artie let out a scalding breath, her body sagging with the aftershocks of too much cortisol racing through her system. She sat back on the sofa before she fell down, her legs shaking, her hands trembling, her mind whirling.

How could this be happening? It was like something out of a period drama. She was being blackmailed into marrying a man she didn't know in order to save her home. What had her father been thinking to plant such a ridiculous idea in Luca Ferrantelli's head? This was nothing but a business deal to Luca but it was her home that was on the line. And not just her home—her security. Her future. She would have nothing to fall back on if she didn't have the *castello*.

It was her heritage.

Her birthright.

Her safety.

How dared Luca Ferrantelli dangle it before her like a plump, juicy carrot in front of a dumb donkey?

She was *not* going to be a pawn in his game. If he thought she was so desperate for a husband she would say yes to the first man who asked her, then he had better think again.

Rosa came back into the salon to collect the coffee cups. 'Your guest left, then. What did he want?' Her eyes went to the ring box on the coffee table. 'Ooh, what's this?'

Artie got up from the sofa and speared her fingers through her hair. 'You wouldn't believe me if I told you. *Grr.* I don't know how I stopped myself from slapping him. He's the most detestable man I've ever met.'

Rosa's look was wry. 'Like you've met heaps of men. Just saying…' She prised open the lid of the ring box and whistled through her teeth. '*Mamma mia.* That is what I call an engagement ring.'

Artie snatched the box off her and snapped it shut and clutched it tightly in her hand. 'If he's representative of the men outside the *castello* walls, then I'm glad I haven't met heaps of them. Do you know what he said? He wants to marry me. For six months. A paper marriage or some such nonsense. And do you know what's worse? Papa put the idea in his head. Luca Ferrantelli will only give me back the *castello*, debt-free, if I marry him.'

'And you said?'

Artie frowned. 'What do you think I said? I said an emphatic, don't-ask-me-again *no*.'

Rosa loaded the coffee percolator onto the tray with

implacable calm. 'Would you say yes if the marriage wasn't on paper?'

'No, of course not.'

'Then what's the problem? Don't you trust him to keep his word?'

Artie put her hands on her hips. She could feel the ring box digging into the soft skin of her palm but did her best to ignore it. She would *not* look at it again. She would not look at those sparkling diamonds and that impossibly blue sapphire and imagine a life free of financial stress.

She would not think of being Luca Ferrantelli's bride.

She. Would. Not.

'Are you seriously telling me I should accept his crazy proposal? Are you out of your mind?' Artie narrowed her gaze and added, 'Wait—do you know something about this? Did Papa talk to you about his scheme to marry me off to a stranger to settle his debts?'

Rosa picked up the coffee tray and held it in front of her body, her expression set in her customary pragmatic lines. 'Your father was worried about you in the weeks before he died—about what would happen to you once he was gone. You gave up your life for him these last few years. He shouldn't have asked it of you and nor should he have run the estate the way he did, but he was never the same after the accident. But you have a chance now to turn things around. To reclaim your life and your inheritance. And Luca Ferrantelli can't be much of a stranger to your father, otherwise he wouldn't have gone to him for help. Why would he have asked Luca if he didn't trust him to do the right thing by you? Six months isn't long. And as long as everything is legally sound, you've got nothing to lose and everything to gain.'

Artie tossed the ring box on the sofa. 'I can't believe you think I should marry that odious man.'

'You can't stay locked away here for ever, Artie. It's not healthy. Your father desperately wanted you to move on with your—'

Artie blew out a breath of exasperation. 'I *can't* leave. I thought you of all people understood. You've seen me at my worst. I feel paralysed with anxiety as soon as I get to the front gates. It's not as if I want to be like this. I can't help it.'

Nothing had helped. Medication. Home visits by a psychologist. Meditation and mindfulness. Nothing had freed her from the curse of her phobia. She had resigned herself to a lifetime of living in isolation.

What else could she do but accept her lot in life?

Rosa shifted her lips from side to side, her dark brown eyes serious. 'You'll have no choice but to leave if the *castello* is sold out from under you.'

The thought of leaving her home, having it taken it away from her by force, made her skin pepper with goosebumps and her heart pound with dread. She had tried so many times to imagine a life outside of Castello Mireille. But it was like a pipedream that never could be realised. It was completely and utterly out of her reach.

Artie glanced at the ring box on the sofa, her heart giving a funny little hopscotch. 'Luca Ferrantelli is an international playboy. He changes lovers every week. What sort of husband is he going to be?'

'You'll never know if you don't marry him, *sì*?' Rosa said. 'Convince him to marry you here at the *castello*—

you won't have to leave at all. It's a marriage in name only so there won't be a honeymoon. In six months, you'll have full ownership again. Plus, a gorgeous ring to keep. Problem solved.'

Eek! She hadn't even thought about a honeymoon. Luca wanted a bride but not *that* sort of bride…or did he? Her lower body tingled at the thought of his hands touching her. His mouth pressing against hers. His body doing things to hers she had only fantasised about and never experienced.

Artie pressed her fingers against her temples once Rosa had left the room. What crazy parallel universe had she stumbled into that even the housekeeper thought she should marry Luca Ferrantelli? She let out a ragged breath and looked around the salon. The black velvet ring box on the white sofa seemed to signify the either/ or choice she had to make. The sofa cushions still contained the impression of Luca's tall athletic body. The air still smelt faintly of his citrus and spice aftershave. Her heartrate was still not quite back to normal.

Would it ever be again?

Meeting Luca Ferrantelli had jolted her into an intense awareness of her femininity. Her body felt alive— tinglingly alive in a way it never had before. Her mind might have decided Luca was the most obnoxious man she'd ever met but her body hadn't got the memo. It was operating off script, responding to him in ways she had never thought possible. Every appraising look he cast her way, every smouldering twinkle in his hazel eyes, every lazy smile, had heated her blood and upped her pulse and fried her brain until even *she* was thinking about accepting his proposal.

Artie walked back to the sofa and picked up the ring box. She curled her fingers around it, telling herself she would put it in the safe until Luca came back tomorrow. But suddenly her fingers were prising open the lid. The ring glinted at her as if to say, *Put me on*.

It was the most beautiful ring she had ever seen. She might not be able to window shop like other people but she did plenty of shopping and browsing online. She ran her fingertip over the top of the arabesque setting, stunned by the ring's exquisite design and breathtaking quality. Money was no object to filthy rich men like Luca Ferrantelli. He thought he could dangle a ridiculously expensive diamond in front of her nose and she would accept his stupid proposal without question.

She stared at the ring some more, turning the box this way so she could see how the diamonds picked up the light coming in from the windows. It was probably too big for her anyway. Artie pulled her lower lip inside her mouth. What would it hurt to try it on just the once? No one had to know. She hadn't been in a bricks-and-mortar jewellery shop since she was a teenager, when her mother bought her a pair of earrings. This was her chance to do what others took for granted.

She took the ring out of the box and set the box down on the table again. She slipped the ring on her left ring finger, pushing it past her second knuckle. It was kind of weird that it was a perfect fit. She couldn't stop staring at it. The sheer brilliance of the diamonds and the deep blue of the sapphire stole her breath clean away.

'Don't get too comfortable there,' Artie addressed the ring. 'I'm not keeping you.'

The ring glinted back at her as if to say, *Are you sure about that?*

Artie took off the ring, placed it back in its velvet box and closed the lid with a definitive snap. She held the box in the middle of her palm, glaring at it like it contained a lethal insect. 'I'm not looking at you again, do you hear me?' She left the box on the coffee table and went to where Rosa was working in the kitchen.

Rosa looked up from where she was preparing vegetables for soup. 'Did the ring fit?'

Artie pursed her lips. 'What makes you think I tried it on?'

Rosa gave a knowing smile. 'It's not every day a girl gets to try on a ring as stunning as that.'

Artie frowned. 'I thought you'd be on my side. Aren't you the least bit concerned about my situation?'

'I'm deeply concerned you're going to lose everything if you don't do what Luca Ferrantelli says,' Rosa said. 'You could do a lot worse than him for a husband. He's handsome and rich and will no doubt spoil you, if that ring is any indication.'

'What if I don't want to be spoilt?'

Rosa picked up an onion and held it in her palm. 'See this? Men like Luca Ferrantelli are like this onion. You're only looking at the surface of him—the façade he shows the world. Peel back the layers and you'll see the man behind the mask. You never know—you might be pleasantly surprised at what you find.'

'And how will I know if peeling back his layers reduces me to tears like that onion will?'

'That's a risk we all take when we get close to someone.' Rosa sliced into the onion with a knife. 'And God knows, you're never going to get close to anyone living on your own here. This is a lifeline and you'd be a fool not to take it.'

Maybe Rosa was right, because, if Artie didn't marry Luca Ferrantelli she would have to leave the *castello*. Permanently.

She couldn't allow that to happen.

No matter what.

But how could she work this to her advantage? What could Luca do for her in return? Apart from buying her a stunningly beautiful engagement ring that just begged to come out of that box and sit proudly on her finger. Artie went back to the salon and picked up the velvet box. She told herself she was going to put it in the safe until Luca returned the following day. But before she could stop herself, she opened the box and took the ring out and placed it back on her finger. She promised herself she would only wear it for a couple of hours, just for the heck of it. Then, once she got tired of it, she would put it back in the box and hand it back to Luca tomorrow with a firm, *Thanks, but no, thanks.*

She couldn't possibly marry him…*could she?*

Later that evening, Artie was doing her embroidery when she suddenly realised the ring wasn't on her finger. She jumped off the sofa and searched around the scatter cushions, her heart racing. Where was it? Had it fallen off somewhere? Oh, God. Oh, God. Oh, God. The ring was worth a fortune. Luca would be furious if she lost his blasted ring. He had no right to buy her such an expensive ring. Her stomach pitched. Would he want her to replace it? Yes, he would.

Rosa came in at that point. 'Look, I know things are

bad financially but surely you don't have to search the back of the sofa for loose change?'

Artie swung around to face her, eyes wide in panic. 'I can't find Luca's wretched engagement ring!'

Rosa frowned. 'Didn't you put it in the safe?'

'No, I stupidly put it on for a couple of hours.' Artie tossed all the scatter cushions on the floor and began lifting off the sofa cushions to no avail. 'What am I going to do?'

Rosa joined in the search. 'You'll have to retrace your steps. Where have you been in the last few hours? Did you go outside to the garden?'

'No, I've only been indoors.'

Artie emptied her embroidery basket onto the floor—thimbles, reels of thread, needles going everywhere. The disorder on the floor in front of her was the same as inside her mind. Chaos. Tangled thoughts. Prickling conscience.

'It must be here somewhere. Oh, God, how could I lose it?'

She stuffed the embroidery items haphazardly back in the basket, pricking her finger with one of her needles.

'Ouch.' She stuck her finger in her mouth and sucked up the droplets of blood. She removed her finger from her mouth and gave Rosa a baleful look. 'He had no right to give me such an expensive ring. I'll have to marry him now.'

But deep down you want to, don't you? Marriage to Luca Ferrantelli just might give you some control over your life. The control you've been seeking for a long time. Money. Freedom. Not to mention a wickedly handsome 'paper' husband...

Rosa bent down and carefully sorted through Artie's basket for a moment. 'Ah, here it is.' She handed Artie the engagement ring. 'You'd better put it back on and leave it on until you give it back to Signor Ferrantelli.'

Give it back?

Lose her one chance of taking back control of her life?

Lose her home?

Artie slipped the ring back on her finger, her thoughts finally untangling. 'I'm not giving it back. Maybe you're right. This is my chance—maybe my only chance—to take control of my life. I'm going to make this work for me. On my terms. It's only for six months—what have I got to lose?'

Rosa raised one brow. 'Your heart?'

Artie set her mouth in a determined line. 'Not going to happen. This is a business deal. If Luca Ferrantelli can keep his emotions out of this, then so can I.'

Luca could not remember looking forward to a meeting more than returning to the Castello Mireille the following day to see Artemisia Bellante. Something about her intrigued him in a way few people did. He'd expected her to be biddable and submissive and instead found her spirited defiance a refreshing change from all the sycophants who surrounded him, pandering to his every whim. He'd found it so hard to take his eyes off her—slim, but with generous curves in all the right places, flashing brown eyes, wild, curly dark brown hair and a ski-slope nose, a stubborn chin and a cherry-red mouth—he'd almost offered her a real marriage. Only joking. No real marriages for him. Ever. He neither wanted nor needed love from a partner. Love was a reckless emotion that had the potential to cause immeasurable harm. He'd had a ringside seat to see just how much harm.

But a six-month hands-off arrangement to give his grandfather the motivation to get chemo was definitely doable. He hadn't been able to save his father or brother but he could save his grandfather. And marrying Artemisia Bellante was the way to do it. The only way.

In all their phone and email conversations, Franco Bellante had told him Artemisia was shy around men. Luca hadn't seen too much shyness. He'd seen sass and spirit and a damped down sensuality that was irresistibly attractive. He'd seen her surreptitious glances at his mouth and felt the supercharged energy in the air when their gazes collided. Did that mean she would be interested in tweaking the terms of their paper marriage?

Don't even think about it.

Luca knew how to control his impulses. He had learned the hard way not to rush into things without careful consideration first. Artemisia Bellante might be the most alluring young woman he'd met in a long time but a deal was a deal and his word was his word. Their paper marriage would last six months and no longer. Nonno's doctors had given him no more than a year to live if he didn't start treatment soon. The clock was ticking on the old man's life and Luca was determined to present him with the perfect choice of bride.

The housekeeper led him to the same salon as yesterday, where Artemisia was waiting for him standing by the windows. Her hands were clasped behind her back, her posture guarded. She looked regal and elegant even though she was wearing casual clothes—blue jeans and a white shirt with a patterned scarf draped artfully around her neck. The jeans highlighted the shapely curves of her hips and the white shirt brought out the creamy tone of her skin. Her chin was at a proud height, her deep brown eyes shining with unmistakable dislike.

Hot and heavy desire tingled in his groin. Her dislike of him was a bigger turn-on than he'd expected. Dating had become a little too easy for him lately—a little too boring and predictable. But nothing about Artemisia Bellante was boring or predictable.

Rein it in, buddy. You're not going there, remember?

Luca gave a sweeping bow. '*Buongiorno*, Artemisia. Have you made your decision?'

Her indrawn breath was like the hiss of a cornered cat. 'I have.'

'And?' Luca was only conscious of holding his breath when his lungs began to tighten. He wanted her as his bride. No one else was going to do. He *had* to have *her*. He couldn't explain his intractable stance other than that something about her ticked all the boxes.

She held his gaze with her icy one, her jaw set, her colour high. 'I will marry you.'

The relief that swept through him momentarily caught him off guard. It wasn't that he'd expected her to say no but somehow he hadn't realised until now how *much* he'd wanted her to say yes. 'Good. I'm glad you see the sense in doing so.'

Her eyebrows rose ever so slightly above her glittering eyes. 'However, I have some conditions on my acceptance of your offer.'

Luca was not one to allow people to push him around

but something about her expression made him make an exception. She stirred him in a way he had never been stirred before. His blood heated with a backbeat of desire, his nostrils flaring to take in the flowery scent of her perfume. 'Go on.'

She unfolded her arms and smoothed her hands down the front of her thighs. He ran his gaze down the slim length of her legs and her neat calves. She was wearing light brown suede ankle boots that gave her an inch or two more height. But even with the benefit of heels, she still wouldn't make it to the top of his shoulder. But that wasn't the only thing she was wearing—his grandmother's engagement ring winked proudly, almost defiantly, on her left hand. The arabesque design chosen so lovingly by his *nonno* to give to the love of his life—Luca's grandmother—suited Artemisia's hand as if designed especially for her. A faint alarm bell sounded at the back of his mind. He would have to be extra careful to keep his emotions out of this arrangement. Their relationship was a business deal and nothing more. There was no point feeling a little sentimental about seeing his grandmother's ring on Artie's hand. There was nothing sentimental about his choice of engagement ring. Sure, he could have bought any other ring but he had deliberately used his *nonna*'s ring knowing it would add authenticity to his committed relationship status in the eyes of his grandfather.

It was his grandfather who was sentimental.

Not him.

'Won't you sit down?' Artie's tone was all cool politeness but her eyes were hard with bitterness.

Luca gestured to the sofa nearest her. 'Ladies first.'

Artie drew in another sharp breath and sat on the sofa, her hands clasped around her crossed knee, her plump mouth tightly set. 'So, I've decided to accept your offer on the proviso we're married here at the *castello*. A quiet wedding, minimal guests.'

It intrigued him why she wanted a low-key wedding. Didn't most young women want to be a princess for the day? He could think of at least half a dozen of his ex-lovers who had dropped enormous hints about their dream wedding. It had killed his interest in them stone-dead. 'Is there any particular reason why you want to be married here and not at one of the local churches?'

Her gaze didn't quite meet his but aimed for the top of his left shoulder. 'My father's funeral was held here, so too was my mother's. It's where many of my ancestors are buried.'

'*Sì*, but a funeral is a little different from a wedding, is it not?'

Her clear brown gaze collided with his. 'Not from my perspective. This isn't a real marriage. I would be uncomfortable desecrating a church by saying vows neither of us intends to keep. It would be disrespectful. Nor do I want a big, flashy wedding with people I don't know and have nothing in common with attending. It would be a waste of money and effort.'

Luca didn't care where they were married as long as they were married. He only hoped Nonno would be well enough to be able to travel from his home in Tuscany, but, since Umbria was a neighbouring region, it wasn't a long journey—just over two hours' drive.

'Fine. We'll marry here. Leave the arrangements to me. I've already applied for a licence so we don't have to wait the six weeks normally required. Your father sent me a copy of your birth certificate and passport before he died. I took the liberty of getting things on the move.'

Her eyes widened and her mouth fell open. 'You were so sure I would accept? But you hadn't even met me in person until yesterday.'

He shrugged one shoulder. 'Your father showed me a photo and he talked about you a lot. I was satisfied you would be suitable.'

She uncrossed her legs and sprang off the sofa, moving some distance away. 'I would have thought a man in your position wouldn't have to resort to finding a mail-order bride.' Scorn underlined every word she spoke. 'What if I'd said no?'

Luca gave a slow smile. 'I would have found some way to change your mind.'

Her chin came up and her eyes flashed. 'I can't believe my father encouraged you in this ridiculous mission to acquire a wife. When did you meet with him? I've never seen you come here before yesterday and I barely left my father's side.'

'I visited your father when he was in hospital with pneumonia late last year. He talked you up so much it intrigued me. I was disappointed not to see you on one of my visits but he said you weren't keen on hospitals since the accident. We emailed or phoned after that.'

She bit her lip and looked away. 'Did he say anything else about me?'

'Just that you were shy and not much of a party girl.'

She gave a snort of humourless laughter. 'Yes, well, that's certainly true.'

Luca rose from the sofa and walked over to a row of

picture frames on a sideboard. He picked up a photo taken when Artie was a child, sitting on her mother's knee. 'Your mother was very beautiful. She was English, *sì*?'

'Y-yes…' There was a slight catch in her voice.

Luca put the photo back on the sideboard and turned to face her. 'It's hard to lose a parent in your teens, especially the same sex parent.' Harder still when you were the cause of their death. And the death of your only brother. The guilt never left him. It sat on his shoulder. It followed him. It prodded him. It never let him forget. It kept him awake at night. His own personal stalker, torturing him with the what-ifs and the if-onlys.

Her brown eyes met his. 'You lost your father and older brother when you were a teenager, didn't you?'

Luca knew there was still stuff about his father and brother's death online. Not so easy to come across these days but it was still there if you did a thorough enough search. It had been a big news story at the time due to his father's high profile in business circles.

He could still see the headlines now—*Property developer CEO and son and heir lost in heavy surf in Argentina.*

There had been nothing about Luca's role in their drowning and he only found out years later it was because his *nonno* had pulled some strings in order to protect him.

Another reason his marriage to Artie had to go ahead and soon. He owed his *nonno* peace in this last stage of his life.

'Yes. When I was thirteen.' He stripped his voice of all emotion—he could have been discussing the stock exchange instead of the worst day of his life.

'I'm sorry.' Artie waited a beat and added, 'Is your mother still alive?'

'Yes. She lives in New York now.'

'Has she remarried?'

'No.'

There was a silence.

Luca could have filled it with all the reasons why his mother no longer lived in Italy. Her unrelenting grief. His strained relationship with her that nothing he said or did could fix. The constant triggers being around him caused her. The empty hole in her life that nothing could fill. The hole he had created by his actions on that fateful day. He hadn't just lost his father and brother on that day—he'd lost his entire family as he'd known it. Even his grandparents—as caring and supportive as they tried to be—had been sideswiped by grief and became shadows of their former selves. His extended family—aunts, uncles, cousins—all of them had been affected by his actions that day.

'So, what changed your mind about marrying me?' Luca decided it was safer to stay on the topic of their upcoming marriage rather than drift into territory he wanted left well alone. 'Let me guess. Was it the engagement ring?'

She swallowed, her cheeks blooming with colour. 'In a way, yes.'

Luca hadn't taken her for a gold-digger but it was a damn fine ring. His eyes flicked to her left hand. 'It looks good on you. But I hope you don't mind it being second hand. It belonged to my grandmother. She left it to me in her will.'

Her eyes widened to the size of dinner plates. 'Your

grandmother's? Oh, my goodness. Just as well I—' She bit her lip and shifted her gaze a fraction, the colour in her cheeks deepening.

'Just as well you…?' Luca prompted, intrigued by her cagey expression.

Her slim throat rose and fell over a swallow and her gaze slipped out of reach of his. 'I—I misplaced it for a couple of hours. But it's your fault for giving me such a ridiculously valuable ring. A priceless heirloom, for pity's sake. What on earth were you thinking? Of course, I'll give it back to you once the six months is up.'

'I don't want it back. It's a gift.'

Her gaze flicked back to his, shock written all over her features. 'I couldn't possibly keep it. It's worth a small fortune, not to mention the sentimental value.'

Luca shrugged. 'It's no skin off my nose what you do with it once our marriage is over. It's just a ring. I will have no further use for it after this. It means nothing to me.'

Her mouth tightened. 'Is there anything that means something to you other than making disgusting amounts of money?'

Luca slanted his mouth into a cynical smile. 'There isn't a law against being successful in business. Money opens a lot of doors.'

'I would imagine it closes others. How would you know if people liked you for you or for your wealth?'

'I'm a good judge of character. I soon weed out the timewasters and hangers-on.'

Her top lip curled and her eyes shone with loathing. 'Well, bully for you.'

CHAPTER THREE

ARTIE WOULDN'T HAVE admitted it even under torture, but she was getting off on sparring with Luca Ferrantelli. Every time they exchanged words, little bubbles of excitement trickled into her bloodstream. He was intelligent and quick-witted and charming and she had to keep on her toes to keep up with him.

She couldn't understand why he had given her his grandmother's engagement ring. *Eek!* Just as well she hadn't lost it. But he didn't seem all that attached to the stunning piece of jewellery, and yet she had fallen in love with it at first sight. Surely he had at least one sentimental bone in his body, or was everything just another business deal?

Luca's brief mention of his father and brother intrigued her. Mostly because he seemed reluctant to dwell on the subject. His expression had given little away, his flat, emotionless tone even less. But still, she sensed there was pain beneath the surface—deep pain that made him distance himself from it whenever he could.

Maybe Rosa was right—Luca Ferrantelli had more than a few layers to his personality that begged to be explored.

But Artie knew all too well about deep emotional pain. Talking about her mother, thinking about the accident and its aftermath sent her into a spiral of despair. Guilt was her constant companion. Wasn't it her fault her father had lost control of his finances? He hadn't been the same after the accident. Losing Artie's mother, and losing the use of his legs as well as an acquired brain injury, had meant he was not the same man—nor ever could be—and she was entirely to blame. Nothing Artie could do would ever change that. It was only fitting that she wed Luca Ferrantelli and reclaim her family's heritage.

It was her penance. The price she must pay. But she would make the best out of the situation by owning her choice to marry Luca rather than feel he had forced her hand.

'We need to discuss the honeymoon.' Luca's expression was inscrutable. 'Do you have somewhere you'd like to go?'

Honeymoon?

Artie widened her eyes so far she thought they might pop right out of her head. She clasped her hand to her throat where her heart now seemed to be lodged. 'A…a honeymoon? Whatever for? You said it's going to be a marriage in name only. Why would we need to go on a honeymoon?' Even saying the word 'honeymoon' made her body go all tingly and her heart race and her blood heat. Heat that stormed into her cheeks and simmered in other more secret places.

One of his dark eyebrows lifted at her stuttering protest, a satirical glint shining in his gaze. 'I'm fine with a quiet wedding here at the *castello* but I insist on

a honeymoon. It will give our marriage more credibil-
ity if we are seen to go away together for a short break.'

Seen? In public? Be in wide open spaces? Rushing
crowds. Traffic. Noise. Busyness. Artie stumbled backwards, her arms wrapping around her body, her breathing tight and laboured. 'No. I can't do that. I don't want
to go. There's no need. It's not a proper marriage and
it's wrong of you to insist on it.'

Breathe. Breathe. Breathe.

Luca frowned. 'Are you worried I'll take advantage
of you? Please be assured that is not going to happen.
I gave you my word.'

'I don't want to go anywhere with you,' Artie said.
'How could you think I would? I don't even like you.'

His eyes dipped to her mouth then back to her gaze.
'Artemisia, we need to be seen together in public. It's
not going to work unless we present as a normal couple.
We'll have to live together most, if not all, of the time.'

Her stomach turned over. 'L-live together?'

'But of course. Isn't that what husbands and wives
do?'

Artie gulped. Her skin prickled, her legs trembled,
her mind raced. Live with Luca Ferrantelli? What would
that entail? She couldn't even leave her own home. How
on earth would she move into his? Should she tell him
about her social phobia? Would he understand? No. Not
likely. Few people did. Even the professionals who had
visited her at the *castello* had more or less given up
on her.

Her gaze moved out of reach of his and she fiddled
with the sleeve of her shirt for something to do with
her hands. 'I'm sorry, but couldn't you move in here?

I mean, this place is huge and you can have your own suite of rooms and we'd hardly have to see each other and no one would ever know we're not—'

'No.' His tone was so adamant the word could have been underlined in thick black ink.

Artie swung away from him, trying to get her breathing back under control. She was light-headed and nauseous, her stomach churning fast enough to make butter. She was going to faint... No, she wasn't. She was going to fight it. Fight *him*. She took a deep breath and turned around to face him. 'I will *not* leave my home. Not for you. A marriage of convenience is supposed to be convenient for both parties. It's not convenient for me to move right now. I've only just buried my father. I'd like more time to...to spend grieving out of the view of the public.' It wasn't completely a lie. She missed her father, not because they were particularly close but because looking after him had given structure and purpose to her life.

Luca studied her for a long moment, his expression giving nothing away. She tried not to squirm under his unnerving scrutiny but it was a mammoth effort and only added to her light-headedness. 'All right. We'll delay the honeymoon.'

Relief swept through her and she brushed back her hair from her face, her hand not quite as steady as she would have liked. 'Thank you.'

She hadn't been in a car since coming home from hospital after the accident. She hadn't been in a plane or train or bus since she was fifteen. She hadn't been around more than two or three people in a decade. Her life was contained within these four ancient stone walls and she couldn't see it changing any time soon.

Luca closed the distance between them and held her gaze for another beat or two. 'I realise your father's financial situation has come as a shock to you. And I understand how resistant you are to my plan to turn things to your advantage. But I want my grandfather to see us married and living as a couple.'

'Why is that so important to you?'

'He's got cancer but he won't agree to treatment.'

'Oh… I'm sorry.'

Luca ran a hand down his face, the sound of his palm scraping over his regrowth loud in the silence. 'Unless he has treatment soon, he will die within a year. His dream has always been to see me settled down with a nice young woman. He disapproves of my casual approach to relationships and has been at pains to let me know at every opportunity. I want him to find a reason to live, knowing I've found a suitable bride.'

A suitable bride.

If only Luca knew how unsuitable she really was. Would he still want to marry her if he knew the truth about her? 'Will your grandfather be well enough to come here for the wedding?'

'I hope so.'

Artie bit her lip. She was conflicted about keeping her social anxiety from Luca but neither could she risk losing her home if he decided to withdraw his offer of marriage. She didn't know him well enough to trust he would make allowances for her. He'd already told her he was a ruthless businessman who didn't allow emotion to cloud his judgement. How could she hope he might be understanding and compassionate about her mental health issues? 'But you only know me as my father presented me. I might be the worst person in the world.'

A lazy smile tilted his mouth and his eyes darkened. 'I like what I've seen so far.'

Artie could feel colour pouring into her cheeks. Could feel a faint hollow ache building, beating between her thighs. Could feel a light tingling in her breasts. His gaze went to her mouth and she couldn't stop herself from sweeping them with the tip of her tongue. His eyes followed the movement of her tongue and liquid warmth spread through her core like warmed treacle. What invisible chemistry was doing this to her? What potent force did Luca Ferrantelli have over her? She had never been so aware of another person. Never so aware of her own body. Her senses were on high alert, her pulse racing.

Suddenly he wasn't standing a metre away but was close enough for her to smell the sharp, clean citrus notes of his aftershave. Had he moved or had she?

She looked into the depths of his gaze and her heart skipped a beat. And another. And another, until it felt like tiny racing footsteps were pounding against the membrane surrounding her heart.

He lifted his hand to her face, trailing his index finger down the slope of her cheek from just above her ear down to the base of her chin. Every nerve in her skin exploded with sensation. Every pore acutely sensitive to his faintest touch.

'You are much more beautiful in person than in the photo your father showed me.' Luca's tone was a bone-melting blend of rough and smooth. Honey and gravel. Temptation and danger.

Artie couldn't take her eyes off his mouth, drawn by a force as old as time. Male and female desire meeting. Wanting. Needing. Tempting. 'I don't get called Artemisia…most people call me Artie.'

Oh, for pity's sake. Couldn't you think of something a little more sophisticated to say?

Luca gave a crooked smile and something warm spread through her chest. 'Artie. It's cute. I like it. Artemisia, Queen of Halicarnassus. She was an ally of the Persian King Xerces in 430 BCE and reputedly brave in battle.'

That's me—brave. Not.

'My mother chose it. She loved Greek history.'

His gaze became hooded and he glanced at her mouth again. 'There will be times when we'll be expected to show affection towards one another. Are you going to be okay with that?'

'W-what sort of affection?'

'Kissing. Holding hands. Touching.'

Her lower body began to throb with a strange kind of ache. She couldn't stop herself thinking about places he might touch her—places that were already tingling in anticipation. How would she cope with a casual brush of his hand? His strong arm around her waist? His mouth pressed to hers? No one had ever touched her with a lover's touch. No one had ever kissed her. The desire to be touched by him was overwhelming. Her body craved it like a drug.

'Okay.'

Okay? Are you out of your mind?

Artie *was* out of her mind—with lust. She had never felt so out of control of her body. It was acting of its own volition, responding to him in ways she had never expected. She didn't even like him. He was arrogant and confident in a way she found irritating. It was as if he expected her to throw herself at him just like any other woman he had encountered. How was she going to resist him if he kissed her? How would it feel to have that firm mouth moving against hers?

Luca continued to look at her with a heart-stopping intensity. 'If you don't want me to kiss you then you need to tell me, because right now I can think of nothing I want to do more.' His voice lowered to a deep bass that sent another wave of heat coursing through her body.

'What makes you think I want you to kiss me now? What would be the point? There's no one here but us.' Artie was proud of her calm and collected tone when inside her body was steaming, simmering, smouldering.

His thumb pressed lightly on the middle of her bottom lip, sending tingles down the length of her spine. 'The way you're looking at me.'

'How am I looking at you?'

Eek. Was that her voice? She had to do something about her voice. None of that whispery, husky rubbish. She had to be brusque and matter-of-fact.

'You must be imagining it.'

He cupped one side of her face with his hand, the slight roughness of his palm making her insides coil and tighten with lust. 'Maybe.' He gave a quick on-off smile and dropped his hand from her face. 'So, the wedding. How does this weekend sound?'

Artie only just managed to suppress a gasp. '*This* weekend? What's the rush?'

'I'm not a fan of long engagements.'

'Funny. But how am I going to find a dress in time? Or are you expecting me to turn up naked?'

Argh. Why did you say that?

A dark glint came into his eyes. 'Now, there's an idea.'

Artie pursed her lips, hoping her cheeks were not glowing as hot as they felt. 'I can safely say I will never, ever be naked in front of you.'

He glided a lazy finger down her burning cheek, a smile in his eyes. 'Have you been naked in front of anyone?'

Artie stepped back, annoyed with herself for not doing so earlier. She *had* to keep her distance. It was dangerous to stand so close to him. She had so little immunity to his sensual power. She had to remember he was a powerful magnet and she was a tiny iron filing.

'I'm not going to discuss my private life with you. It's none of your damn business.'

'We have to know a few things about each other otherwise no one will accept our marriage as the real thing.'

Artie frowned. 'What? Are you going to pretend you're in love with me or something? Who's going to believe it? We're total opposites.'

'Ah, but don't they say opposites attract?' His smile melted her bones—she could feel her legs trembling to keep her upright.

Artie compressed her lips and iced her gaze. 'This may come as a surprise to a man with an ego the size of yours but I'm not attracted to you.'

He gave a deep chuckle. 'Then you're going to have to call on every bit of acting power you possess to convince my grandfather otherwise. Think you can do that, *cara mia*?'

The Italian endearment almost made her swoon. She hoisted her chin. 'Do you, Mr Hardened Cynical Playboy, think *you* can act like a man passionately in love with his bride?'

His gaze held hers in a smouldering lock that made the backs of her knees tingle. 'That will be the easy part.'

CHAPTER FOUR

ARTIE STOOD IN FRONT of the cheval mirror in her bedroom and checked her appearance. She had decided against wearing her mother's wedding dress and chosen a cream satin ballgown of her mother's instead. It was a classic design with a tulle underskirt that emphasised her neat waist, and a close-fitting bodice that hinted at the shape of her breasts without revealing too much cleavage. She hadn't wanted to taint her mother's beautiful wedding gown with her charade of a marriage. Her parents had married for love and lived happily together until Artie insisted on going to a birthday party against their wishes when she was fifteen.

She bit down on her lip until it hurt. Why had she been so adamant about going to that stupid party? Where were those supposed friends of hers now? Only a handful came to visit her in hospital. None had come to the *castello* once she had been released. None had come to her mother's funeral. She had stood beside her father's wheelchair as her mother was lowered into the family plot at the *castello* with her heart in pieces, guilt raining down on her heavier than what was coming from the dismal sky above. How could one teenage decision have so many unforeseen consequences?

Artie plucked at the skirt of her dress, her stomach an ants' nest of nerves. Today was her wedding day. The day she married Luca Ferrantelli in a paper marriage to save her family home. Would this be another decision she would later regret? Or would the consolation of getting the *castello* back into her possession wipe out any misgivings? She glanced at the engagement ring on her hand. The longer she wore it, the more she loved it. She felt strangely connected to Luca's grandmother by wearing her ring. But would the old lady spin in her grave to know Artie was entering into a loveless union with her grandson?

Rosa came in carrying a bouquet of flowers she had picked from the garden. 'You look beautiful, Artie.' She handed her the simple but fragrant bouquet. 'You're not wearing a veil?'

Artie brought the flowers up to her nose and breathed in the heady scent of roses and orange blossom. 'This isn't a proper wedding.'

Rosa frowned. 'But it's still a legal one. You might as well look like a proper bride. And make that handsome groom of yours sit up and take notice.' She went to the large wardrobe and pulled out the long cardboard box where Artie's mother's wedding dress and veil were stored on the top shelf. She placed the box on the bed and lifted the lid and removed the tissue-wrapped heirloom hand-embroidered veil that had been worn by both Artie's mother and grandmother. Rosa shook out the veil and then brought it over to Artie. 'Come on. Indulge me.'

Artie rolled her eyes but gave in, allowing Rosa to fasten the veil on her head, securing it with hair pins. Rosa draped the veil over Artie's face and then stepped back to inspect her handiwork. 'You will knock Luca Ferrantelli's socks off, *sì*?'

Artie turned back to look at her reflection. She did indeed look like a proper bride. She glanced at Rosa. 'Tell me I'm not making the biggest mistake of my life. My second biggest, I mean.'

Rosa grasped one of Artie's hands, her eyes shimmering with tears. 'You have already lost so much. You can't lose the *castello* as well. Sometimes we have to do whatever it takes to make the best of things.' She released Artie's hand and brushed at her eyes and gave a rueful smile. 'Weddings always make me emotional. Just as well I didn't get married myself.'

'Would you have liked to?' Artie was surprised she hadn't thought to ask before now. Rosa was in her sixties and had been a part of the *castello* household for as long as Artie could remember. They had talked about many things over the years but not about the housekeeper's love life or lack thereof.

Rosa made a business of fussing over the arrangement of the skirt of Artie's gown. 'I fell in love once a long time ago. It didn't work out.'

'What happened?'

Rosa bent down lower to pick a fallen rose petal off the floor. She scrunched it in her hand and gave a thin-lipped smile. 'He married someone else. I never found anyone else who measured up.'

'Oh, that's so sad.'

Rosa laughed but it sounded tinny. 'I saved myself a

lot of heartache. Apparently, he's been divorced three times since then.' Her expression suddenly sobered. 'Your parents were lucky to have found each other. I know they didn't have as long together as they would have liked but it's better to have five years with the right one than fifty with the wrong one.'

But what about six months with a man who had only met her a matter of days ago? A man who was so dangerously attractive, her blood raced every time he looked at her?

Luca stood in the *castello*'s chapel, waiting for Artie to appear. His grandfather had been too unwell to travel, but Luca planned to take his new bride to meet him as soon as their marriage was official. Luca had organised for a priest to officiate rather than a celebrant, because he knew it would please his grandfather, who was a deeply religious man—hence his disapproval of Luca's life in the fast lane.

As much as he wanted his grandfather to meet Artie as soon as possible, he was quite glad he would have her to himself for a day or two. They would hardly be convincing as a newly married couple if they didn't look comfortable and at ease with each other.

She was a challenge he was tempted to take on. Her resistance to his charm was potently attractive. Not because he didn't respect and honour the word no when a woman said it. He could take rejection and take it well. He was never so emotionally invested in a relationship that he was particularly cut up when it ended.

But he sensed Artie's interest in him. Sensed the chemistry that swirled in the atmosphere when they were together. Would it be risky to explore that chemistry? She was young and unworldly. What if she didn't accept the terms of the deal and wanted more than he was prepared to give? He couldn't allow that to happen. If she fell in love with him it would change everything.

And if he fell in love with her...

He sidestepped the thought like someone avoiding a sinkhole. Loving her would indeed be a pitfall. For her and for him. Love was a dangerous emotion. Whenever he thought of the possibility of loving someone, his heart would shy away like a horse refusing a jump. Too dangerous. Too risky. Too painful.

The back of Luca's neck started to tingle and he turned to see Artie standing in the portal. He suppressed a gasp, his eyes drinking in the vision of her dressed in a stunning cream ballgown and off-white heirloom veil. The bright golden sunlight backlit her slim frame, making her look like an angel. As she walked towards him carrying a small bouquet of flowers he had to remind himself to breathe. The closer she got, the more his heart pounded, the more his blood thundered. And a strange sensation flowed into his chest. Warmth spreading over something hard and frozen, melting, reshaping, softening.

He gave himself a mental slap. No emotions allowed. This was a business deal. Nothing else. So what if she looked as beautiful as an angel? So what if his body roared with lust at the thought of touching her? This wasn't about him—it was about his grandfather. Giving him the will to live long enough to have treatment that could cure him or at least give him a few more precious years of life.

Artie came to stand beside him, her face behind the veil composed, and yet twin circles of pink glowed in her cheeks. Her make-up highlighted the flawless, creamy texture of her skin, the deep brown of her eyes and the thick ink-black lashes that surrounded them. Her lips shone with a hint of lip gloss, making him ache to press his mouth to hers to see if it tasted as sweet and luscious as it looked. He could smell her perfume, an intoxicating blend of fresh flowers that reminded him of the sweet hope of spring after a long, bleak winter.

'You look breathtaking,' Luca said, taking her hands in his. Her small fingers moved within the embrace of his and a lightning rod of lust almost knocked him off his feet. Maybe he shouldn't have suggested a paper marriage. Maybe he should have insisted on the real deal. The thought of consummating their marriage sent a wave of heat through his body. But his conscience slammed on the brakes. No. No. No. It wouldn't be fair. He wasn't the settling-down type and she had fairytale romance written all over her. Which, ironically, was why she was perfect for the role of his temporary bride. No one else would satisfy his grandfather. It *had* to be her.

'I—I'm nervous…' Her voice trembled and her teeth sank into the plush softness of her bottom lip.

Luca gently squeezed her fingers. 'Don't be.' His voice was so deep and rough it sounded like it had come from the centre of the earth. He didn't like admitting it, but he was nervous too. Not about repeating the vows and signing the register—those were formalities he could easily compartmentalise in his brain. He was worried his promise to keep their relationship on paper was going to be the real kicker. He gave her hand another light squeeze and smiled. 'Let's do this.'

And they turned to face the priest and the service began...

'I, Artemisia Elisabetta, take you, Luca Benedetto, to be my husband...' Artie repeated her vows with a slight quaver in her voice. 'I promise to be true to you in good times and bad, in sickness and in health.' She swallowed and continued, conscious of Luca's dark gaze holding hers, 'I will love and honour you all the days of my life.'

She wasn't a particularly religious person but saying words she didn't mean made her wonder if she was in danger of a lightning strike. The only lightning strike she had suffered so far had been the tingling zap coursing through her body when Luca first took her hand. Every cell of her body was aware of him. Dressed in a mid-blue morning suit, he looked like he had just stepped off a billboard advertisement for designer menswear. She could smell the lemon and lime of his aftershave—it teased her nostrils, sending her senses into a tailspin. How could a man smell so damn delicious?

Eek! How could a man look so damn attractive?

Double eek! How could she be marrying him?

Luca's hand took her left one and slipped on the wedding ring as he repeated his vows. 'I, Luca Benedetto, take you, Artemisia Elisabetta, to be my wife. I promise to be true to you in good times and bad, in sickness and in health.' He paused for a beat and continued with a rough edge to his voice, 'I will love and honour you all the days of my life.'

Artie blinked back moisture gathering in her eyes.

He sounded so convincing. He even looked convincing with his gaze so focused on her, his mouth smiling at her as if she was the most amazing woman who had ever walked upon the face of the earth.

It's an act. Don't be fooled by it. None of this means anything to him and neither should it mean anything to you.

'You may kiss the bride.'

The priest's words startled Artie out of her reverie and she only had time to snatch in a breath before Luca's hands settled on her hips and drew her closer, his mouth descending inexorably towards hers. The first warm, firm press of his lips sent a jolt of electricity through her body. A jolt that travelled all the way down her spine and fizzed like a sparkler deep in her core. He lifted his lips off hers for an infinitesimal moment as if time had suddenly paused. Then he brought his mouth back to hers and sensations rippled through her as his lips moved against hers with increasing pressure, his hands on her hips bringing her even closer to the hard heat of his stirring body.

One of his hands left her hip to cradle one side of her face, his touch gentle, almost reverent, and yet his mouth was pure sin. Tempting, teasing, tantalising. She opened to him and his tongue touched hers and her insides quaked and throbbed with longing. She pressed closer, her arms going around his neck, her senses reeling as his tongue invited hers in an erotic dance. Every nerve in her lips and mouth awakened to his kiss, flowering open like soft petals to strong sunshine. She became aware of her body in a way she never had before—its needs, urges, flagrantly responding to the dark primal call of his.

Luca angled his head to change position, his tongue stroking against hers, a low, deep groan sounding in his throat. It thrilled her to know he was as undone by their kiss as she was. Thrilled and excited her to realise her own sensual power. Power she hadn't known she possessed until now.

The priest cleared his throat and Luca pulled back from her with a dazed look on his face. Artie suspected she was looking just as shell-shocked as him. Her mouth felt swollen, her feminine core agitated with a roaring hunger he alone had awakened.

Luca blinked a couple of times as if to reset his equilibrium. 'Well, hello there, Signora Ferrantelli.' His voice was rusty, his gaze drifting to her mouth as if he couldn't quite believe what had happened between them moments before.

Artie licked her lips and tasted the salty sexiness of his. 'Hello…'

Luca spoke briefly to the priest, thanking him for his services, and then led Artie to where Rosa had set up refreshments in the garden. She sensed him pulling up a drawbridge, a pulling back into himself. He stood without touching her, his expression inscrutable.

'Right. Time to celebrate. And then tomorrow we'll go and visit my grandfather.'

A wave of ice-cold dread washed over her. 'But can't we leave it a while? I mean, wouldn't he expect us to be on our honeymoon and—?'

'I can't afford to leave it too long before I introduce

you to him,' Luca said, frowning. 'He's in a vulnerable state of health.'

Artie chewed at her lip and lowered her gaze. 'I understand all that but I need more time to get used to being your…wife. I'm worried I'll do or say something that will make your grandfather suspicious.'

Luca gave her a smouldering look. 'If you kiss me like you did just then, any doubts he has will disappear.'

Artie could feel her cheeks firing up. 'I was only following your lead. I haven't been kissed before, so—'

'Really?' His eyebrows shot up in surprise.

She pulled away from him and hugged her arms around her body. 'Go on, mock me for being a twenty-five-year-old virgin. I must seem like a pariah to someone like you who changes lovers daily.'

Her conscience rolled its eyes. *I can't believe you just told him you're a virgin.*

He scraped a hand through his hair, making it tousled. 'Look, I kind of figured from your father that you were lacking in experience but I didn't realise you've never had a boyfriend, even as a teenager. Did your father forbid you from going out or something?'

Artie averted her gaze. 'No. I was busy looking after him after the accident that killed my mother and seriously injured him. There wasn't time for dating.'

His deep frown brought his dark eyebrows together. 'Why were you the one looking after him? Why didn't he employ a nurse or carer?'

Artie turned slightly so she was facing the view over the estate. Luca's penetrating gaze was too unsettling, too unnerving. How could she explain her reasons for taking care of her father? How could she explain the guilt that had chained her to his side? The guilt that still plagued her and had led her to marry Luca in order to save her family's home? The home that was the only thing she had left of her family. 'It was my choice to look after him. I was happy to do it.'

Luca came up behind her and placed his hands on the tops of her shoulders and turned her to face him. He expression was still etched in a frown, his hazel eyes gentle with concern. 'You were just a child when the accident occurred. It was unfair of your father to allow you to sacrifice yourself in such a way. But what about school? Surely you would have had plenty of opportunity to mix with people your own age?'

Artie pressed her lips together for a moment. 'I finished my education online. I was given special permission. I didn't want to leave my father to the care of strangers. He was stricken with grief after losing my mother. We both were. It was my choice to take care of him—no one forced me to do it.'

His hands began a gentle massaging movement that made the tense muscles in her neck and shoulders melt like snow under warm sunshine. 'I think what you did for your father was admirable and yet I can't help feeling he exploited you. You should've had more time to yourself doing all the things teenagers and young adults do.'

Artie stepped out of his hold and interlaced her fingers in front of her body. She glanced to where Rosa was hovering with a bottle of champagne. 'Shouldn't we be mingling with Father Pasquale and our two other guests?' She didn't wait for him to answer and turned and walked towards the housekeeper standing with the priest and the other witness, who worked part-time on the Castello Mireille estate.

Luca watched Artie pick up a glass of champagne from the silver tray the housekeeper was holding. Her expression was now coolly composed but he sensed he had pressed on a nerve when discussing her role of caring for her father. He'd already suspected she was a virgin—her father had intimated as such—but no way had he suspected she had zero experience when it came to dating.

No one had kissed her before him.

She had never had a boyfriend, not even during her teens. How had her father allowed that to happen? Surely he must have realised his daughter was missing out on socialising with people her age?

Luca ran his tongue over his lips and tasted the sweet, fruity residue of her lip gloss. He could still feel the soft imprint of her lips on his, could still feel the throb of desire kissing her had evoked in his body, the deep pulses in his groin, the tingles in his thighs and lower spine.

He had kissed many women, too many to recall in any detail, but he knew he would never forget his first kiss with Artie. It was embedded in his memory. He could recall every contour of her soft mouth, every brush and glide of her tongue, her sweet vanilla and wild-strawberry taste.

But he would have to find some way to forget, for theirs was to be a paper marriage. A six-month time frame to achieve his goal of setting his grandfather's mind at peace. Knowing Artie had so little experience was an even bigger reason to stick to his plan of a hands-off arrangement. It wouldn't be fair to explore the physical chemistry between them, because it might raise her expectations on their relationship.

He didn't *do* relationships. And certainly not *that* type of relationship.

Long-term relationships required commitment and responsibility for the health and safety of your partner. His track record on keeping those he loved safe was appalling. It was easier not to love. Easier to keep his emotions in check, to freeze them so deep inside himself they could never be thawed. To imagine oneself falling in love just because of a bit of scorching hot chemistry was a foolish and reckless thing to do. He no longer did anything reckless and foolish.

Luca glanced at Artie and something pinched in his chest. She was standing next to the ancient stone fountain, the tinkling of water and the sound of birds chirping in the shrubbery a perfect backdrop for her old-world beauty. The sunlight brought out the glossy sheen of her dark brown hair, the light breeze playing with a curl that had worked its way loose from her elegant up-do. She was looking into the distance, a small frown on her forehead, and every now and again the tip of her tongue came out and swept across her lips where his had recently pressed. She turned her head and caught him staring at her, and her cheeks pooled with a delicate shade of pink.

Had he made a mistake in choosing her to be his temporary bride? She was so innocent, so untouched and other-worldly, like she had been transported from another time in history or straight out of a classic fairy tale. And yet he'd felt a connection with her from the moment he met her. A powerful connection that no amount of logic and rationality could dismiss. His brain said *Don't go there* and yet his body roared with primal hunger.

But he would have to get his self-control back in shape, and fast, because falling for his sweet and innocent bride would be the most reckless and foolish thing of all.

CHAPTER FIVE

ARTIE WAS AWARE of Luca's gaze resting on her every time she glanced his way. Aware of the way her body responded to his lightest touch. The merest brush of his fingers set off spot fires in her flesh, sending heat travelling to every secret place in her body. Smouldering there like hot coals just waiting for a breath of oxygen to fan them into vibrant life.

His kiss...

Best not to think too much about his kiss. They were supposed to be keeping their relationship platonic, but nothing about Luca's kiss was platonic. It was sensory overload and she wondered if she would ever recover. Or stop wanting him to kiss her again. And why stop at kisses? He had woken something in her, something hungry and needy that begged to be assuaged. The idea of asking Luca to tweak the rules of their marriage slipped into her mind like an uninvited guest. It would be an ideal opportunity for her to get some experience on board. A six-month marriage where she could indulge in the delights of the flesh. What was there to lose other than her virginity?

Your pride? her conscience piped up. *He can have*

anyone. You're not even his type. How do you think you could ever satisfy him for six minutes, let alone six months?

Luca took a glass of champagne off Rosa and came over to where Artie was standing near the fountain. He glanced towards the priest and then back to her. 'Father Pasquale is having a good time indulging in Rosa's food. How long has she been working here?'

'Since I was a baby,' Artie said. 'This is her home as much as it is mine.'

'So, what would she do if you were to sell up and move away?'

Artie raised her chin. 'I would never sell the *castello*. And I don't want to live anywhere but here.'

I can't live anywhere but here.

Luca held her gaze for a long moment. 'How will you maintain the estate? It needs a lot of work, and sooner rather than later.'

She drained her champagne glass and sent him a narrowed glance. 'Is this the right time to discuss this? It's our wedding day.'

His brows drew together in a frown. 'Do I have to remind you of the terms of our marriage?'

'No.' She flashed him a pointed look. 'Do *you* need reminding? That kiss was a little enthusiastic for someone who insisted on keeping things on paper.'

His gaze went to her mouth, and the atmosphere throbbed with heightened intensity. 'Maybe, but it wasn't a one-way kiss, was it, *cara*? You were with me all the way.' His tone was so deep and rough it sent a tingle down her spine. And his eyes contained a glint that made something warm and liquid spill between her thighs.

Artie went to swing away from him but his hand came down on her arm. A shiver coursed through her body at the feel of his long, strong, tanned fingers encircling her wrist. She looked down at his hand on her flesh and the warm, liquid sensation in her lower body spread like fire throughout her pelvis. She lifted her gaze to his and raised her eyebrows in a haughty manner. 'W-what are you doing?' Her tone was breathless rather than offended.

His broad thumb began a slow caress over the pulse point on her wrist, the fast-paced throb of her blood betraying her even further. She breathed in the scent of him—the exotic mix of citrus and clean, warm male, her senses reeling from his closeness.

'We're married, *cara*. People will expect us to touch each other.'

Her heart skipped like it was trying to break some sort of record. 'I'm not used to people touching me.'

Luca brushed his bent knuckles against the curve of her cheek, his gaze holding hers in a sensual lock that made her insides quake with desire. 'But you like it when I touch you, *sì*?' His thumb moved from her pulse point and stroked along her lower lip. 'You like it very much.'

Artie wanted to deny it but she had hardly helped her case by kissing him back the way she had earlier. Nor was she helping it now by not pulling away from his loose hold. Her willpower had completely deserted her—she wanted his touch, craved it like an addict craved a forbidden substance. She couldn't take her eyes off his mouth, couldn't stop thinking about the warm, sensual pleasure of it moving against hers. Couldn't stop thinking about the stroke and glide of his tongue and how it had sent torrents of need racing through her body.

She drew in a ragged breath and forced her gaze back to his. 'I'm sorry if I keep giving you mixed messages. It wasn't my intention at all.'

He brought her hand up to his mouth and pressed a barely-there kiss to her bent knuckles, his gaze unwavering on hers. 'You're not the only one sending mixed messages.' He dropped her hand and gave a rueful smile. 'I'm not going to change the terms of our marriage. It wouldn't be fair to you.'

Not fair? What was fair about denying her body the fulfilment it craved? 'Are you worried I might fall in love with you?' The question popped out before she could stop it.

His dark eyes dipped to her mouth for a moment, his forehead creasing in a frown as if he was quietly considering the possibility of her developing feelings for him. When his gaze came back to hers it was shuttered. Screened with secret thoughts. 'It would be very foolish of you to do so.' His voice contained a note of gravity that made the hairs on the back of her neck tingle.

'Have you ever been in love with anyone?'

'No.' His answer was fast and flat.

Artie twirled the empty champagne glass in her hand. 'I didn't realise it was possible to prevent oneself from falling in love. From what I've heard it just happens and there's nothing you can do to stop it. Maybe you haven't met the right person yet.'

'I have no doubt such feelings exist between other people but I have no interest in feeling that way about someone.'

'Why?'

Luca shrugged one broad shoulder, his gaze still inscrutable. 'It seems to me an impossible task to be someone's soulmate. To be everything they need and want you to be. I know I can't be that person. I'm too selfish.'

Artie wondered if that was entirely true. He was prepared to marry a virtual stranger to keep his grandfather alive for a few more years. How was that selfish? And he was prepared to hand her back the *castello* at the end of six months instead of keeping his ninetenths ownership. Hardly the actions of a self-serving man, surely?

Rosa approached at that moment carrying a tray with fresh glasses of champagne. 'Another quick one before the official photos are taken?' she asked with a smile. 'The photographer is setting up near the rose garden.'

Artie put her used glass on the tray and took a new one. *'Grazie.'*

'And you, Signor Ferrantelli?' Rosa turned to Luca, offering him a fresh glass off the tray.

He shook his head. 'Not for me, thanks. One is enough. And please call me Luca.' He took Artie's free hand and nodded in the direction of the photographer. 'Shall we?'

Once a small set of photos were taken, Artie helped Rosa tidy away the refreshments after the priest and photographer had left. But when the housekeeper announced she was going to have an early night, Artie was left at a loose end. She hadn't seen Luca since the photo session—he'd said he wanted to check a few things out on the estate and hadn't yet returned. She'd thought about what he'd said back at the fountain and his reasons for saying it. The more she got to know him, the more she wanted to know. Why was he so adamant about keeping his emotions in check? What was so threatening about loving someone that made him so unwilling to experience it for himself? She might not have any experience when it came to falling in love, but she knew enough from her parents and books and movies it was a real and powerful emotion that was impossible to block once it happened. But since the accident, she had given up on the hope of one day finding true love. Any love she felt would be one-sided, for how could anyone return her love once they knew the destruction she had caused?

Luca had warned her about falling in love with him—*'It would be very foolish of you to do so.'* But how could she stop something that was so beyond her control? She was already aware of her vulnerability where he was concerned. He was so suave and sophisticated, and occupied a world she hadn't been party to her entire adult life. Hadn't his passionate, heart-stopping kiss shown her how at risk she was to developing feelings towards him?

Artie circled her wrist where his fingers had held her. A shiver shimmied down her spine as she recalled the tensile strength in his hand, the springy black masculine hairs that peppered his skin, the way his touch spoke to her flesh, awakening it, enlivening it, enticing it. He was temptation personified and she would be a fool indeed to allow her feelings to get the better of her. He had been clear about the terms of their relationship.

Why, then, did she ache for more of his touch? Why, then, did she want to feel his mouth on hers again?

Artie sat in the main salon with her embroidery on her lap, when Luca came in. His hair looked tousled from the wind or the passage of his fingers or both. And he had changed out of his morning suit into jeans and a white cotton shirt, the sleeves rolled back to reveal his strong wrists and forearms. The white shirt highlighted his olive-toned tan, the blue jeans the muscled length of his legs. He brought in with him the fresh smell of outdoors and something else…something that made her female hormones sit up straighter and her senses to go on high alert.

She put the sampler she was working on to one side and crossed one leg over the other, working hard to keep her features neutral. 'I wasn't sure of your plans, so I got Rosa to make up one of the guest rooms for you. It's on the second floor—the green suite overlooking the vineyard.'

His gaze held hers with a watchful intensity. 'So, she knows our marriage is a hands-off affair?'

Artie moistened her lips, conscious of the slow crawl of heat in her cheeks. 'Yes, well, I thought it best. I'm not the best actor when it comes to playing charades, and she's known me a long time and would sense any hint of inauthenticity.'

'I would prefer you not to tell anyone else about the terms of our relationship.' His tone was firm. 'I don't want any idle gossip getting back to my grandfather.'

'Rosa is the soul of discretion. She would never betray a confidence.' It was the one thing Artie could rely on—the housekeeper was loyal and trustworthy to a fault. Rosa had never revealed Artie's struggles to anyone and had always been as supportive as possible.

Luca came over to the sofa where she was sitting and leaned down and picked up the sampler she'd been working on. He ran his fingers over the tiny flower buds and leaves she had embroidered. 'This is exquisite work. Have you been doing it long?' he asked.

Artie shrugged off the compliment but inside she was glowing from his praise. No one apart from her father and Rosa had ever seen her work. 'It's just a hobby. I started doing embroidery after I got out of hospital. I'm self-taught, which you can probably tell.'

He turned the sampler over and inspected the other side, where the stitches were almost as neat and precise as on the front. 'You undersell yourself, *cara*. You could start a small business doing this sort of thing. Bespoke embroidery. There's a big swing away from factory-produced or sweatshop items. What people want these days is the personal touch.'

'Yes, well, I'm not sure I'm ready for that.' Artie took the sampler out of his hand and folded it and put it inside her embroidery basket, then closed the lid with a definitive movement.

'What's stopping you?'

I'm stopping me.

Her fear of the big, wide world outside the *castello* was stopping her from reaching her potential. She knew it but didn't know how she could do anything to change it. How could she run a business locked away here? She met his probing gaze for a moment before looking away again. The thought of revealing her phobia to him made her blood run cold. What would he think of her? She had effectively married him under false pretences. 'I'm happy leaving it as a hobby, that's all. I don't want to put myself under pressure of deadlines.'

'Speaking of deadlines…' Luca rubbed a hand down his face, the raspy sound of his palm against his light stubble making her recall how it had felt against her skin when he'd kissed her. 'I'd like to make an early start in the morning. My grandfather gets tired easily, so the first part of the day is better for him to receive visitors.'

Artie blinked. Blinked again. Her pulse began to quicken. Her breathing to shorten. Her skin to tighten. She rose from the sofa on unsteady legs and moved to the bank of windows on the other side of the room. She turned her back to the room and grasped the window-sill with white-knuckled force. 'Maybe you should go alone. I need more time before I—'

'There isn't time to waste.' The intransigent edge to his tone was a chilling reminder of his forceful, goal-directed personality.

Artie swallowed a tight lump in her throat and gripped the windowsill even harder. 'I… I can't go with you.'

There was a beat or two of intense silence. A silence so thick it seemed to be pressing in on her from all four walls and even the ceiling. A silence that echoed in her head and roared in her ears and reminded her she was way out of her depth.

'What do you mean, you can't? We made an agreement, Artie. I expect you to adhere to it.' His voice throbbed with frustration. 'Be ready at seven thirty. I'm not taking no for an answer.'

Artie released her grip on the windowsill and turned

to face him. Her stomach was roiling, her skin damp with perspiration, her mind reeling at the thought of going beyond the *castello* gates. 'Luca, please don't do this.' Her voice came out sandpaper-hoarse.

He gave a savage frown. 'Don't do what? All I'm asking is for you to uphold your side of our agreement. Which, I might remind you, is a legal one. You signed the papers my lawyer prepared—remember?'

Artie steepled her hands against her nose and mouth, trying to control her breathing. Her heart was doing cartwheels and star jumps and back flips and her pulse was off the charts. 'It's not that I don't want to go…'

'Then what is it?'

She lowered her hands from her face and pressed her lips together to stop them from trembling. She clasped her hands in front of her body, her fingers tightly inter-laced to the point of discomfort. She couldn't bring her gaze up to meet his, so instead aimed it at the carpet near his feet. 'There's something I haven't told you… something important.'

Luca crossed the room until he was standing in front of her. He lifted her chin with the end of his finger and meshed his gaze with hers. His frown was still in place but was more concerned now than angry. 'What?' His tone was disarmingly gentle and his touch on her chin light but strangely soothing. 'Tell me what's going on. I want the truth, *cara*.'

Artie bit the inside of her mouth, trying to find the words to describe her condition. Her weakness. Her shame. 'I… I haven't been outside the *castello* grounds since I was fifteen years old. It's not that I don't want to leave it—I can't.'

His hand fell away from her face, his forehead creased in lines of puzzlement. 'Why can't you? What's stopping you?'

She gave a hollow, self-deprecating laugh and pointed a finger at her chest. '*I'm* stopping me.' She stepped back from him and wrapped her arms around her body. 'I have crippling social anxiety. I can't cope with crowds and busy, bustling places. I literally freeze or have a meltdown—a full-blown panic attack.'

He opened and closed his mouth as if trying to think of something to say.

'I'm sorry,' Artie said. 'I should have told you before now but I was too embarrassed and—'

'Please. Don't apologise.' His voice was husky, his expression etched with concern. He shook his head like he was trying to get his muddled thoughts in some sort of order. 'Why didn't your father say something to me? He led me to believe you were—'

'Normal?' She raised her brows in an arch manner. 'Is that the word you were looking for? I'm hardly that, am I?'

Luca made a rough sound at the back of his throat. '*Cara*, please don't run yourself down like that. Have you seen a health professional about it?'

'Four.'

'And?'

Artie spread her hands outwards. 'And nothing. I couldn't cope with the side effects of medication. Meditation and mindfulness helped initially but not enough to get me outside the *castello* grounds. Talk therapy helped too at first but it was expensive and I didn't have the time with my caring responsibilities with Papa to keep going with it.' She gave a sigh and added, 'I found it exhausting, to be honest. Talking about stuff I didn't really want to talk about.'

'The accident?'

Artie nodded, her gaze slipping out of reach of his. 'So, there you have it. My life in a nutshell—no pun intended.'

Luca brushed a finger down her cheek. 'Look at me, *cara*.' It was a command but so gently delivered it made something move inside her chest like the slow flow of warm honey.

Artie raised her eyes back to his, the tip of her tongue sneaking out to sweep over her lips. 'I'm sorry for misleading you. You probably wouldn't have married me if you'd known. But I was so desperate to keep the *castello*. I don't know what I'd do without it. It's the only home I've ever known and if I'm forced to leave...' She bit her lip until she winced. 'I can't leave. I just can't.'

He touched her lip with the pad of his thumb. 'Stop doing that. You'll make it bleed.' His tone was gruff and gently reproving, his gaze surprisingly tender. 'We'll find a way to manage this.'

'How? If your grandfather is too ill to travel, then how will I ever get to meet him?'

'Technology to the rescue.' He gave a quick smile and patted his jeans pocket, where his phone was housed. 'We can set up a video call. Nonno's eyesight isn't great and he's not keen on mobile phones but it will be better than nothing.'

Artie moved a step or two away, her arms crossing over her body, her hands rubbing up and down her upper arms as if warding off a chill. 'You're being very understanding about this… I wouldn't blame you if you tore up the agreement and took full possession of the *castello*.'

Please God, don't let him do that. Please. Please. Please.

Luca came up behind her and placed his hands on her shoulders. 'That's not going to happen.' She suppressed a shiver as the movement of air when he spoke disturbed the loose strands of her hair around her neck. 'We'll work together to solve this.'

Artie turned to face him with a frown. 'Why are you being so generous? You said earlier today you're a selfish man, but I'm not seeing it.'

His smile was lopsided and his hands gently squeezed the tops of her shoulders. 'I can be extremely selfish when it comes to getting what I want.' His gaze drifted to her mouth and her heart skipped a beat. After a moment, his eyes came back to hers. Dark. Lustrous. Intense. The air suddenly vibrating with crackling energy as if all the oxygen particles had been disturbed.

'Luca?' Her voice was barely audible, whisper-soft. Her hand crept up to touch his lean jaw, her fingers trailing over the light prickle of his stubble. She sent her index finger around the firm contours of his mouth, the top lip and then the slightly fuller lower one. He drew in a sharp breath as if her touch excited him, thrilled him, tempted him.

His hand came up and his fingers wrapped around her slim wrist as if to pull her hand from his face. But then he made a low, deep sound at the back of his throat and his head came down and his mouth set fire to hers.

CHAPTER SIX

LUCA KNEW HE should stop the kiss before it got out of control. Knew he shouldn't draw her closer to his body where his blood was swelling him fit to burst. Knew he was forty times a fool to be tempted to change the rules on their paper marriage. But right then, all he could do was explore her soft mouth and let his senses run wild with the sweet, tempting taste of her lips. She opened to him on a breathless sigh and the base of his spine tingled when her tongue met his—shy and yet playful, innocent and yet daring. Need drove him to kiss her more deeply, to hold her more closely, to forget about the restrictions he'd placed on their relationship. Call him reckless, call him foolish, but right now he would die without the sweet temptation of her mouth responding to his.

Artie pressed herself against him, her arms winding around his neck, her young, slim body fitting against him as if fashioned specially for him. He ached to explore the soft perfection of her breasts, to glide his hands over her skin, to breathe in the scent of her, to taste her in the most intimate way possible.

His hands settled on her hips, holding her to the aching throb in his pelvis, his conscience at war with his body. He finally managed to find the willpower to drag his mouth off hers, but he couldn't quite bring himself to let her go.

'You know this can't happen.' His voice was so rough it sounded like he'd swallowed ground glass.

She looked up at him with eyes bright and shining with arousal. 'Why can't it? We're both consenting adults.'

Luca placed his hands around her wrists and pulled her arms from around his neck, but he still didn't release her. His fingers circled her wrists in a loose hold, his desire for her chomping at the bit like a bolting thoroughbred stallion. 'You know why.'

Her mouth tightened, her cheeks pooling with twin circles of pink. 'Because I'm a virgin? Is that it?'

Luca released her wrists and stepped away, dragging a hand through his hair in an effort to get his pulse rate to go back to somewhere near normal. 'It's not just about that.'

'Are you saying you don't find me attractive? Not desirable?' Self-doubt quavered in her tone.

Luca let out a gusty sigh. 'I find you extremely attractive and desirable but that's not why I married you. It's not part of the deal. It will make things too complicated when we end it.'

'How do you know that? People have flings all the time without falling in love with each other. Why not us?'

Luca put some distance between their bodies, but even a metre or so away he could still feel the magnetic pull of hers. 'You're young, Artie. Not just in chronological years but in experience. You said it yourself—you haven't been outside the *castello* for ten years. Those were ten valuable growing-up years.'

Her expression soured and hurt coloured her tone. 'You think I'm immature. A child in an adult's body? Is that what you're saying?'

Luca pressed his lips together, fighting to keep his self-control in check. Her adult body was temptation personified but he had to keep his hands off her. It wouldn't be fair to take things to another level, not now he knew how limited her experience. He was the first man to kiss her, to touch her, to expose her to male desire. She was like a teenager experiencing her first crush. A physical crush that had to stop before it got started. 'I'm saying I'm not the right man for you.'

'Consider my offer withdrawn.' She folded her arms around her body and sent him a sideways glance. 'Sorry if I offended you by being so brazen. Believe me, I surprised myself. I don't know what came over me.'

Luca fought back a wry smile. 'We should keep kissing to the absolute minimum.'

Artie gave an indifferent shrug but her eyes displayed her disappointment. 'Fine by me.'

The silence throbbed with a dangerous energy. An energy Luca could feel in every cell of his body. Humming, thrumming sensual energy, awakened, stirred, unsatisfied.

It would be so easy to take back everything he had said and gather her in his arms, to assuage the longing that burned in his body with hot, flicking tongues of flame, to teach her the wonder of sexual compatibility— for he was sure they would be compatible.

He had not felt such electrifying chemistry from kissing someone before. He had not felt such a rush of lust from holding someone close to his body. He had not felt so dangerously tempted to throw caution to the wind and sink his body into the soft silk of another's.

Artie released her arms from around her middle and absently toyed with her wedding ring. 'If you don't mind, I think I'll go to bed.' Her cheeks reddened and she hastily added, 'Alone, I mean. I wasn't suggesting you join—'

'Goodnight, *cara*.'

Artie bolted up the stairs as if she were being chased by a ghost. *Eek.* How could she have been so gauche as to practically beg Luca to make love to her? She couldn't understand why she had been so wanton in her behaviour. Was there something wrong with her? Had her lack of socialising with people her own age affected her development? Her body had woken from a long sleep the moment he kissed her at the wedding. His mouth had sent shivers of longing to every pore of her skin, made her aware of her female needs and desires, made her hungry for a deeper, more powerful connection. A physical connection that would ease the tight, dragging ache in her core.

She closed her bedroom door behind her, letting out a ragged breath. *Fool. Fool. Fool.* He had laid down the rules—a paper marriage with no emotional attachment. A business contract that was convenient and for both parties. But what was convenient about the way she felt about Luca? The heat and fire of his touch made her greedy for more. She had felt his physical response to her, so why was he denying them both the pleasure they both craved?

Because he doesn't want you to fall in love with him.

Artie walked over to her bed and sank onto the mattress with another sigh. Luca thought her too young and innocent for him, too inexperienced in the ways of the world for their relationship to be on an equal footing. But the way her body responded to him made her feel more than his equal. It made her feel alive and feminine and powerful in a way she had never imagined she could feel.

She looked down at the engagement and wedding rings on her left hand, the symbol of their union as a married couple. She was tied to him by law but not by love. And she was fine with that. Mostly. What she wanted was to be tied to him in desire, to explore the electrifying chemistry between them, to indulge herself in the world of heady sensuality.

Artie bounced off the bed and went to her bathroom, staring at her reflection in the mirror above the marble basin. Her eyes were overly bright, her lips still pink and swollen from Luca's passionate kiss. She touched her lower lip with her fingers, amazed at how sensitive it was, as if his kiss had released every one of her nerve endings from a deep freeze.

Artie touched a hand to the ache in the middle of her chest. So, this was what rejection felt like. The humiliation of wanting someone who didn't want you back.

Why am I so unlucky in the lottery of life?

Luca wasn't a drinker, but right then he wanted to down a bottle of Scotch and throw the empty bottle at the wall.

He wanted to stride upstairs to Artie's bedroom and take her in his arms and show her how much he wanted her. He wanted to breathe in the scent of her skin, taste the sweet nectar of her lips, glide his hands over her beautiful body and take them both to paradise. But the hard lessons learned from his father's and brother's death had made him super-cautious when it came to doing things that couldn't be undone.

Making love with Artie would change everything about their relationship. It would change the dynamic between them, pitching them into new territory, dangerous territory that clashed with his six-month time limit.

He had thought himself a good judge of character, someone who didn't miss important details. And yet he hadn't picked up on Artie's social phobia, but it all made perfect sense now. Why she hadn't been at the hospital when he'd visited her father. Why she'd insisted on the wedding being held at the *castello* instead of at one of the local churches. Why she had such a guarded air about her, closed off almost, as if she was uncomfortable around people she didn't know. He still couldn't get his head around the fact that she had spent ten years living almost in isolation. Ten years! It was unthinkable to someone like him, who was rarely in the same city two nights in a row. He lived out of hotels rather than at his villa in Tuscany. He lived in the fast lane because slowing down made him think too much, ruminate too much, hurt too much.

It was easier to block it out with work.

Work was his panacea for all ills. He had built his father's business into a behemoth of success. He had brokered deals all over the world and cashed in on every one of them. Big time. He had more money than he knew what to do with. It didn't buy him happiness but it did buy him freedom. Freedom from the ties that bound others into dead-end jobs, going-nowhere relationships and the drudgery of duty-bound responsibilities.

Luca walked over to the windows of his suite at the *castello*. The moon was full and cast the *castello* grounds in an ethereal light. The centuries-old trees, the gnarled vines, the rambling roses were testament to how many generations of Artie's family had lived and loved here.

Love. The trickiest of emotions. The one he avoided, because loving people and then letting them down was soul destroying. The stuff of nightmares, a living torture he could do without.

Luca watched as a barn owl flew past the window on silent wings. Nature going about its business under the cloak of moonlight. The *castello* could be restored into a showcase of antiquity. The gardens tended to and nurtured back into their former glory, the ancient vines grafted and replanted to produce award-winning wine. It would cost money...lots of money—money Artie clearly didn't have. But it would be his gift to her for the time she had given up to be married to him.

Six months, and day one was just about over. A day when he had discovered his bride was an introverted social phobic who had never been kissed until his mouth touched hers. A young woman who had not socialised with her peers outside the walls of the *castello*. A young woman who was still a virgin at the age of twenty-five. A modern-day Sleeping Beauty who had yet to be woken to the pleasures of sex.

Stop thinking about sex.

But how could he when the taste of her mouth was still on his lips? The feel of her body pressed against him was branded on his flesh. The ache of desire still hot and tight and heavy in his groin.

The *castello* was huge, and Artie's bedroom was a long, wide corridor away from his, but his awareness of her had never been more heightened and his self-control never more tested. What was it about her that made him so tempted to throw his rules to one side? Her unworldly youth? Her innocence? Her sensual allure? It was all those things and more besides. Things he couldn't quite name but he was aware of them all the same. He felt it in his body when he kissed her. A sense of rightness, as if every kiss he'd experienced before had been erased from his memory so that her mouth could be the new benchmark of what a kiss should be. He felt it when he touched her face and the creamy perfection of her skin made his fingers tingle in a way they had never done when touching anyone else. He felt it when he held her close to his body, the sense that her body was a perfect match for his.

Luca turned away from the window with a sigh of frustration. He needed his laptop so he could immerse himself in work but he'd left it in the car. He knew there wouldn't be too many bridegrooms tapping away on their laptops on their wedding night, but he was not a normal bridegroom.

And he needed to keep reminding his body of that too.

When Artie came downstairs the following morning, Rosa was laying out breakfast in the morning room, but not with her usual energy and vigour. Her face was pale and there were lines of tiredness around her eyes.

'Are you okay?' Artie asked, going to her.

Rosa put a hand to her forehead and winced. 'I have the most dreadful headache.'

'Then you must go straight back to bed. I'll call the doctor and—'

'No, I'll be fine. It's just a headache. I've had them before.'

Artie frowned at the housekeeper's pallor and blood-shot eyes. 'You don't look at all well. I insist you go up-stairs to bed. I'll manage things down here. It's about time you had some time to yourself. You've been going non-stop since Papa died. And well before that too.' Artie didn't like admitting how dependent she had be-come on the housekeeper but she wouldn't have been able to cope without Rosa running errands for her.

Rosa began to untie her apron, her expression etched with uncertainty. 'Are you sure?'

Artie took the apron from the housekeeper and tossed it to one side. 'Upstairs. Now. I'll check on you in a couple of hours. And if you're not feeling better by then, I'm calling the doctor.'

'*Sì, sì*, Signora Ferrantelli.' Rosa mock-saluted Artie and then she left the room.

Artie released a sigh and pulled out a chair to sit down at the breakfast table but her appetite had com-pletely deserted her. What *would* she do without Rosa? The housekeeper was her link to the outside world. Her only true friend. If anything happened to Rosa she would be even more isolated.

Stranded.

But you have a husband now...

The sound of firm footsteps approaching sent a tingle down Artie's spine. She swivelled in her chair to see Luca enter the breakfast room. His hair was still damp from a shower, his face cleanly shaven, the sharp tang of his citrus-based aftershave teasing her nostrils. He was wearing blue jeans and a white T-shirt that lovingly hugged his muscular chest and ridged abdomen.

'Good morning.' Her tone was betrayingly breathless and her cheeks grew warm. 'Did you sleep well?'

'Morning.' He pulled out the chair opposite, sat down and spread his napkin over his lap. 'I ran into Rosa when I was coming down. She didn't look well.'

Artie picked up the jug of fresh orange juice and poured some into her glass. 'I've sent her back to bed. She's got a bad headache. She gets them occasionally.' She offered him the juice but he shook his head and reached for the coffee pot. The rich aroma of freshly brewed coffee filled the air.

Luca picked up his cup, glancing at her over the rim. 'Has she got plans to retire? This is a big place to take care of. Does anyone come in to help her?'

Artie chewed at the side of her mouth. 'They used to but we had to cut back the staff a while back. I help her. I enjoy it, actually. It's a way of thanking her for helping me all these years.'

'And how does she help you?' His gaze was unwavering, almost interrogating in its intensity.

Artie lowered her gaze and stared at the beads of condensation on her glass of orange juice. 'Rosa runs errands for me. She picks up shopping for me, the stuff

I can't get online, I mean. She's been with my family for a long time. This is her home. Here, with me.'

Luca put down his cup with a clatter on the saucer. 'She can't stay here for ever, Artie. And neither can you.' His tone was gentle but firm, speaking a truth she recognised but didn't want to face.

She pushed back her chair and tossed her napkin on the table. 'Will you excuse me? I want to check on Rosa.'

'Sit down, *cara.*' There was a thread of steel underlining each word. The same steel glinting in his eyes and in the uncompromising line of his jaw.

Artie toyed with the idea of defying him, a secret thrill shooting through her at the thought of what he might do to stop her flouncing out of the room. Grasp her by the wrists? Hold her to his tempting body? Bring that firm mouth down on hers in another toe-curlingly passionate kiss? She held his gaze for a heart-stopping moment, her pulse picking up its pace, the backs of her knees fizzing. But then she sat heavily in the chair, whipped her napkin across her lap and threw him a look so sour it could have curdled the milk in the jug. 'I hope you're not going to make a habit of ordering me about like I'm some sort of submissive slave.'

His eyes continued to hold hers in a battle of wills. 'I want to talk to you about your relationship with Rosa. I get that she's been supportive for a long time and you see her as a friend you can rely on, but what if she's actually holding you back from developing more autonomy?'

Artie curled her lip. 'I didn't know you had a psychology degree amongst your other impressive achievements.'

'I don't need a psychology degree to see what's happening here.' He picked up a teaspoon and stirred his coffee even though he didn't take sugar or milk. He put the teaspoon down again and continued. 'I know it's hard for you but—'

'How do you know anything of what it's like for me?' She banged her hand on the table, rattling the cups and saucers. 'You're not me. You don't live in my mind, in my body. I'm the only one who knows what this is like for me.' Her chest was tightening, her breathing becoming laboured, her skin breaking out in a sweat. She could feel the pressure building. The fear climbing up her spine. The dread roiling in her stomach. The hammering of her heart. The panic spreading, growing, expanding, threatening to explode inside her head.

Luca rose from his seat and came around to her side of the table and crouched down beside her chair. He took one of her hands in his, enclosing it within the warm shelter of his. 'Breathe, *cara*. Take a slow, deep breath and let it out on the count of three. One. Two. Three. And again. That's it. Nice and slow.'

Artie concentrated on her breathing, holding tightly to the solid anchor of his hand, drawing comfort from his deep and calming tone. The panic gradually subsided, retreating like a wild beast that had been temporarily subdued by a much bigger, stronger opponent. After a long moment, she let out a rattling sigh. 'I'm okay now… I think…' She tried to remove her hand but he kept a firm but gentle hold on her, stroking the back of her hand with his thumb in slow, soothing strokes that made every overwrought cell in her body quieten.

'Take your time, *mia piccola*.'

Artie chanced a glance at his concerned gaze. 'I suppose you think I'm crazy. A mad person who can't walk out of her own front gate.'

Luca placed his other hand beneath her chin and locked her gaze on his. His eyes were darkened by his wide pupils, the green and brown flecks in his irises reminding her of a nature-themed mosaic. 'I don't think any such thing.' He gave a rueful twist of his mouth and continued. 'When my father and brother drowned, I didn't leave the house for a month after their funeral.' A shadow passed across his face like scudding grey clouds. 'I couldn't face the real world without them in it. It was a terrible time.' His tone was weighted with gravitas, his expression drawn in lines of deep sadness.

Artie squeezed his hand. 'It must have been so tragic for you and your mother. How did you survive such awful loss?'

One side of his mouth came up in a smile that wasn't quite a smile. 'There are different types of survival, *sì*? I chose to concentrate on forging my way through the morass of grief by studying hard, acing my exams and taking over my father's company. I taught myself not to think about my father and brother. Nothing could bring them back, but I figured I could make my father proud by taking up the reins of his business even though it was never my aspiration to do so. That was my brother's dream.' His half-smile faded and the shadow was back in his gaze.

Artie ached for what he had been through, knowing first-hand how such tragic loss impacted on a person. The way it hit you at odd moments like a sudden stab, doubling you over with unbearable pain. The ongoing reminders—birthdays, anniversaries, Christmas, Mother's Day. So many days of the year when it was impossible to forget. And then there was the guilt that never went away. It hovered over her every single day of her life. 'How did your mother cope with her grief?'

Luca released her hand and straightened to his full height. Artie could sense him withdrawing into himself as if the mention of his mother pained him more than he wanted to admit. 'Enough miserable talk for now. Finish your breakfast, *cara*. And after that, we will call my grandfather and I'll introduce you to him.'

Her stomach fluttered with nerves. 'What if he doesn't accept me? What if he doesn't like me or think I'm suitable?'

Luca stroked his hand over the top of her head, his expression inscrutable. 'Don't worry. He will adore you the minute he meets you.'

CHAPTER SEVEN

LUCA CALLED HIS GRANDFATHER on his phone a short time later and selected the video-call option. He sat with Artie on the sofa in the salon and draped an arm around her waist to keep her in the range of the camera. The fragrance of her perfume wafted around his nostrils, her curly hair tickling his jaw when she leaned closer. His grandfather's image came up on the screen and Luca felt Artie tense beside him. He gave her a gentle squeeze and smiled at her before turning back to face his grandfather.

'Nonno, allow me to introduce you to my beautiful wife Artemisia—Artie for short. We were married yesterday.'

The old man frowned. 'Your wife? *Pah!* You think I'm a doddering old fool or something? You said you were never getting married and now you present me with a wife? Why didn't you bring her here to meet me in person?'

'We're on our honeymoon, Nonno,' Luca said, wishing, not for the first time, it was true. 'But soon, *sì*?'

'*Buongiorno*, Signor Ferrantelli,' Artie said. 'I'm sorry you've been ill. It must be so frustrating for you.'

'I'll tell you what's frustrating—having my only

grandson gadding about all these years as a free-dom-loving playboy, when all I want is to see a great-grandchild before I leave this world. It's his duty, his responsibility to carry on the proud family name by producing a new generation.'

Luca gave a light laugh. 'We've only just got married, Nonno. Give us time.' He suddenly realised he didn't want to share Artie with anyone. He wanted to spend time alone with her, getting to know her better. He wanted her with an ache that wouldn't go away. Ever since he'd kissed her it had smouldered like hot coals inside him. The need to explore her body, to awaken her to the explosive pleasure he knew they would experience together. But he refused to even think about the cosy domestic future his grandfather hoped for him. Babies? A new generation of Ferrantellis? Not going to happen.

'You've wasted so much time already,' Nonno said, scowling. 'Your father was married to your mother and had Angelo and you well before your age.'

'*Sì*, I know.' Luca tried to ignore the dart of pain in his chest at the mention of his father and brother. And his mother, of course. He could barely think of his mother without feeling a tsunami of guilt for how his actions had destroyed her life. Grandchildren might soften the blow for his mother, but how could he allow himself to think about providing them? Family life was something he had never envisaged for himself. How could he when he had effectively destroyed his own family of origin?

'Luca is everything I ever dreamed of in a husband,' Artie piped up in a proud little voice that made something in his chest ping. 'He's definitely worth waiting for.'

Nonno gave a grunt, his frown still in place. 'Did you give her your grandmother's engagement ring?' he asked Luca.

'*Sì,*' Luca said.

Artie lifted her hand to the camera. 'I love it. It's the most gorgeous ring I've ever seen. I feel incredibly honoured to be wearing it. I wish I could have met your wife. You must miss her terribly.'

'Every day.' Nonno shifted his mouth from side to side, his frown softening its grip on his weathered features. 'Don't leave it too long before you come and see me in person, Artie. I haven't got all the time in the world.'

'You'd have more time if you follow your doctor's advice,' Luca said.

'I'd love to meet you,' Artie said. 'Luca's told me so much about you.'

'Yes, well, he's told me virtually nothing about you,' Nonno said, disapproval ripe in his tone. 'How did you meet?'

'I met Artie through her father,' Luca said. 'I knew she was the one for me as soon as I laid eyes on her.' It wasn't a lie. He had known straight up that Artie was the only young woman his grandfather would approve of as his bride.

Nonno gave another grunt. 'Let's hope you can handle him, Artie. He's a Ferrantelli. We are not easy to live with but if you love him it will certainly help.'

'I think he's the most amazing man I've ever met,' Artie said, softly. 'Take care of yourself, Signor Ferrantelli. I hope to meet you in person soon.'

The most amazing man she'd ever met? Luca mentally laughed off the compliment. Artie had met so few men it wasn't hard to impress her. What he wanted to do was help her get over her phobia. Not just because he wanted her to meet his grandfather but because he knew it would open up opportunities and experiences for her that had been denied her for way too long. But would she trust him enough to guide her through what would no doubt be a difficult and frightening journey for her?

Artie turned to face Luca once the call had ended. His arm was still around her waist and every nerve beneath her skin was acutely aware of its solid warm presence. 'I'm not so sure we convinced him. Are you?'

Luca's expression was etched in frowning lines. 'Who knows?' His features relaxed slightly and he added, 'You did well. That was a nice touch about me being your dream husband. It's kind of scary how convincing you sounded.' He brushed a stray strand of hair away from her face, his gaze darkening.

Artie disguised a swallow, her heart giving a little kick when his eyes drifted to her mouth. 'Yes, well, I surprised myself, actually.' She frowned and glanced down at the engagement and wedding rings on her hand and then lifted her gaze back to his. 'I feel like I'm letting you down by not being able to leave the *castello*. If we'd gone in person to see him, or even better, married somewhere closer so your grandfather could have attended…'

'You're not letting me down at all,' Luca said. 'But what if I tried to help you? We could start small and see how it goes—baby steps.'

'I've had help before and it hasn't worked.'

'But you haven't had my help.' He smiled and took her hand, running his thumb over the back of it in gentle strokes. 'It's worth a try, surely?'

Panic crawled up her spine and sent icicles tiptoeing across her scalp. 'What, now?'

'No time like the present.'

Artie compressed her lips, trying to control her breathing. 'I don't know…'

He raised her chin with the end of his finger. 'Trust me, *cara*. I won't push you further than you can manage. We will take it one step at a time.'

Artie swallowed and then let out a long, ragged breath. 'Okay. I'll try but don't be mad at me if I don't get very far.'

He leaned down and pressed a light kiss to the middle of her forehead. 'I won't get mad at you, *mia piccola*. I'm a very patient man.'

A few minutes later, Artie stood with Luca on the front steps of the *castello*, her gaze focussed on the long walk to the brass gates in the distance. Her heart was beating so fast she could feel its echo in her ears. Her skin was already damp with perspiration, and her legs trembling like a newborn foal's. She desperately wanted to conquer her fear, now more than ever. She wanted to meet Luca's grandfather, to uphold her side of their marriage deal but what if she failed yet again? She had failed every single time she had tried to leave the *castello*. It was like a thick glass wall was blocking her exit. She could see the other side to freedom but couldn't bring herself to step over the boundary lines. The *castello* was safe. She was safe here. Other people on the outside were safe from *her*.

What would happen if she went past her self-imposed boundary?

Luca took her hand and smiled down at her. 'Ready? One step at a time. Take all the time you need.'

Artie sucked in a deep breath and went down the steps to the footpath. So far, so good. 'I've done this before, heaps of times, and I always fail.'

'Don't talk yourself into failure, *cara*.' His tone was gently reproving. 'Believe you can do something and you'll do it.'

'Easy for you to say.' Artie flicked him a glance. 'You're confident and run a successful business. You've got runs on the board. What do I have? A big fat nothing.'

Luca stopped and turned her so she was facing him, his hands holding her by the upper arms. 'You have cared for your father for a decade. You quite likely extended his life by doing so. Plus, you're a gifted embroiderer. I have never seen such detailed and beautiful work. You have to start believing in yourself, *cara*. I believe in you.'

Artie glanced past his broad shoulder to the front gates, fear curdling her insides. She let out another stuttering breath and met his gaze once more. 'Okay, let's keep going. I have to do this. I *can* do this.'

'That's my girl,' Luca said, smiling and taking her by the hand again. 'I'm with you every step of the way.'

Artie took two steps, then three, four, five until she lost count. The gates loomed closer and closer, the outside world and freedom beckoning. But just as she got to about two-thirds of the way down the path a bird suddenly flew up out of the nearby shrubbery and Artie was so startled she lost her footing and would have tripped if Luca hadn't been holding her hand. 'Oh!' she gasped.

'You're okay, it was just a bird.'

Artie glanced at the front gates, her heart still banging against her breastbone. 'I think I'm done for one day.'

He frowned. 'You don't want to try a little more? We're almost there. Just a few more steps.'

She turned back to face the safety of the *castello*, breathing hard. 'I'm sorry but I can't do any more. I'll try again tomorrow.'

And I'll fail just like every other time.

Luca stroked his hand over the back of her head. 'You did well, *mia piccola*.'

Artie gave him a rueful look. 'I failed.'

He stroked her cheek with a lazy finger, his gaze unwavering. 'Failure is when you give up trying.' He took her hand again with another smile. 'Come on. It's thirsty work wrestling demons, *si*?'

Once they were back inside the *castello* in the salon, Artie let out a sigh. 'It's not that I don't want to go outside…'

He handed her a glass of mineral water. 'What are you most frightened of?'

She took the glass from him and set it on the table next to her, carefully avoiding his gaze. 'I'm frightened of hurting people.'

'Why do you think you'll hurt someone?'

Artie lifted her eyes to his. 'It was my fault we had the accident.'

Luca frowned and came over to sit beside her, taking her hands in his. 'But you weren't driving, surely? You were only fifteen, *si*?'

She looked down at their joined hands, her chest feeling so leaden it was almost impossible to take in another breath. 'I wanted to go to a party. My parents didn't want me to go but like teenagers do, I wouldn't take no for an answer. They relented and I went to the party, which wasn't as much fun as I'd hoped. And when my parents picked me up that night...well, my father was tired because it was late and he didn't see the car drifting into his lane in time to take evasive action. I woke up in hospital after being in a coma for a month to find my mother had died instantly and my father was in a wheelchair.'

Luca put his arms around Artie and held her close. 'I'm sorry. I know there are no words to take away the guilt and sadness but you were just a kid.'

Artie eased back to look up at him through blurry vision. 'I haven't ever met anyone else who truly understood.' She twisted her mouth wryly, 'Not that I've met a lot of people in the last ten years.' She lifted her hand to his face and stroked his lean jaw and added. 'But I think you do understand.'

A shadow passed through his gaze and he pulled her hand down from his face. 'You don't know me, *cara*. You don't know what I'm capable of.' His voice contained a note of self-loathing that made the back of her neck prickle.

'Why do you say that?'

He sprang off the sofa in an agitated fashion. 'I haven't told you everything about the day my father and brother died.'

She swallowed tightly. 'Do you want to tell me now?' Her voice came out whisper-soft.

Luca pulled at one side of his mouth with his straight white teeth, his hands planted on his slim hips. Then he released a ragged breath. 'It was my fault they drowned. We were on holiday in Argentina. We had gone to an isolated beach because I'd heard the waves were best there. I wanted to go back in for another surf even though the conditions had changed. I didn't listen to my father. I just raced back in and soon got into trouble.' He winced as if recalling that day caused him immeasurable pain. 'My father came in after me and then my brother. The rip took them both out to sea. I somehow survived. I can never forgive myself for my role in their deaths. I was selfish and reckless, and in trying to save me, they both lost their lives.'

Artie went to him and grasped him by both hands. 'Oh, Luca, you were only a child. Kids do stuff like that all the time, especially teenage boys. You mustn't blame yourself. But I understand how you do…you see, I blame myself for my mother's death and my dad's disability.'

'I do understand.' His eyes were full of pain. 'There were times when I wished I had been the one to die. I'm sure you wished the same. But that doesn't help anyone, does it?'

'No…' She leaned her head against the solid wall of his chest, slipping her arms back around his waist. 'Thank you.'

'For?' The deep, low rumble of his voice reverberated next to her ear.

Artie looked back up at him. 'For listening. For understanding. For not judging.' She took a little hitching breath and added, 'For wanting me when I thought no one ever could.'

Luca brushed his thumb over the fullness of her lower lip, setting off a firestorm in her flesh. 'I want you. I've tried ignoring it, denying it, resisting it, but it won't go away.' His voice dropped to a lower pitch, tortured almost, as if he was fighting a battle within himself between what he should do and what he shouldn't.

Artie licked her lips and encountered the saltiness of his thumb. 'I want you too.' She touched his firm jaw with her hand. 'I don't see why we have to stick to the rules. We are attracted to each other physically. Why not enjoy the opportunity? How else am I going to gain experience? I'm hardly going to meet anyone whilst living here, and we're married anyway, so why not?' She could hardly believe how brave she was being, speaking her needs out loud. But something about Luca made her feel brave and courageous. His desire for her spoke to her on a cellular level, making her aware of her body and its needs in a way she hadn't thought possible.

Luca cupped one side of her face in his hand, his thumb stroking over her cheek in slow, measured strokes. A frown settled between his brows, his eyes darker than she had ever seen them. 'Is that really want you want? A physical relationship, knowing it will end after six months?'

Maybe it won't end.

Artie didn't say it out loud—she was shocked enough at hearing it inside her head.

Since the accident, she had denied herself any dreams of one day finding love, of marrying and having a family. She had destroyed her family, so why should she have one of her own? But now she had met Luca, she realised what she was missing out on. The thrill of being attracted to someone and knowing they desired you back. The perfectly normal needs within her body she had ignored for so long were fully awake and wanting, begging to be assuaged. 'I want to know what it is like to make love with a man,' Artie said. 'I want that man to be you. I trust you to take care of me. To treat me with respect.'

He stroked her hair back from her forehead, his eyes dark and lustrous. 'I can't think of a time when I wanted someone more. But I told myself I wasn't going to take advantage of the situation—of you. I don't think it would be fair to give you false hope that this could lead to anything…more permanent.'

She leaned closer, winding her arms around his neck. 'Stop overthinking it. Do what your heart is telling you, not your head. Make love to me, Luca.'

Luca placed his hands on her hips and bent his head down so their lips were within touching distance. 'Are you sure? There's still time to change your mind.'

Artie pressed her lips against his, once, twice, three times. 'I'm not changing my mind. I want this. I want you.'

He stood and drew her to her feet, dropping a warm, firm kiss to her lips. 'Not here. Upstairs. I want everything to be perfect for you.'

A short time later, they were in Luca's bedroom. He closed the door softly behind them and ran his gaze over Artie. She had expected to feel shy, self-conscious about her body, but as soon as he began to undo the buttons on her top, she shivered with longing, desperate to be naked with him, to feel his skin against her own.

He kissed her lingeringly, taking his time nudging and nibbling her lips, teasing her with his tongue, tantalising her senses with his taste and his touch. His mouth moved down to just below her ear and she shivered as his lips touched her sensitive skin. One of his hands slipped beneath her unbuttoned top, gliding along the skin of her ribcage to cup one of her breasts. His touch was gentle and yet it created a tumultuous storm in her flesh. Her nipple tightened, her breast tingled, her legs weakened as desire shot through her like a missile strike.

'I want to touch you all over.' His tone had a sexy rough edge that made her senses whirl.

'I want to touch you too.' Artie tugged his T-shirt out of his jeans and slid her hands under the fabric to stroke his muscular chest. His warm, hard flesh felt foreign, exotically foreign, unlike anything she had touched before. She explored the hard planes and ridged contours of his hair-roughened chest, marvelling at the difference between their bodies. A difference that excited her, made her crazy with longing, eager to discover more.

Luca unclipped her bra and gazed at her breasts for a long moment, his eyes dark and shining with unmistakable desire. 'So beautiful.' His thumbs rolled over each of her nipples, his gaze intent, as if he found her breasts the most fascinating things he'd ever seen. Before this moment Artie had more or less ignored her breasts other than to do her monthly breast check. But now she was aware of the thousands of nerve-endings that were responding to Luca's touch. Aware of the way her tender flesh tingled and tautened under his touch. Aware of the primal need it triggered in her feminine core—of the ache that longed to feel the hard male presence of his body.

Artie gasped as Luca brought his mouth to her breasts, her hands gripping him by the waist, not trusting her legs to keep her upright as the sensations washed through her. His tongue teased her nipple into a tight point, and then he circled it with a slow sweep of his tongue.

The slight roughness of his tongue against her softer skin evoked another breathless and shuddering gasp from her. 'Oh… *Oh*...'

Luca lifted his mouth off her breast and smiled a bone-melting smile. 'You like that?'

Artie leaned closer, the feel of her naked breasts pressing against his muscular chest sending another riot of tingling sensations through her body. 'I love it when you touch me. I can't get enough of it.'

He slid his hands down to the waistband of her jeans, his fingers warm against her belly as he undid the snap button. Who knew such an action could cause such a torrent of heat in her body? Artie could barely stop her legs from shaking in anticipation. He held her gaze in a sensual lock that made her heart skip and trip. He slid his hand beneath the loosened waistband, cupping her mound through the thin, lacy barrier of her knickers. Her body responded with humid heat, slickening, moistening with the dew of desire.

'I can't seem to get enough of you either,' he said. 'But I don't want to rush you. I want to go slowly to make it good for you.'

Artie placed her hands on the waistband of his jeans. 'Can I?'

His eyes gleamed. 'Go for it.'

She held her breath and undid the fastening and slid down the zipper. She peeled back his underwear and drank in the potent sight of him engorged with blood, thickened with longing. Longing for *her*.

Luca drew in a sharp breath as her fingers skated over his erection. He removed her hand and returned his mouth to hers in a spine-tingling kiss that spoke of the primal need pulsing through his body. The flicker of his tongue against hers, the increasing urgency and pressure of his mouth drew from her a fevered response she hadn't thought possible.

Within a few breathless moments they were both naked and lying on the bed together, Luca's eyes roving over her body in glinting hunger. He placed a hand on her hip, turning her towards him, his expression becoming sober. 'There's something we need to discuss. Protection. We can't let any accidents happen, especially given the terms of our relationship.'

Artie knew he was being reasonable and responsible but a secret part of her flinched at his adamant stance on the six-month time frame. An accidental pregnancy would change everything. It would tie them together for the next eighteen years…possibly for ever. 'I understand. I wouldn't want any…accidents either.' She had not allowed herself to think of one day having a baby but now a vision popped into her head of a gorgeous, dark-haired baby… Luca's baby.

Don't get any ideas. You know the terms. Six months and six months only.

Her conscience had an annoying habit of reminding her of the deal she had made with Luca. A deal she hoped she wouldn't end up regretting in the end.

Luca stroked his hand down the flank of her thigh, his gaze centred on hers. 'It's important to me that you enjoy our lovemaking. I want you to feel comfortable, so please tell me if something isn't working for you or you want to stop at any point.'

Artie traced the shape of his lower lip with her finger. 'I've liked everything so far. I thought I'd be nervous about being naked with someone but this feels completely natural, as if we've done this before in another lifetime. Does that make sense?'

He smiled and captured her hand and pressed a kiss to each of her fingertips, his eyes holding hers. 'In a strange way, yes, although I have to say I've never made love to a virgin before.'

'Are *you* nervous?'

His mouth twisted into a rueful grimace. 'A bit.'

'Don't be.' She pressed her lips to his in a soft kiss. 'I want you to make love to me. I feel like I've been waiting all my life for this moment.'

Luca brought his mouth back to hers in a kiss that drugged her senses and ramped up her desire for him until she was arching her back and whimpering. His hands explored her breasts in soft strokes, his lips and tongue caressing her until she was breathless with longing. The ache between her legs intensified, a hot, throbbing ache that travelled through her pelvis like the spread of fire.

He moved down her body with a series of kisses from her breasts to her belly and then to the heart of her femininity. Artie drew in a breath, tense with excitement as his fingers spread her, his lips and tongue exploring her, teasing a response from her that shook her body into a cataclysmic orgasm. It swept her up in its rolling waves, the pulsations carrying her into a place beyond the reach of thought or even full consciousness. Blissful sensations washed over her, peace flooding her being—the quiet after the storm.

'I had no idea it could be like…like *that*…' Artie could barely get her voice to work and a sudden shyness swept over her.

Luca moved back up her body to plant a kiss to her lips. She could taste herself on his lips and it added a whole new layer of disturbing but delightful intimacy. 'It will only get better.' He brushed his knuckles over her warm cheeks. 'Don't be shy, *cara*.'

Artie bit her lip. 'Easy for you to say. You've probably done this a hundred times, possibly more. I'm a complete novice.'

He smoothed her hair back from her face, his expression suddenly serious. 'The press makes a big thing out of my lifestyle but I haven't been as profligate as they make out. Unfortunately, my grandfather believes what he reads in the press.' His mouth twisted ruefully. 'I've had relationships—fleeting ones that were entirely transactional. And I've always tried not to deliberately hurt anyone. But of course, it still does happen occasionally.'

I hope I don't get hurt.

The potential to get hurt once their relationship came to its inevitable end was a real and present worry, but even so, Artie couldn't bring herself to stop things before they got any more complicated. He had revealed things about himself that made her hungry to learn more about him. His workaholism, his carefully guarded heart, his history of short-term, going-nowhere relationships. He was imprisoned by his lifestyle in the same way she was imprisoned by the *castello*. Would he go back to his playboy existence once they parted?

Artie lifted her hand and stroked his stubbly jaw. 'I want you to make love to me. I want you to experience pleasure too.'

Luca's eyes were dark and hooded as he gazed at her mouth. 'Everything about you brings me pleasure, *cara*. Absolutely everything.' And his mouth came down and sealed hers.

The kiss was long and intense and Artie could feel the tension rising in his body as well as her own. His legs were entangled with hers, his aroused body pressing urgently against her, his breathing as ragged as hers. His mouth moved down to her breasts, subjecting them to a passionate exploration that left her squirming and whimpering with need. She slid her hand down from his chest to his taut abdomen, desperate to explore the hard contours of his body. He drew in a quick breath when her hand encountered his erection and it made her all the bolder in her caresses. He was velvet-wrapped steel, so exotically, erotically different from her, and she couldn't wait to experience those differences inside her body.

Luca eased back and reached for a condom, swiftly applying it before coming back to her, his gaze meshing with hers. 'I'll go slowly but please tell me if you want to stop at any point. I don't want to hurt you.'

Artie brushed his hair back from his forehead, her

lower body so aware of his thick male presence at her entrance. 'You won't hurt me.' Her tone was breathless with anticipation, her body aching for his possession.

He gently nudged apart her feminine folds, allowing her time to get used to him as he progressed. Slow, shallow, sensual. Her body welcomed him, wrapping around him without pain, without resistance.

'Are you okay?' he asked, pausing in his movements.

'More than okay.' Artie sighed with pure pleasure, her hands going to his taut buttocks to hold him to her.

He thrust a little deeper, still keeping his movements slow and measured. She arched her hips to take more of him in, her body tingling with darts and arrows of pleasure as his body moved within hers. His breathing rate changed, becoming more laboured as his pace increased. She was swept up into his rhythm, her senses reeling as the tension built to an exquisite crescendo. She was almost at the pinnacle, hovering in the infinitesimal moment before total fulfilment. Wanting, aching, needing to fly but not sure how to do it.

Luca reached down between their bodies and coaxed her swollen feminine flesh into an earth-shattering orgasm. Spirals of intense pleasure burst through her body, ripples and waves and darts of bliss, throwing her senses into a tailspin and her mind into disarray.

Luca reached his release soon after, an agonised groan escaping his lips as his body convulsed and spilled. Artie held him close, breathing in the scent of their lovemaking, thrilled to have brought him to a place of blissful satiation.

Artie lay with him in the peaceful aftermath, her thoughts drifting... The boundaries between the physical and the emotional were becoming increasingly blurred. She knew she would always remember this moment as a pivotal one in her life as a woman.

Luca Ferrantelli. Her husband. Her first lover.

The presence of his body, the desire that drew them together bonded her to him in a way that was beyond the physical. The chemistry between her and Luca was so powerful, so magical it had produced a cataclysmic reaction. An explosion of pleasure she could still feel reverberating throughout her body.

How could she have thought he was arrogant and unyielding? He had taken such respectful care of her every step of the way. He had held back his own release in order to make sure she was satisfied first. She couldn't have asked for a more considerate and generous lover.

But it didn't mean she was falling in love with him.

Artie knew the rules and had accepted them. She could be modern and hip about their arrangement. Sure she could. This was about a physical connection so intense, so rapturous she wanted to make the most of it.

Luca leaned up on one elbow and slowly withdrew from her body, carefully disposing of the condom. He rolled back to cradle one side of her face with his hand, his eyes searching hers. 'How do you feel?' His voice had a husky edge, his expression tender in a way she hadn't been expecting. Had he too been affected by her first time and their first time together?

'I'm fine.'

A frown pulled at his brow. 'I didn't hurt you?'

'Not at all.' She smoothed away his frown with her fingertip. 'Thanks for being so gentle with me.'

His hand brushed back the hair from her face in the

tenderest of movements. 'Your enjoyment is top priority for me. I don't want you to feel you ever have to service my needs above your own.'

Artie ran her fingertip over the fullness of his bottom lip, not quite able to meet his gaze. 'Was it good for you too?'

He tipped up her chin and smiled, and her chest felt like it was cracking open. 'Off the charts.' He leaned down to press a soft, lingering kiss to her lips. He lifted off again, his expression becoming thoughtful. 'I've never been a virgin trophy hunter. A woman's virginity is not something I consider a prize to be claimed or a conquest to be sought.' He captured a loose strand of her hair and tucked it back behind her ear. 'But I have to say I feel privileged to have made love with you.'

Artie wrapped her arms around his waist and leaned her cheek against the wall of his chest. 'I feel privileged too. You made it so special.'

There was a moment or two of silence.

Luca stroked his hand down between Artie's shoulder blades to the base of her spine. 'I should let you get up and get dressed.'

Artie lifted her head off his chest to smile at him. 'Is that what you really want me to do right now?'

He grinned and pressed her back down on the bed with his weight playfully pinning her. 'Not right now.' And he brought his mouth back down to hers.

CHAPTER EIGHT

LATER THAT MORNING, Luca had to convince himself to get out of bed with Artie. He couldn't remember a time when he had spent a morning more pleasurably. Making love with her for the first time had affected him in a way he hadn't been expecting. The mutual passion they had shared had been beyond anything he had experienced before. And that was deeply troubling.

Why was it so special? Because she was innocent and he so worldly and jaded that making love with her was something completely different from the shallow hook-ups he preferred? Or was it the exquisite feel of her skin next to his? Her mouth beneath his? Her touch, her sighs, her gasps and cries that made him feel more of a man than he ever had before?

The trust she had shown in him had touched him deeply. And he had honoured that trust by making sure she was completely satisfied, and yet his own satisfaction had risen to a whole new level of experience. It was as if his body had been asleep before now. Operating on a lower setting that didn't fully register all the nuances of mind-blowing sex. The glide of soft hands on his body, the velvet-soft press of lips on his heated skin, the delicious friction of female flesh against him. Every moment was imprinted on his brain, every kiss, every touch branded on his body.

And he wanted it to continue, which was the most troubling thought of all. He, who never stayed with a lover longer than a week or two. He, who never envisaged a future with anyone. He, who had locked down his emotions so long ago he didn't think he had the capacity to feel anything for anyone any more.

And yet...

Every time Artie looked at him with those big brown eyes, something tugged in his chest. Every time her pillow-soft lips met his, fire spread through his body, a raging fire of lust and longing unlike any he had felt before. Every time she smiled it was like encountering sunshine after a lifetime of darkness.

Luca swung his legs over the side of the bed before he was tempted to make love to her for the third time. He turned and held out a hand to her. 'Come on. Time for some more exposure therapy.'

Artie unfolded her limbs and stood in front of him, her hands going to his hips, sending his blood racing. Her eyes were bright and sparkling, her lips swollen from his kisses. 'Let's stay here instead. It'll be more fun.'

Luca gave her a stern look. Exposure therapy was well known to be the pits the first few times but it still had to be endured for results. '*Cara*, you're procrastinating. It's classic avoidance behaviour and it will only make things worse.'

Her gaze lost its playful spark and her mouth tightened. Her hands fell away from his hips and she turned

and snatched up a loose bed sheet and covered her na-
kedness, as if she was suddenly ashamed of her body.
'Last time I looked, you were my temporary husband
and lover, not my therapist. I don't appreciate you trying to fix me.'

Luca suppressed a frustrated sigh. 'I'm not trying
to fix you, *cara*. I'm trying to help you gain the courage to go a little further each day. I'll be with you all
the time and I won't push you into doing anything you
don't want to do. You can trust me, okay?'

Her teeth chewed at her lower lip, her gaze still
guarded. 'Look, I know you mean well, but we tried it
before and I failed.'

'That doesn't mean you'll fail today.'

There was a long moment of silence.

Artie released a long, shuddering breath. 'Okay... I'll
give it another try.' She swallowed and glanced at him,
her cheeks tinged with pink. 'Do you mind if I have a
quick shower first?'

Luca waved his hand towards the bathroom. 'Go
right ahead. I'll meet you downstairs in half an hour.'
He needed to put some space between them before he
was tempted to join her in the shower.

She walked to the door of the bathroom, then stopped
and turned to look back at him with a frown between
her eyes. 'Did you only make love to me to make me
more amenable to going outside the *castello* grounds
with you?'

'I made love with you because I wanted you and you
wanted me.'

And I still want you. Badly.

Her teeth did another nibble of her lip, uncertainty

etched on her features. 'I hope I don't disappoint you this time…'

Luca came over to her and tipped up her chin and planted a soft kiss to her lips. 'You could never disappoint me.'

Artie showered and changed with her mind reeling at what Luca wanted her to do. She had failed so many times. Why should this time be any different? Panic flapped its wings in her brain and her belly, fear chilled her skin and sent a tremble through her legs. But she took comfort in the fact he promised to stay with her, to support her as she confronted her fear—a fear she had lived with so long it was a part of her identity. She literally didn't know who she was now without it. But making love with Luca had given her the confidence to step outside her comfort zone. Her skin still sang with the magic of his touch, the slightly tender muscles in her core reminding her of the power and potency of his body.

Luca was waiting for her downstairs and took her hand at the front door. 'Ready? Our goal is to go farther than we went yesterday—even if we don't make it outside the gates it will still be an improvement. That's the way to approach difficult tasks—break them up into smaller, achievable segments.'

Artie drew in a shaky breath, her chest feeling as if a flock of frightened finches were trapped inside. 'Sounds like a sensible plan. Okay, let's give it a go.'

The sun was shining and white fluffy clouds were scudding across the sky. A light breeze scented with old-world roses danced past Artie's face. Luca's fingers wrapped around hers, strong, warm, supportive, and she glanced up at him and gave a wobbly smile. 'Thanks for being so patient.'

He looped her arm through his, holding her close as they walked slowly but surely down the cobbled footpath to the wrought-iron front gates. 'I probably made you go too fast the first time. Let's slow it down a bit. We've got plenty of time to stop and smell the roses.'

Artie walked beside him and tried to concentrate on the spicy fragrance of the roses rather than the fear crawling over her skin. She was conscious of Luca's muscular arm linked with hers and the way he matched his stride to hers. She flicked him another self-conscious glance. 'You must think this is completely ridiculous. That *I'm* completely ridiculous.'

He gave her a light squeeze. 'I don't think that at all. Fear is a very powerful emotion. It can be paralysing. Fear of failure, fear of success, fear of—'

'Commitment,' Artie offered.

There was a slight pause before he answered. 'That too.'

'Fear of love.' She was on a roll, hardly noticing how many cobblestones there were to go to the front gate.

There was another silence, longer this time, punctured only by the sound of the whispering breeze and twittering birds in the overgrown shrubbery.

'Fear of not being capable of loving.' His tone contained a rueful note.

Artie stopped walking to look up at his mask-like expression. 'Why do you think you're not capable of loving someone? You love your grandfather, don't you?'

Luca gave a twisted smile that didn't quite reach

his eyes. 'Familial love is an entirely different sort of love. However, choosing to love someone for the rest of my life is not something I feel capable of doing. I would only end up hurting them by letting them down in the end.'

'But is loving someone a choice?' Artie asked. 'I mean, I haven't fallen in love myself but I've always understood it to be outside of one's control. It just happens.'

He captured a loose tendril of her hair and tucked it back behind her ear. His touch was light and yet electrifying, his gaze dark and inscrutable. 'A lucky few find love for a lifetime. But some lives are tragically cut short and then that same love becomes a torture for the one left behind.'

'Is that what happened to your mother?'

Luca's gaze drifted into the distance, his expression becoming shadowed. 'I will never forget the look of utter devastation on my mother's face when she was told my father and brother had drowned. She didn't come with us that day and when only I came home…' He swallowed tightly and continued in a tone rough and husky with banked-down emotion. 'For months, years, she couldn't look at me without crying. I found it easier to keep my distance. I hated seeing her like that, knowing I was responsible for what happened.'

Artie wrapped her arms around his waist and hugged him. 'Oh, Luca, you have to learn to forgive yourself. I'm sure your mother doesn't blame you. You were a young teenager. She was probably relieved you hadn't been taken as well. It could have happened. You could have all been drowned.'

He eased out of her hug and gave her a grim look. 'There were times in the early days when I wished I had been taken with them. But then I realised I owed it to my father and brother to live the best life I could to honour them.'

A life of hard work. A life with no love. No commitment. No emotional vulnerability. A life of isolation... not unlike her own.

A life of isolation she would go back to once their marriage was over.

Artie glanced at the front gates of the *castello* and drew in a shuddering breath. The verdigris-covered gates blurred in front of her into a grotesque vision of blue and green twisted metal. The sun disappeared behind a cloud and the birds suddenly went quiet as if disturbed by a menacing predator lurking in the shadows.

'Luca, I don't think I can go any further...'

He took her hand and looped her arm through his once more. 'You'll be fine. We're almost there. We've gone farther than yesterday. Just a few more steps and we'll be—'

'No.' Artie pulled out of his hold and took a few stumbling steps back towards the *castello*. 'I can't.'

Luca captured her by the wrist and brought her back to face him, his expression concerned. 'Whoa there. Slow down or you'll trip and twist your ankle.'

Her chest was so restricted she couldn't take a breath. Her stomach was churning, her knees shaking, her skin breaking out in a clammy sweat. She closed her eyes and a school of silverfish swam behind her eyelids. She opened her eyes but she couldn't see past the sting of tears. She tried to gulp in a breath but her throat wouldn't open enough for it to get through.

I'm going to die. I'm going to die. I'm going to die.

The words raced through her mind as if they were being chased by the formless fear that consumed her.

Luca gathered her close to his chest and stroked her stiff back and shoulders with slow, soothing strokes. 'Breathe, *cara*. Take a deep breath and let it out on the count of three. One. Two. Three. And again. One. Two. Three. Keep going, *mia piccola*. One. Two. Three.'

His gently chanted words and the stroke of his hands began to quieten the storm inside her body. The fog in Artie's brain slowly lifted, the fear gradually subsiding as the oxygen returned to her bloodstream.

She was aware of every point of contact with his body—her breasts pressed against his chest, the weight of his arm around her back, his other hand moving up and down between her shoulder blades in those wonderfully soothing strokes, his pelvis warm and unmistakably male against hers, his chin resting on the top of her head. She was aware of the steady *thud, thud, thud* of his heart against her chest, the intoxicating smell of his skin, the need awakening anew in her body. Pulses, contractions, flickers and tingles deep in her core.

Luca lifted his chin off her head and held her slightly aloft, his gaze tender. 'You did well—it's only our second try. Don't feel bad you didn't make it all the way. We'll try again tomorrow.'

Artie chewed her lip, ashamed she hadn't gone further. 'What if I'm never able to do it? What if I—?'

His finger pressed softly down on her lips to silence her self-destruction beliefs. 'Don't talk yourself into failure, *cara*. I know you can do it. You want to get better and that's half the battle, is it not?'

Artie gave a tremulous smile, heartened by his belief in her. Comforted by his commitment to helping her. Touched by his concern and patience and support. 'I do want to get better. I'm tired of living like this. I want to experience life outside the walls of the *castello*.'

He cupped one side of her face in his hand. 'And I can't wait to show you life outside these walls. There are so many things we can do together—dinner, dancing, sightseeing, skiing, trekking. I will enjoy showing you all my favourite places.'

Artie gave a self-deprecating smile. 'I have a lot of catching up to do. And only six months in which to do it.'

Luca's hand fell away from her face, his expression tightening as if her mentioning the time limit on their relationship was jarring to him. 'Of course, the most important thing we need to do is introduce you to my grandfather. I can't use the excuse of being on honeymoon for weeks or months on end.'

'Maybe he'll be well enough to come here soon.' It was a lame hope but she articulated it anyway.

His hand scraped back his hair in a distracted manner. 'There's no guarantee that's going to happen. Besides, I have work to see to. I can't stay here indefinitely.'

'I'm not stopping you from doing your work,' Artie said. 'You can leave any time you like.'

His gaze met hers. Strong. Determined. Intractable. 'I want you with me.'

A frisson scooted down her spine at the dark glint in

his eyes. The glint that spoke of the desire still smouldering inside him—the same desire smouldering inside her. She could feel the crackle of their chemistry in the air. Invisible currents of electricity that zapped and fizzed each time their eyes met and each time they touched. He stepped closer and slid his hand beneath the curtain of her hair, making her skin tingle and her blood race. His gaze lowered to her mouth, the sound of his breath hitching sending another shiver cascading down her spine.

'I didn't think it was possible that I could want someone so much.' His tone was rough around the edges.

Artie moved closer, her hands resting on the hard wall of his chest, her hips clamped to his, heat pooling in her core. 'I want you too.'

He rested his forehead on hers, their breath mingling in the space between their mouths. 'It's too soon for you. You'll be sore.' His voice was low, his hands resting on her hips.

Artie brought her mouth closer to his, pressing a soft kiss to his lips. 'I'm not sore at all. You were so gentle with me.'

He groaned and drew her closer, his mouth coming down on hers in a kiss that spoke of banked-down longing. She opened to the commanding thrust of his tongue, her senses whirling as he called her tongue into sensual play. Need fired through her body, hot streaks of need that left no part of her unaffected. Tingles shot down her spine and through her pelvis, heating her to boiling point. Her intimate muscles responded with flickers and fizzes of delight, her bones all but melting. One of his hands moved from her hip to cup her breast through her clothes, sending another fiery tingle through her body.

He deepened the kiss even further, his hand going beneath her top and bra to cup her skin on skin. The warmth of his palm and the possessive weight of his fingers sent her pulse soaring. He stroked her nipple into a tight bud of exquisite sensations, powerful sensations for such a small area of her body. He lifted his mouth off hers and lowered his lips to her breast, his tongue swirling over her engorged nipple, his teeth gently tugging and releasing in a passionate onslaught that made her gasp with delight.

The sound of Luca's phone ringing from inside his trouser pocket evoked a curt swear word from him as he lifted his mouth off her breast. 'I'd better get this. It's the ringtone I set up for Nonno's carer.' He pulled out his phone and took the call, a frown pulling at his forehead.

Artie rearranged her clothes and tried not to eavesdrop but it was impossible not to get the gist of the conversation. His grandfather had suffered a fall and was being taken to hospital with a suspected broken hip. Luca ended the call after reassuring his grandfather's carer he would leave for the hospital straight away.

He slipped the phone back in his pocket and gave Artie a grave look. 'You heard most of that?'

Artie placed her hand on his forearm. 'I'm so sorry. Is he going to be okay?'

He shrugged one shoulder, the almost casual action at odds with the dark shadows in his eyes. 'Who knows? Nonno is eighty-three. A broken hip is a big deal for someone of that age.' He released a breath and continued. 'I'm going to the hospital now. I want to speak to the orthopaedic surgeon. I want to make sure Nonno gets the very best of care.' He held her gaze for a moment. 'This might be your only chance to meet him.' His voice was husky with carefully contained emotion but she could sense the effort it took. His jaw was locked tight, his nostrils flaring as he fought to control his breathing.

Artie's throat tightened. 'I wish I could go with you, Luca. I really do.'

He gave a movement of his lips that wasn't quite a smile. He reached for her hand and gave it a gentle press. 'I'll be back as soon as I can.'

'Please send my best wishes for a speedy recovery.' Artie knew the words were little more than useless platitudes when all Luca wanted was her by his side. She was never more aware of letting down her side of the bargain. Letting *him* down. It pained her she was unable to harness her fear for his sake.

She watched as he drove away, her heart feeling as if it was torn in two. It felt wrong not to be with him—wrong in a way she hadn't expected to feel. As if part of her was missing now he was gone. The *castello* had never been more of a prison, her fear never more of a burden. Why couldn't she feel the fear and do it anyway? Was she to be imprisoned within these walls for the rest of her life? Luca needed her and she wasn't able to be with him, and yet she wanted nothing more than to be by his side.

She wanted to be with him because she loved him.

Artie could no longer suppress or deny her feelings about him. She had fallen in love with him in spite of his rules, in spite of her own efforts to keep her heart out of their arrangement. But her heart had been in it from the moment Luca kissed her. He had awoken her out of a psychological coma, inspiring her to live life in a full and vibrant way. How could she let him down now when he needed her? How could she not fight through her fears for him?

Rosa came out to join her, shading her eyes from the blinding sunshine. 'Do you know when he'll be back?'

Artie gave a despondent sigh. 'No. I feel so bad I wasn't able to go with him. What sort of wife am I that I can't even be by my husband's side when he needs me most?'

Rosa gave her a thoughtful look. 'I guess you have to measure up which thing is bigger—your fear of leaving here or your fear of not being there for him.'

Artie bit her lip, struggling to hold back a tumult of negative emotion. Her sense of failure, her lack of courage, her inability to overcome her phobia.

You're hopeless. A failure. An embarrassment.

Her harsh internal critic rained down abuse until she wanted to curl up into a tiny ball and hide away. But hiding never solved anything, did it? She had hidden here for ten years and nothing had changed.

And yet…something *had* changed. Luca had changed her. Awakening her to feelings and sensations she hadn't thought possible a few days ago. Feelings she could no longer hide from—feelings that were not part of Luca's rules but she felt them anyway. How could she not? He was the light to her darkness, the healing salve to her psychological wound, the promise of a life outside these cold stone walls. He was her gateway to the outside world, the world that had frightened and terrified her so much because she didn't trust it to keep her safe.

But she trusted Luca.

She had trusted him with her body, giving herself to him, responding to him with a powerful passion she could still feel in her most intimate flesh. Her love for him was bigger than her fear. Much bigger. That was what she would cling to as she stared down her demons. She had the will, she had the motivation, she had her love for him to empower her in a way nothing had been able to before. Luca was outside her prison walls, and the only way she could be with him in his hour of need was to leave the *castello*, propelled, empowered, galvanised by the love she felt for him.

Love was supposed to conquer all.

She would damn well prove it.

CHAPTER NINE

Luca GOT TO the hospital in time to speak to his grandfather before he was taken for surgery. Nonno looked ashen and there was a large purple and black bruise on his face as well as his wrist and elbow where he had tried to break his fall. Luca took the old man's papery hand and tried to reassure him. 'I'll be here when you come out of theatre. Try not to worry.'

Nonno grimaced in pain and his eyes watered. 'When am I going to meet this new wife of yours? You'd better hurry up and bring her to me before I fall off my perch.'

'Soon,' Luca said, hoping it was true. 'When you're feeling better. You don't want to scare her off with all those bruises, do you?'

A wry smile played with the corners of Nonno's mouth. 'It's good that you've settled down, Luca. I've been worried about you since…well, for a long time now.'

'I know you have.' Luca patted his grandfather's hand, his chest tightening as if it were in a vice. 'I was waiting for the right one to come along. Just like you did with Nonna.'

The strange thing was, Artie did feel right. Right

in so many ways. He couldn't imagine making love to anyone else, which was kind of weird, given there was a time limit on their relationship. A six-month time limit he insisted on because no way was he interested in being in for the long haul. Not with his track record of destroying people's lives.

'Your grandmother was a wonderful woman,' Nonno said, with a wistful look on his weathered features. 'I miss her every day.'

'I know you do, Nonno. I miss Nonna too.'

Another good reason not to love someone—the pain of losing them wrecked your life, leaving you alone and heartsore for years on end. If that wasn't a form of torture, what was? None Luca wanted any part of, not if he could help it.

He was already missing Artie, and he'd only been away from her the couple of hours it took to drive to the hospital. He'd wanted her to come with him to meet his grandfather but that wasn't the only reason. He genuinely enjoyed being with her, which was another new experience for him. The women he'd dated in the past were nice enough people, but no one had made him feel the way Artie did.

Making love with her had been like making love for the first time, discovering things about his body as well as hers. Being tuned in to his body in a totally different way, as if his response settings had been changed, ramped up, intensified, so he would want no one other than her. No one else could trigger the same need and drive. No one else would satisfy him the way she did. He ached for her now. What he would give to see her smile, to feel her hand slide into his and her body nestle against him.

His grandfather turned his head to lock gazes with Luca. 'I've been hard on you, Luca, over the years. I see it now when it's too late to do anything about it. I've expected a lot of you. You had to grow up too fast after your father and Angelo died.' He sighed and continued. 'You've worked hard, too hard really, but I know your father would be proud of your achievements. You've carried on his legacy and turned Ferrantelli Enterprises into a massive success.' He gave a tired smile. 'I've only ever wanted you to be happy. Success is good, but personal fulfilment is what life is really about.'

The hospital orderly arrived at that point to take Nonno down to the operating theatre.

Luca grasped his grandfather's hand and gave it a gentle squeeze. 'Try and get well again, Nonno. I'll be waiting here for you when you come back.'

Once his grandfather had been wheeled out of the room, Luca leaned back in the visitors' chair in his grandfather's private room and stretched out his legs and closed his eyes. Hospitals stirred emotions in him he didn't want to feel. It was a trigger response to tragedy. Being surrounded by death and disease and uncertainty caused an existential crisis in even the most level-headed of people. Being reminded of a loved one's mortality and your own. It would be a long wait until Nonno came out of theatre and then recovery but he wanted to be here when his grandfather came back. His gut churned and his heart squeezed and his breath caught.

If he came back…

* * *

Artie put her small overnight case in the back of Rosa's car and pressed the button to close the boot. She took a deep breath and mentally counted to three on releasing it. She came around to the passenger side and took another breath. 'Okay. I can do this.'

I have to do this. For Luca. For myself. For his grandfather.

She got in the car and pulled the seatbelt into place, her heart pounding, her skin prickling with beads of perspiration.

Rosa started the engine and shifted the gearstick into 'drive'. 'Are you sure about this?'

Artie nodded with grim determination. 'I'm sure. It won't be easy but I want to be with Luca. I need to be with him.'

Rosa drove towards the bronze gates, which opened automatically because of the sensors set on either side of the crushed limestone driveway. Artie concentrated on her breathing, trying to ignore the fear that was like thousands of sticky-footed ants crawling over her skin. Her chest was tight, her heart hammering like some sort of malfunctioning construction machinery, but she was okay…well, a little bit okay.

Rosa flicked a worried glance her way. 'How are you doing?'

Artie gripped the strap of the seatbelt that crossed her chest. Her stomach had ditched the butterflies and recruited bats instead. Frantically flapping bats. 'So far, so good. Keep going. We're nearly outside.'

They drove the rest of the way out of the gates and Artie held her breath, anticipating a crippling flood of panic. But instead of the silent screams of terror inside her head, she heard Luca's calm, deep voice, coaching her through the waves of dread.

'Breathe, cara. *One. Two. Three.'*

It wasn't the first time someone had taught her breath control—two of the therapists had done so with minimal results. But for some reason Luca's voice was the one she listened to now. It gave her the courage to go further than she had gone in over a decade. Out through the *castello* gates and into the outside world.

Artie looked at Rosa and laughed. 'I did it! I'm out!'

Rosa blinked away tears. '*Sì,* you're out.'

Artie wished she could say the rest of the journey was easy. It was not. They had to stop so many times for her to get control of her panic. The nausea at one stage was so bad she thought she was going to vomit. She distracted herself with the sights and sounds along the way. Looking at views she never thought she would see again—the rolling, verdant fields, the lush forests and the mountains, the vineyards and orchards and olive groves of Umbria. Scenes from her childhood, places she had travelled past with her parents. The memories were happy and sad, poignant and painful, and yet also gave her a sense of closure. It was time to move on. Luca had given her the tools and the motivation to change her thinking, to shift her focus. And the further away from the *castello* they got, the easier it became, because she knew she was getting closer to Luca.

But then they came to the hospital.

Artie had forgotten about the hospital. Hospitals. Busyness. Crowds. People rushing about. Patients, staff, cleaners, security personnel. The dead, the dying and the injured. A vision of her mother's lifeless, bruised and broken body flashed into her brain. A vision of her father in the Critical Care Spinal Unit, his shattered spine no longer able to keep him upright.

Her fault. Her fault. Her fault.

She had destroyed her family.

Artie gripped the edges of her seat, her heart threatening to pound its way out of her chest. 'I can't go in there. I can't.'

Rosa parked the car in the visitor's parking area and turned off the engine. 'You've come this far.'

'It was a mistake.' Artie closed her eyes so she didn't have to look at the front entrance. 'I can't do this. I'm not ready.'

I will never be ready.

'What if I call Luca to come out and get you?'

Artie opened her eyes and took a deep breath and slowly released it. Luca was inside that building. She was only a few metres away from him. She had come this far, further than she had in ten years. All she had to do was get to Luca. 'No. I'm not giving up now. I want to be with Luca more than anything. But I need to do this last bit on my own. You can go home and I'll talk to you in a few days once we know what's happening with Luca's grandfather.' She released her tight grip on the car seat and smoothed her damp palms down her thighs. 'I'm ready. I'm going in. Wish me luck?'

Rosa smiled and brushed some tears away from her eyes with the back of her hand. 'You've got this.'

Luca opened his eyes when he heard the door of his grandfather's room open, but instead of seeing a nurse come in he saw Artie. For a moment he thought he was dreaming. He blinked and blinked again then sprang out of the chair, taking her by the arms to make sure she was actually real and not a figment of his imagination. '*Cara?* How did you get here? I can barely believe my eyes.'

She smiled, her eyes bright, her cheeks flushed pink. 'Rosa brought me. I wanted to be with you. I forced myself to get here. I can't say it was easy. It was awful, actually. But I kept doing the slow breathing thing and somehow I made it.'

Luca gathered her close to his chest, breathing in the flowery scent of her hair where it tickled his chin. He was overcome with emotion, thinking about the effort it must have cost her to stare down her fears.

For him?

Fears she had lived with for ten years and she had pushed through them to get to his side. To be with him while he faced the very real possibility of losing his grandfather. He wasn't sure how it made him feel… awed, honoured, touched in a way he had rarely been touched. He was used to having entirely transactional relationships with people. He took what he wanted and they did too.

But Artie had given him something no one had ever done before—her complete trust.

'You were very brave, *mia piccola*. It's so good to have you here.' He held her apart from him to smile down at her, a locked space inside his chest flaring open. 'I still can't believe it.' He brushed his bent knuckles down her cheek. 'Nonno will be so pleased to meet you.'

Her forehead creased in concern. 'How is he? Did you get to speak to him before—?'

'Yes, he's in Theatre, or maybe in Recovery by now.' Luca took both of her hands in his. 'I've missed you.'

'I've missed you too.' Her voice whisper-soft, her gaze luminous.

He released her hands and gathered her close again, lowering his mouth to hers in a kiss that sent scorching streaks of heat shooting through his body. She pressed herself closer, her mouth opening to the probe of his tongue. Tingles went down the backs of his legs, blood thundered to his groin, rampant need pounding in his system. Her lips tasted of strawberries and milk with a touch of cinnamon, her little gasps of delight sweet music to his ears and fuel for his desire. A desire that burned and boiled and blistered with incendiary heat right throughout his body in pummelling waves. How could one kiss do so much damage? Light such a fire in his flesh?

Because it was *her* kiss.

Her mouth.

Her.

Luca lifted his mouth off hers to look down at her flushed features and shimmering eyes. 'If we weren't in my grandfather's hospital room, I would show you just how much I've missed you right here and now.'

Her cheeks went a delightful shade of pink. 'I've sent Rosa back home. It's okay for me to stay with you, isn't it?'

Luca smiled. 'I can think of nothing I'd like more. My villa is only half an hour from here.'

She stroked his face with her fingers, sending darts

of pleasure through his body. 'Thank you for helping me move past my fear. I know it's still early days, and I know I'll probably have lots of setbacks, but I feel like I'm finally moving in the right direction.'

Luca tucked a loose strand of her hair back behind her ear, feeling like someone had spilled warm honey into his chest cavity. 'I'm so proud of you right now. The first steps are always the hardest in any difficult journey.'

Artie toyed with the open collar of his shirt, her eyes not quite meeting his. 'I found it helped to shift my focus off myself and put it on you instead. I knew you wanted me with you and I wanted to be with you too. So, so much. That had to be a bigger driver than my fear of leaving the *castello*. And thankfully, it was.'

Luca framed her face in his hands, meshing his gaze with hers. 'Once Nonno is out of danger, I am going to introduce you to everything you've only dreamed of until now.'

She wound her arms around his neck and stepped up on tiptoe to plant a soft kiss to his mouth. 'I can hardly wait.'

A short time later, Luca's grandfather was wheeled back into the room. Artie held on to Luca's hand, feeling nervous at meeting the old man for the first time. She had met so few people over the last decade and had lost the art of making small talk. But she drew strength from having Luca by her side and basked in his pride in her for making it to the hospital. Something had shifted in their relationship, a subtle shift that gave her more confidence around him. He might not love her but he wanted her with him and that was more than enough for now.

It *had* to be enough.

Her love for him might seem sudden, but wasn't that how it happened for some people? An instant attraction, a chemistry that couldn't be denied, an unstoppable force. Luca didn't believe himself capable of loving someone, but then, she hadn't believed herself capable of being able to leave the *castello*. But she had left. She had found the courage within to do so. Would it not be the same for him? He would need to find the courage to love without fear.

Nonno groaned and cranked one eye open. 'Luca?'

Luca moved forward, taking Artie with him. He took his grandfather's hand in his. 'I'm here, Nonno. And so is Artie.'

The old man turned his head on the pillow and his sleepy gaze brightened. 'Ah, my dear girl. I'm so glad to meet you in person. I hope you'll be as happy with Luca as I was with my Marietta.'

Artie stepped closer. '*Buongiorno*, Signor Ferrantelli. It is so lovely to meet you face to face.'

The old man grasped her hand. 'Call me Nonno. You're family now, *sì*?'

Family. If only Nonno knew how short a time she would be a part of the Ferrantelli family. Artie smiled and squeezed his hand back in a gesture of warm affection. 'Yes, Nonno. I'm family now.'

An hour or so later, Luca drove Artie to his sprawling estate in Tuscany a few kilometres from the town of San Gimignano, where fourteen of the once seventy-two medieval towers created an ancient skyline. The countryside outside the medieval town was filled with sloping hills and lush valleys interspersed with slopes of grapevines and olive groves and fields of bright red poppies. Tall pines stood like sentries overlooking the verdant fields and the lowering sun cast a golden glow over the landscape, the angle of light catching the edges of the cumulous clouds and sending shafts and bolts of gold down to the earth in a spectacular fashion.

Artie drank in the view, feeling overawed by the beauty to the point of tears. She brushed at her eyes and swallowed a lump in her throat. 'It's so beautiful… the colours, the light—everything. I can't believe I'm seeing it in real time instead of through a screen or the pages of a book or magazine.' She turned to him. 'Do you mind if we stop for a minute? I want to stand by the roadside and smell the air and listen to the sounds of nature.'

'Sure.' Luca stopped the car and came around to open her door. He took her hand and helped her out of the car, a smile playing at the corners of his mouth, creating attractive crinkles near his eyes. 'It's an amazing part of the country, isn't it?'

'It sure is.' Artie stood beside him on the roadside and lifted her face to feel the dance of the evening breeze. She breathed in the scent of wild grasses and sun-warmed pine trees. Listened to the twittering of birds, watched an osprey ride the warm currents of air as it searched for prey below. A swell of emotion filled Artie's chest that Luca had helped her leave the prison of her past. 'I never thought I'd be able to do things like this again.'

Luca put an arm around her waist and gathered her closer against his side. 'I'm proud of you. It can't have been easy, but look at you now.'

She glanced up at him and smiled. 'I don't know how to thank you.'

'I can think of a way.' His eyes darkened and his mouth came down to press a lingering kiss to hers. After a few breathless moments, he lifted his mouth from hers and smiled. 'We'd better get going before it gets dark.'

Once they were back in the car and on their way again, he placed her hand on the top of his thigh and her fingers tingled at the hard warmth of his toned muscles beneath her palm. 'Thank you for being so sweet to Nonno,' he went on. 'He already loves you. You remind him of my grandmother.'

Artie basked in the glow of his compliment. 'What was she like? Were you close to her?'

His expression was like the sky outside—shifting shadows as the light gradually faded. 'I was close to her in the early days, before my father and brother drowned. Their deaths hit her hard and she lost her spark and never quite got it back.' His hands tightened on the steering wheel, making his knuckles bulge to white knobs of tension. 'Like my mother, being around me reminded her too much of what she'd lost. I was always relieved when it was time to go back to boarding school and even more so when I moved away for university.'

Artie stroked his thigh in a comforting fashion, her heart contracting for the way he had suffered as a young teenager. She was all too familiar with how grief and guilt were a deadly combination. Destroying hope, suffocating any sense of happiness or fulfilment. 'I can only imagine how hard it was for all of you, navigating your way through so much grief. But what about your mother? You said she lives in New York now. Do you ever see her?'

'Occasionally, when I'm there for work.' His mouth twisted. 'It's…difficult being with her, as it is for her to be with me.'

'I don't find it hard to be with you.' The words were out of her mouth before she could stop them. She bit her lip and mentally cringed as heat flooded her cheeks. Next she would be blurting out how much she loved him. Words he clearly didn't want to hear. Love wasn't part of their six-month arrangement. Romantic love wasn't part of his life, period.

Luca glanced her way, a smile tilting the edges of his mouth and his eyes dark and warm. 'I don't find it hard to be with you either.' His voice was low and deep and husky and made her long to be back in his arms. To feel the sensual power of his body, the physical expression of his need, even if love wasn't part of why he desired her. But she realised now her desire was a physical manifestation of her love for him. A love that had awakened the first time his lips touched hers, waking her from a psychological coma. A coma where she had denied herself the right to fully engage in life and relationships. Locking herself away out of fear. But she was free now, freed by Luca's passion for her and hers for him.

'Will I get to meet your mother? I mean, is that something you'd like me to do?' Artie asked.

A frown formed a double crease between his eyes.
'I'm not sure it will achieve much.'

'But what if I'd like to?'

He flicked her a brief unreadable glance. 'Why do
you want to?'

Artie sighed. 'I lost my mother when I was fifteen.
It left such a hole in my life. I can barely watch a tele-
vision show or commercials or movies with mothers
in them because it makes me miss my mother all the
more.'

'You have no need to be envious of my relationship
with my mother,' Luca said in a weighted tone.

'At least you still have her.'

There was a protracted silence.

Luca released a heavy breath. 'Look, I know you are
only trying to help but some family dynamics are best
left alone. Nothing can be changed now.'

'But that's what I thought about my fear of leaving
the *castello*,' Artie said. 'I lost years of my life by giving in to my fears, allowing them to control me instead
of me controlling them. I never thought I could do it,
but you helped me see that I could. Maybe it's the same
with your relationship with your mother. You shouldn't
give up on trying to improve the relationship just because it's been a little difficult so far. What you went
through as a family was horrendously tragic. But you
still have a family, Luca. You have your mother and
your grandfather. I have no one now.'

Luca reached for her hand and brought it up to his
mouth, pressing a soft kiss to her fingers. 'You have
me, *cara*.' His voice had a note of tenderness that made
her heart contract.

But for how long? Six months and no longer.

And then she would be alone again.

A short time later, Luca drove through the gates of his estate and pulled up in front of the imposing medieval villa.

Built like a fortress with four storeys, a central dome and several turrets, it was surrounded by landscaped gardens with a tinkling fountain at the front. 'Don't be put off by the grim façade,' he said, turning off the engine. 'I've done extensive renovations inside.'

'I try never to judge a book or a person by their cover,' Artie said. 'Not that I've met a lot of people lately, but still. Hopefully that's going to change.'

Luca's eyes glinted. 'I'm not sure I want to share you with anyone just yet. This is our honeymoon, *si*?'

A shiver coursed down Artie's spine and a pool of liquid fire simmered in her core. She sent him a shy smile. 'So, we'll be alone here? Just you and me?'

He leaned closer across the gear shaft and, putting a hand to the back of her head, brought her closer to his descending mouth. 'Just you and me.'

CHAPTER TEN

ARTIE WOKE THE next morning to find her head tucked against Luca's chest and his arms around her and her legs tangled with his. One of his hands was moving up and down her spine in a slow stroking motion that made her pelvis start to tingle. His hand went lower, to the curve of her bottom, and every nerve in her skin did a happy dance. Her inner muscles woke to his touch, instantly recalling the magic of the night before and wanting more. Would she ever tire of feeling his hands on her body? His touch was gentle and yet created a storm in her flesh. A tumult of sensations that made her ache for closer, deeper, more intimate contact.

Luca turned her onto her back and leaned on one elbow to gaze down at her. He brushed some wayward strands of her hair back from her face, his eyes darkly hooded, a lazy smile tipping up one side of his mouth. 'Well, look who's been sleeping in my bed.' His voice had a sexy early-morning rasp to it that made something in her belly turn over.

Artie traced a straight line down his strong nose, a playful smile tilting her own mouth. 'I don't know that I did much sleeping.' Her finger began to circle his stubble-surrounded mouth and chin. 'Unless I was dreaming about you making love to me…how many times was it?'

His eyes darkened. 'Three.' He stroked her bottom lip with his thumb, a small frown settling between his brows. 'I would have gone for four or even five but I didn't want to make you sore. This is all so new to you and…'

Artie smoothed his frown away with her finger. 'New, but wonderful.' She looked deep into his eyes, holding her hand against his prickly jaw. 'I didn't think it would be so…so wonderful. Is it always like this?'

Luca held her gaze for a long moment, his eyes moving between each of hers before lowering to her mouth. He released a soft gust of air, his lopsided smile returning. 'No. It's not always as good as this.'

'Really? Are you just saying that to make me feel good?'

He picked up one of her hands and turned it over to plant a kiss to the middle of her palm, his eyes holding hers. 'I'm saying it because it's true. It feels…different with you.'

'In what way?'

He interlaced his fingers with hers, a contemplative frown interrupting his features. 'I can't explain it. It just feels different.'

Artie aimed her gaze at his mouth rather than meet his eyes. 'Is it because of my lack of experience? I must seem a bit of a novelty to someone like you who's had so many lovers.'

He tipped up her chin and his eyes met hers, and something shifted in the atmosphere. A new, electric energy, a background hum, as if each and every oxygen particle had paused to take a breath.

'I'm not going to dismiss any of my past lovers to faceless bodies who didn't leave a single impression on me, because it's simply not true.'

He stroked his thumb over her lower lip again—a slow-motion stroke that set her mouth buzzing.

'But with you...it feels like I'm discovering sex for the first time. Feeling things on a different level. A more intense level.'

Artie toyed with the hair at the back of his neck, her lower body tinglingly aware of the growing ridge of his erection. Aware of the potent energy that pulsed and throbbed between them. 'I couldn't have asked for a better first lover.'

His mouth came down and sealed hers in a mind-altering kiss that set her pulse racing. His fingers splayed through her hair, his tongue meeting hers in a playful dance with distinctive erotic overtones. Her lower body quaked with longing, her flesh recognising the primal call to connect in the most physically intimate way of all. Her legs tangled with his rougher ones, her breasts crushed against the firm wall of his chest, her nipples already tightening into pert buds.

One of Luca's hands cradled one of her breasts, his touch light, and yet it sent shockwaves of need coursing through her body. Molten heat was licking along her flesh...lightning-fast zaps and tingles that made her groan in pleasure. She moved closer, pressing her mound to his erection, opening her legs for him, desperate to have him inside her.

'Not so impatient, *cara*.' He gave a light laugh and

reached for protection, deftly applying it before coming back to her, his eyes gleaming with the fiery desire she could feel roaring through her own body.

Artie framed his head in her hands, her breathing erratic. 'I want you so much it's like pain.'

'I want you too. Badly.' He kissed her mouth in a kiss that spoke of his own thrumming desire, his lips firm, insistent, hungry.

He moved down her body, kissing her breasts, her belly, and to the secret heart of her womanhood. He separated her and anointed her with his lips and tongue, making her writhe and gasp with bone-melting pleasure. The wave broke over her in a rush, sending her spinning into a place of sheer physical bliss. The storm in her flesh slowly abated but then he created another one by moving up her body again, entering her with a slow, deep thrust that made every hair on her head tingle and tighten at the roots. Her back arched, her thighs trembled, her breath stalled and then came out in a rush of rapturous delight. Delicious sensations rippled through her as he continued to thrust, his breathing rate increasing along with his pace, his touch like fire where his hand was holding her hip, tilting her to him. The pressure built in her body, the primal need a drumbeat working its way up to a powerful crescendo. Blood pounded through her veins, a hot rush fuelled by the intense sensations activated by the erotic friction of his hard male body.

Artie lifted her hips to get him where she most wanted him but it was still not quite the pressure she needed. 'I'm so close…so damn close…'

'Relax, *mia piccola*. Don't fight it.' Luca slipped a

hand between their bodies and stroked the swollen heart of her flesh, sending her over the edge into a cataclysmic orgasm that surpassed everything she had enjoyed so far. Starlight burst behind her eyelids, fireworks exploded in her body, heat pouring like liquid flames all through her pelvis and down her legs to curl her toes.

'Oh, God. Oh, God. Oh, God,' she panted, like she had run a marathon, her heart pounding, her flesh tinglingly alive with mind-smashing ecstasy.

Luca's release followed hers and swept her up in its power and intensity. His entire body seemed to tighten as if he were poised on the edge of a vertiginous cliff. And then he gave an agonised groan and shuddered as if consumed with a rabid fever, his essence spilling, his body finally relaxing against hers.

Artie stroked her hands down his back where his firm flesh was still peppered with goosebumps. The in and out of his breath tickled the side of her neck but she didn't want to move in case it broke the magical spell washing over her, binding her to him in a way no words could possibly describe. There was a rightness about their union—a sense of belonging together for all time.

But you've only got six months, remember?

The prod of her conscience froze her breath and stopped her heart for a moment. It wasn't long enough. Six months was a joke. She wanted for ever. She wanted to be in his arms like this for the rest of her life. How could she ever move on from her relationship with him? Who would ever measure up? How could she love anyone else when he had stolen her heart from the first time he kissed her?

She didn't want to love anyone else. Her heart belonged to him and only him.

Luca must have sensed the subtle change in her mood, and quickly disposed of the condom, and then leaned up on one elbow to look at her, his hand idly brushing her wild hair out of her face. 'What's wrong?' His tone and gaze were gently probing.

Artie painted a smile on her lips. 'Nothing.'

His eyes moved between each of hers like a powerful searchlight looking for something hidden in the shadows. His thumb began to stroke the pillow of her lower lip in slow movements that sent hot tingles through every corridor of her flesh. 'I've been around long enough to know that "nothing" usually means "something". Talk to me, *cara*. Tell me what's worrying you.'

She aimed her gaze at his Adam's apple, her heart skipping rope in her chest. How could she be honest with him without relaying how she felt? He might call an end to their physical relationship and go back to the paper marriage he'd first insisted on. 'I'm just wondering how I will ever find another lover who makes me feel the way you do. I mean, in the future, when we're done.'

There was a beat or two of thick silence.

Then Luca's hand fell away from her face and he released a heavy sigh and rolled onto his back, one arm flung over the edge of the bed, the other coming up to cover his eyes. 'The last thing I want to think about right now is you with someone else.' There was a rough quality to his voice that hinted at a fine thread of anger running under the surface.

'But it's going to happen one day,' Artie said. 'We're

both going to move on with our lives. Isn't that what you planned? What you insisted on?'

He removed his arm from across his face and sat upright, the muscles of his abdomen rippling like coils of steel. He swung his legs over the edge of the bed, his hands resting on either side of his thighs, his back towards her, his head and shoulders hunched forward as if he was fighting to control his emotions.

There was another tight silence.

Artie swallowed, wondering if she had pushed him too far. 'Luca?' She reached out and stroked her hand down between his tense shoulder blades, and he flinched as if her touch burned him. 'What's wrong?'

'Nothing.' The word was bitten out. Hard. Blunt. *Keep-away* curt.

She had a strange desire to smile—her lips twitched as she tried to control it. What was sauce for the goose and all that. 'You know, someone told me recently that "nothing" usually means "something".'

Luca let out a gush of air and gave a deep, self-deprecating chuckle. He turned back to face her. 'Touché.' He took her nearest hand and brought it up to his mouth, locking his gaze with hers. He bit down gently on the end of her index finger and then drew it into his mouth, sucking on it erotically. She shivered and a wave of heat passed through her body, simmering, smouldering like hot coals in her core.

He released her finger from his mouth and returned to holding her hand in his. 'Sometimes I wonder if I need my head read for allowing this to go this far between us.' His thumb stroked over the fleshy part of her thumb, the back-and-forth motion making her stomach do a flip turn. 'But I can't seem to stop myself from wanting you.'

Artie leaned closer, placing her free hand on the rock-hard wall of his chest, her mouth just below his. 'Want me all you like.' She pressed her lips to his in a barely-there kiss, pulling back to gaze into his eyes. 'We've got six months.'

She kept her tone light. *I'm-totally-cool-with-having-a-time-limit-on-our-relationship* light.

He held her gaze for a long moment, shadows shifting in his eyes like filtered sunlight moving across a forest floor. Then his eyes lowered to her mouth, a muscle in his cheek pulsing as if something wasn't quite at peace within him. 'Then let's make the most of it,' he said and covered her mouth with his.

The following evening, after spending some time visiting Nonno, Luca took Artie out for dinner at a restaurant in San Gimignano with a spectacular view over the region. She sat opposite him at a table at the window at the front of the restaurant, feeling both nervous and excited about her first meal out at a restaurant since she was a teenager.

Artie took a sip of the crisp white wine Luca had ordered, and then surveyed the menu. 'So much to choose from…'

'Take your time.' His tone was indulgent, as if he sensed how overawed she was feeling.

Once their orders were taken by the waiter, Artie glanced up at Luca with a rueful expression. 'I'm frightened I might use the wrong cutlery or something. It's been so long since I've eaten in public. I'm glad the restaurant isn't busy tonight.'

He reached for her hand across the table, holding it gently in the cradle of his. 'I made sure it wasn't busy. I know the owner. I asked him to keep this part of the restaurant clear for us.'

Artie blinked at him in surprise. 'Really? But wouldn't that have incurred a considerable loss of income for him?'

Luca shrugged one broad shoulder. 'Don't worry. I've more than compensated him.'

She chewed at the side of her mouth, touched that Luca had gone to so much trouble and expense for her comfort. 'I guess I can hardly call myself a cheap date, now, can I?'

His fingers squeezed hers, a smile playing about his mouth. 'You're worth more than you realise, *cara*. My grandfather certainly thinks so—he was in much better spirits today. Meeting you has done him the power of good. He told me when you were using the bathroom earlier today that he's decided to go ahead with the chemo for his cancer. I have you to thank for his change in attitude. He wants to live now. You've given him a reason to.'

'I'm so glad,' Artie said. 'But I hope the chemo won't be too gruelling. He's not a young man.'

'No, but he's a tough old guy.' Luca stroked his thumb over the back of her hand and added in a heavy tone, 'It's something I've been dreading—losing him. He's the last link to my father and brother, apart from my mother, of course.'

Artie could sense the deep love he had for his grandfather and it gave her hope that he might one day learn to embrace other forms of love—romantic love. Love-for-a-lifetime love. *Her* love.

'Has your mother been to see Nonno recently?'

His mouth twisted, a shadow passing through his gaze. 'They talk on the phone now and again. My mother hates flying back to Italy. It reminds her too much of our flight back from Argentina with my father's and brother's bodies.' He released her hand and picked up his wine glass, staring at the golden liquid with a frowning expression.

Artie placed her hand on his other forearm where it was resting on the table. 'I can only imagine how devastated you both were on that trip home. I can relate to it with my own journey home from hospital after the accident. It felt surreal, like I was having a nightmare or something. I kept expecting my mother to be there when I got home, but of course she wasn't. And my father was a shell of himself. A broken shell. I blamed myself, just as you did and still do.'

Luca leaned forward and took both of her hands in his. 'We've both suffered terrible tragedies. Nothing is going to change the past. It's done and can't be undone. But it's important to live your own life.'

Artie looked down at their joined hands. 'At least I'm living my life now, thanks to you. I think I was asleep to myself for the last ten years.' She raised her gaze to his and continued, 'I didn't realise how much I'd let my fear control me. It kind of crept up on me until I was completely imprisoned by it. But somehow you got me to change my focus, to shift my thinking. How can I ever thank you for that?'

'You don't have to thank me. You did it all by your-self.' Luca idly stroked her hands with his thumbs. 'You're doing so well now. I can't tell you how shocked and delighted I was to see you appear at the hospital the other day. I thought I was dreaming.'

'I was sick with nerves,' Artie confessed. 'But know-ing you were there at the end of my journey really helped. It gave me a clear goal to aim for.'

Luca smiled and released one of her hands, then took a flat rectangular jewellery box out of his jacket pocket. 'I have something for you.' He placed the box on the table between them. 'Open it.'

Artie prised open the lid to find a beautiful dia-mond and sapphire pendant and matching earrings. 'Oh, Luca, they're absolutely gorgeous!' She picked up one of the dangling earrings. 'But they're the same design as your grandmother's engagement ring. Does that mean they're—?'

'*Sì*, they were Nonna's. I want you to have the whole collection.'

'But they're priceless heirlooms. Why are you giv-ing them to me?'

'Don't you think you're worth it?'

She put the earring back in the box, and ran her fin-gertip over the fine gold chain of the pendant. 'It's not that so much...' She glanced up at him. 'It's more that I feel uncomfortable with you being so generous to me when we're only going to be together for six months. I mean, I seem to be the biggest winner in this arrange-ment of ours. I get to keep the *castello* and all this amaz-ing jewellery, and what do you get?'

His eyes held hers in a strange little lock that made

the hairs on the back of her neck tingle. 'I get some wonderful memories of our time together. Plus, my grandfather will hopefully recover now he's agreed to go ahead with the treatment.'

Artie frowned. 'But don't you want more than that?'

A screen came up in his gaze. 'What more could I want?'

Me. You could want me, for ever.

Artie couldn't bring herself to say it out loud but she wondered if he could hear her hopes in the ringing silence. 'Don't you want to keep your grandmother's jewellery in case one day you change your mind about marrying someone else?'

'Not going to happen.' He sat back in his chair, lifted his wine glass from the table and took a measured sip. 'I have no plans of that nature.'

Not going to happen.

The words taunted her for the rest of the meal.

Not going to happen.

He was so adamant about never falling in love.

Not going to happen.

How could he be so confident it wouldn't happen?

And how could she be so hopeful it would? That he would fall in love with her?

CHAPTER ELEVEN

ONCE DINNER WAS OVER, Luca led the way back to his car past a wine bar where live music was being played. The sweet strains of a well-known Italian love song filled the night air. He glanced down at Artie's wistful expression, and stopped in front of the entrance. 'Do you fancy going in for a bit?'

She shifted from foot to foot, looking like she was torn between running away and going in and letting her hair down. 'I haven't heard live music before. And I've never been to a wine bar. Or danced with anyone before.'

He took her hand and looped it through his arm. 'Come on, then. Let's dance.'

A short time later, Luca held Artie in his arms as they slow-waltzed to another old love song. Her head was resting against his chest, her hair tickling his chin, her flowery fragrance teasing his nostrils. Her body moved in perfect time with his, as if they had been dancing together for ever. The naturalness of their motion reminded him of the natural rhythm of their love-making. It was as if their bodies were in tune with each other, recognising the other as the perfect partner.

Perfect partner? You're hardly that.

The sharp prod of his conscience made him miss a step and he had to gather Artie closer to stop her from bumping into another couple on the small dance floor. 'Sorry,' he said. 'I lost my concentration.' Or maybe he'd momentarily lost his mind, thinking about the possibility of a future with her.

A future he couldn't offer her.

When he'd first offered her a six-month marriage it had seemed an inordinately long time to be tied to someone, and yet now it didn't seem long enough. He avoided thinking about their inevitable divorce. Avoided thinking about a time when she wouldn't be in his life. Avoided thinking about her with someone else. He felt sick to his guts at the thought of her making love with some other man. He'd never considered himself the jealous type but he couldn't stomach the thought of her with someone else. What if they didn't treat her with respect? What if they weren't patient with her struggles in public? What if they didn't understand how sensitive and caring she was?

Artie looked up at him with luminous eyes, her face wreathed in smiles. 'This is so much fun. Can we do this another night soon?'

Luca smiled and bent his head to kiss her. 'I can think of nothing I'd like more.'

The next couple of weeks passed in a whirlwind of activity where Artie's feet barely touched the ground. There were visits to the hospital to see Luca's grandfather, who was making good progress after his hip surgery. Then there were trips to various sightseeing spots, and picnics in the countryside overlooking the hills and valleys of the region. Luca taught her about the skill of wine-making and olive production and showed her the vines and groves on his estate. He took her for romantic dinners in award-winning restaurants as well as less famous ones, where the food was just as fabulous and the atmosphere intimate and cosy. Luca took her shopping and spoilt her with a completely new wardrobe of clothes, including a collection of swimsuits and gorgeous lingerie.

But it was the nights at home she enjoyed the most. Just being with him, sitting in the salon chatting, watching a movie or listening to music together, her head resting on his chest and his arms around her. It gave her a glimpse of what life could be like if they stayed together longer than the six months he'd stipulated. He was still driven by work and was often on the phone or answering emails, but she noticed he was more relaxed than before and seemed to smile and laugh more. Was it because his grandfather was on the mend and had decided to go ahead with his cancer treatment? Or was it because she had helped Luca to see there was more to life than work? That being in a romantic relationship could be positive rather than negative?

Artie had to bite her tongue so many times to stop herself from confessing how she felt about him but she let her actions do the talking instead. Every time she kissed him, she let her lips communicate her love. Every touch of her hands, every stroke of her fingers, every press of her body on his, love poured out of her. But she wanted to say it out loud. She needed to say it out loud. She needed him to hear the words—I love you.

They were sitting on the sofa watching the moon rise through the salon windows after a day of sightseeing. The moonlight cast a silver light over the surface of the infinity pool outside on the terrace overlooking the vineyard. Luca's arm was around her shoulders, her head resting on his shoulder, and soft music was playing through the sound system—cellos, violins and the sweetly lilting tones of a flute. A romantic ballad that tugged at her heartstrings and made her wish there wasn't a limit on their time together.

'Luca?'

'Mmm?' One of his hands began to play with her hair, sending shivers coursing down her spine.

Artie tilted her head to look at him. 'Luca, I want to talk to you about something. Something important.'

He brushed an imaginary hair away from her face, his eyes dark and serious. 'Go on.' His tone held a note of caution, unease, guardedness, but she refused to let it daunt her.

She swallowed a tight knot in her throat. 'There's so much I enjoy about being with you. You've spoilt me like a princess. You've treated me with so much patience and kindness and helped me build my confidence.'

He gave a half-smile, some of the wariness in his gaze fading. 'I like seeing you blossom, *cara*. You're a beautiful person who's been hiding away for too long.'

Artie touched his face with her fingers, her love for him taking up all the room in her chest so she could barely take a breath. 'I never thought I'd meet someone like you. And not just because I was locked away in the *castello*. But because I didn't think people as wonderful as you existed.'

Luca took her by the upper arms in a firm grip, his expression clouding. 'Look, don't go making me out to be a hero, Artie. I'm hardly that. You're confusing good chemistry with…other feelings.' Even the way he hesitated over the rest of his sentence showed how reluctant he was to the notion of love, but Artie pressed on regardless.

'Luca…' She took a deep breath and plunged in. 'I don't want our relationship to be temporary. I want more, and deep down I think you do too.'

His hands fell away from her arms and he sprang off the sofa to put some distance between them. 'You're wrong, Artie. That's not what I want. I've never wanted that. We made an agreement—'

Artie jumped off the sofa as well and stood in front of him. 'We made an agreement and then we changed it to what it is now—a physical relationship that works on every level but the one that means the most to me. I can't make love with you and keep my feelings to one side. They *are* the reason I want to make love with you. The only reason. I love you.'

Luca drew in a harsh-sounding breath and released it in a stuttered stream. He placed his hands on his hips, his shoulders hunched forward. 'You're young and inexperienced, of course, you're going to think the first person who makes love to you is the love of your life. But believe me, I am not that person.' His expression was like a walled fortress. Closed. Locked.

Keep out or face the consequences.

'You are that person.' Artie choked over the words as emotion welled in her throat. 'You've been that person from the moment we kissed at our wedding.

Something happened that day—I knew it on a cellular level. And—'

'Will you listen to yourself?' His tone had a cutting edge that sliced at her self-esteem like a switchblade. 'You're spouting forth a fairy-tale fantasy. It's not real, Artie. You've fashioned me into some sort of romantic hero who ticks all the boxes for you. You need more life experience. You need to date other men so you can gain more perspective. You'll thank me in the end. Tying yourself to me indefinitely would be a mistake. A mistake you'll regret for the rest of your life.' He turned away from her, drawing in another ragged breath, his tone softening. 'Let's leave this for now. I don't want to upset you.'

Artie swallowed a tight restriction in her throat, tears stinging at the backs of her eyes. 'But you've already upset me by not accepting that I love you. You've dismissed it as if I don't know my own mind. I know what I feel.' She banged her fist against her chest for emphasis. 'I can't deny my feelings or ignore them as you seem to do. They're here with me all the time.'

Luca turned back around and opened and closed his eyes in a slow, *God-give-me-strength* blink. 'Look, you're one of the nicest people I've ever met, *cara*. You have so much to offer and I want you to be happy. I really do. But I'm not the person to make you happy. It's not in my skill set. I don't want the same things as you.'

Artie pressed her lips together for a moment to stop them from trembling. 'I think you do want the same things but you don't feel you deserve them because of what happened to your father and brother. I understand that more than most people, because I've experienced the same guilt for the last ten years. It completely imprisoned me, kept me from having a life of my own. But meeting you changed that. You freed me from my prison of fear and showed me I could have more than I ever thought possible.' She came up to him and placed her hand on his forearm. 'I know you have deep feelings locked away inside you. I feel it every time you kiss me. I feel it every time you make love to me.'

Luca brushed off her arm as if it was soiling his sleeve, his gaze hard, his mouth tight, his firewall still up. 'You're mistaking good sex for something else. It's an easy mistake to make, especially when you're not very experienced. But in time, you'll gain experience and realise this is just a crush, an infatuation that can't last.'

'I don't have to be experienced to know how I feel,' Artie said. 'They're *my* feelings. I feel them. I own them.'

'And I know how I feel and it doesn't include the sort of love you're talking about.' He ran a hand over his face and continued, 'I care about you, of course. I enjoy being with you but that's all it is—companionship and mutual desire that has an end point, as per our agreement.'

Artie's heart gave a painful spasm, and for a moment she couldn't locate her voice. He cared about her and enjoyed being with her but that was all it was? How could she have got it so wrong? She was sure he was developing feelings for her—sure enough to reveal her own. He thought her young and gauche, a girl in the throes of her first crush. How could she get through to him? How could she prove she loved him? Or was it pointless? Was she fooling herself that he would one day change? Didn't so many deluded women fall for that fantasy? The vain hope that in time, enough love would change their difficult men to the man of their dreams?

But what if Luca never changed?

What if he was incapable of it?

'Luca, I took a huge risk in leaving the *castello* for you,' Artie said. 'Why can't you take a risk and allow yourself to feel what I know is in your heart? I know it's scary to admit how much you care about someone. And I know the last thing you want to do is be reckless and spontaneous but we've connected in a way people rarely do. Surely you can't deny it? We have so much in common, can't you see that? We're perfect for each other.'

Luca turned his back, drawing in a deep breath, his hands on his hips in a braced position. 'Stop it, Artie. This is a pointless discussion. You're making me out to be someone I can never be.'

Artie ran her tongue over her dry lips, tasting the metallic bitterness of disappointment. She clasped her hands together in front of her body, trying to contain the emotions rioting through her. 'You'll never be free of the prison of the past unless you learn to let go of control. To allow yourself to be reckless with your heart, to open it to the feelings I know you've buried there. I've let go of control. I've opened my heart to you. Why can't you do it for me? If you won't do it for me, then it wouldn't be fair to either of us to continue in a relationship that is so out of balance.'

'It's not out of balance.' Luca swung back around

to face her. 'I made it so we both get what we want. At the end of six months, you get to keep the *castello* and Nonno completes his chemo. It's a win-win.'

She shook her head at him. 'It's a lose-lose but you can't see it. I would choose love over a run-down old castle any day. And how are you going to explain the end of our marriage to your grandfather?'

He gave a dismissive shrug. 'Marriages break up all the time. It won't matter by then because he'll have finished the course of treatment. As I said—win-win.' His tone had a businesslike ring to it. No emotions. Ticking a box. Deal done.

Artie steepled her fingers around her nose and mouth, concentrating on keeping calm even though inside she was crumbling, the very foundations of her under assault as self-doubts rained down on her. She wasn't worthy of his love. She wasn't good enough. She was defective, damaged. He didn't love her. He would *never* love her. He had only married her as a means to an end, and yet she had fooled herself he was developing feelings for her. She was a fool for thinking he felt more for her than companionship and care.

Her old friend panic crept up behind her...lurking in the background.

You can't survive on your own. Stay with him. Put up and shut up.

Her skin prickled, fear slid into her stomach and coiled around her intestines, squeezing, tightening.

You'll lose the castello if you leave him now.

But Artie knew she couldn't lock herself in another prison. Staying with Luca in a loveless marriage for the next few months would be the same as locking herself in the *castello*. Shutting herself away from her hopes and dreams. From her potential.

From love.

She couldn't go back to being that frightened person now. She had to forge her way through with the strength and courage Luca had inspired in her. He had awakened her to what she most wanted in life and it would be wrong to go backwards, to silence the hopes and dreams she harboured. She owed it to herself to embrace life. To live life fully instead of living in negative solitude.

Artie lowered her hands from her face and straightened her shoulders, meeting his cold gaze with a sinking feeling in her stomach. 'I don't think there's any point in waiting out the six months. It will only make it harder for me. It's best if I leave now.'

A ripple of tension whipped over his face and his hands clenched into fists by his sides. 'Now? Are you crazy? You can't leave. We made an agreement.' There was a restricted quality to his voice. 'You'll lose everything if you leave now.'

Artie sighed. 'I can't be with you if you don't love me. It wouldn't be healthy for me. It would only reinforce the negative feelings I've had about myself in the past. That I'm not worthy, that I'm somehow the cause of everything bad that happens to me and those I care about. I need to leave that part of my life behind now. I need to embrace life as a fully awakened adult woman who knows what she wants and isn't afraid to ask for it.'

His hand scraped through his hair, leaving tracks in the thick black strands. He muttered a curse word in Italian, his mouth pulled so tight there were white tips at the corners. 'I can't stop you leaving but I should warn you there will be consequences. I'm not going to hand over a property with the potential of Castello Mireille just because you've pulled the plug on our agreement. I will keep it. I will develop it into a hotel and then I'll sell it.' His eyes flashed with green and brown sparks of anger. An anger so palpable it crackled in the air.

Artie ground her teeth, fighting to keep control of her own anger. 'Do what you need to do, Luca. I won't stand in your way. And I don't expect you to stand in mine.' She moved across to where she had left her phone. 'I'm going to call Rosa to come and get me.'

'Don't be ridiculous,' Luca said. 'It'll take her hours to get here.'

Artie faced him, phone in hand, eyebrows arched. 'Will you drive me?'

His top lip curled and his eyes turned to flint. 'You must be joking.'

Her chin came up. 'I'm not.'

He released a savage breath and muttered another curse. 'I'll organise a driver.' He took out his own phone and selected a number from his contacts.

Artie turned away as he told his employee to come and collect her for the journey back to Umbria. There was nothing in his tone to suggest he was shattered by her decision to leave him. He was angry, yes, but not devastated. Not as devastated as she was feeling. But how could he be? He didn't love her, so why would he feel anything but anger that she was pulling out of their agreement? His plans had been disrupted. His heart was unaffected.

Luca slipped the phone back in his pocket, his expression set in cold, emotionless lines. 'Done. Emilio will be here in five minutes.'

Artie moistened her parchment-dry lips again. Was this really happening? He was letting her go without a fight? It validated her decision to leave now, before she got even more invested in their relationship. But how much more invested could she be than what she was now? She loved him with her entire being and yet he felt nothing more for her than he would for a pet or a pot plant. He *cared* about her. That wasn't enough for her. It would never be enough. 'Thank you. I'd better go and pack a few things.' She turned for the door, waiting, hoping for him to call her back. She even slowed her steps, giving him plenty of time to do so. One step. Two steps. Three steps. Four…

'Artie.'

Her heart lifted like a helium balloon and she spun around. Had he changed his mind? Would he beg her to rethink her decision?

Oh, please, beg me to stay. Tell me you love me.

'Yes?'

His expression was mask-like but his throat rose and fell over a tight swallow. 'Keep safe.' His tone was gruff.

An ache pressed down on her chest, an avalanche of emotion that made it impossible for her to take a breath. Her eyes burned with unshed tears. She. Would. Not. Cry. Not now. She would not make herself look any more gauche and desperate. She would take a dignified stance. She would take a leaf from his relationship playbook—she would be cool and calm and collected, detached. Their business deal was over and she would move on. End of story. 'You too. And thanks for…everything.' She pulled the heirloom engagement ring off her finger as well as the wedding band and held them out to him. 'You'd better take the rings back. The earrings and pendant are upstairs. I'll leave them on the dressing table.'

'Keep them.'

'But they're family heirlooms—'

'I said, keep them.' The words were bitten out through a paper-thin slit between his lips, a savage frown pleating his brow.

Artie put the rings on one of the side tables and then turned and walked out of the room, closing the door softly but firmly behind her.

CHAPTER TWELVE

AS SOON AS the car carrying her away disappeared from
sight Luca sucked in a breath that tore at his throat like
wolf claws. What did she expect him to do? Run after
her and beg her to stay? He had told her the terms from
the outset. He had made it clear where his boundaries were.

But you shifted the boundaries. You slept with her.

He dragged a hand down his face, his gut clenching
with self-disgust. Yes, he had shifted the boundaries and
he should have known better. Artie was so young and
inexperienced, and sleeping with him had made things
so much worse. It had fuelled her romantic fantasies
about him, fantasies he could never live up to. But he
hadn't been able to help himself. He'd wanted her the
moment he met her, maybe even before that.

She was light and he was darkness.

She was naïve and trusting and he was ruthless and
cynical.

She was in touch with her emotions and he had
none…well, none that he wanted to acknowledge. Emotions were not his currency. It was a language he didn't
speak and nor did he want any fluency in it.

Luca picked up the engagement and wedding rings from the side table, curling his fingers around them so he didn't have to look at the mocking, accusing eyes of the diamonds. He rattled them in his hand like dice and tossed them back on the table, turning away with an expletive.

He was not going to go after her. He. Was. Not. He was *not* going after her. His old self would have run up the stairs even before she packed and got down on bended knee and begged her to stay.

But he was not that reckless teenage boy any more. He was able to regulate his reactions, to think logically and carefully about his actions. He was able to weigh the checks and balances and act accordingly…except when it came to making love with her. That had been reckless and ill-advised and yet he had done it anyway. Done it and enjoyed every pulse-racing second of it. Artie had got to him in a way no one else ever had.

He *felt* different.

Something inside him had changed and he wasn't sure he could dial it back. But he was damn well going to try.

Artie spent the first month back at Castello Mireille vainly waiting for the phone to ring. She longed to hear Luca's voice, she longed to feel his touch, to be in his arms again. She was suffering terrible withdrawal symptoms, missing the stroke and glide of his body within hers, the passionate press of his lips on her mouth, her breasts and her body. She reached for him in the middle of the night, her heart sinking when she found the other side of the bed cold and empty.

She realised with a sickening jolt that this was what her father had gone through after the accident. He had grieved both physically and emotionally for her mother. The loss of an intimate partner was felt on so many levels, little stabs and arrows every time you were reminded of the person, every time a memory was triggered by sight, sound, taste, touch or hearing.

Losing Luca was like a death. He was gone from her life and she couldn't get him back, not unless she compromised herself in the process. And hadn't she compromised herself enough for the last decade? Denying herself any sort of life, any sort of enjoyment and happiness out of guilt?

She was no longer the girl in a psychological coma. She was awake to her potential, awake to what she wanted and no longer afraid to aim for it, even if it meant suffering heartbreak along the way. Luca was everything she wanted in a husband, but if he didn't love her, then how could she ever be happy settling for anything less than his whole heart?

Artie was working in the morning room on a christening gown for one of the villager's baby, waiting for Rosa to bring in morning tea. There was a certain sadness in working on babies' clothes when it was highly likely she would never have a baby now. How could she without Luca, the only man she wanted to have children with? The only man she could ever love? She placed another neat stitch in the christening gown, wondering what he was doing now. Working, no doubt. Visiting his grandfather. Taking a new lover to replace her... Her insides revolted at the thought of him making love to someone else. Artie forced herself to concentrate on her embroidery rather than torturing herself. The weeks since coming home, she had decided to pour her energy into her craft and had even set up a social media page and website. To take it from a hobby to a business. She had orders coming in so quickly she could barely keep up. But it gave her the distraction she needed to take her mind off Luca and their broken marriage.

Rosa came in carrying a tray with their refreshments. She set it on the table in front of Artie and then sat down beside her, taking a cup of tea for herself off the tray. 'I'm thinking about taking a little holiday. I know my timing isn't good, given the situation with you and Luca, but I thought it was time I saw a bit of the world outside these walls now you're a little more independent.'

Artie put the christening gown to one side, wrapping it in the white muslin cloth she used to protect it. 'Oh, Rosa, I feel bad you've been stuck here with me for so long. But you don't have to worry about me now. I've been to the village several times this week on my own and even had coffee at the café a couple of times. I can't say it's easy, but I do it and feel better for it.'

'I'm so glad you're able to do more.' Rosa sighed and continued, 'While you were staying with Luca, I realised I might have been holding you back. Don't get me wrong—I wanted to help you, but I think my reasons were not as altruistic as you think.'

Artie frowned. 'What do you mean?'

Rosa looked a little shamefaced. 'When I got my heart broken all those years ago, I locked myself away here working for your family. It was my way of avoiding being hurt again. But I worry that I might have inadvertently held you back by allowing you to become dependent on me.'

'You haven't done any such thing,' Artie said. 'I held myself back and now I'm moving forward. But I can't thank you enough for being there when I needed you.'

Rosa's expression was tender with concern. 'Have you heard from Luca?'

Artie sighed and shook her head. 'No. Nothing.'

'Have you called or texted him?'

Artie leaned forward to reach for a teacup. 'What would be the point? I told him how I feel and he didn't feel the same, so end of story. I have to move on with my life. Without him.'

Rosa toyed with the hem of her flowered dress in an abstracted manner. 'What will you do if or when he sells the *castello*?'

'I'll find somewhere else to live. I can't live in a place this big. It's not practical.' Artie's shoulders went down on a sigh. 'I'll always have wonderful memories of being here with Mama and Papa before the accident but it's well and truly time to move on. Someone else can live here and make their own memories.'

Rosa straightened the folds of her dress over her knees. 'The holiday I was telling you about…? I'm going with a…a friend.'

Artie's interest was piqued by the housekeeper's sheepish tone. She put the teacup back down on the table in front of her. 'Who is the friend?'

Twin spots of colour appeared in Rosa's cheeks. 'Remember I told you about the love of my life who got away? Well, Sergio and I met up while you were staying with Luca. We've been seeing each other now and again since. He's asked me to go away with him for a short holiday. I won't go if you need me here, though.'

Artie leaned over to give Rosa a hug. 'I'm so happy for you.' She leaned back to look at her. 'I will always need you, Rosa, but as a friend, not as a babysitter.'

Rosa grimaced. 'You don't think I'm too old to be galivanting off with a man?'

Artie smiled. 'Not if you love him and he loves you.'

If only I should be so lucky.

Luca put off telling his grandfather about Artie leaving him for as long as he could because he didn't want to say the words out loud. *She left me.* But when Nonno was released from hospital and transferred into a cancer therapy unit, Luca had to explain why Artie wasn't with him. *She left me.* Those three words were like bullet wounds in his chest, raw, seeping, deep.

Nonno's distress at hearing Luca's news about his marriage was almost as bad as his own. 'But why? She's perfect for you, Luca. Why haven't you gone after her and brought her back?'

'Nonno, gone are the days when a man can carry a woman back to his cave,' Luca said. 'I can't force her to stay with me. She made the choice to leave.'

Nonno scowled. 'If you loved Artie like I loved your grandmother, nothing would stop you from doing everything in your power to get her back. A man in love is a force to be reckoned with.'

The silence was telling.

Luca loosened the collar of his shirt and leaned forward to rest his forearms on his thighs. 'Enough about my dramas. Is there anything I can get you?'

Nonno shook his head and closed his eyes. 'No. I just need to sleep.'

Luca stood from the bedside and laid a gentle hand on his grandfather's weathered arm. 'I'll be in again tomorrow.'

He was on his way out of the hospital when his phone rang with his mother's ring tone and his chest seized with the all too familiar dread. But instead of letting his phone go to message service as he often did, this time he answered it. 'Mama.'

'Luca, how is Nonno? I tried calling him but he must have his phone off. His carer rang to tell me he had a fall a week or two ago. She also told me you're married. Is that true? Why didn't you invite me to your wedding?'

Guilt gnawed at his conscience. 'Nonno's doing okay. As to my marriage—it's a long story and I hate to tell you it hasn't got a happy ending.'

'Oh, Luca.' His mother's sigh only intensified the pain riddling his chest. 'What's happened to us that you didn't want me to be there on your special day?'

Luca cleared his suddenly blocked throat and stepped out of the way of visitors coming through the hospital entrance. He pinched the bridge of his nose, scrunching his eyes closed briefly. 'It's not you. It's me. It's always been me that's the problem.'

'You're too hard on yourself,' his mother said. 'You're so like your father it's uncanny.' She sighed again and went on, 'It's why I found it increasingly difficult to be around you as you grew into a man. I couldn't look at you without seeing him. It reminded me of my role in what happened.'

Luca frowned, his hand going back to his side. 'Your

role? What are you talking about? I was the one who entered the surf that day. You weren't even at the beach.'

'No.' Her voice was ragged. 'I wasn't there. I went shopping instead of spending the day with my family as your father wanted. Do you know how much I regret that now? It's tortured me for years. What if I had gone along? I could've called for help instead of you trying to do it on your own. I can't bear to think of you running along that deserted beach, half drowned yourself, trying to find someone to help.' She began to sob. 'Whenever I've looked at you since, I've seen that traumatised, terrified young boy and felt how I let you and your papa and Angelo down.'

Luca blinked away stinging moisture from his eyes. He swallowed deeply against the boulder-sized lump in his throat. 'Mama, please don't cry. Please don't blame yourself. I'm sorry I haven't called you. I'm sorry I've let you suffer like this without being there for you. It was selfish of me.'

'You haven't got a selfish bone in your body,' his mother said. 'Your father was the same. Too generous for words, always hard-working, trying to make the world a better place. But tell me, what's going on with your marriage? It breaks my heart to think of you missing out on finding the love of your life. I'm so grateful I had those precious years with your father. They have sustained me through the long years since. I live off the memories.'

Luca gave a serrated sigh and pushed his hair back off his forehead. 'I'd rather not talk about it now, but next time I'm in New York do you want to catch up over dinner?'

'I would love that.' His mother's voice was thick with emotion. 'Give Nonno my best wishes.'

'Sì,' Luca said. 'I will.'

Luca tried not to think about Artie in the next couple of weeks and he mostly succeeded. Mostly. He blocked his memories of her smile, her touch and her kiss with a punishing regime of work that left him feeling ragged at the end of each day. One would think he would stumble into bed and fall instantly asleep out of sheer exhaustion, but no, that was when the real torture got going. The sense of emptiness could be staved off during the day but at night it taunted him with a vengeance. He tossed, he turned, he paced, he swore, he thumped the pillows and doggedly ignored the vacant side of the bed where Artie had once lain. He did his best to ignore the fragrance of her perfume that stubbornly lingered in the air at his villa as if to taunt him. He did his best to ignore the pain that sat low and heavy in his chest, dragging on his organs like a tow rope.

She left you.

But then more words joined in the mocking chorus. *You let her go.*

He allowed them some traction occasionally, using them as a rationalisation exercise. Of course he'd let her go. It was the right thing to do. She wanted more than he could give, so it was only fair that he set her free.

But you're not free.

What was it with his conscience lately? Reminding him of things he didn't want reminding about. No, he didn't feel free and—even more worrying—he didn't *want* to feel free. He wanted to feel connected, bonded to Artie, because when he was with her, he felt like a fully functioning human being. He felt things he hadn't felt before. Things he didn't think he was capable of feeling. Things that were terrifying because they made him vulnerable in a way he had avoided feeling for most of his adult life.

He had shut down his emotional centre.

Bludgeoned it into a coma.

But since his conversation with his mother there were tiny flickers of life deep in his chest like the faint trace of a heartbeat on an electrocardiograph. A pulse of something he had thought long dead. A need he had denied for so long he had fooled himself he wasn't capable of feeling it.

The need to love and be loved.

Three more words popped into his head like a blinding flash of light.

You love her.

Luca let them sit for a moment, for once not rushing to block them or erase them or deny them.

You love her.

And then he tweaked them, substituting the 'you' for 'I'.

I love her.

Bringing himself inexorably closer to the truth, step by step.

I. Love. Her.

He embraced the truth of those words like someone sucking in oxygen after near strangulation.

I love her.

His chest ballooned with hope, positive energy zapping round his body.

I love her.

Luca snatched up his car keys and the wedding and engagement rings from the bedside table. He'd placed them there as a form of self-torture but now he couldn't wait to see them back on Artie's finger where they belonged. Nonno was right. Luca's love for Artie was a force to be reckoned with—nothing would stop him from bringing her home.

Artie heard a car roaring through the *castello* gates and her heart turned over. She peered through the window in the sitting room and saw Luca unfold his tall, athletic figure from his car. Her pulse picked up its pace, her heart slamming into her breastbone, her skin tingling all over.

He's here.

She walked as calmly as she could to open the front door, schooling her features into a mask of cool politeness. After all, there was no point setting her hopes too high—he hadn't made a single effort to contact her over the past month. 'Luca. What brings you here?' She was proud of her impersonal tone. It belied the tumult of emotions in her chest.

He stepped through the open doorway with brisk efficiency, closing it with a click behind him. 'You bring me here, *cara*. You and only you.' He stood there with his hands by his sides and his expression set in grave lines. He looked tired around the eyes and his face hadn't seen a razor in a couple of days. 'I need to talk to you.'

Artie took a step back, her arms folding across her chest, her chin lifting. 'To say what?'

He unpeeled her arms from around her body, taking her hands in his. 'I've been such a fool. It's taken me the best part of a month to realise what's been there all the time.' He squeezed her hands. 'I love you, *mia piccola*. I love you so damn much it hurts. I can't believe I let you go. Can you ever forgive me?' He blinked a couple of times and she was surprised to see moisture in his eyes. 'I made a terrible mistake in not telling you sooner. But I wasn't able to recognise it until it was too late.' He drew her closer, holding her hands against his chest. 'Tell me it's not too late. I love you and want to spend the rest of my life with you. Please say yes. Please say you'll come back to me. Please give me another chance to prove how much I adore you.'

Artie brought one of her hands up to his prickly jaw, stroking it lovingly. 'I never thought I'd hear you say those words to me. I had given up hope, especially over the last few weeks.'

He grimaced and hugged her tightly to his chest. 'Don't remind me what a stubborn fool I've been. I can never forgive myself for that. I was in such denial that I couldn't even bring up your name on my phone. I knew it would hurt too much, so I didn't do it. Classic avoidance behaviour.'

Artie eased back to smile up at him. 'You're here now, so that's the main thing. I've missed you so much. I felt only half alive without you.'

He framed her face with his hands. 'You're everything I could ever want in a life partner. You complete me, complement me and challenge me to be the best man I can be. I can barely find the words to describe how much you mean to me.'

'I love you too, more than I can say.'

Luca lowered his mouth to hers and happiness exploded through her being. He was here. He loved her. He wanted to spend the rest of his life with her. His kiss communicated it all, passionately, fervently, devotedly. Even the steady thud of his heartbeat under her hand seemed to say the same. *I love you. I love you. I love you.*

After a moment, Luca lifted his mouth off hers and took something out of his trouser pocket. He held the wedding and engagement rings between his fingers. 'I think it's time these were put back where they belong, don't you?'

'Yes, please.' Artie held out her hand for him to slip them back on her ring finger. 'I'm never taking those rings off again.'

Luca smiled. 'I want you to meet my mother. Will you come to New York with me as soon as possible?'

Artie raised her eyebrows in delight. 'You've spoken to her?'

His face lit up with happiness. 'We had a chat about things and I realised how blinkered I'd been all these years, reading things into her behaviour that weren't accurate at all. You've taught me so much about myself, *cara*. I can never thank you enough for that. I hope you won't mind sharing my mother with me? I should warn you that she'll very likely shower you with love.'

'I won't mind sharing her at all. I can't wait to meet her.' Artie lifted her face for his kiss, her heart swelling with love. Her sad, closed-off life had somehow turned into a fairy tale. She was free from her self-imposed prison, and Luca, the man of her dreams, her Prince Charming, had claimed her as the love of his life.

Luca finally lifted his head and looked down at her with heart-stopping tenderness. 'Will you come away for a honeymoon with me after we visit my mother?'

'Just try and stop me.'

He stroked the curve of her cheek with his finger. 'I wasn't going to sell Castello Mireille.'

Artie smiled and gave him a fierce hug. 'I think on some level I knew that.' She eased back to look at him again. 'But I don't need it any more. What I need is you. It doesn't matter where I live as long as you're there with me.'

His eyes shimmered with emotion and her heart swelled with love to see how in touch with his feelings he was now. 'I've spent most of my life avoiding feeling like this—loving someone so much it hurts to think of ever losing them. I was in denial of my feelings from the moment I met you. You woke me to the needs I'd shut down inside myself. The need to love and be loved by an intimate partner. I can't believe how lucky I am to have found you.'

Artie pressed a soft kiss to his mouth. 'I'm lucky to have been found by *you*. If it hadn't been for you, I might still be locked away from all that life has to offer.'

Luca smiled, his eyes twinkling. 'I know it's early days, but maybe we can think about having those bambinos Nonno was talking about?'

She beamed with unfettered joy. 'Really? You want to have children?'

'Why not?' He kissed the tip of her nose. 'Building a

family with you will be a wonderful experience. You'll be the best mother in the world.'

'I think you'll be an amazing father,' Artie said. 'I can't wait to hold our baby in my arms. I never thought I wanted to have a family until I met you. I didn't allow myself to think about it. But now it's like a dream come true.'

Luca gazed down at her with love shining in his eyes. 'Thank you for being you. Adorable, sweet, amazing you.'

Artie gave him a teasing smile. 'So, you don't think I'm too naïve and innocent for you now?'

'You're perfect for me.' He planted a smacking kiss on her lips. 'And as to remaining innocent, well, I'll soon take care of that.'

Artie laughed and flung her arms around his neck. 'Bring it on.'

* * * * *

COMING SOON!

We really hope you enjoyed reading this book. If you're looking for more romance, be sure to head to the shops when new books are available on

Thursday 11th June

To see which titles are coming soon, please visit

millsandboon.co.uk/nextmonth

MILLS & BOON

Coming next month

REVELATIONS OF HIS RUNAWAY BRIDE
Kali Anthony

'This marriage is a sham.'

In some ways, he agreed with her. Yet here he stood, with a gold wedding band prickling on his finger. Thea still held her rings. He needed her to put them on. If she did, he'd won—for tonight.

'You're asking me to return you to the tender care of your father?' A man Christo suspected didn't have a sentimental, loving bone in his body.

Thea grabbed the back of a spindly chair, clutching it till her fingers blanched. 'I'm asking you to let me go.'

'No.'

Christo had heard whispers about Tito Lambros. He was reported to be cruel and vindictive. The bitter burn of loathing coursed like poison through his veins. That his father's negligence had allowed such a man to hold Christo's future in his hands...

There was a great deal he needed to learn about Thea's family—some of which he might be able to use. But that could wait. Now it was time to give her something to cling to. *Hope.*

'You'll come with me as my wife and we'll discuss the situation in which we find ourselves. That's my promise. But we're leaving now.'

She looked down at her clothes and back at him. Her liquid amber eyes glowed in the soft lights. 'I can't go dressed like this!'

No more delays. She glanced at the door again. He didn't want a scene. Her tantrums could occur at his home, where any witnesses would be paid to hold their silence.

'You look perfect,' he said, waving his hand in her direction. 'It shows a flair for the dramatic—which you've proved to have in abundance tonight. Our exit will be unforgettable.'

She seemed to compose herself. Thrust her chin high, all glorious defiance. 'But my hat... I told everyone about it. I can't disappoint them.'

'Life's full of disappointments. Tell them it wouldn't fit over your magnificent hair.'

Thea's lips twitched in a barely suppressed sneer, her eyes narrow and glacial. The look she threw him would have slayed a mere mortal. Luckily for the most part he felt barely human.

'Rings,' he said.

She jammed them carelessly on her finger. *Victory*. He held out the crook of his arm and she hesitated before slipping hers through it. All stiff and severe. But her body still fitted into his in a way which enticed him. Caused his heart to thrum, his blood to roar. Strange. Intoxicating. All Thea.

'Now, smile,' he said.

She plastered on a mocking grimace.

He leaned down and whispered in her ear. 'Like you mean it, *koukla mou*.'

'I'll smile when you say *that* like you mean it, Christo.'

And he laughed.

This second laugh was more practised. More familiar— like an old memory. But the warmth growing in his chest was real. Beyond all expectations, he was enjoying her. For his sanity, perhaps a little too much...

Continue reading
REVELATIONS OF HIS RUNAWAY BRIDE
Kali Anthony

Available next month
www.millsandboon.co.uk

LET'S TALK
Romance

For exclusive extracts, competitions
and special offers, find us online:

 facebook.com/millsandboon

 @MillsandBoon

 @MillsandBoonUK

Get in touch on 01413 063232

For all the latest titles coming soon, visit
millsandboon.co.uk/nextmonth

MILLS & BOON

THE HEART OF ROMANCE

A ROMANCE FOR EVERY KIND OF READER

MODERN

Prepare to be swept off your feet by sophisticated, sexy and seductive heroes, in some of the world's most glamourous and romantic locations, where power and passion collide.
8 stories per month.

HISTORICAL

Escape with historical heroes from time gone by. Whether your passion is for wicked Regency Rakes, muscled Vikings or rugged Highlanders, awaken the romance of the past.
6 stories per month.

MEDICAL

Set your pulse racing with dedicated, delectable doctors in the high-pressure world of medicine, where emotions run high and passion, comfort and love are the best medicine.
6 stories per month.

True Love

Celebrate true love with tender stories of heartfelt romance, from the rush of falling in love to the joy a new baby can bring, and a focus on the emotional heart of a relationship.
8 stories per month.

Desire

Indulge in secrets and scandal, intense drama and plenty of sizzling hot action with powerful and passionate heroes who have it all: wealth, status, good looks…everything but the right woman.
6 stories per month.

HEROES

Experience all the excitement of a gripping thriller, with an intense romance at its heart. Resourceful, true-to-life women and strong, fearless men face danger and desire - a killer combination!
8 stories per month.

DARE

Sensual love stories featuring smart, sassy heroines you'd want as a best friend, and compelling intense heroes who are worthy of them.
4 stories per month.

To see which titles are coming soon, please visit

millsandboon.co.uk/nextmonth

JOIN US ON SOCIAL MEDIA!

Stay up to date with our latest releases, author
news and gossip, special offers and discounts, and
all the behind-the-scenes action
from Mills & Boon...

 millsandboon

 millsandboonuk

 millsandboon

It might just be true love...